GOBSMACKED!

GOBSMACKED!

A HAMILTON ST. JAMES MYSTERY

PETER CLEVELAND

IGUANA

Publisher: Meghan Behse
Editor: Lee Parpart
Front cover design: Jonathan Relph
Author photo: Lindsey Gibeau

ISBN 978-1-77180-573-5 (paperback)
ISBN 978-1-77180-572-8 (epub)

This is an original print edition of *Gobsmacked!*

For Judy

Chapter 1

Detective Chief Inspector David Kingston removed his tailor-made suitcoat and draped it over the back of a soft leather chair. With a fresh cup of black coffee and a copy of the *Metro*, he settled behind his cherrywood desk to spend the first half hour of the day scouring articles about his department's cases. Were the facts accurately reported or were liberties taken that Kingston would have to set straight?

Detective Inspector Phyllis Joy stuck her head around Kingston's doorjamb.

"Good morning, sir." She grinned and pointed at the paper. "Any howlers today?"

Kingston looked up from his task and took in the short, slim redhead.

"Nothing yet. In fact it all looks quite accurate for a change," he said in his middle-class British accent. "I can park my verbal cricket bat for another day."

Joy chuckled and hovered in the door. "I take it we're still meeting later this morning to review cases?"

Kingston was about to answer when the hallway filled with voices. From the sounds of it, two detective sergeants were chasing down case leads by phone.

"Absolutely," Kingston said, raising his voice a little. "I've booked the meeting room down the hall."

Joy nodded and smiled as she took her leave.

Kingston heard her crisp voice trailing as she moved through the hall exchanging pleasantries with a couple of colleagues on her way to her own office. It was easy to see why Joy — Phyllis —had been promoted to DI in just two years. She was well-liked and an up-and-comer — a tough, tenacious investigator with just enough charm to be disarming when she needed to be. Kingston's predecessor had obviously seen all of that and put her on the fast track. *Good thing too*, he mused.

Kingston felt his cell vibrate.

"Kingston."

"David, it's John Taylor."

Kingston leaned back in his chair and smiled.

"John! Great to hear from you. Been yonks since we had a pint or two."

Son of Taylor Supermarkets' founder Ralph Taylor, John was CEO of the fourth-largest multi-supermarket chain in the United Kingdom. Taylor and Kingston had struck up a friendship after meeting at Lord's Cricket Ground a couple of years before. They'd vowed to meet at the Westminster Arms for Guinness a couple of times a year, and that, it turned out, was the reason for Taylor's call.

"This afternoon at four, the Westminster it is, John," Kingston said jovially.

For the remainder of the day, Kingston reviewed cases inherited from his predecessor with his staff. He was keen to understand every detail in the files, and he made sure to confirm facts and conclusions with Joy and the detective sergeants who'd been assigned to the Criminal Investigation Department's fraud unit before he was appointed DCI.

At 3:40 p.m., Kingston grabbed his coat and umbrella and left the Yard to make the fifteen-minute trek to Westminster Arms on Storey's Gate.

It was the first week of July, and an early morning fog had slowly burned off, turning the day sunny. Bright bunches of red and coral geraniums and tufts of light-blue lobelia popped from second-storey flower boxes, their delicate scents periodically overtaken by the herbal, woody aroma of marijuana. In the distance, sirens combined with Big Ben's chime.

Turning onto Birdcage Walk, Kingston shielded his eyes from debris stirred by the whirling rotors of one of the Metropolitan Police Services' three helicopters, while the pilot hovered as low as he dared.

The crowded, narrow Storey's Gate was jammed with motorists blaring their horns as they manoeuvred around large tour buses. From these double-decker obstacles, wave after wave of passengers spilled into the street, anxious to join the next parliamentary tour.

Just as Kingston walked under the blue awning at Westminster Arms, the parliamentary division bell rang. Several MPs bolted through the door and hurried past him on their way to the nearby House of Commons to honour the call for a vote.

A favourite of lords, members of parliament, actors and journalists, Westminster's solid, well-appointed chestnut-oak bar stood guard over thirty or so liquors resting on ornate glass shelving. The room was brimming with loud chatter and the smell of hops.

Kingston spotted Taylor leaning against the far end of the busy bar, nursing a Guinness.

"Good to see you, you old sod!" Kingston said, slapping the tall, lanky, sandy-haired Taylor on the back.

Taylor's preference for plain black suits, solemn ties and black brogues reminded Kingston of a mortician. The distracted, almost glum look on Taylor's face as he stared into his beer did nothing to dispel that impression. But as soon as he saw Kingston, he turned with a broad smile and stuck out his hand.

"Been too long, mate," Taylor said.

"Indeed, it has."

Kingston smiled and summoned a pint from the bartender.

"How's life at the Yard?" Taylor asked. "You settling in?"

"Getting there. But there's always more business than I can manage. Can't seem to get out in front of it all."

"Good God, man, you've only been in the position a short time. You can't expect instant success."

"Yes, well, fraudsters outnumber us many times over. I have a great team of DSs but could use a few more. The Yard's short of good talent at the moment."

"I have the same problem," Taylor said, shaking his head. "Can't seem to find strong, profit-driven store managers. The ones we have manage store activities all right, but with little thought to creative cost control."

Kingston nodded. "Well, I might sound old school, but people don't seem to care anymore. No pride in a job well done. It's all about collecting a paycheque and tweeting about life-work balance."

Taylor chuckled, and Kingston took a swig of Guinness.

"You speak the truth, my friend."

Kingston grinned as if to change the subject. "How's the food business?"

"Turnover's up over last year, but profit's down. Has me a bit worried. Can't seem to put my finger on why."

He took a pull of stout.

"Ah, finance will figure that out." Kingston wiped the froth from his lips.

"They're working on it, but nothing so far. We're meeting tomorrow morning to discuss it. We'll see what that brings."

***

The following day Kingston arrived at the Yard at his usual time. After his coffee-and-newspaper ritual, he met with DI Joy and the three detective sergeants to discuss cases. It was their habit to go around the room, starting with Joy.

"I'll soon wrap up the Ponzi investigation," she said.

Kingston looked at her, impressed. "When you're happy, let's review the case together. If we're on solid ground, I'll ask the Serious Fraud Office to consider prosecution."

Joy nodded and the tall, broad-shouldered DS Yvonne Davies leaned forward to open her dossier. "As you and DI Joy requested, sir, I've begun investigating the potential Middle East arms deal. I might need your help, sir, to bring in the foreign secretary."

"Yes, of course. And because of the political implications, I'm going to need closer involvement, Davies," Kingston said.

"Yes, sir."

Davies sat back and rested a file in front of her grey knee-length skirt.

A young detective constable stepped forward. "I'm looking into a possible share-ramping scheme," he said, then shot a look at DI Joy. "DI Joy has been guiding me through the initial investigation. We need to get a bit further into it before meeting with you, sir."

"We'll keep you posted, sir," Joy said. She smiled encouragingly at her underling, who shrank back to his desk.

"Thank you," Kingston said.

"I'm gathering evidence on a telephone scheme," a second junior detective said, speaking only to Kingston. "Looks like money is being seduced from elderly people through a suspicious church."

DI Joy flushed slightly and intervened. "That's still to be determined, sir," she said to Kingston, who nodded and levelled his gaze at the young man.

"I'd like you to work closely with DI Joy on this one, Detective," Kingston said.

"Yes, sir," the junior detective said, slightly deflated.

After Kingston had heard all the details and given his troops what he hoped was enough encouragement to forge ahead on their cases, he retreated to his office. He pulled a ham-and-cheese sandwich out of a plastic container he'd brought from home and ate at his desk while pecking away at a summary of what he'd accomplished in his first weeks on the job. His new boss, Superintendent Callaghan, was expecting the report later in the day.

At 1:15 p.m., his cell vibrated. He wiped his hands on a cotton napkin from home and answered.

"Kingston."

"David, it's John."

"I didn't expect to hear from you so soon," said a surprised Kingston.

"David, can you spare an hour this afternoon?"

Kingston heard stress in his friend's voice.

"Something wrong, John?"

"There may be, but I'd prefer to speak in person. Would you mind coming to me?"

Chapter 2

DCI Kingston made his way to Taylor's flagship store and headquarters on Rupert Street in Soho. He walked along a well-stocked aisle of the brightly lit store through crowds of Friday afternoon shoppers to a set of dark wooden stairs at the back. A slim, attractive twenty-something brunette wearing a light-blue skirt — one Kingston thought too short for proper office attire — met him at the top stair and escorted him into Taylor's second-floor corporate office.

Inside, he faced Taylor's vice presidents: Cindy Woods, a plump VP finance with short blond hair; Daniel Sauvé, the tall, slim, pale VP operations; and Lucas Vanderbilt, Taylor's scruffy-looking VP information technology.

The three sat facing Taylor's desk in solid wooden chairs that looked like they were badly in need of varnish. One wall was dominated by a black-and-white photograph of three generations of Taylors; another featured an oil painting of Ralph Taylor. Apart from the care invested in displaying those family images, the office looked tired, outdated. Taylor himself looked tired and anxious. Kingston noticed but didn't want to say anything in front of his friend's employees.

"What seems to be the problem?" the DCI asked, once he'd settled into a faded wing chair next to the VPs.

Taylor sighed heavily from behind his small desk and laced his long fingers together. "We seem to have misplaced £185,000."

Kingston looked puzzled. "How is that possible?"

"That's just it. I have no idea. Monthly financials year-to-date showed £185,000 less profit than forecasted."

"So the £185,000 shortfall is up to June thirtieth?"

"Yes. Our year-end is December thirty-first, so it represents half a year."

After giving this some thought, Kingston said, "Your business is not seasonal. People usually buy food at the same rate year round. Demand is not cyclical."

"Right. Habitual buyers."

"Habitual?"

"Yes. They tend to buy the same items most of the time, as they run out."

"I see. That would mean replenishing products would naturally reflect the same pattern. So it wouldn't be unreasonable to assume that if profit shrinkage continued for the balance of the year it could approach £370,000?"

Taylor looked blankly at Kingston. "Reasonable conclusion, yes."

"Not a small sum, especially if declines continue for longer than the current year." Kingston thought for a moment. "What have you looked into so far?"

Taylor explained the team's investigation into profit decline during the past ten days and said that nothing had come of it.

"To be honest, we're flummoxed," he said.

When Kingston asked for more specifics about the internal investigation, Taylor gestured to Cindy Woods.

Woods straightened a little in her chair and spoke to Kingston while glancing periodically at her boss. "We analyzed inventory purchases for the past year and found every one matched corresponding purchase orders and vendor contracts within a reasonable tolerance of error. Nothing major out of the ordinary that we could see. Then we went through customer sales, searching for errors in pricing and quantities. Following that, we analyzed overheads and reviewed bank reconciliations."

Kingston noticed Vanderbilt scratching his greasy head. The young man took a strand of hair, which was almost down to his jawline, and moved it behind one ear. Next to him, Sauvé stared off, seemingly uninterested in the conversation.

"And?" Kingston said with an anxious look.

"Everything checked out," Woods said.

Kingston stroked his square chin and turned to Taylor. "I'm not exactly sure how I can help, John. In the absence of a crime or anything suspicious, there's nothing to justify police involvement."

Taylor slowly nodded as if he hadn't heard Kingston. He looked first at Sauvé and then Vanderbilt. "Do either of you have anything to add?"

"No. Cindy covered it," Sauvé replied blandly.

Vanderbilt nodded his agreement with Sauvé.

"Thank you," Taylor said to the three. "Now I need time alone with DCI Kingston."

Taking their cue, the team rose, shook Kingston's hand one by one, and left.

An unhappy Taylor turned to Kingston. "None of this makes sense, David!"

Kingston ignored Taylor's conclusion. "The other two didn't seem very interested in your problem."

Taylor shrugged. "They usually let Cindy talk unless I have a technical question she can't answer. I don't know what to do next to solve this profit problem."

Kingston got up and paced, then helped himself to some water from a bubbler.

"Sorry, David, I should have offered you something. I'm so distracted."

"Not to worry," Kingston said, sipping and thinking. "Have you spoken with your accountants?"

"First call I made. They would conduct the same investigation as management, but it would cost a lot." Taylor paused for several seconds. "Why? Do you know of anyone who might help?"

Kingston stared at the faded white ceiling, noticing a water stain. Finally, he looked Taylor in the eye.

"Yes, I do."

Chapter 3

"Who?" Taylor asked anxiously.

"A man I've worked with many times over the years. Very capable."

"That sounds promising. What are his qualifications?"

"I would call them gifts rather than qualifications, though he has those too," Kingston said. "Let's just say he has a unique skill for detecting wrongdoing in companies. If it's there, he ferrets it out, identifies who caused it, how and why."

Taylor's forehead furrowed. "I thought that's what you did!"

"I'm afraid you misunderstand the Criminal Investigation Department, John. That's the reason I said I wasn't sure how I could help. If you report fraud, we investigate and bring justice where we can prove it. It's not our role to go looking for unknown fraud. As I said, there has to be a law broken or at least a reasonable expectation someone has done something wrong for us to be involved. This gentleman and his team look for fraud and, in many cases, create the evidence we need to prosecute. Essentially, he looks for the pain you feel but can't see."

Taylor's despair ramped. "But I could spend a lot of money, and this guy finds nothing."

"Yes, but you'd eliminate most wrongdoings as a reason for the profit decline. And, since your team already conducted a financial investigation that uncovered nothing, this is the logical next step."

Taylor peered at Kingston over crossed arms. "What's your guy's background?"

"Harvard MBA. CPA. Runs a commercial investigation practice. He works with both law enforcement and companies tormented by the unknown."

"Well there's no question I'm tormented," Taylor muttered. He picked up a glass paperweight and turned it around in his hand. "My management team is very competent. So, whatever this is, it's out of the ordinary."

Kingston nodded. He was a bit surprised to hear greasy-haired Vanderbilt and spacey Sauvé described as competent but was willing to give his friend the benefit of the doubt. And Cindy Woods certainly seemed capable.

There was a knock on the door.

"Yes," Taylor called out.

The door opened slightly, and the young woman who had escorted Kingston into Taylor's office poked her head in.

"Mr. Taylor, there's a call for you on line four."

"Thanks, Deborah. Tell whoever it is, I'll call them back this afternoon."

Deborah nodded and closed the door.

"Is your fellow located here in the United Kingdom?"

"No. He lives in Ottawa."

Taylor stared. "Ottawa … Canada?"

Kingston laughed and said, "Yes, the last time I checked, Ottawa was in Canada."

Taylor smirked at him, and Kingston forged ahead, pretending that he hadn't just seen his friend's look of concern about working with someone from the colonies.

"He teaches commercial crime detection at a university there."

Taylor shook his head. "An academic won't work. I need someone who lives business every day."

"He's not an academic," Kingston said quickly. "He's a commercial crime detective who happens to teach part time, not the other way around. He had to be convinced to take time away from his investigations to teach. A friend at the business school finally talked him into sharing his expertise with the next generation."

Taylor thought for a moment. "Is he expensive?"

Kingston grinned. "Very."

An exaggerated frown washed over Taylor's face. It was a long time before he let out a loud grumble. "Guess I have no choice. Can you see if he's available?"

"Smart move. I'll call him and let you know."

"By the way, does this fellow have a name?" Taylor asked as Kingston rose to leave.

"Hamilton St. James."

Chapter 4

Gerhard Becker shoved a dilapidated wooden chair beneath his rickety blue desk — one of several finds from a junkyard outside London. With a dirty forefinger, he rapped the cracked tabletop.

"Friedrich," he barked in course German. "Dump the box here."

Friedrich Schmidt slowly bent over a box of stolen computer equipment he'd just off-loaded from a rusty grey-and-white 1995 Vauxhall Vivaro. A tall, thin man, partially disabled by a construction accident, he winced as he struggled to carry the load across the concrete floor of the cinder-block self-storage unit Becker had rented, just off the A12.

Limping with every step, Schmidt finally plunked the box down on Becker's desk. The junkyard rescue wobbled under its weight.

"There you go, Gerhard."

"Good," said Becker brusquely, stroking his black moustache. "Now I'll see if I can open this damn thing."

Becker's resemblance to Super Mario was uncanny. His moustache was so vast as to impede eating; his mouth was barely visible under what looked like a small street broom attached to his face. Just over five feet tall, Becker's dark-brown eyes were sunken and bookended by small deformed ears. His right cheek was disfigured by two scars from a knife fight.

Outside, the wind howled. Driving rain pinged as it ricocheted off the uninsulated tin roof.

Schmidt repositioned his soiled ball cap. "What do you think's on it?"

"Where the money is, fool!" Becker snarled. "Think we risked breaking into that guy's flat for the good of our health?"

Schmidt shrugged as he sat on an old inverted wooden packing crate.

The poorly lit room smelled of old motor oil. Broken wooden chairs leaned against one wall, and a roll of maroon carpeting hugged another. Piled in the centre was an aluminum extension ladder resting atop pieces of discarded slab wood from an old construction site.

"Have to open this thing before Schneider calls," Becker mumbled. "He'll be mad as hell if I haven't."

Becker removed the brown-and-white lid from a well-used bankers box, took out a silver laptop and placed it on the decaying desk. Pulling a crumpled piece of white paper from a coverall pocket, he used the edge of the desk to smooth out the wrinkles with scarred hands.

When the laptop came to life and the screen asked for a password, Becker typed in a series of numbers and letters written on the paper.

Password incorrect flashed on the screen.

Instantly flustered, Becker re-entered the numbers and letters in the reverse order.

Password incorrect. He growled and tried again, putting all the numbers in ascending order first, followed by the letters in alphabetical order.

Password incorrect. Finally, he tried the numbers in descending order and the letters in reverse alphabetical order.

Password incorrect. A heavy bout of cursing followed as Becker tried a few more combinations, his face reddening.

Rubbing an ache in his bad leg, Schmidt said, "What made you think it was the password in the first place?"

Becker looked up from the screen and scowled. "Because, idiot, when I lifted the laptop off the guy's desk, this piece of paper was inside an envelope marked *password*, and the envelope was taped to the bottom of the machine."

"Why would someone be stupid enough to do that? You may as well not have a password at all if you're going to make it that easy."

"What do you know?" Becker shot back.

Who's the idiot now? Schmidt thought, looking away.

Becker's cell vibrated. "Yeah."

"You get that laptop from Chamberlain's flat yet?" The voice on the other end of the line was clipped and impatient.

"Oh, Mr. Schneider, it's you," blurted Becker awkwardly.

"Who the hell else would it be, Becker?"

"No one, sir."

"Well?"

"Yes, we have it. But I'm having trouble with the password."

"What password?" Schneider snarled. "There wouldn't be a password lying around the guy's flat for anyone to use, you moron."

"Well, sir, I have a piece of paper with a bunch of letters and numbers on it. It came from an envelope marked *password*."

"Don't touch that damn computer!" Schneider yelled. "You're too stupid to open it properly. You'll ruin everything. I'll find someone who knows what they're doing."

Schneider hung up without another word.

Chapter 5

Schneider stood nervously in front of Harry Fischer's ornate desk, waiting for his boss to break his stony silence.

Fischer rose from behind the desk and ambled over to a window overlooking Gottlieb-Daimler Straße. When he finally spoke, it was to a cedar hedge, not his second-in-command.

"Did those two morons you hired actually steal Chamberlain's laptop?"

"Yes," Schneider said. "They have it in the London warehouse."

"A couple of our people have had the pleasure of ... *interacting* with them," Fischer said with heavy sarcasm. "They're wondering why you risked the project on two men who can barely find their way out of a lit room."

"Well, sir ... I didn't hire them for their intellect," Schneider said defensively.

"Good thing," Fischer barked.

Schneider ignored the jab. "All they do is break into properties and steal. They come recommended for that kind of work only. Nothing else."

The bald, round-faced Fischer sighed and began cleaning his rimless glasses. "I'm unhappy about this, Wilhelm. I don't believe they're smart enough to keep their mouths shut."

"Precisely why I didn't give them any information about the project," Schneider said.

"I don't care!" Fischer yelled. "They're loose ends. They can be traced to you. As soon as we have that laptop I want them dealt with. Terminated, understand?"

"I understand, sir."

Fischer stared at his employee as though he wasn't sure what to do with him.

"Do I have to remind you of how vital security is to our entire operation? To our very survival?"

"No, sir," Schneider said, forcing himself to meet his boss's eyes.

In fact, Schneider knew very well that security was Fischer's single biggest preoccupation and the most important feature of the network of businesses that made up his conglomerate, IEI.

Fischer had purchased the small white-brick building in Gundelsheim, Germany, a short walk from the Neckar River, ten years earlier, with the goal to operate as far under the radar as possible. He would create and run a business in a small town without anyone in the community thinking twice about its existence or knowing that it was staffed by highly skilled specialists from around the world.

Maintaining this level of secrecy required elaborate rules and controls, beginning with the hiring process. Fischer demanded advanced computer skills unnatural to Gundelsheim's economy. So his first challenge was to source and woo an advanced talent pool willing to work in an environment less glamorous than those found in any of the world's big technology centres.

Once a team was committed, Fischer had to figure out how to move thirty people from around the world into Gundelsheim, again without being noticed.

His solution was to stagger flights into Stuttgart, an hour-and-a-half drive from Gundelsheim. He brought in two employees a day until all thirty were present at head office. Transportation from Flughafen Stuttgart to Gundelsheim alternated between train and automobile. Two people travelling together would look like tourists rather than the foundation for a highly skilled technical team.

Fischer didn't want too many members of the team walking around Gundelsheim, a town of only eight thousand, at the same time. Thirty new residents in a group would draw attention and risk exposing the operation. Regular tourists spent only a couple of days at most — long enough to sightsee, walk the medieval cobblestone streets, eye the town's significant timber architecture, and poke around a few shops. If Fischer's team lodged in town, they wouldn't be conducting such tourist activities. They'd disappear every day to work at head office. It would be only natural for locals to wonder what the new people were doing.

To keep them out of town and away from prying eyes, Fischer bought a brick farmhouse south of Gundelsheim and housed his team there. He hired a cook, a handyman and three maids to maintain the old brown building. Every employee had to sign an agreement accepting immediate dismissal without liability to IEI if they violated company secrecy rules for any reason.

In exchange for being stuck in a remote tourist town and having their freedom of movement controlled, Fischer's employees earned substantial premiums — about thirty percent more than the going private sector rate. Then there were the travel perks. Once every six to eight weeks, Fischer flew rotating groups of employees anywhere in the world for an all-expenses-paid week off. These mini-vacations were designed to preserve mental health and loyalty, and they did the trick. The operation was extremely expensive to maintain, but the obscene amounts of cash it generated made it worthwhile to Fischer. Every precaution kept IEI alive and shielded the company from scrutiny.

He extended the same care and scrutiny to the building and grounds. Employees weren't to mill about outside, park vehicles in front, or conduct other activities that could pique local curiosity and encourage unwanted questions. There was no such thing as a smoke break at IEI; employees were strictly forbidden to stand outside long enough to be seen from the road. No more than four employees were permitted to travel to and from the farm at any one time. Fischer believed any more than that would attract undesirable attention.

The building itself was completely ordinary looking, if a little rundown; its faded exterior needed a fresh coat of paint, and its asphalt lot was ribboned with cracks, through which tufts of grass and the occasional dandelion appeared. A row of windows on the first floor had been blacked out with opaque screening. Above the main door, a large weather-beaten plaque read Internationale Unternehmen. Below it, the English translation — International Enterprises — appeared in large black letters. There had been considerable discussion about whether to add a sign to the building. Fischer had finally decided that it might attract more attention to leave one off.

Inside was a completely different world. Every wall and most other surfaces had been painted white. In a large open-concept room that made up the main workspace, a beehive of computers and thirty or so people of all ethnicities and nationalities scurried about, mumbling into headsets and tapping the latest cell phones. Everyone was driving a piece of company business somewhere in the world.

To the outside world, Fischer described IEI as an importer-exporter of East and Southeast Asian goods — textiles, clothing, antiquities and crafts.

He'd invested millions in computer systems, all of it financed with money swindled from several organizations. Their "donations" bought IEI all the equipment and cybersecurity needed to ensure that no one, no matter how smart, could hack into the operation. Fischer referred to his cyber creation as Fischerlock, and thought of it as the internet version of Fort Knox.

As Fischer's second-in-command for the past eight years, Schneider knew all of this well. He also knew that when Fischer was unhappy or felt that security was being compromised in any way, it was better to stay with him than leave him to ruminate. So the muscular blond-haired security director sat down in a white leather chair facing his boss's desk and waited.

Fischer straightened some loose paper on his desk, then picked up a paper weight shaped like a racing car and centred it on top of the pile. Finally, he looked at Schneider. "How soon can you get into Chamberlain's hard drive?" he demanded. "I want to know right away whether Chamberlain was skimming from us, and if so, where the money is."

"I plan to find an expert to deal with all that," Schneider said evenly.

"You don't know enough to pick the best," Fischer snarled.

Schneider tried not to look stung. "I'll use one of our own experts to help define, source and screen potential candidates."

"Okay" — Fischer wagged a finger — "but don't keep our best money-generators off the job too long."

"I won't," Schneider said.

Fischer stared off. "Assuming you find an expert to open Chamberlain's hard drive, and there's money to be found, how will you go about finding it?"

"I won't know that until we see what information's on there. Could be we find elaborate records that answer those questions."

"Doubt it," Fischer said. "Chamberlain's not that stupid."

Schneider shrugged. "We'll see."

Chapter 6

Kingston punched in Hamilton St. James's Ottawa telephone number as soon as he returned to Scotland Yard from Taylor's office.

"Hamilton, you old dog. How've you been?" Kingston chirped.

St. James's voice came across as smooth as ever — the aural equivalent of his tall dark-complexioned self. "Between cases and the university, I'm busy as hell, David. It's been — what's that British word for *ages* — since we worked together."

"*Yonks!* It's yonks since we worked together, is what you would say. Thought you Canadians spoke the Queen's English," Kingston poked.

"We do, but we threw out the silly words before we adopted it."

"Fighting words, Hamilton. Fighting words. I'll let you off this time."

"To what do I owe the pleasure?"

"Well, I have a friend in the supermarket business who might need your help."

"Ah. What's the issue?"

"He's being tormented by an unexplained dive in profits, and his management team can't seem to isolate the problem."

"Any leads at all so far?"

"Nothing yet. As you know, I can't help him until or unless someone is shown to have broken the law. Taylor told me he thinks it's just poor management at the store level rather than wrongdoing—"

"Could be both. Poor management often leaves the door wide open for wrongdoing to go undetected."

"Indeed."

"Is it a chain?"

"Yes. Multiple supermarkets."

"Revenue? *Turnover*, as you call it."

"Seventy-five million pounds annually."

"Big enough to manage my cost, then," St. James said arrogantly.

"Yes, but he's extremely, extremely cost-sensitive."

"Wow! Average Brit usually has only one *extremely* before *cost-sensitive*. To have two is quite something. You sure he's not Scottish?"

Kingston chuckled. "Quite sure."

"The company?"

"Taylor Supermarkets. Family-owned business. CEO is John Taylor."

"How urgent is this?"

"Judging by John's anxiety level this afternoon, I would say *very*."

St. James thought for a moment. "Why don't we have a group call tomorrow morning, say ten o'clock my time, to make sure we're on the same page. The last thing I need is to fly to London for nothing."

"Perfect. I'll set it up."

***

Saturday afternoon at three o'clock, Kingston conferenced in John Taylor and Hamilton St. James by Zoom and introduced them to one another.

Kingston launched into his role as self-appointed chair. "John, why don't you start with an overview and history of the business?"

"Sure," Taylor said lightly.

Over the next few minutes, he took them through the company's history, from the one supermarket his father managed fifty years ago to the chain's current complement of thirty-four stores. He explained that annual turnover had grown from a meagre £250,000 to £75 million during the same period, and that the company now employed 1,300 part-time and full-time staff. This expansion had been made possible through three rounds of financing, arranged by Taylor since he took control of the business from his father.

"When did you notice the profit decline?" St. James asked.

"I began noticing large discrepancies during my financial review a month ago."

"What do you call large?"

"Actual net income typically differs from the forecast by no more than plus or minus two percent. Year-to-date actual net income is twenty percent less than forecast. Too great a difference to blame on my forecasting. Has to be something else going on."

"Like what?" St. James said bluntly.

Taylor became slightly impatient. "I don't know. That's why I'm talking to you."

St. James grimaced but said nothing.

Taylor ran through the details of his senior team's analysis during the past ten days, their findings and conclusions.

St. James stayed mostly silent, with the occasional *hmm* as he took it all in.

"Hamilton, tell John what you do. Give him a picture of what to expect."

St. James went through his personal history, different cases he had worked on and how he went about investigations. He knew Taylor was anxious about cost, so he outlined how he billed, and listed the members of his team and their skillsets.

Taylor stayed silent for a long moment, quietly calculating the damage. Finally, he exhaled and said, "Okay, Hamilton. All I ask is that you be as efficient as possible doing what you need to do. Keep the cost to a minimum."

"Fair enough. Are all your systems fully automated, computerized?"

"Cradle to grave."

"Then I'll bring my computer guy with me."

Taylor cut in swiftly: "We have lots of those here in London, you know. No need to incur extra travel cost."

St. James went silent for a moment. "You may have 'lots of those,' but I don't know them. I've worked with this man many times. We are a hand-in-glove team. I won't be as efficient if I have to train someone new."

"But the airfare, the hotel, everything…"

"I assure you, it would cost a lot more to do it that way than to incur a little extra travel."

When Taylor went silent, St. James pressed on. "Then there's my reputation. I'm afraid if you don't accept my computer guy, I can't take on the contract. I won't work with an unknown."

Taylor mulled this over for a full minute. St. James could almost hear the man squirming in his seat. Finally, Taylor said, "Okay. When can you be here?"

"Let's see … today's Saturday. I have a few things to clear up on my last case. Normally, I'd have to arrange for someone to take over my university class, but that's not an issue since it's summer break. Barring any flight problems, I can leave here Wednesday night and be in London Thursday morning."

They agreed, and St. James disconnected, leaving Kingston and Taylor on the call.

"Arrogant fellow, David."

"Maybe a little, but he's the best at what he does."

Chapter 7

The Wednesday after the conference call, St. James and Louis Smythe boarded the 9:05 p.m. WestJet flight from Toronto to London Heathrow and arrived Thursday at 9:05 a.m.

Smythe's green plaid sports coat and yellow plaid pants turned heads like dominoes as he walked down the aisle to take his seat at the back of the plane. Both men had managed to fit all their personal items into carry-on suitcases, but Smythe was also weighed down with a messenger bag full of computer equipment: two laptops, charger cables and a couple of Type G power adapters for plugging into British electrical outlets.

At 11:15 a.m., they checked into the weathered-stone Thistle Piccadilly Hotel on Coventry, a short walk from Taylor Supermarkets' head office on Rupert.

Riding the lift to their fourth-floor rooms, St. James said, "I couldn't sleep a wink on the plane, Louis. I need a couple of hours rest."

"Me too," Smythe said with a yawn.

St. James eyed Smythe's attire. "I know you're sensitive about your wardrobe, but the British can be stuffy, prim and proper people with an overdeveloped sense of class. I'm not sure how they'll take to your sartorial choices."

"Up yours!"

"Your usual response, but I felt compelled to forewarn you."

The lift doors opened to the fourth floor and they stepped out.

"I don't care what the British say," Smythe countered. "I am who I am and I have no intention of changing."

St. James shrugged as if to say, at least I warned you.

The Thistle's rooms were standard fare, with double beds and a single grey fabric chair. Knowing that he would have to do a lot of in-room work, St. James arranged for a small desk and chair to be included in his room. Smythe didn't feel the same need.

Before flopping onto the bed, St. James took the time to phone Kingston to let him know they'd arrived.

"If you're not too jet-lagged, Carolyn and I would like you and Louis to come to dinner tonight," Kingston suggested.

"That would be wonderful, David."

"We usually eat around six. Call me when you're ready, and I'll come around to collect you.

"Excellent."

St. James also phoned Taylor to let him know that he and Smythe had landed and would be in his office Friday morning at nine if that was quite convenient. That was perfect for Taylor.

After a power nap, St. James texted Kingston at 4:45 p.m. to say he and Smythe were ready for dinner. Fifteen minutes later, he and Smythe were climbing into the back of Kingston's dark-blue Jaguar.

Whereas St. James could have been mistaken for a London professor on a casual night out, Louis looked like he'd escaped from a clown convention. Dressed entirely in plaid, he'd managed to combine most of the colour wheel into a single ensemble. Moreover, he looked like he hadn't had a haircut in a couple of years; a long front lock flopped over one eye.

Kingston chuckled to himself at the sight of the computer expert, then turned to his old friend St. James. "Good to see you, Hamilton," he said as he drove off in the direction of his family home in Dulwich Village, south of London.

"Good to see you too," Hamilton said as he settled in. "Thank you for coming to get us. We were rather worn out."

"Of course."

St. James turned and began brushing his hand across his forehead, a gesture to encourage his partner to fix his wild hair.

"What?" Smythe said, playing dumb.

When St. James glared at him, Smythe shot him a weary smile and made a half-hearted attempt to reposition his lopsided comb-over.

Kingston kept looking at Louis in the rearview mirror, until St. James felt compelled to explain his partner's odd presentation.

"I guess there aren't many Brits wearing clashing plaid these days, David," St. James said with a grin.

"Oh, we have a few, but they're all on drugs."

"See, Louis?" St. James joked. "I told you you'd be in good company."

Kingston laughed and shifted down to stop at a red light. St. James took the opportunity to set the record straight about his associate.

"Louis is rather … eccentric…"

"I can see that," Kingston said, still smiling into the rearview mirror.

"…and wishes to set himself apart from others in his profession. This is how it turned out."

Kingston stole another look.

"Well, Louis, I would say you succeeded," he said lightly. "Welcome to London."

"Thank you," Smythe said. "First time here. Excited to see the city."

"We'll see if we can accommodate that while you're here."

At last, they pulled up to the Kingstons' beautiful two-storey traditional home. St. James had already filled Smythe in on the history of the place, explaining back at the hotel that David had inherited the estate from his father, Sir Joshua Kingston, who had been knighted for outstanding service to the crown following World War II. Even with this preparation, Smythe's eyes went wide at the sight of Kingston's impressive family home.

St. James had dined with the Kingstons on numerous occasions while working cases in the United Kingdom. He'd gotten to know Carolyn fairly well and wasn't surprised to receive one of her warm, substantial hugs when they all converged in the home's spacious foyer. He introduced Smythe.

"Nice to meet you, Louis," she said.

"My pleasure, Carolyn."

Carolyn turned back to St. James. "So good to see you, Hamilton. We always enjoy having you visit," she said with great enthusiasm.

"Wonderful to be here. Looking forward to another of your fabulous home-cooked meals, Carolyn."

"How's Anna? Any wedding bells in the offing?" she said, her grin devilish.

St. James recoiled with pained laughter. "No, Carolyn. And don't you start on me too. It's bad enough my friends at home are needling me to pop the question."

"All right, all right. But you know how I feel. That young woman is a jewel."

"Oh, I know…"

"What is it you say in North America? That she's 'the whole package'? Beauty, brains, a sense of humour … and to think, she's also your chief researcher. You're almost too lucky."

Any more of this and St. James was going to blush or bolt. All he could do was repeat his agreement. "I know," he said as meaningfully as he could manage.

St. James had expected this onslaught. Anna Strauss tended to make a strong impression on people. The Kingstons had met her the previous summer when the two were holidaying in the United Kingdom, and Carolyn had been completely taken with the charming and beautiful young woman.

Desperate to change the subject, St. James pointed to Carolyn and looked at Smythe. "You're in for a treat, my friend. The lady is chef material."

"Looking forward to it."

Carolyn smiled. "Stop it, Hamilton! You're ramping up expectations. It's sure to jinx the meal, and you're making me blush."

St. James laughed apologetically. *That makes two of us*, he thought.

A bit taller than her husband, Carolyn was rail thin with short auburn hair and delicate features. Her accent was slightly more upper crust than her husband's, and yet her natural warmth made one forget her origins. St. James had only begun to plumb the depths of all these gradations in class and education during his time in England. He knew enough not to ask about their upbringings.

Carolyn avoided all mention of Smythe's unusual outfit, and St. James silently thanked her for sparing him the need to explain Smythe's appearance again. He knew he didn't *have* to, but he always felt somewhat obligated to explain why Louis looked like the Joker, minus the lipstick.

Kingston jumped in to take drink orders — red wine for Louis and scotch for Hamilton, on the rocks. Then he offered Carolyn her usual glass of white wine, earning himself a sweet look and a "Thank you, darling."

Smythe peered into the sitting room. A nineteenth-century Edwardian cabinet, in pristine condition, occupied one wall, flanked by a pair of crisply carved Louis-style armchairs. An eighteenth-century beige button-back sofa occupied another wall. On either side of a red-brick fireplace stood two brown Moroccan leather armchairs. The walls were a soft blue-and-white floral.

When Kingston disappeared into the dining room to prepare drinks, Carolyn set out to learn what she could about Smythe.

"What is it you *do*, Louis?" she asked. "I've heard a little from David about how terribly indispensable you are to Hamilton, but I haven't been told at *what*."

"Most everything that revolves around computers," he said, happy to have been asked. "Code breaking, fraud detection, proof of transactions, that sort of thing." As soon as he said the words, he thought they probably sounded dull to a non-computer person, but Carolyn seemed riveted.

"That sounds like fascinating work," she said with genuine interest. "Essential too. Tell me, how did you and Hamilton team up?"

"Well, I was doing a project for a company in Toronto at the same time Hamilton was advising them on a fraud matter. We met there and ended up working a couple of cases together. We made a good team, so we made it official and became partners."

"Now if only he would make things more official with someone else on his team," Carolyn teased, not letting go of the Anna question. That got a smile out of Smythe, but he kept quiet.

At last, Carolyn looked at Smythe kindly and said, "May I ask a personal question?"

"Absolutely."

"How ... did you come to choose your rather unique ... style of dress?"

Smythe began answering as if Carolyn had asked about corporate branding.

"It was a process of elimination. I have a friend who's an image consultant. He suggested I wear bow ties and suits the same colour. He thought if I looked classy when everyone in my profession dressed like sloppy teenagers, it would generate a more positive impression. I tried it for a while, but everyone thought I was a lawyer. We tried different themes, but it soon became clear I needed something much bolder." Smythe arced both thumbs toward his chest. "And voila," he said with a huge grin.

Carolyn laughed. "Louis, I've only just met you, but I can already tell you're priceless."

Carolyn's assessment pleased him.

Kingston returned with everyone's drinks on a silver tray. He handed them out, then sat in one of the leather armchairs and raised a glass of scotch to propose a toast.

"To the successful resolution of John Taylor's business problem, whatever it may be."

Everyone raised their glasses in unison and drank.

St. James spoke up from the couch. "What can you tell us about Taylor?"

Before Kingston could answer, Carolyn raised her hand and excused herself. "While you gentlemen talk business, I'll see to dinner so I don't fail to live up to Mr. St. James's high praise. I'm now under savage pressure," she said lightheartedly.

"Yell if you need help, Carolyn," Smythe offered, as if they were old friends.

Kingston turned to St. James. "John is forty-five and tall, like you, Hamilton. About six-four. Very smart, also like you. Oxford man. Degree in business."

"Oh, so he didn't just inherit the business and learn on the job."

"Actually, he did both. He trained in the supermarket business from the age of sixteen. His father, Ralph Taylor, taught him everything. John became CEO at thirty-three and has managed to make money every year since. Ralph Taylor stayed on as chair of the board long enough to make sure John was on solid footing before retiring at seventy-seven."

Kingston drank his scotch.

"Personality?" St. James said.

"Nice man, makes friends easily. Well-liked. As you know, he worries a lot about the business. He can be nervous, especially when dealing with the unknown. A bit obsessive-compulsive."

St. James nodded slowly, nursing his scotch. "How so?"

"The business made approximately £750,000 for the first six months of this year."

"Christ, if it's doing that well, why the hell are we here?" St. James said.

Kingston laughed. "That's the OCD part. He figures it should have been higher."

"I suppose for a CEO of a £75 million business, a little OCD could be an asset," St. James said thoughtfully.

"That's how he's managed to increase profits every year. He's brilliant and usually sees problems coming in plenty of time to react. He didn't see a £185,000 profit reduction coming. That ruins his profit performance as CEO. Tantamount to failure in his mind, but not in anyone else's, I assure you. Most other CEOs would walk barefoot over burning coals to have his performance record. There's a lot of pride and ego romping around in that brilliant mind of his," Kingston said.

St. James nodded as if he'd heard this before. "No one is successful without pride and ego. I'd be concerned if he didn't have it."

Carolyn poked her head in. "Supper is ready," she announced. "Let's move to the dining room. David, would you be a dear and carve?"

"Yes, ma'am," Kingston said obediently before downing the last of his scotch.

Quickly finishing their drinks, St. James and Smythe moved to the dining table, which was set with the Kingstons' best china, silverware and crystal. Kingston rolled up his sleeves and began allocating slices of beautifully tender roast pork to each plate while Carolyn distributed bowls of roasted potato and mixed vegetables for everyone to help themselves.

Kingston, fork and electric carving knife in hand, said, "Hamilton would you do the honours with wine?"

"Delighted to assist." St. James walked around the table, filling each goblet from a crystal carafe.

Dinner conversation centred mainly around David and Carolyn's two sons, now at university.

"Cost is brutal," Kingston said, forking vegetables. "Can't believe how much tuition has risen since I went to university."

"This is fabulous, Carolyn," Smythe said with warmth. "Hamilton wasn't exaggerating. You are chef material."

"Thank you, Louis. You're too kind," she said modestly.

Dessert was hot bread pudding with drizzled vanilla sauce.

Wine glasses were refilled, and they moved back to the sitting room.

Kingston said, "Tomorrow, gentlemen, you'll meet three other senior people at Taylor's. The vice president of finance is Cindy Woods, who seems competent enough, but you can judge for yourselves. It bothers me she found nothing to help John identify the shortfall. The second person is the vice president of operations, Daniel Sauvé. I don't have a good read on him. He didn't say much during last week's meeting."

"Perhaps, he's intimidated by authority figures," St. James said with a devilish grin.

Kingston returned the smile. "I doubt if I'm that intimidating."

"I don't know about that," Carolyn poked.

Smythe took a sip of wine and stayed out of it.

"You said 'three,'" St. James reminded.

"The third is a Dutch fellow from Utrecht. Lucas Vanderbilt, vice president of information technology. He said even less than Sauvé. He looks like a bit of a goofball. I have no idea how competent he is."

It was ten thirty when St. James and Smythe walked into the hotel lobby. Smythe elected to go straight to bed. St. James entered the bar, pulled a small notebook from a coat pocket and began planning how to tackle Taylor Supermarkets.

Chapter 8

Wilhelm Schneider sat behind a small wooden desk in a cramped green office on the first floor of IEI headquarters. With help from one of the company's own computer experts, he'd spent the afternoon researching code crackers who might be capable of breaking into the laptop Gerhard Becker and Friedrich Schmidt had stolen from Nigel Chamberlain, a wealthy British businessman in London.

The irony didn't escape Schneider. At least ten people sitting outside his office door were capable of doing the job Fischer needed doing in London — what Schneider referred to as "phase two" of his plan.

But Fischer had strict rules. No one working at headquarters was allowed to work in any other location. The more employees moved around, the greater the chance they'd be recognized by someone they'd worked for in the past. God forbid they be peppered with questions about their current employment and end up leading someone back to Gundelsheim. It was a risk Fischer wasn't prepared to take.

With one long, scarred finger, Schneider tapped Fischer's extension into his phone.

"Harry, we've found five people we believe have the skills to carry out phase two. Three in Europe, two in North America."

"How will you narrow the search?" an impatient Fischer challenged.

"By tightening the selection criteria."

"Well, what are you waiting for, man?"

Schneider hung up and made an unpleasant noise. "Someday, I might have to kill that garden gnome," he mumbled.

By seven that evening, he had the five potential experts whittled down to two and decided to source both in case there was a problem with one. He called his most dependable lieutenant to find the two by the next afternoon.

Chapter 9

Friday morning, St. James and Smythe made the short trek to Taylor Supermarkets' largest store on Rupert Street.

The day was sunny and bright, and the streets were full of pedestrians and cyclists taking advantage of the fabulous weather.

As Kington had instructed, St. James and Smythe walked to the back of the meticulously maintained, well-stocked store and climbed the stairs to the second-floor corporate office where the receptionist, Ms. Singent-Smythe escorted them into Taylor's office. Introductions were made, and Taylor gestured for the two to sit in a pair of older wooden chairs facing his desk. Taylor made no mention of Smythe's attire, which was a slightly less clashing version of what he'd worn the night before, with one fewer plaid pattern in play.

"How would you like to proceed, Hamilton?" said the tall, thin sandy-haired retailer.

St. James noted an odd disconnect between Taylor's deep, baritone voice and his soft hazel eyes, thin eyebrows and chalky features.

"I'd like to start by spending some time with you while Louis gets to know the company systems and programs. And of course, we'll need a place to work. Do you have a spare office?"

"I anticipated that, so I booked the small meeting room two doors down for as long as you need it."

"Great."

"Why don't you take a moment to settle in first. Then I'll introduce Louis to Lucas Vanderbilt, my VP of IT, so they can get started." Smythe nodded, and Taylor turned to St. James. "After that, you and I can spend as much time as you wish here in my office."

Taylor escorted the two men down the hall and let them into a small meeting room. The walls were bare, and the few pieces of furniture were all of the outdated blond-wood variety. St. James and Smythe set up laptops, pulled notepads from travel cases and plugged in their cell phones to recharge.

St. James shook his head at the décor. *Must be his father's original stuff.*

Taylor then escorted Smythe to the last office on the right and introduced him to Lucas Vanderbilt. Taylor returned to collect St. James from the drab meeting room, and they settled in the CEO's office.

Taylor's office was almost as sparse as the meeting room, with a veneered desk, walls in need of paint, and several cracked floor tiles. Head office felt more like a company spiralling into bankruptcy than a thriving supermarket chain. But St. James had encountered extremely frugal business leaders before, and he decided not to read too much into the bleak surroundings.

Taylor looked at him from across the desk. "Where would you like to start, Hamilton?"

"Well, you gave me the corporate history on the call last week. No need to cover that again. Let's start with your assessment of the management team. Strengths and weaknesses, performance, that sort of thing. Perhaps we could begin with your VP operations."

"Okay. Daniel Sauvé has been with me for about ten years. Does an excellent job managing logistics and sourcing products at good prices, taking advantage of the purchasing power that comes from having our thirty-four stores."

St. James nodded for Taylor to continue.

"He's particularly good at maintaining consistent policies and procedures across our locations. I don't think he's tough enough on accountability. Stores with less than stellar performance are crying for improvement." Taylor reflected for a second. "But, in fairness, good managers are hard to come by. He's afraid if he's too tough, they might quit, and he'd be worse off. He's not big on communication. That bothers me some days more than others."

St. James nodded and made a note. "Is a store manager's remuneration equal to, lower or greater than the competition's?"

"A bit lower, but not significantly. Less than five percent, I think."

"When managers leave, do they usually go to the competition?"

"We don't have much turnover here. Maybe one or two every couple of years. The job market in the food industry is quite tight in the UK. There aren't that many places for them to go."

St. James persisted. "But when they do go, do they go to the competition?"

"Mostly. We've lost a few of our best managers that way."

"They can poach because they pay more," St. James said bluntly.

"That's part of it."

St. James pulled a list from his attaché case. "I'll need an organization chart and a list of employees, together with performance ratings and remuneration, if that's not too much trouble."

Taylor pulled a pad from the top right-hand desk drawer. "I'll start a list for Deborah to gather."

"Deborah?"

"Singent-Smythe, the lady who met you at the top stair. If I'm not available for some reason, you can ask her for anything. The staff know who you are. I had an office meeting yesterday afternoon to explain what you would be doing and instructed everyone to cooperate fully."

"Excellent. Thank you. How about Cindy Woods?"

"Vice president finance. Chartered accountant. Went through the CA program with our auditors, worked on our account. That's how we got to know her. When she was made redundant, we snapped her up."

"Has she performed well?"

"Very well. I have to say, though, I am a bit disappointed she didn't find anything during the investigation. Sometimes she's a bit officious and tries to dominate management meetings, but I think that's more a personality thing than a performance issue."

St. James made notes. "I can appreciate that. How's she viewed by people reporting to her?"

"Mostly positive. Woods can be snappy when the pressure is on."

"So can I," St. James said quickly with a grin.

Taylor smiled. "Guess that goes for all of us."

"How about Lucas Vanderbilt?"

"Bit of an oddball, but he knows his stuff. Loner. Has trouble socializing. Been with us for three years. I've spoken to him a couple of times about his appearance."

"Appearance?"

"Dresses like a bum, and I'm not sure his hair's been washed since he joined us."

St. James laughed. "David mentioned something to that effect last night. I'm surprised you put up with it."

"There are good reasons why I do. He has a master's in computer science and came first in his university graduating year. Extremely high IQ. Had experience with the same software we used when he worked for a supermarket chain in the Netherlands. So he knows the program inside out and has extensive programming experience if we need special reporting over and above what the program package provides. Chances of finding someone else with the same credentials would be close to zero."

Taylor smiled and added, "No one outside the company knows he works here. He never represents us in public. So his image doesn't affect us, and everyone here is oblivious to how he looks. So what would be the point."

"Makes sense."

Taylor shrugged as if to say, I guess so.

"Are the three married?"

"Sauvé and Woods are. They each have school-age children. I don't think a woman would go near Vanderbilt."

St. James grinned. "Any financial issues with them?"

"Seems an odd question."

"Goes to the heart of motivation to do wrong," St. James reasoned.

"Okay. None that I am aware of."

"Drugs? Alcohol? Vices that could cloud judgment or strain family budgets?"

Taylor looked startled. "Never crossed my mind!"

"Necessary questions, I'm afraid, to complete the mandate properly," St. James said dryly.

"I understand — I think. The only thing I'm aware of is Sauvé is a recovering alcoholic. But that's never been a problem in all the years he's been with us."

St. James noted the response. "Did the team make a written report of the investigation?"

"Just an email summarizing procedures and conclusions."

"Okay. I'll need a copy of that."

St. James handed Taylor a list of documents he required for the investigation.

For the next hour or so, St. James grilled Taylor on various aspects of operations, possible systems weaknesses and who had the authority to approve and do what.

When St. James returned to the meeting room, Smythe was still interviewing Vanderbilt, so he used the privacy to call Anna.

She just about squealed when she heard his voice. It had been two days since they'd spoken. "How's your first day going over there?" she asked.

St. James could feel her smile.

"Just getting cranked up. Spent the last couple of hours with the CEO, gathering answers to the usual questions, you know, the ones you've heard a dozen times and are sick of."

"Oh no," she teased. "I'm not sick of the questions at all. Why don't you take me through every detail?"

St. James laughed. He could almost see the sweet smile Anna always flashed after a playful jab.

"How about Louis?" she said. "Is he working and playing well with others? Making a good impression?"

St. James made a noise that said he wasn't sure. "Hope so. He's meeting with the head of IT at the moment."

"What's next for you, then?"

"I should be getting several documents from Taylor's executive assistant this afternoon. That'll keep me busy for a while."

"Anything you want me to do?"

"Really? You're not too busy?"

"I'm fine. Put me to work."

"That would be amazing. I'd love it if you could do a bit of digging. Find everything you can on Taylor Supermarkets, John Taylor, Daniel Sauvé, Lucas Vanderbilt and Cindy Woods, all located in the United Kingdom. Vanderbilt is an ex-pat from Utrecht, Netherlands."

"Any particular focus?"

"Usual stuff. Background, financial information, run-ins with the law, skeletons in the closet."

"You've got it, boss."

"You know what it does to me when you call me that," St. James joked.

"Hush," Anna said. "Talk to you later tonight."

Chapter 10

Smythe made himself comfortable in the only guest chair in front of Vanderbilt's antiquated desk, then opened his notebook to a clean page and began pumping the VP for every aspect of the company's information technology.

Vanderbilt pushed gunmetal octagon glasses back on his square nose and brushed long greasy strands of black hair away from his green eyes and unshaven face. He leaned back in his chair, crossed his arms in front of the old red sweatshirt that passed for his business attire that day and cleared his throat.

"Our system consists of the latest, most advanced, secure supermarket end-to-end POS software, requiring minimal human touch once purchase orders are approved. Automatic repurchase notifications pop up in sufficient lead time to allow for timely restocking when items dwindle, preventing lost sales due to late reordering, one of a supermarket's greatest concerns."

Vanderbilt drank from a coffee mug that looked like it might not have been washed in months. Smythe felt a little queasy just looking at it.

"Items scanned through checkouts automatically flow into electronic daily sales reports, and accumulate monthly into profit-and-loss statements. Minimal human touch reduces the opportunity for error. Sales on accounts for commercial customers such as restaurants, hospitals and private clubs automatically generate invoices. There are various approval levels for expenses. Recurring standard monthly expenses are pre-approved at the beginning of the year, and cheques are issued automatically on the last day of the month. Those expenses don't require further approval unless for some reason amounts or quantities change," Vanderbilt explained.

"How are approval levels allocated above that?" Smythe asked, his notetaking trying to keep pace with Vanderbilt's rapid explanations.

Vanderbilt cleared his throat. "Expenses up to £2,000 that are not pre-approved can be authorized by any one of the three vice presidents on their own. From £2,000 to £6,000 they must be approved by Cindy Woods plus either myself or Daniel Sauvé. Anything from £6,000 to £9,000 requires the signatures of all three vice presidents. Anything above that needs Mr. Taylor's signature."

Smythe gently adjusted his comb-over. "Seems like reasonably good control."

Vanderbilt nodded. "Think so."

"How do you prevent hacking from outside?"

"I wasn't entirely happy with the safeguards built into the programs we purchased. So I wrote an add-on program to make it even more difficult for hackers."

Smythe brightened. "Always interested in add-ons. I usually learn something."

"I took the best of Enhanced Mitigation, Reason Core, and Anti-Hacker and incorporated them into a single program. From there, I added more robust components to create a superior hacker-blocker that runs as an extra layer of security between the firewall and anti-virus software. Like Reason Core, it doesn't slow system performance."

"Impressive," Smythe said. "Does the add-on alter the manufacturer's program in any way?"

"No, that's why I went the add-on route. Tweaking the manufacturer's program could cause issues with service. Invalidate manufacturer support."

Smythe nodded. "Did you have manufacturer support check the add-on to make sure it didn't violate your contract?"

"Didn't think it was necessary."

Smythe's trepidation was obvious. "It would be smart to get written approval to avoid service arguments down the road."

Vanderbilt just shrugged.

"Okay. Does Taylor know you've done this?"

"He knows I've created the add-on and feels more secure with it being part of the system, but he doesn't know how I did it."

"And he hasn't asked you to explain it to him?"

"No. He leaves everything related to systems and security to me."

An expressionless Vanderbilt lightly scratched his three-day-old growth. "I'd be glad to show you when we're finished here."

Smythe nodded. "How many people in your department?"

"Five — a senior developer, two juniors, one admin person, and me."

"Odd to have a senior developer on staff with a VP of your calibre and fully developed systems functioning well. Seems like a duplication — an unnecessary expense."

"I like to be prepared if we discover some aspect of the system is not producing reliable data. But the main reason is I would like to move back to Utrecht soon, and he's my succession plan."

Smythe noted the response. "Now would be an excellent time to show me the system. Perhaps a demonstration at the same time?"

Vanderbilt stood up, pulled his ratty sweatshirt down over the waist of his worn jeans and motioned to the door. "Come with me."

Smythe followed Vanderbilt down a faded blue hall lined with a series of discoloured photographs of London from what looked like the 1970s. Smythe smiled to himself as he listened to the squeak of Vanderbilt's bright-blue runners making contact with the linoleum floor.

At the end of the hall, Vanderbilt unlocked a door and invited Smythe into what he referred to as his "coding room." The room housed several laptops, printers and computer accessories. One wall was completely taken up with books and computer manuals, and the other held Vanderbilt's university degrees and advanced course certificates. Smythe took in the framed diplomas.

Well, he's certainly qualified.

For the next hour and a half, Vanderbilt demonstrated every aspect of the company's computer network and cybersecurity systems, paying particular attention to the add-on he had created.

At noon Singent-Smythe arrived with an assortment of sandwiches and bottled water. She placed them on a vacant desk and left without a word. The two helped themselves to a quick lunch before continuing to test the system.

After a few hours of this, Smythe sat back and said, "What you've created is immensely powerful, Lucas. You must be proud."

Vanderbilt smiled slightly for the first time.

As he looked through the coding, Smythe noticed one section of the add-on that didn't seem to enhance security.

"What does this do?"

"It's a performance booster to make what I extracted from Reason Core even faster."

Smythe studied it for a long moment. He wondered if it was a phishing program of some sort, a vehicle for diverting customers' personal information or siphoning off company data for nefarious purposes. Digital subterfuge. He'd have to run the program himself to determine if it did any of those things.

"Is it possible to load a blank version of the software on my laptop, create a dummy company and run through a few artificial transactions? That way, I can see how the program behaves without contaminating company data," Smythe said.

"I think I can manage something along those lines."

Vanderbilt pointed to a small desk and chair in a corner of the room. "I can set you up there."

Smythe eyed the meagre workspace. "That'll do. I'll grab my laptop and files from the meeting room. Do you have time to help?"

"I'll make time," said a stoned-faced Vanderbilt.

For the next two and half hours, Vanderbilt and Smythe sat side by side in the coding room while Vanderbilt led Smythe through the program, set up a dummy company and provided a list of typical supermarket transactions.

Smythe didn't say what he was looking for, and Vanderbilt didn't ask.

Chapter 11

Monday was the second full day running data through the dummy company, and Smythe had found nothing unusual. No programming, data compilation or report-generation flaws. But Smythe would run every aspect of the system until he found a defect or was absolutely sure one didn't exist. It was a work ethic St. James greatly admired. Smythe's conclusions never let him down.

St. James wandered down the hall to Vanderbilt's coding room to check on Smythe's progress.

"How's it going there, snappy dresser?"

"Up yours, Hamilton."

"Louis, it's about time you came up with a new insult. 'Up yours' is wearing thin."

"So is mocking my clothes."

"Touché. Do you want to break for coffee?"

Smythe brightened. "Good idea. Let's get out of here."

They ended up at an ice cream shop called Amorino on Old Compton Street, a few minutes' walk from Rupert. There they ordered two black coffees and settled at a small table. As they enjoyed some of the best coffee either of them had tasted since arriving in London, Hamilton asked Louis about Vanderbilt's system.

"Well, he's created an elaborate add-on program. He says it gives the chain an extra layer of security, to ward off hacking attempts."

"And does it?"

Smythe breathed in the coffee before taking another sip. "I think so. I've been playing with it using a dummy company on my laptop, and I can't find any bugs. I believe it probably does what it's supposed to." Smythe stared at an attractive brunette who was standing at the counter, waiting to pay for a heavily sauced waffle. "There's potentially a bigger problem."

"What's that?"

Smythe leaned forward so no one could hear. "The add-on program could render off-the-shelf programs invalid for manufacturer support."

St. James finished his coffee and rested his chin on a palm. "In what way?"

Still whispering, Smythe said, "Programs could malfunction because of the add-on. Without a manufacturer's written approval when it's installed, your service agreement could be toast."

"Jesus. Does Taylor know this?"

"Don't think so," Smythe said. Then he looked at St. James and shared his other concern. "An even bigger issue is there's no check on Vanderbilt himself. He has free rein."

St. James nodded gravely.

The two sat in silence for a long moment, considering the risk of all this. Then Smythe said, "What have you found?"

"Not much," St. James said with a frown. "I reviewed Woods's investigation report in the form of a loosely worded email. I didn't find it very complete, but what was there didn't cause me any great concern."

"You don't sound very confident."

St. James rolled his eyes. "Let me put it this way, I wouldn't want to go to court on the strength of it."

Smythe smiled slightly. "You're being too polite, Hamilton. It doesn't look good on you. What you're trying hard not to say is that it's not worth a damn."

St. James smiled. "Sounds about right."

"Thought so."

"I read the performance reviews Taylor conducted for his three senior people," St. James offered. "Ratings were middle of the road. Nothing terrible. Nothing outstanding. And the three didn't commit to any personal improvement actions. Looks to me like they weren't worth doing. I still have to dig behind Woods's analysis of the £185,000 profit discrepancy."

Smythe smiled as he watched the brunette glide from the counter to the table behind St. James to begin eating her high-calorie waffle. "I don't know what, if anything, we'll find here, Hamilton," Smythe said mindlessly.

St. James stared into his empty coffee cup. "Thinking the same thing, Louis."

With that, they walked back to Taylor's head office.

Chapter 12

When they returned from Amorino, St. James went to the meeting room, and Smythe went back to the coding room.

St. James's cell buzzed.

"Anna! I am so glad it's you. I am missing you *a* lot!"

"Why? You have Louis there," Anna said, mirth in her voice.

"I assure you, my dear, it is not the same."

Anna laughed.

"Everything all right at home?"

"Everything's fine here. Been doing some of that digging you asked for. Want to hear what I have so far?"

"You bet."

"Everything you told me about John Taylor checks out. Oxford business, third in his class. He started working with his father, Ralph, when he was sixteen and has worked for the chain continuously, except for his Oxford years. He made CEO at thirty-three. He has no police record—"

"Nice to know."

"—and no negative press, except some find him to be a bit of a fuddy-duddy. He's highly regarded and welcome in all the right social circles. Not much to go on for the world's most renowned commercial crime sleuth."

"Hilarious, Anna," St. James said. "What about Daniel Sauvé?"

"Daniel Sauvé…" she said, shuffling her notes. "Born in Nice. Thirty-eight years old. Worked for Taylor the last ten years, started as a checkout boy, promoted to store manager after five years, VP operations after eight. Fired from a previous job for a drinking problem. According to police records, he was responsible for a car accident resulting in a woman becoming paralyzed for life. Quadriplegic. That set off the drinking. Our Daniel signed himself into a monastery to dry out eight months later, and he appears to have been clean ever since. At least I have no indication that he's fallen off the wagon."

"What happened to the woman?"

"She's still alive. Looked after by the University Hospital Rechts der Isar in Munich. They have an excellent reputation for treating spinal cord damage."

"Name?"

"Gerda Wagner. Fifty-two. She was in the hospital for a while. Then transferred to a long-term care facility close by so the hospital could continue treating her as needed."

St. James paused a beat. "Who's funding the health care?"

"Don't know."

"Can you find out?"

"Do my best."

"Thank you, darling."

"You're welcome, darling."

"What about Cindy Woods?"

"Articled with a medium-size London accounting firm, earned her CA there. Five years ago, she was made redundant and joined Taylor as a controller, later promoted to vice president. On her second marriage. No kids from the first, three from the second. When she's not at the office, she's all about family. Her husband is often in and out of jobs and prefers pubs over home."

"How do you find this stuff out?" said a stunned St. James. "It isn't information you'd find in public records."

St. James pictured her smirk.

"Like you always say, Hamilton, I have my methods, and they serve me well."

St. James smiled as Anna threw his own words back at him. "Okay, what else did you find?"

"Well she does have one not-so-little mark against her. She was caught shoplifting a few years back and ended up being reported to the police by the store owner. She got off by making restitution, paying for whatever she took, but she's banned from the store for life."

"Hmm. Could be useful information," St. James mumbled, obviously deep in thought. "What about our mangy IT guy?"

"Lucas Vanderbilt?"

"Yes."

"Moved from Utrecht to London three years ago to accept the IT position with Taylor, promoted to senior programmer after twelve months. Became vice president just last year. Considered a social misfit but brilliant. Master of Computer Science, first in his class. Nobody seems to know anything about his personal life. A loner, I guess."

"Great start, Anna. Dig deeper, if you can. There's enough smoke buried in what you found so far to justify more time."

"Right, boss."

"Oh, you…"

Chapter 13

St. James and Smythe strolled back to their rooms at the Thistle Piccadilly Hotel at four thirty to freshen up. They met at the bar downstairs at five fifteen.

"So what do you think, Hamilton?" Smythe said, adjusting his hair.

A thin, long-haired bartender took a hard look at Smythe and shook his head as he plunked down drinks.

"Well, Louis, we've not been at it exceedingly long, but so far, I see nothing seriously wrong. I'm not sure why we're here."

Louis nodded. "Me neither. The investigation is beginning to feel like no investigation. We may have to fire ourselves if we don't soon get a whiff of impropriety."

An attractive blond lady at the other end of the bar studied St. James. She scribbled something on a white cocktail napkin and said something to the scrawny bartender, who promptly dropped it in front of St. James.

St. James looked at it.

Smythe looked on. "Why doesn't that ever happen to me?"

St. James just raised his eyebrows and looked pointedly at Smythe's ensemble, which was especially eye popping. Louis responded by rolling his eyes.

St. James pulled a pen out of his blazer, scribbled on the back of the napkin and asked the bartender to pass it back to the lady. The blond woman took a second to read, waved to St. James with a small smile of respect, slid off her stool and left.

"What did you say to her?" Smythe said anxiously.

"That I was happily attached and not interested."

"You could have put in a good word for me."

"You're right, Louis. I should have. Thoughtless of me. We look so much alike that she probably wouldn't have noticed the difference."

"Up yours."

"Now what did I say about that?"

Smythe shrugged and ignored the retort. "What are you doing tomorrow?"

"I plan to interview the three senior people under Taylor, or at least get a start on it. You?"

"I'll spend the day working the program."

St. James brought Smythe up to date on Anna's findings as he drank scotch.

Smythe had a thought. "What if Sauvé is tapped from contributing to this Gerda Wagner's care? Maybe he's selling Taylor's information to help with the health-care costs."

St. James nodded. "Well, Cindy Woods is married to a guy who can't keep a job and likes pubs. Her budget may have a few stretch marks."

"Either one could have the motive to grab money over and above legitimate paycheques," Louis offered, drinking the last of his wine.

St. James stared off for a beat. "Then there's our mystery meat, Vanderbilt."

"Not really mystery meat. More like roadkill. Saves a lot of money on shampoo and clothes," Smythe said with a huge grin. "His budget's probably not stretched at all."

"Could have a drug addiction or a gambling problem. Right now, Vanderbilt's world is wide open to almost anything. As far as Anna can tell, he just exists."

With that, they went into the dining room and had dinner.

When they finished, St. James said, "I think I'll go to my room and call Anna."

"I'm going for a walk," said Smythe. "All day inside that software gave me a headache."

St. James nodded, and they went their separate ways.

Smythe crossed Wardour Street to Swiss Court and decided to explore the well-treed Leicester Square. A large fountain supporting a statue of William Shakespeare reminded him how much he'd hated *Hamlet* in high school.

It was a beautiful summer evening, and the city was filled with people strolling and enjoying food and drink on patios. Lovers walked hand in hand. Others sat idly on park benches, people-watching. Double-decker buses roared past on all four streets enveloping the park.

Around the square were statues of famous movie characters — Harry Potter, Mary Poppins, Batman, Mr. Bean.

For a time, Smythe settled on a bench in front of a stand of trees. As he watched people come and go, he was struck by the presence of so many seemingly happy couples. He wondered what they talked about. Maybe life goals? Passions? Experiences, certainly. Suddenly he felt empty. Sad. For a time, his mind drifted as he wondered if he would ever find a compatible partner. Someone who'd accept him for who he was, with his quirks and eccentricities.

What type of woman would he appeal to? Who would she be? She wouldn't have to be the most beautiful woman in the world. He was, after all, realistic. He was no Hamilton St. James in the looks department. But he was kind, gentle and generous and, most importantly, honest and loyal. *That should count for something with women.*

An Ottawa real estate agent had once shown him a house in need of significant repairs. A "handyman special," she had called it. "Who the hell would buy this mess?" he'd said to her. "Every house has a buyer," she'd said. "The trick is to find them."

At that moment, Smythe felt like that house. He was the mess that hadn't found its buyer, the right woman.

He was still musing over this when he felt a prick in the neck. A moment later, he felt nothing at all.

Chapter 14

Smythe woke in darkness, with a large black hood covering his head. He was sitting upright in a chair.

Behind him, two men were arguing in what sounded like German. His head throbbed, and he felt as though some sort of drug was gradually ebbing out of his system.

He tried moving his hands but they were bound tightly behind his back with what felt like hard plastic zip-tie handcuffs. His feet were also tied to the front legs of the chair he occupied.

"Friedrich," one of the men barked, "pull his hood off."

Schmidt limped over and roughly yanked the hood from Smythe's head, exposing him to a harsh overhead light that left him squinting as his eyes adjusted. He looked around the damp green room. It was empty except for a rickety blue desk, a couple of chairs that'd seen better days, some random pieces of wood and a few packing crates.

The dimly lit room was quiet except for a generator-like sound resonating behind him. As his head began to clear, he heard sounds of heavy traffic. *Close to an A or M route*, he thought.

He focused on his two mangy captors. "Why are you doing this?" he said, then began to cough from the dryness in his throat.

"We have a job for you," Becker snapped.

When the coughing got worse, the taller of the two men finally limped over and held a half-full water bottle up to Smythe's lips. Smythe looked suspicious but opened his mouth and accepted a little water.

When he could speak again, he said, "Who are you?"

The shorter man rubbed his bushy moustache and pointed to a laptop sitting on the blue desk. "We want you to hack into that computer."

Smythe looked over at the laptop, beads of sweat running down his face.

"Why me? I've only been in London a couple of days. Never been here in my life," Smythe said, his voice ladened with anxiety.

"Friedrich," Becker growled, "show him we mean business."

Schmidt shuffled closer to Smythe, still holding the bottle of water in his left hand, and walloped him with his right fist. Smythe's head snapped back with such force it ricocheted forward and bounced off his chest.

Blood ran from his nose.

"Now — does that convince you to cooperate?" Becker said gruffly.

Smythe was doing his best not to cry out from the pain that was radiating from his nose through his skull and into the back of his neck. His mind was racing so much that he couldn't think of anything to say. He only had a vague sense that he needed to stay calm to save his own life.

Becker relaxed his tone. "I'm going to untie you so you can work on that computer. If you try anything funny, I'll have Friedrich work you over real good. Understand?"

Smythe didn't answer.

Schmidt hit him a second time, harder than before. "Answer the man!"

Blood spattered as Smythe nodded.

Schmidt untied him, handed Smythe tissues from a small white box on the desk, then hauled him over to the chair tucked behind.

Becker passed the paper bearing a series of letters and numbers to Smythe. "Make this password work."

Smythe's cloudy vision focused on the paper for a long moment.

"Well?" snapped the impatient Becker.

"Not a password," said Smythe, voice gurgling from blood in his throat.

"What do you mean, not a password. It was in an envelope marked *password.*"

Smythe managed a faint smile.

"Nobody mocks me, especially dressed like you," Becker shouted, pointing to Smythe's clothes. "Look at you. You're pathetic."

"At least I don't look like a Nintendo character," Smythe whispered.

Becker hit Smythe harder than Schmidt. "For a scrawny little guy, you sure do like hurt," Becker said, scratching his head. He pointed to the paper. "If this isn't a password, what is it?"

"Encryption key," Smythe mumbled.

"What the hell's that?" Becker said as a confused Schmidt looked on.

Trying to formulate an answer, Smythe wiped the blood from his face. "Unlocks a data vault in a hard drive," he said, voice barely audible.

"Thought that's what the password did," Becker said stupidly.

"Passwords identify users. Encryption keys locate and open secured data areas," Smythe managed to get out, wincing with pain.

"Identifies users?"

Smythe took more tissues from the box and wiped the blood from his face. "Pet's name, birth date, something like that."

"How the hell am I supposed to find that out?"

"Beat the guy like you're beating me," Smythe said sarcastically.

Becker hit him again.

Chapter 15

Tuesday morning St. James was up at the usual time, down for breakfast by eight o'clock.

By eight fifteen, he wondered why Smythe hadn't shown.

St. James called Smythe's cell. No answer. He went upstairs and pounded on the door. No answer. At the far end of the hall, he spotted a short dark-haired woman wearing a light-brown maid outfit. She was opening the door to clean a room. He rushed down and persuaded her to unlock Smythe's door.

Smythe wasn't in his room, and the bed was still intact. *Not like Louis,* St. James thought. He went back to the maid, described Smythe and asked if she had seen him.

"No. I'd remember someone dressed like that," she said, dragging a vacuum into the room.

St. James ran downstairs and described Louis to the hotel manager, then remembered that he had a recent picture of Smythe on his phone, taken as they were killing time at the airport on their way to London. He showed the manager the photo, and the manager shook his head. "No, I'd remember him."

Grimacing, St. James rushed back to his room and phoned Kingston.

Right away, Kingston assigned DS Joy to head up a search. St. James forwarded the picture of Smythe to her.

Joy's eyebrows rose when she saw the photograph. "Be easy to pick out in a crowd," she mumbled.

Joy mobilized a ground search, sending Smythe's picture to everyone on the force and ordering any information concerning Smythe be texted to her, day or night.

St. James called John Taylor to explain the situation. An understanding Taylor told him to take whatever time needed to find Smythe.

Several hours passed with no word from police. St. James called Smythe's drinking buddies in Canada. No one had heard from him since the two left Ottawa. He gave Smythe's Facebook, Twitter, Snapchat and Instagram accounts to Joy.

St. James paused to think what he should do next. He called Anna.

"What about Dozer? Did you call him?" she said anxiously after listening to what happened.

"No, I haven't. With all of Scotland Yard looking for him, they'd get in each other's way."

"You surprise me, Hamilton," Anna said. "I would have bet Dozer was the first call you made."

"Hmm." St. James thought for a time.

"You still there?"

"Yes. Just thinking about what you said."

"Call him, Hamilton. You have more confidence in him than Scotland Yard."

St. James's smile was faint and nervous. "Better not let David hear you say that."

When they clicked off, he tapped the telephone number for White Investigations in Toronto.

CEO Erasmus White was a member of St. James's investigative team who got the nickname Bulldozer playing football in university. St. James shortened it to Dozer when they worked together on a case in Texas.

Always immaculately dressed and perfectly manicured, Dozer was a larger, muscular LL Cool J. He had been St. James's go-to man for protection. But there had been no need for protection. Anna's admonishment was a stark reminder that the need could arise anytime, as much as St. James hated to think about it.

He filled Dozer in on everything that had happened since he and Smythe had landed at Heathrow.

"Jesus, Hamilton. It's not like Louis to wander off for no reason. Want me to catch the next available flight?"

"Would you?" St. James was instantly grateful and relieved.

***

Eight o'clock Wednesday morning, Dozer landed at Heathrow, groggily wandered off the plane carrying a duffel bag and made his way through the crowd to the baggage area. He rescued his luggage when it slid down the carousel and headed for the car rental kiosk he'd called the night before. While he was waiting for the agent to complete paperwork, a stunning young lady tapped Dozer on the back and with great excitement said, "Mr. Cool J, may I have your autograph?"

Dozer's smile was huge as he turned to face the young lady. Without the slightest hesitation, he said, "I would be delighted to, dear lady. Anything for a fan. What's your name?"

"Emily," she said with glee.

With that, Dozer took the paper Emily was holding and wrote *Best wishes, Emily. You are adorable. LL Cool J.* Emily's face was beyond jubilant as she clenched the autograph close to her heart and rushed off to show her friends.

The rental agent took in the exchange and haughtily said, "You're not LL Cool J!"

"No, I'm not," he said as he took the keys and rental contract from her. "I can't help it if I look like him. I get that a lot."

"You misled that poor girl," the agent scolded.

Dozer's expression clouded. "No, I didn't," he said curtly. "I made this the happiest day of her life. She has something exciting to share with her friends. And, lady, you had better stick to the rental business, 'cause you don't know jack shit about making people feel good."

Dozer wheeled around and walked away before the agent could respond.

When Dozer checked into the same hotel where St. James and Smythe lodged, it was ten thirty. He called St. James right away to let him know he'd meet him at Scotland Yard at one o'clock.

By one thirty, Dozer, St. James and DI Joy were sitting around a chestnut-brown table in a small white Scotland Yard meeting room, surrounded by pictures of prime ministers since Winston Churchill.

Joy took them through procedures she initiated to mobilize the thirty thousand police officers patrolling London's 626 square miles and to get them working with Smythe's description. Thus far, no one had reported any Smythe sightings. Nor had anything been communicated by Smythe's friends. Social media accounts hadn't yielded any leads.

A sturdy-looking middle-aged assistant named Margaret poked her head in the meeting room. She wore a baggy patterned skirt and grey blouse and had a kind face.

"Mr. St. James, is Mr. Smythe's phone an Android?" Margaret asked.

"Yes, it is."

"Would you by chance have his account information?"

"Yes, I have that for all my team in case of emergency."

Dozer frowned. "In case you haven't noticed, brother, this is a damn emergency!"

St. James shrugged as he pulled up Smythe's Google credentials and gave them to Margaret .

"Have your team members consented to cell phone tracker apps?" Margaret said.

"Yes, they all have."

"Great."

Joy's cell vibrated. "DI Joy, speaking … uh-huh … uh-huh. Excellent. Just off the A12, you say?" Joy hauled a writing pad closer. "Repeat the address, please." Joy scribbled on the pad and ended the call.

"Gentlemen, we may have gotten a lucky break. Constable Brown's beat includes a light industrial area off the A12. Ten minutes ago, he saw three men get into a nineties-something Vauxhall van, one wearing clothes matching Smythe's. I'll get men up there right away."

Joy rushed out to dispatch officers to the address given by Brown.

Dozer and St. James looked at one another.

Dozer whispered, "Kidnapped?"

"Sounds like it. But we've only been here a couple of days. Louis has never been to the United Kingdom. He's not a wealthy man, so money can't be a motive, and he wouldn't have enemies here, so why would anyone target him?"

"Maybe he's already too close to something on your client, making someone nervous," Dozer suggested.

"Possible, I suppose."

Joy returned.

Dozer looked at Joy. "Did the officer say Louis looked like he was being restrained or taken against his will?"

Joy stared at her cell, hoping for a follow-up call. "He wasn't close enough to see if his hands were bound, but I believe he was. A man on either side pushed him into the back of the van."

"Kidnapped!" St. James and Dozer said simultaneously.

While they waited for Joy's search results, St. James and Dozer each took one of Smythe's social media pages and searched for any activity that may have occurred that morning. Nothing. St. James logged on to Smythe's email account. Nothing.

Several minutes later, Margaret reappeared in the doorway. "I've had some success with a couple of tracking apps. They show Mr. Smythe's device creeping southwest on the A12."

"Let me see," DI Joy said abruptly.

She handed the cell to Joy.

"This isn't far from the address Brown just gave me."

St. James loaded the tracking app on his cell and set it to follow Smythe's phone on Google Maps.

"I need some fresh air, Phyllis," St. James said innocently. "Please excuse us. Dozer, let's go for a walk."

Her mind elsewhere, Joy looked at them briefly and nodded as they left the room.

Dozer looked as if St. James had just grown a second head. "Really, Hamilton? A walk?" he whispered incredulously.

"Need to clear my head," St. James said duplicitously.

When they stepped outside Scotland Yard, Dozer grabbed St. James by the arm and brought him to a halt.

"You're not fooling me, Hamilton," said Dozer. He pointed to the Thames. "You no more want a walk than to jump in that river."

St. James smiled. "I knew you'd understand, Dozer."

Dozer raised his voice. "Understand what, man? Have you lost it?"

St. James stared into Dozer's dark-brown eyes without saying a word.

Suddenly Dozer's face lit up. "We're going after these bastards, aren't we?" he said excitedly. "Chase them down like the animals they are and take Louis back even if we have to beat them to death."

St. James smiled. "Now that's the kind, gentle, sweet Dozer I've come to know and love."

Chapter 16

Shortly after three o'clock, St. James hailed a cab on Victoria Embankment and told the driver to cross Waterloo Bridge to the Enterprise car-hire office. He requested a Volvo XC60 and insured it to the hilt. The Volvo was large enough to withstand a sizable crash, should things end up that way before the day was out. A strong chassis and extra coverage were good things to have whenever St. James was in a chase.

Dozer drove so St. James could follow Smythe's phone on the app. Weaving through traffic, they made their way across Southwark Bridge, followed the A3200 up to the A1203, taking several turns before reaching the A12.

"Do we stay on the A12?" Dozer asked as he rounded a turn, watching his speed. The last thing they needed was to be pulled over.

Staring at the cell, St. James raised a hand. "Just a second. They're turning left on the B112. According to this, it's Homerton Road."

They followed what they assumed was the van that Constable Brown had spotted earlier and ended up in a poorer area around Camden Station. Dozer brought the Volvo to an abrupt halt in front of a rundown property with a rusty grey-and-white Vauxhall Vivaro parked in front. The house's weather-beaten clapboard was cracked, split and desperately needed paint.

"Nice house," St. James said facetiously, studying the property's overgrown grass. "Looks like they haven't mowed it since the Battle of Britain."

"That fits the bill," Dozer said, pointing to the aged vehicle.

"Yes, it does."

"What do you want to do?" Dozer said, studying the property, trying to guess what dangers might be lurking.

"Well, we should phone DI Joy and give her the plate number to find who owns that piece of junk…"

Sensing St. James was conflicted about calling Joy, Dozer shot him a huge grin showing perfectly white teeth. "I feel a rather large *but* coming on."

"Yes, Dozer, a monumental *but*! If you recall, as far as Joy's concerned, we went for a walk to clear our heads almost three and a half hours ago now. We've effectively gone around her and Kingston by renting a car and chasing the kidnappers. Remember, they've gone out of their way to help us find Louis."

Dozer wagged a finger in St. James's direction. "What do you mean *we*, white man? You were the one who wanted to clear your head. My head was perfectly clear. Louis gone missing is the reason I'm here, where my focus is and should be."

St. James smiled distractedly and nodded as if he hadn't heard.

"Well, what do you want to do?" Dozer repeated, staring at the hovel.

St. James ran his fingers through his thick black hair as he thought. "It's dangerous to try to take the place when we're unarmed."

"Agreed. And we don't know how many might be in there or if they're armed," Dozer said. "But sitting here won't accomplish much. Let's at least take a closer look."

They climbed out of the Volvo, and St. James quietly waded through the tall grass toward the right side of the house, while Dozer stayed to the left. When they were almost at the door, they heard glass shattering behind them, across the street. Dozer looked over and spotted a couple of young kids, barely in their teens, throwing rocks through windows of a nearby house.

"Great neighbourhood," he mumbled.

Dozer walked across the street toward the delinquents. When they spotted him, they ran.

"Wait, guys, I'm not the police," Dozer yelled. "I want to give you five pounds each to do a little job for me."

That brought the kids to an abrupt halt. They turned toward Dozer.

"What do we have to do, mister?" the taller of the two asked suspiciously.

Dozer smiled. "Just what you have been doing."

The kids exchanged puzzled looks.

Dozer pointed to the house across the street. "You see that old house with the rusted van in front? I want you to throw rocks through every window in that place."

"What's the catch?" the taller kid said, while the shorter one hung back nervously.

Dozer pulled a wallet from his back pocket and said, "No catch, boys. This should convince you." He handed them each a five-pound note.

A huge smile washed over each kid's face as they grabbed the bills.

"Wait for my signal," Dozer said, "then give it all you've got."

The boys nodded, and Dozer walked back across the street to his position on the left side of the house. He signalled to St. James to stay where he was and keep low.

When Dozer nodded, the boys crossed over to the property and started pelting rocks at the four front windows, shattering them in quick succession. Then they ran down the street.

The front door flew open and two men ran out onto the driveway. One of them was short and muscular with a huge black moustache; the other was tall and skinny and hopped with a limp. Dozer and St. James were on them within seconds, tackling them from behind and shoving their faces to the pavement. Dozer took the moustache guy , who looked like he had a little more power in him. St. James took the beanpole.

"Anyone else in there?" Dozer said aggressively, his knee on the stockier guy's back. The man wriggled and grunted until he realized he was pinned.

"I asked you a question," Dozer said, leaning harder on the man's spine.

"Unconscious guy," the man said, then spat onto the driveway.

"Weapons?" St. James barked.

"No," said the beanpole.

Dozer and St. James looked at each other and yanked the two men to their feet at the same time. Dozer's man suddenly broke free enough to kick Dozer in the groin. Dozer doubled over but quickly recovered, drew back his meaty fist and hit the man squarely on the chin, dropping him to the ground. St. James's man was less agile and put up much less of a fight. There was a lot of swearing in German from the two as Dozer and St. James tied their hands behind their backs with a pair of zip ties that Dozer quickly produced from a coat pocket. Once they'd neutralized the men, they dragged them into the house.

Dozer led as they carefully cased each room and moved through the space. The inside was just as derelict as the outside, and the main floor had two rooms, a kitchen and a bathroom. The whole place was filthy and littered with plastic cups, cigarette butts on the floor, and other garbage.

In the far corner of a larger green room, they found Smythe slumped against a wall, head hanging to one side. His hands were tied behind his back and he was covered in blood.

"Jesus," St. James said. He ran to his friend, leaving the skinny captive standing there, hands tied, next to Dozer and the other guy.

"Louis," St. James said, kneeling. Smythe was unresponsive. His eyes were swollen almost shut, his cheeks were puffy and bruised, and his nose was almost certainly broken. He was still wearing his plaid blazer, but it was now covered in dirt and blood.

As he studied Smythe's condition, St. James looked back at Dozer. He could see the man's rage building. Dozer was about to head-butt the shorter guy when St. James held up his hand to signal him to stop.

"Dozer," he said firmly, "there'll be time for revenge later. For now, you watch these two idiots. I'll look after Louis."

Dozer gave a reluctant nod as he pushed the restrained kidnappers down onto a pair of well-worn chairs around a plywood table. While Dozer stood over them, St. James found some paper towels in the kitchen, drenched one in cool water and brought it to Smythe. Kneeling on the filthy floor in front of his friend, he began dabbing at Smythe's bloody face until the battered computer specialist came around.

"Hamilton," Smythe whispered, "what took you so long, man?"

"I know, Louis ... I know. I'm so sorry."

"Water," Smythe mumbled.

"Water, of course. I'll be right back."

St. James thoroughly rinsed a plastic cup he found in the kitchen, filled it with fresh water and held it to Smythe's lips.

Dozer glared at the two thugs, who were pitched forward on the chairs and squirming from the restraints. "Take a good look at Louis, fellas. He's *GQ* material compared to what you're going to look like when this is over."

Fear washed over their scraped faces.

"Please don't hurt us," the man with the limp pleaded.

"We'll see how much you cooperate," Dozer said. "That'll determine how much hurt you get."

A look of panic crossed the man's face. The one with the large moustache remained quiet and showed no emotion.

"One way or another you are going to tell me who you work for and why you kidnapped our friend," Dozer barked.

Moustache finally spoke. "You won't get anything out of us."

Dozer smiled. "We'll see about that."

St. James sat on the floor next to Louis. "Anything broken, buddy?"

"My nose, I think. And my head hurts."

"Think you can walk?"

"Think so. Give me a few minutes."

St. James nodded. "We should get you to the hospital, but then we'd have to turn these two over to the police before we knew who and what is behind all this."

Smythe slowly sat straight and pointed to a laptop sitting on the plywood table. "They wanted me to get into the hard drive to find information about money, but they don't have the owner's password."

St. James looked at Smythe quizzically. "Since when has that stopped you?"

Smythe managed a faint smile. "Kidnapped and beaten, I seemed to have forgotten everything I ever knew about computers."

"Took guts, Louis. I'm proud of you."

Chapter 17

It took about five minutes for Smythe to recover enough to stand. He looked down at his multi-plaid outfit.

"Jesus, Hamilton, look what they did to my clothes. My best outfit — and my most expensive too."

St. James was struggling to refrain from sarcasm when his cell vibrated. Joy's number.

"I can't talk to her right now," he mumbled.

Smythe caught a whiff of himself. "I need a shower in the worst way, but I think the bathroom here is probably dirtier than I am."

"We can wait until you get to a clean one, Louis," St. James assured with a wink. "For the good of both of us, though, let's take a walk. Might help to air you out and work out some of the hurt. It'll also help us see whether you need immediate medical attention."

St. James turned to Dozer, who was still babysitting the idiots. "Why don't you take them into the smaller room and see what you can get out of them. I want to know who hired them and why — and why they wanted Louis." Dozer nodded, and St. James eyed the two thugs. "This doesn't stop here. They're the little fish. We want the big fish, the one who ordered this."

"I'll get it out of them," Dozer said, his fists clenched and ready.

"And, Dozer — don't leave a mess I'll have to explain to the Metropolitan Police. As it is now, I'll have to beg forgiveness for what we did today."

Dozer smiled. "I'd pay to see that. Never witnessed you grovelling before."

St. James flashed a sarcastic smile at Dozer as he led Smythe out the front door for a slow walk around the neighbourhood.

St. James's cell vibrated again. Kingston. He ignored the call.

Smythe put one tentative foot in front of the other. His head wounds had stopped bleeding, and nothing besides his nose seemed broken. But still, St. James kept a close eye on his friend's every move to make sure a doctor could wait.

When they returned to the house ten minutes later, Dozer had moved the kidnappers to the small blue room adjacent to the larger one where they had found Smythe. Their faces had already experienced some of Dozer's hospitality.

Dozer smiled when St. James and Smythe entered the room. He pointed to the one wearing coveralls. "Super Mario here is Gerhard Becker. The gimpy one is Friedrich Schmidt. Both work for Wilhelm Schneider."

St. James nodded. "Where is Schneider?"

"Germany, a small town called Gundelsheim," Dozer said, looking pleased with his handywork. "I took their phones and the laptop. I figured Louis and Scotland Yard might find a lead."

St. James nodded and looked at Smythe. "Louis is good to go."

Smythe grinned. "I've been saved!" he said with as much passion as he could muster, both palms open to heaven.

"Well," said Dozer with a smile, "at least they didn't beat the sense of humour out of you."

St. James frowned. His watch said 9:45 p.m. "It's time for me to face the music. I'm going outside to call David."

Chapter 18

"I'm very disappointed in you, Hamilton," Kingston said tersely. "I had DI Joy drop everything to help you find Louis, and you ducked out to take the law into your own hands."

"I'm deeply sorry, David. There is no excuse for doing what we did, but there is a reason."

"And what might that be?"

"The kidnappers were on the move. We had to strike fast," said St. James.

"Not good enough, Hamilton. Following kidnappers with an app is not exclusive to you. I'm sure Joy could have and would have done the same."

"I agree, but we have the kidnappers here and we're holding them for Joy to make the arrest." St. James gave Kingston the address. "We also have preliminary information connecting these thugs to a guy in Gundelsheim, Germany."

After a long pause, Kingston said, "I'll try to smooth it over with Joy, but right now, she's hopping mad, and you wouldn't get her vote if you were running for street cleaner."

Kingston hung up without a word.

By the time Joy arrived with four other officers to arrest Becker and Schmidt, it was close to midnight. She walked past St. James without a word and hauled the two away swiftly while Smythe and Dozer quietly looked on.

Joy left it to another officer to deliver a message to St. James.

"Mr. St. James, DCI Kingston would like to see you and your colleagues in his office tomorrow morning at ten."

St. James nodded. "We'll be there."

***

Ten o'clock Thursday morning, St. James, Smythe and Dozer walked into Kingston's office single file, like students called to the principal's office.

Kingston hadn't met Dozer, so St. James took a moment to introduce them.

Kingston's attention turned to Smythe. "They banged you up badly, Louis. Do you want me to arrange a doctor?"

"No, thank you, David. The hotel made an appointment for three this afternoon," Smythe said quietly.

Kingston nodded. "Good." He turned to St. James. "The two men Joy arrested last night look worse than Louis. Was that the result of your persuasion techniques?"

"Mine," Dozer confessed quickly.

Kingston nodded, looking thoughtful, trying to choose his words carefully. He looked at Dozer. "I suppose your methods may have yielded more information than the civilized ones we are restricted to by law. I don't accept what you have done, but if you have information from those two, I'd be a fool not to take advantage of it. Rest assured, Dozer, if it happens again, I'll be forced to charge you with assault."

"I understand, sir," Dozer said solemnly.

Kingston's tone became less authoritative. "Now tell me what you know."

Dozer told Kingston everything he had gotten from the two he interrogated, and Smythe recounted his kidnapping experience and what the kidnappers wanted him to do with the laptop. Kingston listened quietly without interrupting. "Did you manage to get into the computer?"

"No, sir."

"So our two houseguests downstairs still don't know what's on it?"

"No, they don't, sir," Smythe said.

"Good. Can you access it without the owner's personal information?" Kingston said.

"Absolutely," Smythe said confidently.

Kingston turned to St. James. "Here's the deal, Hamilton. You work with us — and I mean *really* work with us — to solve this, whatever this is, and what you did yesterday never happened." Kingston's deep-blue eyes darted back and forth between the three sitting before him. "Deal's off if any one of you pulls another stunt like yesterday. Agreed?"

"Agreed. Thank you, David," Hamilton said.

Smythe and Dozer nodded in unison.

"Good. We can start by finding out what's on that laptop. Louis, Joy will set you up at a workstation so you can go at it until your doctor's appointment. She's expecting you."

Kingston looked at Hamilton and Dozer. "We're short two DSs, so I'd like you two to take their places, work with Joy to find out whatever is going on here. So that we understand one another, when you receive a request from Joy, it's the same as if it were coming from me. Okay?"

St. James and Dozer both nodded.

"Good." Kingston buzzed Joy, and she immediately came around to collect them.

As they left Kingston's office, Dozer turned to St. James. "Look at the shit you got me into, man. One call to the Canadian authorities by Kingston and I could lose my PI licence."

"Well, then, it's a good thing the DCI is a friend of mine."

Chapter 19

After being chastised by Kingston, St. James thought that, if he had to work closely with Joy, he'd better make amends, and fast. He started by apologizing profusely.

"What I did was wrong, Joy," St. James said quietly. "I am so sorry to have snubbed you. You went full out to help me find Louis, and in the wake of my thoughtless actions, I humiliated you. What can I do to make it up to you?"

"It will take me a long time to get over this one," Joy said coldly. "If you actually worked for me, I'd have you transferred and write a strong demerit comment in your file."

"Yes, I know. I deserve your anger. Do you want me off the file?"

Joy thought for a long moment. "No," she said finally. "DCI Kingston wants your help. And I need your skills to help solve this thing."

Not knowing what to say, St. James just nodded.

Joy stared sharply into his blue eyes. "But I can't live with looking over my shoulder at your every turn. You are either with me or you are not — on my team or out. No half-measures. Understand?"

"Perfectly," he said.

Joy walked away.

St. James knew he had a long way to go to regain her trust.

Joy found a vacant cubicle where she set Smythe up and ensured he had everything he needed to get the job done.

She pointed to the laptop. "Louis, we have to find out what's on it quickly. We're obligated to return it to Chamberlain as soon as possible."

"Understand," Smythe said. "I'll work as quickly as possible."

"Thank you," Joy said and left to meet with St. James and Dozer.

The space Joy had assigned to Smythe was small but workable for the task he had to complete. Smythe plugged in the orphaned computer and put it into safe mode, took the necessary steps to open the laptop and worked the encryption key he got from Becker to open the data vault.

Joy sat with St. James and Dozer in the same meeting room as before.

"Hamilton, I'd like you to research everything you can on this Schneider fellow and anyone you find associated with him."

St. James nodded and filled Joy in on his investigation at Taylor Supermarkets and his obligations to Kingston's friend.

"Mostly, it's Louis that's needed over there," he said cautiously, so as not to upset her.

"I think we can spare him once we have whatever that laptop holds," Joy said.

"Excellent. I'll tell Taylor."

Joy turned to Dozer.

"Dozer, I would like you to go to Gundelsheim, snoop around, see what you can find without being too obvious. I would send one of my officers, but we'd have to go through proper channels with the German authorities. As a private citizen, you're free of all the bureaucratic nonsense that comes with being a police officer from another country. They don't have to know you're an acting DS."

Dozer nodded, then left to check out of the hotel and make travel arrangements. Since he was on his way to Germany, Dozer wouldn't need the car he'd hired at the airport, so he gave the concierge fifty pounds to have the vehicle returned.

St. James returned to his temporary office and phoned John Taylor.

"I am so glad you found Louis. How is he?" Taylor said with genuine concern.

"He's banged up but okay. He'll be back in your office early next week."

"Great," said Taylor, sounding relieved. "And you?"

"I'll be a couple more days, but I would have to wait on Louis anyway. So there'll be no time lost."

They clicked off, and St. James called Anna.

"Hamilton!" she babbled. "It's six thirty in the morning! I was sound asleep."

Hamilton looked at his watch on London time. "Oops. Sorry, darling."

"What can be so important at this hour?" she growled.

St. James apologized a second time. "I need some searches done."

"Give me a moment to get to the study," she said in a less-than-forgiving tone. Still half-asleep, she hauled herself out of bed and picked up the study phone extension seconds later. "Go ahead," she said.

"We need everything you can find out on Wilhelm Schneider. Who he works for and anyone connected to him."

"When do you need this?"

"Yesterday."

"Very funny."

St. James told Anna about Louis's torture and capturing his kidnappers. She gasped with every new detail.

"My God. Is he all right?"

"He's fine now. A lot braver about it all than I would have expected."

"Wow, this case has certainly morphed into a lot more than Taylor's lower profit."

"Sure as hell has."

Just as Anna and St. James disconnected, Smythe appeared at St. James's door, holding the laptop.

"I am into the vault. Some interesting stuff here," he said. "It's all about megabucks, £50 million to be exact. The laptop belongs to a Nigel Chamberlain, a wealthy businessman here in London."

"Let me see," St. James said anxiously.

Smythe pulled a chair next to St. James and showed him what he'd discovered on the hard drive.

"Looks like he's hidden money somewhere," Smythe suggested. "But why would a wealthy man hide money?"

"I can think of three reasons right off the bat, Louis."

Smythe looked at St. James quizzically. "And they would be — what?"

"The money isn't his, and the rightful owner wants it back; or he's in the middle of a nasty divorce and wants to hide it from an estranged wife; or Her Majesty's Revenue and Customs is after him for income taxes." St. James thought for a moment. "But it could just be that someone without any connection to him at all is trying to steal it."

"Someone like Wilhelm Schneider?" Smythe mused.

"Well, the two who worked you over said they worked for him. And they did steal the laptop we now know belongs to Nigel Chamberlain. And they did kidnap you to gain access to whatever information was on the laptop. And when you did, it was all about the hidden money. That's a rather good trail, Louis. Now while you continue burrowing into the hard drive, I'm going to check whether the three usual reasons to hide money are plausible in Nigel Chamberlain's case."

Smythe nodded and returned to the cubicle and continued poking through Chamberlain's hard drive until 2:30 p.m., when he left Scotland Yard for his doctor's appointment.

St. James buzzed Kingston's extension. "Does the name Nigel Chamberlain mean anything to you, David?"

Kingston was quiet for a few seconds. "I don't know him, but I've heard of him. Papers say he made a fortune in international trade. Why do you ask?"

"The laptop appears to belong to him."

"Oh — that's interesting," Kingston said slowly, trying to think what significance that could have.

"Very interesting. Do you happen to know anyone at Her Majesty's Revenue and Customs?"

"No, but one of my DSs does. Why?"

"I'd like to know if Chamberlain is under investigation for any reason."

"Tricky question. Let me see what I can do. Aside from it being his laptop, what does Chamberlain have to do with this Schneider fellow?"

"Don't know. Just following a lead."

Kingston nodded at the phone. "Okay."

"Final question. How could I find out if Chamberlain has marital problems?" said St. James.

"Call Carolyn," Kingston said without a beat.

"Carolyn?"

"Yes, she reads the social pages, tabloids and anything else that covers useless high-society information," Kingston said.

St. James wasn't sure how to react to Kingston's view of his wife's interests. "Okay."

St. James called the Kingston home, greeted Carolyn jovially and explained what he needed to know and why.

"Nigel Chamberlain isn't married," Carolyn said quickly.

Chapter 20

Smythe and St. James were sitting in the hotel bar at five o'clock on Thursday. Smythe's nose was straight again but swollen and had turned from red to purple, and his cheeks sported a couple of butterfly bandages.

Louis caught his reflection in the bar mirror and cast a long-suffering look at St. James, who tried to cheer him up with humour.

"Well, Louis, you've always been into mixing and matching your colours. I don't see how this is any different."

"Ha-ha."

"How bad was it when she reset your nose?"

"Take a wild guess."

"Oh dear. That bad," St. James said, lathering on the sympathy. "What else did she say?"

"Just that I'll live. She gave me a prescription for a cream to clear up my face. Nothing to be concerned about."

"Could have been much worse," St. James said, shaking his head. "So how far did you get with the laptop before you left for the doctor?"

Smythe sipped his wine. "Not far. There's a trail involving banks, how many or for what I don't know yet. There's the name of a law firm here in London, but I haven't found what service they provided. Confusion was part of this guy's strategy. A lot of information scattered about in no particular order."

"Scrambling information in case someone like you got hold of the laptop, no doubt," St. James said, taking another swig of scotch.

"Think so."

***

On Friday, Smythe hibernated in the cubicle all day. St. James didn't see or hear from him until about three in the afternoon when he asked for a meeting with him and Joy. They agreed to convene at four thirty.

Shortly after four, Kingston showed up at St. James's door.

"My DS finally got through to his Revenue and Customs contact to ask about Chamberlain."

"And?"

"The fellow wouldn't say much. Not permitted to speak to anyone outside the department. Policy strictly enforced. Penalty's immediate termination," said Kingston grimly.

"Well, did we learn anything at all?"

Kingston smiled slightly. "The department opened a file on Chamberlain thirty days ago in connection with another investigation."

"What other investigation?"

Kingston shrugged. "He wouldn't talk. What I expected."

"That's *all* he got?"

"That's *what* he got."

St. James reflected for a moment, lightly massaging his square jaw. "Well it's not much, but I guess it's something. They don't open files on a whim. There has to be some smoke around Chamberlain somewhere. All we have to do is find where and trace it back to fire."

"Hamilton, I don't get why you're spending time on a guy just because his laptop's stolen. Your focus is supposed to be on Taylor."

"Okay. The two thugs said they worked for Wilhelm Schneider. So Schneider would have ordered them to steal Chamberlain's laptop. At first we thought Louis might be getting too close to something at Taylor's, something someone didn't want him to find, but that wasn't it. Schneider wanted an experienced computer person to open a stolen laptop for information concerning a substantial amount of money, £50 million to be exact. So Chamberlain's connected to Schneider in some way. I have to find out how."

"Chamberlain hid the money. Not typical for wealthy people unless it belongs to someone else or they're hiding it from a spouse's divorce lawyer or the tax authorities are investigating for unpaid taxes."

"We eliminated the divorce explanation right away. Chamberlain isn't married. Revenue and Customs have opened a file on him, making tax avoidance a possible lead. But my instincts tell me there's something more here than meets the eye."

"So what could be the connection?" Kingston mused.

"Perhaps the department's open file is meant to determine just that. Maybe it's this Schneider fellow they're after, and Chamberlain's caught in the crosshairs."

Kingston shook his head. "Doesn't make sense. Why would our Revenue and Customs have an interest in a German nationalist living in Germany with no business operations that we know of in the United Kingdom?"

"Maybe the German authorities asked Britain for help," St. James ventured. "That could fit if they thought Schneider did have a connection here. They could be running down a lead, opposite what I'm doing for Joy. Starting with Schneider, searching for a connection with someone here, like Chamberlain; while I'm starting with Chamberlain, searching for a connection with someone there, like Schneider."

"Hmm. I see your point," Kingston said. "So what would be a plausible bridge between Chamberlain and Taylor Supermarkets?"

"No idea. Chamberlain could be a hacking into Taylor's system, extracting information or money for personal gain. A long shot, I admit, but I have to explore everything if I'm to do the job properly," St. James said.

Kingston shook his head and walked back to his office.

The meeting Smythe invited St. James and Joy to didn't start until four forty-five. Joy had a call from Washington concerning another case.

When the three finally settled in the meeting room, Smythe opened Chamberlain's laptop and placed his notes on the table.

"I wanted to take you through what I've discovered so far before I went any further," Smythe said, adjusting his comb-over.

"Okay," Joy said.

"Let's hear what you have, Louis," St. James said.

Smythe turned to St. James. "You remember I said the data vault noted a law firm?"

"I remember."

"Well, the firm is Randall & Collins here in London. A year ago in May, Nigel Chamberlain engaged Lisa Randall, the senior partner there, for some advice regarding moving money internationally. Chamberlain's notes said he sent Randall to Switzerland, where she opened a safety deposit box in UBS in Zurich. Randall was to authorize an alternative person to have access. The box was huge, so maybe she deposited some of the £50 million."

Smythe looked at both of them to make sure they were following him, then continued.

"Then Chamberlain said he would send Henry Collins, Randall's partner, to Switzerland a week later to open the same size safety deposit box in Credit Suisse. Just as Randall did, he authorized an alternative person to have access. Then he was to go to UBS and access the box Randall opened the previous week, no indication why. Maybe he took something out or put something in. I don't know. My guess is he took something out because he was supposed to go back to the safety deposit box at Credit Suisse. He wouldn't go back empty-handed. Be no poi—"

"Who were the authorized alternatives?" St. James interrupted.

"Each other. Collins was Randall's alternative, and Randall was Collins's.

"Makes sense," Joy said.

Smythe continued. "Randall and Collins repeated these trips several times."

"I suppose if they were transporting a sizable amount of the £50 million, they'd have to make several trips," St. James added. "If they wanted to take it all at once, it would have to go air cargo."

"What the hell was he doing?" said a frustrated Joy.

"Well, it's time to let Chamberlain know we have his laptop, anyway. So we can ask him in person," St. James suggested.

"I agree. I'll have my assistant track him down."

Chapter 21

Saturday morning, St. James woke to an overcast sky with the promise of rain. Pedestrians scurried about the streets while a row of saplings outside the hotel struggled to survive stronger westerly winds.

As arranged the night before, Joy picked St. James up at nine o'clock in front of the hotel. He climbed into her car and straightened his wind-blown hair as he thanked her for picking him up. Joy flashed a quick smile and got down to business, filling him in on a new development.

"Lindsay discovered Chamberlain owns an upscale flat on Yeoman's Row in Knightsbridge and a large home in Wimbledon," Joy said as they pulled away from the hotel. "She tried two phone numbers registered to Chamberlain three times, but there was no answer."

"Lindsay?"

"My assistant."

"Never heard you call her by name before."

About twenty minutes later, they pulled up at Chamberlain's address on Yeoman's Row. It was a Georgian building, close to the street but shielded from the road by a large boxwood hedge. Joy knocked on the heavy black door. No answer. Her knocks became more aggressive.

After three tries, she said, "Guess he's not home."

"Maybe he is and just not receiving callers," St. James muttered as he pulled a small case from his sports coat pocket.

Joy studied what looked like a compact sewing kit. "I hope that's not what I think it is."

St. James unzipped the case and took out a lock pick. "I'm afraid it is."

"Those things are illegal here. You can't do that, especially in the presence of a police officer," she said bluntly.

"We have probable cause," St. James said as he slipped the tool into the lock.

"What bloody probable cause?" she said, raising her voice. "Bollocks! There's no damn probable cause!"

St. James didn't answer.

After a jiggled turn of the pick, the lock released, and St. James pushed the door open. Joy stood outside, fuming and looking all around, until she finally let out an exasperated burst of air and followed him inside and shut the door.

From the foyer, they could see a cream-toned sitting room decorated with expensive art, plush green carpeting and modern European furniture.

Throughout the room, a pleasant scent of fresh flowers lingered. Everything said wealth.

Joy yelled, "Metropolitan Police! Anyone home? Hello."

No answer.

They moved past the sitting room into a large recently renovated kitchen and dining area with grey marble countertops, a white marble floor and every modern, upper-end appliance imaginable built into walls, including a flat-screen television switched on low to the BBC.

St. James pointed to the screen. "There's your probable cause."

"What kind of crap is that?" Joy snapped. "We couldn't hear that from the sitting room, let alone outside."

St. James smiled.

"You are incorrigible. You know that?"

"Girlfriend tells me that all the time."

"Huh," Joy said, in a tone that St. James couldn't read and decided to let lie.

They slowly moved to the foot of the stairs leading to the second level. Joy looked at St. James and put out her hand to get him to pause, which he did. She called out again, from the bottom stair, identifying herself as a police officer.

Still no response.

At the top of the stairs, they entered a blue room on the right. It looked like a spare bedroom that hadn't been used for some time. Next to it was a smaller pink bedroom. Farther down the hall on the right was a third bedroom that had been converted into a small study. It was furnished with a rolltop desk, a grey metal filing cabinet and a table barely large enough to accommodate a printer.

Across the hall was a larger pale-yellow bedroom that looked like it could be the master. The bed linens were in such a state that St. James thought there must have been a struggle. He opened the closet and studied its contents: expensive suits, Italian shoes and French dress shirts. "Don't think he shops at Walmart."

"Don't think he has to," Joy mumbled as she rooted through a night-table drawer.

St. James made his way around the ransacked king-size bed. On the floor, between the mattress and window overlooking Yeoman's Row, lay a man — or what remained of one. St. James guessed him to be midfifties. It was a dreadful sight. Both hands were missing, and his chest was covered in blood from what appeared to be multiple gunshot wounds. A large pool of blood had seeped around each arm.

St. James caught Joy's gaze and motioned her over to where he stood. She joined him and let out a little cry as she grabbed Hamilton's forearm.

"Dear God," she said quietly.

"I think we can stop arguing about probable cause now," St. James said.

Chapter 22

It was well into a foggy and rainy Saturday afternoon before the coroner finished, the body was confirmed to be that of Nigel Chamberlain and removed, and police had processed the crime scene. St. James and Joy were back at the Yard at four thirty, filling Kingston in on the day.

"Why cut the hands off, for God's sake?" Kingston said with a pained look.

"Don't know," said Joy. "Coroner thinks he was still alive when they were severed, if you can believe that."

Kingston was aghast as he pictured the horrendous torture Chamberlain would have suffered before death.

St. James stared off, deep in thought.

Kingston nodded. "Since this is now a murder investigation, Revenue and Customs will have to give us what they have on Chamberlain."

"Would be helpful," St. James said thoughtfully.

"I'll make an appointment with Randall & Collins, hopefully for Monday," Joy offered.

∗∗∗

Sunday morning St. James called Joy.

"Feel like taking a run at Chamberlain's flat today, Phyllis? Or are you jammed up with personal stuff?"

"Need groceries, but that can wait. Let's scour the place."

"You have the key?"

"Don't need one as long as I have you and your little kit, do I?"

"Illegal in the UK, isn't it?"

"Not if you have probable cause. Cut the crap and let's get going; key's in my pocket."

"Guess I'm never going to live that down."

"Nope. I'll pick you up in front of your hotel in thirty."

When they let themselves into the flat about an hour later, they could see right away that it had been cleaned, top to bottom. There was no sign of blood anywhere in the master bedroom, and the bed was back to normal.

The flat had been declared free of fingerprints, except those of Chamberlain and his cleaning lady. So the best St. James and Joy could hope for was a physical clue of some sort.

Joy went through table and dresser drawers, poking around everything in sight. She found tissues, magazines, toiletries and a manicure kit in one night table and an old paperback copy of *The Great Gatsby* in another. Not much else. In the corner of the blue guest room were two stacks of hard-cover mystery books by different authors, and a complete collection of Agatha Christie's Poirot novels sat on the floor of the small pink bedroom. Closets in the smaller bedrooms were ladened with upscale, fashionable women's clothing.

"With all these expensive women's clothes, it's strange our guys didn't find prints," Joy said.

"What does that tell you?"

"Not sure what to make of it. Maybe Chamberlain was murdered by a deranged unhappy lover or a female relative with anger issues," she mumbled in jest. "But it's unlikely a woman would be capable of cutting off the hands."

"Why wipe your prints and then leave clothes behind? It doesn't make sense. There should be prints from before the murder. Lover or relative, a woman stayed here more than once and expected to return. Otherwise, there'd be no reason to leave clothes," he reasoned.

Joy pulled out her cell and tapped the number for the head of forensics. A man answered right away.

"Phil, it's Joy. I'm at Chamberlain's flat. Your guys couldn't find prints other than Chamberlain's, but there are clothes here belonging to a woman. Did you test those?"

St. James could hear the man's voice but not enough to make out what was said.

"Why the hell not?" Joy barked.

More garbled words.

"Well send someone back here immediately," she said tersely. "I want these clothes taken to the lab and tested for everything!" Joy clicked off before Phil could respond.

"Asshole!" she said sharply.

"Let me guess," said St. James with a smirk, "because he found no one else's prints anywhere in the flat, he skipped the clothes."

Joy nodded. "Sometimes, I wonder about him."

St. James shrugged and made his way across the hall where he sat at Chamberlain's rolltop desk and found various bits of correspondence with a man named Keller. Social exchanges, nothing of importance. He guessed the space on the desk was where the stolen laptop once rested. Printer paper filled a cubbyhole below, and a drawer contained the usual miscellaneous office equipment, nothing much to help the case.

St. James leaned back in the swivel chair and paused for a few seconds, wondering what could be missing besides the laptop.

"Phyllis?"

"Yeah?" she shouted from another room.

"I don't recall seeing a cell phone."

Joy walked down the hall to where St. James was sitting. "Come to think of it, neither do I." She leaned against the doorjamb, arms folded.

"What about the forensic guys? They mention a phone?"

"No, they didn't." Joy pondered for a long moment. "Only the man's wallet was on his body."

"They went through Chamberlain's Rolls at the same time. Did they find anything there?"

Joy looked annoyed with herself for the oversight. "Nothing."

St. James stared at her. "Everyone has a cell, especially someone importing and exporting goods around the world."

Joy nodded. "Killer might have taken it thinking it held something incriminating."

"Possible."

They opened and closed every door and drawer throughout the flat for the next hour and a half but found nothing resembling a clue.

"Maybe the woman's clothes will tell us something when the lab report comes back," Joy said hopefully.

Walking back to her green Fiat, Joy paused. "We may as well do the Wimbledon home while we're at it."

St. James nodded.

The drive to Wimbledon took about forty minutes. After getting lost twice, they finally found Chamberlain's large three-storey Victorian mansion on Parkside Avenue, where Joy said houses sold for £1,300 per square foot.

St. James whistled. "What would that translate into?"

Joy looked over at him and smiled. "Two million pounds might get you a fixer-upper."

"How the other half lives, I guess."

When they climbed out of the Fiat, Joy flashed her badge to a caretaker named Earl and told him they were there to search the house. Earl, who had been told of Chamberlain's death, was in shock and just waved them on.

Jones, a tall, heavy-set butler, greeted them when they knocked on the door, dressed in a traditional black morning coat worn by butlers throughout history. He had been briefly interviewed by police and had passed the horrible news on to staff. Everyone was appalled at Chamberlain's ghastly death and worried about their jobs. Jones remained calm in light of his leadership role with the staff, but stress and strain were clearly showing.

Jones managed a grand tour of the mansion — eight bedrooms, six bathrooms, a main floor snooker room — twenty rooms in all.

St. James eyed a large wood-panelled study on the main floor, off a wide hallway covered in thick green carpeting.

One wall was floor-to-ceiling books, and a large oak desk sat in the centre of the room. Dark paintings of the English countryside occupied the remaining walls; the other furniture included a perfectly restored mid-Victorian divan and several reading chairs.

"Elegant," Joy said.

St. James turned to the butler. "Jones, we didn't find a cell phone in Mr. Chamberlain's flat. Do you have any idea where it could be?"

"Yes, Mr. St. James. Mr. Chamberlain found the cell beginning to dominate his life far too much and chose to spend the odd day without it. Yesterday was one of those days. He gave it to me for safekeeping when he wished to be without it."

Jones pointed to a painting of the Midlands. "There is a safe behind that one. I keep his cell there. Mr. Chamberlain received many confidential communications regarding sensitive matters, you know. It's not good to leave it lying around for curiosity to get the better of staff."

"I see," said St. James. "Can you open it?"

"By all means, sir."

St. James glanced at Joy, surprised Jones knew the combination.

Jones glided over to the picture, tapped one corner, and the painting flipped open. He entered the combination, and the safe opened smoothly on its own. Jones reached in, pulled out a cell and handed it to St. James.

"Chamberlain must have trusted you a lot to give you the combination," Joy said with a slight smile.

"I have been with him for many years, miss, and I have never given him a reason to distrust. I imagine he thought I earned it."

"What will you do now that he's gone?" Joy asked empathetically.

Jones's stone-cold face showed a trace of pain. "I honestly don't know, miss. Being a butler here is all I've ever known." With that, Jones turned and left the room.

"Poor sod," Joy said, shaking her head. "No longer has a purpose."

St. James ignored Joy's assessment. "Phyllis, I'll spend my time here. It's the logical place to find clues to help my end of the investigation — if there are any to find."

Joy looked at him with raised eyebrows. "You're doing it again, Hamilton."

"Doing what?"

"Being annoying."

A puzzled St. James blankly said, "I don't understand."

"You've highjacked the study as your search ground and expect me to cover the other nineteen rooms," she said in a slightly raised voice.

"I don't expect you to do anything, Phyllis! I'm just saying, if there's anything important for what I'm trying to do for you, it's most likely here, in this room."

"Argh!" Joy said, shaking her head as she walked out.

St. James frowned as he sat behind Chamberlain's large desk to examine the cell.

The unlocked cell clarified why Jones didn't leave it where wondering eyes could get a glimpse of anything confidential.

No need for a password, I guess; it's either on Chamberlain's person or in the safe, he thought.

For the next half hour, he scrolled through emails and text messages Chamberlain had with numerous people. Grabbing his attention was a running exchange with Wilhelm Schneider, the man who hired Becker and Schmidt to steal Chamberlain's computer. It proved at least one connection between the two men St. James was hoping to find, but it was conflicted. Chamberlain and Schneider were discussing business together. St. James considered this for a beat. *On one hand, they're talking about working together. On the other, Schneider just had Chamberlain's computer stolen.*

"What would give rise to that?" he mumbled.

"Who are you talking to?" Joy said as she returned to the large study.

"Myself."

"How's that working?"

St. James ignored the jab. "Come look at this."

He showed her the exchange between Schneider and Chamberlain.

"Odd," she said. "Wonder what happened between them."

Joy scrolled further. "A fellow named Harry Fischer is copied on everything. Who's he, I wonder?"

"Don't know. I'll have Anna research him."

"Anna? A good researcher?" Joy said, continuing to scroll.

"The best."

Joy handed the phone back to him. "I'll see what else's in the safe."

She found a stack of papers, but more importantly, a second laptop hidden beneath those papers.

"Looks like we have another job for Louis," she said, holding the computer up for St. James to see.

"Hope it holds more than we have now. Let's bag the phone and laptop for your people and Louis to examine. I'll go through the file cabinets and desk drawers."

"I'll read through the papers," Joy said, sounding more agreeable than when she left earlier.

They spent another two hours going through filing cabinets and drawers, bagging everything that remotely looked relevant to Chamberlain's murder and his connection with Wilhelm Schneider.

Seven o'clock that evening, Joy dropped St. James off at the Thistle Piccadilly Hotel on Coventry.

"Productive day, Hamilton. Thank you. Tomorrow we'll get people working on what we found and see if Randall and Collins can meet."

"Sounds good, Phyllis. Enjoy the remaining hours of your weekend," St. James said as he slid out of the Fiat.

Chapter 23

When Joy called first thing Monday morning, Lisa Randall said her day was relatively straightforward, and she could meet with her and St. James at ten.

It was the beginning of the third week of July. Steady rain on Sunday had given way to a bright sunny Monday morning, and the city was alive with people looking to begin another week.

Joy and St. James met outside the old brick building on Fleet Street where Randall & Collins kept their second-floor offices. They climbed the stairs and entered a modern, renovated space filled with Urban Office flexible workspaces and modular sofas and chairs.

An older receptionist stood up behind her desk. "Detective Joy, is it? And..." She looked down at a piece of paper. "Mr. St. James?"

The woman's colourful plaid skirt reminded St. James of Smythe.

"That's right," Joy said while St. James nodded and smiled.

The receptionist wasted no time announcing their arrival to Randall, who appeared a few minutes later to collect them.

Everything about Lisa Randall said *upper-class*, from her slim build and her beige suit to her shoulder-length black hair with its tasteful streak of white. She smiled pleasantly as she shook their hands and welcomed them into her office.

She motioned to two blue leather chairs, then settled herself behind an average-size maple desk.

"Now," Randall said in a slightly deeper voice than her countenance suggested, "how can I be of help?"

"No doubt you've heard the news about your client, Nigel Chamberlain," St. James said solemnly.

"I have," Randall said sadly. "Dreadful turn of events. Nasty business. He was a lovely man and an excellent client. Do you know what happened?"

Joy wasn't about to go into gory details, not just yet anyway. "The investigation's just begun. We're here," she said, watching Randall's face carefully for her reaction, "because you made several trips on Mr. Chamberlain's behalf to two different banks in Switzerland. We'd like to know what for, what service you provided."

"You know we are bound by solicitor-client privilege," Randall said in a haughty tone.

Joy stiffened. "Mrs. Randall, this is a murder investigation. You no longer have a client nor the power to withhold evidence in your possession. Now we could handle this like professionals, or I could force you with a court order. And

I dare say that once a judge hears Chamberlain had both hands cut off while he was still alive, your chances of squashing a motion would be slim to none."

"Hands cut off!" Randall said, covering her face with both hands. "Jesus, who would do such a thing?"

"You didn't know?" St. James said doubtfully.

Randall brought her hands down and dropped them in her lap. She looked ashen. "No details, just that he was murdered."

"He was shot eight times too," St. James said, hoping the extra shock value would speed up cooperation.

Randall was stunned. "My God!"

Without another word, she rose from behind the desk, opened the door and asked her assistant to fetch Chamberlain's files and to call in Henry Collins.

A couple of minutes later, a short, plump Collins entered Randall's office. He wore a three-piece grey suit with a red bow tie and peered at them through half-glasses that rested on the end of his nose. One arm held Chamberlain's files, and the other cradled a laptop. Introductions were made, and they moved to a larger table where they could spread out.

Joy explained Chamberlain's gory murder for Collins's benefit.

Collins closed his eyes and said nothing, as though he were observing a minute of silence on Remembrance Day. When his eyes opened, Collins booted up the laptop and flipped open files chronicling the firm's work for Chamberlain.

"We made several trips to Zurich to deposit packages in large safety deposit boxes," Randall began, speaking slowly and deliberately.

"What exactly was in the packages?" Joy asked.

Collins took the lead. "Even though the packages were the size and shape of pound notes, we never knew what they contained. Our instructions were clear. We were to rent safety deposit boxes and deposit packages. Lisa and I were to take turns to avoid the suspicion of one person making multiple trips. We weren't to ask questions. And we weren't to open the packages. We were each given a power of attorney to facilitate everything."

"The two of you?" St. James said.

Collins scratched his bald head. "Yes. Mr. Chamberlain wanted both of us empowered in case one or the other wasn't able to go for some reason."

"I see," said Joy. "Weren't you the least bit curious about what you were transporting? Curious enough to open a package?"

"Absolutely not," Randall said emphatically. "We signed a contract saying we wouldn't, and we honoured that contract to the letter."

"Were you not concerned you could be doing something illegal?" St. James pressed.

"Not in the least," Collins said. "We were acting only as couriers. We didn't know what we were carrying and didn't want to know. We had no part in assembling the contents."

"Did you do any other work for Chamberlain? Normal legal work, I mean," said Joy.

"Usual things," said Randall. "Real estate purchase and sale agreements, deeds, work contracts."

"What line of work was he in?" asked St. James.

"Import/export," replied Collins.

"Of what?" asked Joy.

"Carpets, carvings, collectibles and antiquities from East and Southeast Asia," Collins replied.

"Pretty big sandbox," St. James mused.

"Yes, it is," Randall agreed.

"Were you given any other instructions by Chamberlain?" St. James said.

"Not that I recall," Collins said, trying to remember as he spoke.

"Can't think of anything," Randall said.

Joy changed course. "How long had Chamberlain been a client?"

"Five or six years," Randall said.

"Was he ever accused of criminal activity?" St. James said.

"By whom?" Collins said abruptly.

"Anyone."

"None this firm's aware of," Randall assured. "Doesn't mean another firm didn't handle a situation."

"Of course. Lawsuits?" St. James said.

"The odd nuisance suit. You know, the kind launched more for negotiating purposes than to recover actual damages," Randall responded.

St. James nodded. "Did either of you notice anyone following you during your travels to and from Zurich?"

Randall and Collins each stared out the window simultaneously, working to recall movements and who, if anyone, might have stood out or looked suspicious during their travels.

"There was one fellow who stood out a little," said Randall slowly. "Wore a long grey coat and matching hat. Aviator sunglasses."

"Do you remember when you first noticed him?" Joy asked.

Randall worked her memory again. "I believe it was at the airport gate here in London, waiting to board a Zurich flight."

"Was he on the same flight?" St. James asked.

"I didn't see him on the plane, but he was sitting in the same lounge area as me. So I would assume he would be. The area was only for the one flight."

"And did you see him after that?" Joy said.

"Maybe strolling between Paradeplatz 6 and Paradeplatz 8 streets when I was heading to the UBS, but I can't be certain. Memory's a little fuzzy."

"Did this fellow approach you at all, show any interest in you and what you were doing?" St. James pressed.

"Never approached me. As for showing interest, I wouldn't know because of the sunglasses."

St. James turned to Collins. "How about you, Mr. Collins?"

Collins shook his head. "I am afraid I'm nowhere near as observant as Lisa. I don't remember the grey-coat fellow or anyone else for that matter. That doesn't mean they weren't there. I was so focused on what I had to do for Mr. Chamberlain that I paid no attention to anything else."

Joy dominated the meeting with typical murder-investigation questions for the next forty-five minutes. When she had filled a notebook and run out of questions for the time being, they thanked Randall and Collins for their time and cooperation and headed back to Scotland Yard.

Chapter 24

Tuesday morning, Joy called a meeting of everyone working on Chamberlain's murder case. She and St. James were focused primarily on the fraud side, so additional resources had to be assigned to ensure a proper investigation into Chamberlain's death.

Karen Saunders, a small plain-featured pathologist, sat opposite Joy. A heavy-set DS Bert Billings, in charge of Chamberlain's murder investigation, sat on Joy's right. Two of Billings's junior officers were also in attendance.

"Karen, what can you confirm at this stage?" Joy asked.

"His hands were severed before he died, for sure."

"What do you think was used?" Joy said.

"Hacksaw, maybe."

Joy shuddered. "Anything other than the severed hands?"

Bruises on the back of his head, probably from a struggle," Saunders reported.

"Blunt force?" Joy asked.

"No. More likely pushed backward into something. Slammed up against a door casing, something like that."

"What about the weapon?"

"Odd choice for a murder weapon," Saunders said. "Bullets came from a Ruger SR22, a popular target pistol but not the usual choice of a killer."

"Why is that?" asked a junior.

"The gun has to be aimed at a specific part of the body to kill instantly; heart or head. Otherwise, it could take multiple shots to end a life," Saunders explained.

"Could explain the eight shots," Joy offered.

"Given that his hands were severed, the number of shots is academic. He'd have been dead before he was shot. Bleed out in seconds," Billings said gruffly.

"True," said Joy. "But it could tell us something about the killer."

Saunders nodded. "Amateur, most likely. Not professional."

"I agree," Joy said.

Billings nodded. "So we're probably looking for a novice, first-time killer. No point in searching databases for professionals, then. Waste of time."

"Unless that's what the killer wants us to think," Saunders suggested.

"Possible, I suppose," Joy said thoughtfully. "But my experience is professional killers don't care. They only care that nothing can be traced back to them."

"Would a novice killer sever hands?" Sanders asked. "Doesn't seem realistic. A first-time killer would be frightened enough using a gun, let alone hacksawing hands from a person still breathing."

"Good point, Karen," Joy said.

"Maybe more than one person involved," Sanders suggested.

"Maybe," Billings said, rubbing his fleshy neck.

Joy nodded.

Billings stared off in thought for a couple of beats. "If they're a first-time killer, odds are they may not have owned a gun. More likely a recent purchase," Billings reasoned. "I'll check for Rugers purchased during the last six months."

"Thanks, Bert. Keep me posted," Joy said.

"Absolutely," Billings said.

"Fingerprints?" Joy asked.

"Like I said last Saturday, everything was wiped clean. The only prints we found belonged to Chamberlain and his cleaning lady, who I have on my list to interview," Billings said.

"What about the woman's clothes, Bert? Lab come up with anything?"

"Only that they were all European size thirty-nine — North American size seven. Nothing on the clothes we can use. There were DNA traces but they were damaged to the point of being useless."

"How could that happen?" Joy said abruptly.

Billings shrugged. "The lab says if you expose *E. coli* to low concentrations of hydrogen peroxide, it damages DNA. They think that's what happened here."

"A lot simpler to dispose of the clothes," Joy said, shaking her head.

"I agree," Billings said.

"Bert, can you speed things up by using the lads?" Joy asked, nodding to the two junior officers.

"They'll be with me until I nail this sucker. I'll have them track down anyone in Chamberlain's circle — friends, business relationships, family, acquaintances, that sort of thing."

They batted around additional theories about the killer's profile before ending the meeting.

Chapter 25

Smythe was feeling better when he arrived back at Taylor Supermarkets on Tuesday morning. The cuts on his face were healing well, as was his broken nose, and the bruises were fading. The pain had all but subsided thanks to whatever magic was in the doctor's prescription.

Vanderbilt had taken the day off, and the senior programmer was attending a computer conference for most of the day at a Heathrow hotel. Smythe had the coding room all to himself.

Instead of working dummy transactions in the fabricated company on his laptop, Smythe asked one of the juniors to log him on to the system so he could check for malware.

Smythe put the computer into safe mode and searched for suspicious files in the list of programs. Nothing obvious. Everything looked legitimate. Just the normal programs one would expect for a supermarket chain.

Then something caught Smythe's eye. A program called Pay Validation, which didn't identify with any major software producer.

Smythe began burrowing, looking for traffic related to Pay Validation to learn more about how the system worked. Hours of probing and exploring consumed Tuesday and Wednesday.

On Thursday morning, he discovered a thread. Pay Validation seemed to focus on purchase orders and invoices from a company called Baker Sugars, processing shipments and payments in return.

By Friday night, four straight days of probing had fried Smythe's brain. Exhausted after putting in another fourteen-hour day, he opted to dine alone in his room and turn in early.

He heard banging on the hotel door at seven o'clock on Friday evening and found St. James standing in the hallway.

"There is no way you're eating alone in your room again tonight, Louis," St. James said slowly, but with such authority, Smythe knew resistance was futile.

Smythe raised both hands to surrender.

"Get your coat, Louis. We're getting drunk."

Fifteen minutes later, they were seated at a window table at the Romulo Café and Restaurant on Kensington High Street. Smythe was dressed in a plain grey tracksuit — a massive departure from his usual technicolour plaid ensembles.

St. James looked at him with concern and ordered a double shot of Macallan. Smythe skipped his usual glass of wine in favour of a gin and tonic.

Smythe looked at Hamilton with faint suspicion. "I thought you only drank Macallan to celebrate surviving an attempt on your life," he said, slowly pointing to St. James's glass.

"I've expanded my ritual to include attempts on a team member's life. This double is in honour of you surviving the beating."

"Very kind, Hamilton, thank you." Smythe raised his drink for a small toast, and the two men clinked glasses.

St. James studied Smythe's face. "Speaking of beatings, you're looking better."

Smythe flashed a wan smile.

"Thanks. Feels better too. Doesn't hurt as much. Whatever the doctor prescribed is good stuff."

"That's great," St. James said encouragingly, before a look of concern crossed his face.

He looked out the window and noticed a walking tour of Japanese tourists crowded around a guide. The guide wore a large-brimmed hat and was gesturing to places of interest as the pack moved along.

"What?" Louis asked, noticing Hamilton's worried expression.

"I've never seen you work this hard, Louis. I'm actually a bit concerned."

"Well, I guess that makes two of us. This case is the hardest thing I have ever had to solve. I'm exhausted."

"You say that about every case."

"This time I mean it."

"I can see the stress in your face. Where are you with it?"

Smythe explained the Pay Validation program, the processing of food invoices from Baker Sugars, and the subsequent payment of those invoices.

"I'll get Anna to check out the company. Anything else?"

"The complexity is huge."

"How so?"

"When I finished this afternoon, I was fairly certain Baker was the only account paid at certain intervals, when the account grew to certain levels. Every other major supplier is on negotiated credit terms. It was extremely difficult to catch Baker as the only exception. I was out of my mind by the end of yesterday."

"I can see why. Not only tedious but almost impossible to detect," St. James consoled. "Does this have anything to do with Vanderbilt's add-on program?"

"No. Pretty well ruled that out with dummy transactions in the company he set up on my laptop. The add-on sped up performance, as Vanderbilt said. Baker Sugars' activity, I'm sure, is driven by the Pay Validation program. Nothing to do with Vanderbilt's add-on."

St. James nodded, then sighed. "Do we know if the Baker transactions are bona fide?"

"Not yet. I'm hoping Anna's research sheds light on that."

A short, thin server with fake eyelashes arrived at the table.

St. James leaned in to read her name tag. "Hello, Bernila," he said, with a big smile that was immediately returned.

"What a pretty name," Smythe said, looking a little brighter. "Out of curiosity, what is its origin?"

"Filipino. My dad owns part of the restaurant. He talked me into coming to London to help him run it."

"Wonderful!" St. James said.

For the next two hours, they placed themselves in Bernila's capable hands; the two old friends lingered over a beautiful supper, killing two bottles of Chateau du Puy Bonnet in the process, and sharing stories that they hadn't thought about for a while. As the drinks and conversation flowed, Smythe became noticeably more relaxed.

Later, strolling to the hotel, Smythe said, "Tonight has been just what I needed, Hamilton. I feel a lot better. Thank you!"

St. James's smile was huge. "You should, my friend, with all that booze in you."

Chapter 26

St. James was a walker. His choice of exercise. At home, he had an eleven-kilometre route that took him three to four hours to complete. He used the time to think and work through cases, plan strategy and next steps. This was especially helpful when he hit a wall with an investigation.

Since landing in London his walking time had been limited, and on Saturday morning, he was determined to reverse the trend. After breakfast he pulled up London streets on Google Maps and laid out a route that took him to St. Anne's Court, over to Dean, down to Gerrard and right to hook back up to Wardour — a rectangular walk, somewhere between three and a half and four kilometres. Nothing close to his Ottawa route, but he didn't know London that well.

The walk took him through Chinatown, past sidewalk vegetable stands, shops and restaurants, and under strings of red lanterns and a large colourful arch near Wardour and Shaftesbury. In front of St. Anne's churchyard, he sat on the grass for a time, watching pedestrian and vehicle traffic and thinking about Taylor's case. His mind slowly drifted into a state of unrest, causing him to second-guess his instinct that Chamberlain's murder was somehow connected to Taylor's profit conundrum.

I'm gambling that Chamberlain, Schneider and Fischer have a connection that affects Taylor somehow, but with no evidence. Why do I think they're one case? It's just a hunch, and it could end badly. We could blow the whole case, following a weak idea down a dark hole, without so much as a single irregularity in Taylor's business to show for it. Huge reputation risk.

And then the most worrying thought of all: *Maybe this time my luck will run out.*

When some tourists passed close by him in matching yellow coats, the odd sight jarred him back into the present moment, and he shook off the negativity. An optimist by nature, the sudden shift to gloom concerned him. His instincts had served him well on many other cases. Why the sudden self-doubt? He shook his head again, rose from the grass, brushed himself off and continued on. It was noon when he arrived back at the hotel and pounded on Smythe's door.

He smiled when he saw Smythe's mismatched plaid pyjamas: red and yellow on top, green and black on bottom.

"Have you eaten, Louis?"

Smythe shook his head.

"Get dressed and meet me in the bar. I'll buy you a beer and a sandwich. This afternoon we'll take a tour of London."

The prospect of seeing London brightened Smythe's manner.

"Excellent, Hamilton. Give me ten minutes."

***

That afternoon, St. James took Smythe on an extensive tour of London's more famous sights — Big Ben, the Tower of London, the National Gallery, Piccadilly Circus, Trafalgar Square, and the London Eye, to name a few. At six o'clock, they landed at Wiltons Restaurant on Jermyn Street to enjoy a traditional British steak dinner and a bottle of Saint-Joseph red.

As they waited for their entrees, Smythe was ebullient, telling St. James what a great afternoon he'd had and thanking him twice.

St. James was slightly surprised by Smythe's out-of-character response. He'd witnessed the man's excitement when he decrypted a problematic code, but never for something as simple as a tour.

"You're most welcome, Louis. You've worked hard, not to mention suffering a horrific beating at the hands of two thugs who were defective from birth. You deserved some fun."

Smythe ignored St. James's assessment, his mind reliving the day. "You know, I remember a lot of British history from school. Seeing it in person is like living a history lesson."

The conversation turned to human behaviour they both found vexing. After the second bottle of wine, St. James paid the bill, and they strolled back to the hotel.

Back in the room, St. James called Anna.

"I love you, Hamilton," she said without so much as a hello.

"I love you too, Anna," he said.

"If you don't come home soon, I'm coming to London," she said with determination.

St. James laughed. "Is that a threat?"

"Absolutely."

"You are more than welcome to come, but it could be boring with me at Scotland Yard all day."

"Maybe Carolyn Kingston would like to shop with me," Anna said facetiously.

"Five days a week?" he cackled.

Anna ignored the jab to share some gripping information she'd unearthed about Wilhelm Schneider. "He's had several assault charges, but nothing has stuck. He was charged with first-degree murder five years ago, but his lawyer managed to get him off. No convictions on record."

"All good to know. By the way, Dozer's in Germany trying to find more on Schneider from that end," St. James said, almost as an afterthought.

"Maybe he'll shine a brighter light than what I've found."

"Regardless, Schneider doesn't sound like a charming fellow. Anything else on him?"

"He's associated somehow with a Harry Fischer."

St. James recounted the brutal death of Nigel Chamberlain, the searches he and Joy had conducted at Chamberlain's two residences, the text exchanges between Chamberlain and Schneider copied to the Harry Fischer Anna just referred to, and the discovery of the second laptop.

"Wow!" said a surprised Anna. "This case gets more complicated with every turn."

"Not looking for more complication, I assure you."

Anna changed topics. "Gerda Wagner's health care?"

"Yes, please."

"I spoke to someone named Helmut Müller in the German civil service. He confirmed that the government covers seventy-five percent of Wagner's health care and said her private insurance plan pays fifteen percent."

"Hmm. What about the other ten percent?"

"Müller believes that's coming from a settlement Sauvé negotiated with Wagner's family after the accident. Restitution for the hurt and damage he caused. I asked if this was an ongoing obligation of Sauvé's."

"And?"

"He said the investigator at the time made detailed notes showing Sauvé lost everything to help fund her care. Nothing about ongoing obligations."

"Hmm." St. James paused, then said, "Will you see what you can find on the British company Baker Sugars, as well as Chamberlain and Fischer?"

"On the case, dear."

Chapter 27

St. James woke up early Sunday morning feeling stressed about all the loose ends on the Taylor Supermarkets case. It bothered him that with Smythe's kidnapping and rescue and Chamberlain's murder, he hadn't had time to review Cindy Woods's analysis of the £185,000 profit shortfall.

He had all the documents with him in the hotel room. So there was no reason he couldn't review what Woods had done then and there.

He flipped open the laptop and clicked on a folder called Taylor Files, scrolled down the list of documents and opened one titled Woods Analysis. He pulled a file of paper documents from his case, again titled Woods, and began referencing information in each document to the calculations on the screen. After an hour, he concluded that everything checked out. Then one by one, he checked formulas contained within the analysis, clicking to study cell sources and mathematical calculations within those formulas. When he came to the last cell, his forehead scrunched.

"My God!" he said aloud. "How the hell do I handle this?"

***

St. James walked down the hall in sock feet and banged on Smythe's door. Smythe answered almost immediately. St. James was somewhat surprised to find him already dressed.

"Come with me," St. James said, beckoning Smythe with a forefinger.

Smythe nodded and followed him back to his room. St. James motioned for him to sit at the small wooden desk and refreshed the laptop screen, revealing the forecast profit analysis.

"What do you see, Louis?"

Smythe stared at the screen for a long moment. Suddenly his eyes bulged to impossible proportions. St. James had seen this *eureka* look on Louis's face before, and it always reminded him of Don Knotts.

"Holy shit," Smythe blurted. "Her forecast is wrong. The final profit forecast is higher than what the analysis supports. What does this do to our investigation, Hamilton?" he said with a look of dismay.

"I'll tell you what it means, Louis." St. James's voice reflected the magnitude of the situation. "Taylor may have paid us to fly over here to investigate a profit decline that doesn't exist!"

"I don't follow," Smythe said with a puzzled look.

St. James cleared his throat. "Taylor always looks at the forecast as gospel, the benchmark to compare to and judge actual profit performance. So when actual profit is materially lower than the forecast, he assumes the forecast is formula-correct and that actual results are the problem, either due to poor operating performance or accounting errors."

"Wouldn't that have come out in Woods's investigation?"

"Not necessarily. When profit is less than forecast, Taylor directs management to find underperforming financial results. But, in this case, the mistake is buried in the forecast formula, so his benchmark is faulty, not the actual financial results. The forecast is higher than it should be because it double counts subtotals. Management didn't find errors in actual performance, because there probably weren't any to find."

Smythe shook his head. "You're the accountant, Hamilton, but this makes no sense to me. Wouldn't Woods compare the actual numbers with the forecast numbers line by line? Find errors that way?"

"When I ran my finger down both the forecast and the actual columns at the same time, the numbers matched within a reasonable margin of error. There will always be some differences between the two because a forecast is just that, a prediction."

"Here, the difference is too large to ignore. Unless you open the formula for the net profit forecast and follow the components back to every subtotal comprising it, you'd never know some subtotals were included twice."

"What would total forecast profit be without the double counting if you subtotalled individual revenue and expense lines and netted the two?" Smythe said. "Do it like you used to, before spreadsheets. Bypass the bottom formula altogether, see what the profit forecast should have been."

"Let's see." St. James pulled a calculator from his attaché case and began tapping in numbers from each forecast line to arrive at the correct total. Smythe leaned in, watching him do his old-school work. After a few minutes of this, including some pauses to write out subtotals on a yellow legal pad, St. James put down the calculator.

"So it looks like the difference averaged approximately £25,000 a month, amounting to £148,000 over six months," he said. "Not the £185,000 Taylor thinks he's lost, but it's eighty percent of it. The balance could easily be the normal difference between forecast and actual. Like I said, they'd never be the same."

"Shit. What do we do now?" Smythe said blankly.

"Well, you know what I do when the facts blindside me…"

Louis looked puzzled for a moment, then knew what he meant. "Thinkin' 'n drinkin'?"

"You know me so well."

"I'm still recovering from last night, but okay, if we must."

"We must."

They headed to Waxy O'Connor's, the famous Irish pub on Rupert Street, and settled on red leather stools at the main-floor bar. St. James ordered a Guinness, and Smythe a glass of Chateau Cos d'Estournel.

They took a minute to soak up the ambience of the unique Chinatown pub, with its multiple bars and tall tree touching a beamed ceiling. A combination of brick, stone and solid dark wood contributed to the opulence.

When their drinks arrived, St. James raised his glass for a quick toast, then got down to business.

"Now that we're where we should be on a Sunday afternoon, let's take inventory of what we have so far."

"Inventory. Always a good place to start thinkin' 'n drinkin'."

"All right then," St. James said. "We came here looking for wrongdoing. Right?"

With a mouthful of wine, Smythe could only nod.

"And wrongdoing was defined for us in advance by Taylor, in the form of disappearing profit. Our mistake was accepting that premise upfront, allowing him to highjack our objectivity. I'm annoyed with myself for letting that happen."

St. James drank some of his beer.

"I guess that's right," Louis said.

"And you ruled out any wrongdoing that might have been caused by Vanderbilt's add-on program."

Louis nodded and drank, listening to St. James lay out the terrain.

"Then we have Chamberlain's murder, and Dozer in Germany chasing a would-be suspect for a crime we don't know was committed."

"Also true."

"Now we have an error in the profit forecast that accounts for approximately £148,000 of the £185,000 Taylor thinks he's lost. But it's not an actual loss. It's an error in the forecasting model that Taylor assumed he could trust. The way his mind works, the actual financial results should be where the problem is, if there is a problem at all."

"Still confusing," Smythe said, shaking his head. "And even if I wasn't confused, Taylor is an Oxford graduate, a very bright man. Believing a forecast is flawless is not the kind of mistake a bright Oxford businessman makes."

St. James smiled. "Taylor reviews and approves the forecast a month before a fiscal year commences, before any actual financial results have occurred. But he only looks at revenues and expenses forecasted, asking himself if they represent a reasonable expectation of what will happen in the coming year, all else being equal. If they do, that's what makes him think the forecast is flawless — and it is, *until* you get to the last formula, where the total net profit includes the subtotals twice. It wouldn't dawn on him to check the formulas. That's what he pays Woods for, to check her work or have someone do it for her. So Woods either missed the error, or the version she sent me was a draft that was corrected before she sent it to Taylor for final approval."

Smythe played with a cocktail napkin as he considered what St. James said.

"Could be what happened, I suppose," Smythe said.

"And we have the mysterious supplier, Baker Sugars, and the Pay Validation program processing multiple invoices each month, right?"

"Yes."

St. James told Smythe about the search of Chamberlain's properties, the cell phone exchanges with Schneider, and about Harry Fischer and the second laptop.

"Sounds like more work for me," Smythe said with a slightly sad look.

"Chin up, Louis. There could be stuff in there that makes your job easier."

Smythe considered everything for a couple of seconds. "I think we don't tell Taylor what we found right away. Give me time to learn more about Pay Validation and Baker Sugars, and Anna to determine who owns Baker."

"I agree," St. James said and smiled. "See how effective thinkin' 'n drinkin' can be, Louis? We just rationalized ourselves out of a mess."

Smythe raised his glass. "Here's to thinkin' 'n drinkin'."

Chapter 28

Monday morning, Louis dove back into the Pay Validation program and the Baker Sugars transactions. As agreed, he left the higher-level corporate research on Baker Sugars to Anna and concentrated on what transpired between Baker Sugars and Taylor.

He looked at the number of times Taylor paid Baker Sugars, and the average amounts, then summarized the findings for St. James to interpret.

While Smythe was doing all that, St. James met Joy at the Yard.

"I gave the second laptop and Chamberlain's cell to one of our techies and asked him to arrange a meeting with Louis to look at what's on each device," Joy said.

This reminded St. James of something. "I forgot to ask: What's on Becker and Schmidt's cells?"

"Mostly gibberish. Those two are morons," Joy said, shaking her head. "That's why I didn't bother you with it. Too stupid."

St. James smiled. "You mean they're not going to set the world on fire?"

"They couldn't set the world on fire if it was soaked in petrol and they each had a fist full of matches."

St. James laughed, then turned to more serious things.

"I think the only way we're going to move further with this case is to see what's in those safety deposit boxes in Zurich."

Joy smoothed a few strands of rogue red hair and stared at him. "As much as I hate to admit it, I think you're right."

"You know what that means, right?"

"Another visit to Randall & Collins."

St. James nodded.

"I'll set it up."

Joy's gregarious self was beginning to creep back, even in St. James's presence. He wasn't sure it equated to forgiveness for what he and Dozer had done, but he hoped it was a sign of better things to come.

***

By early Monday afternoon, St. James and Joy were sitting in Lisa Randall's office, and Henry Collins had joined them.

"We have to see what's in those safety deposit boxes in Zurich," Joy said authoritatively.

Randall smiled. "I was expecting that. Henry and I have already discussed who would go with you to open them. I have a client in Switzerland — Geneva, not Zurich. He's been after me to attend one of their board meetings for some time. There's one this Thursday. So I can go to Zurich tomorrow, arrange for you to access the boxes, spend the night with a university girlfriend and hire a car to drive to Geneva on Wednesday. Should take about three hours. How does the timing sound to you two?"

"Perfect," said St. James without looking at Joy.

Joy waited until they were outside the building to unload on St. James.

"What part of being on my team didn't you get?" Joy said bluntly.

"What do mean? You led the interview. I didn't contradict you or cut you off."

"You were doing just fine until we got to Randall's travel plans. Then you decided to agree with her without involving me," she barked. "That made Randall think you were the lead detective, not me."

"Agreeing to travel plans doesn't make me the lead investigator," St. James countered.

"It certainly does when the actual lead investigator is sitting beside you and you ignore her."

St. James shrugged.

"You have been working alone for so long you don't know how to be a team player," she said tersely.

"I play well with my own team."

"That's because they take orders from you, not the other way around. You don't want to, or can't, take orders from anyone else. We have a ranking system at the Metropolitan Police. A hierarchy that respects orders. And you're not part of it. You're here at the pleasure of DCI Kingston. No other reason. You don't get that. You think you can just continue to operate the way you always do. But it's different when you're on someone else's team."

"But no orders were involved here," St. James argued. "We were just organizing a trip."

"Maybe *orders* is the wrong word," she said with a disgusted look. "Maybe the word's *respect*."

Without another word, Joy turned toward the street and hailed a cab.

Chapter 29

Tuesday morning DCI Kingston found a report on his desk regarding the contents of Chamberlain's cell phone and second laptop. A yellow sticky on top said Smythe had yet to examine the devices.

"Bollocks!" Kingston barked. "Joy left specific instructions for them to be examined *with* Smythe, not without him."

Kingston tapped the extension number for Herb Johnson, the head of Scotland Yard's technical group.

"This was supposed to be done with Louis Smythe, as Joy requested," Kingston said curtly.

"We didn't see the need for outside help, sir," said Johnson.

"You don't ignore the request of a senior officer. If you plan to have a career with the Metropolitan Police, you better learn to follow orders, you got that?"

"Yes, sir," Johnson said timidly.

"Now I'm leaving this unfinished report with my assistant. I suggest you come up and take it back right away and set up a meeting with Smythe to examine the devices together. I have no intention of wasting my time reading a report not properly vetted." Kingston hung up before Johnson could respond.

Kingston shook his head. "Bloody stupid."

Joy stuck her head into Kingston's office. "St. James and I are heading to Zurich with Chamberlain's lawyer to see what's in those safety deposit boxes."

"Excellent," said Kingston, shuffling papers on his desk. "Hope what you find shines some light on this whole mess."

Kingston told Joy about the premature report on the contents of Chamberlain's devices.

Joy's irritation was more visible than Kingston's. "I specifically told them Smythe had to be part of it."

"I know, I know, Joy. I reamed Johnson out."

"Thank you, sir. St. James will make sure Smythe comes back from Taylor's to work on it with our guys. By the way, Dozer didn't get anywhere ferreting information on Schneider in Gundelsheim. No one had even heard of him. So I asked Dozer to meet us in Zurich in case we need help."

"Good," said Kingston as he picked up another report. "Travel safe."

Joy nodded and left the Yard to be ready for Switzerland.

***

Right after Smythe promised he'd meet Scotland Yard's technical group, St. James left for Heathrow. He found Joy standing in front of the Swiss Air gate for flight 319 to Zurich. Randall was already in Zurich, having travelled earlier that morning. The three planned to rendezvous in front of the UBS Bank in Paradeplatz 6 at 4:15 p.m.

St. James texted the meeting time and place so Dozer could catch a flight in time to meet them.

The noon flight was smooth and on time. St. James and Joy made it to the UBS rendezvous point by 4:10 p.m., with five minutes to spare. Dozer was already there, standing in front of the four-storey stone building, checking emails on his iPhone. Randall had not yet arrived.

At four thirty, they spotted Randall running toward them.

"I am so sorry, everyone," she panted. "I misjudged the traffic."

"The important thing is that you're here," Joy said, sounding impatient without meaning to. "Let's get on with it, shall we?"

St. James introduced Randall to Dozer, and they walked into the bank.

Although the outside reflected its European history, the interior was completely modern, with a long white service counter, glass artwork and marble floors.

Randall led them to the safety deposit box area and made the necessary arrangements to enter the secure section. The location was lavish, with upscale private rooms for the most wealthy, modest ones for the moderately rich, and walls of safety deposit boxes stretching from floor to ceiling.

Randall followed the supervisor until they found the box she had opened for Chamberlain months before. Randall stood aside while the supervisor inserted the bank's key into Chamberlain's box. They watched him make a half-turn before removing it and doing the same with a second key Randall took from her purse.

"May we have a private meeting room, please?" she said to the supervisor.

He pointed to a nearby room large enough to accommodate the four of them. "You may use that one, madam."

Randall thanked him and turned to Dozer. "I am anticipating this will be too heavy for me; would you mind?"

"Not at all, Miss Randall. Happy to help," Dozer said with a huge smile.

"That's Mrs. Randall, if you don't mind," Randall said haughtily.

Dozer's smile dissipated as he nodded. *Snob.*

St. James smiled at Randall's rebuke.

Dozer pulled the box from its place of rest, and they went into a meeting room furnished with a large mahogany table, matching chairs, and expensive oil paintings of well-known Swiss mountains — Jungfrau, Matterhorn and the Dufourspitze.

For a moment, they stared at one another with anxious anticipation.

Then Joy said to Randall, "Open it quickly, please."

Randall lifted the box's cover, removed several packages and began peeling wrappers from each one.

The room suddenly went silent.

Chapter 30

"Holy shit!" Dozer blurted.

Randall was stunned. "My God! I made all those trips to deposit blank paper," she said. "What the hell was Chamberlain doing?"

"Just when I thought the case couldn't be more difficult," St. James mumbled.

"I am at a complete loss," an exasperated Joy said.

Randall looked at her, and then at St. James. "Why would Chamberlain do this?"

Joy shrugged.

St. James stared off for a time and then back at the box's contents, deep in thought.

It took time for everyone to come back to the present and finish venting about the time and money wasted to make the trip.

St. James wanted everyone to get a grip.

"Let's get back to the task at hand, folks. We have to check the Credit Suisse safety deposit box too," he reminded.

Everyone reluctantly agreed, but the grumbling continued across Paradeplatz to Credit Swisse.

When they entered Credit Suisse, Randall went through the same security procedures and unwrapped similar brick-shaped packages to find the same contents that they found at UBS: bundles of plain white paper the size of pound notes.

"I need a drink," said a discouraged Joy.

Randall looked at the other three. "I've had it! My girlfriend keeps a boatload of wine in the house, and the way I feel, I could drink it all."

Randall wished them safe travels back to London and left.

The others left a few minutes later. Dozer hailed a cab. He, St. James and Joy climbed in, and the vehicle headed for the airport. On the way, Dozer changed their flights from Heathrow to London City Airport, conveniently leaving an hour and a half of bar time before boarding.

When they settled in the airport bar, St. James said, "Dozer, you've been quiet, bro."

"Been thinkin'," Dozer said, staring at the travellers rushing to catch flights.

"About what?" Joy said.

"Well, if we put together what we have on this case, it makes me think of Jim Croce."

"Huh?" Joy said with a puzzled look.

St. James smiled. "She's younger than us, Dozer. Probably never heard of Jim Croce."

"He wrote a song, 'Bad, Bad Leroy Brown,'" Dozer said. "Top of the charts in 1973, coincidentally the year he died. The song includes a memorable line about a jigsaw puzzle that's missing some pieces. That's what this case feels like — a jigsaw puzzle, minus a couple of key pieces."

Joy's shrug said, *what the hell.*

"Let's try to put the puzzle together with the pieces we are gathering," St. James suggested.

Dozer and Joy nodded.

St. James sipped Lagavulin.

"Let's start with Taylor's supermarket chain. Louis sent me a text today, saying he's finished the system analysis and prepared a report I'll review tomorrow," St. James said, then turned to Joy. "Tomorrow, he goes back to Scotland Yard to work with your technical people on Chamberlain's cell phone and second laptop."

"Not including him in the first place pissed me off."

St. James nodded. "I heard."

Dozer smiled.

St. James continued. "Wilhelm Schneider, a man charged with several assaults and one murder, orders two thugs to steal Chamberlain's laptop. At the same time, Chamberlain's cell shows a conversation with Schneider about partnering. So the question is, is Schneider setting Chamberlain up for a double-cross of some sort, or what?"

Dozer shrugged.

"And every exchange between the two is copied to Fischer, who so far is an unknown," Joy added.

"Anna's researching Fischer now, so we should have something on him soon." St. James turned to Dozer. "No one you questioned in Gundelsheim had heard of this Wilhelm Schneider, correct?"

Dozer nodded, which prompted St. James to add, "So if he is there, he's hiding or incognito."

"Or both," Joy said quickly.

"Whoever and wherever Schneider is, we have him tied to Chamberlain," St. James said as they finished drinks. He looked at his watch. "We have time for a second before the flight."

Dozer signalled the server.

"Then someone chops off Chamberlain's hands. Maybe Schneider, torturing him for information, where the money is, how to access it, that sort of thing. When Schneider couldn't extract the information he needed, he could have shot Chamberlain eight times just from rage," St. James said.

Joy's eyebrows furrowed. "Hell, guys, Chamberlain would already be dead or at least passed out from the pain when his hands were severed. He'd be incapable of saying anything, even if he did know something."

"But the murderer would have assumed Chamberlain was holding out. As I said to Kingston, maybe chopping off his hands is punishment for that," St. James suggested.

"Could be," Dozer said thoughtfully.

Joy nodded. "Here's what's troubling me: How did you make the giant leap from Taylor's profit conundrum to Chamberlain and Schneider? You talk as if they are the same case."

"I don't know that they're not one case," St. James said. "The one thing we know for certain is Schneider ordered Louis to be kidnapped, presumably for his ability to open Chamberlain's encrypted data vault."

"I know that," Joy said, mildly irritated. "My point is Schneider probably had someone search for experts to crack the laptop. They just happened to land on Louis for his talent not his connection to Taylor. Nowhere in this investigation have we found Taylor, Schneider or Fischer crossing paths."

"Agreed," said St. James calmly. "But it's not my nature to drop theories before they are proven wrong."

"You could waste a lot of police time going down that road," Joy said impatiently.

"Remember, it was the police who asked for my team's involvement because you're shorthanded at the Yard," St. James countered.

"You were *asked*, as you put it, because you took the law into your own hands and ended up in the middle of the case," Joy said bluntly.

St. James ignored her and concentrated on his scotch.

Dozer intervened. "Let's get back on track, folks. Going down a rat hole won't help."

St. James nodded, and Joy, fuming, stared off in the distance.

"Then, of course, we have this wasted trip producing nothing but massive amounts of blank paper," St. James said.

Joy remained silent, focusing on her second Chablis but looking too annoyed to enjoy it.

"My thinking is someone must have been following Chamberlain. So he thought blank paper packaged like real money would throw whoever off the scent. Money secured in the Swiss banking system would be out of reach. Deterrence for the pursuer, encourage him to give up," Dozer said.

St. James drank scotch. "Could be, Dozer," he said thoughtfully.

Dozer stared across the room, watching three attractive thirty-something women drinking wine at the bar.

St. James's cell vibrated with an incoming text. "It's Anna. She has information on Chamberlain, Baker Sugars and this fellow Harry Fischer."

The London flight was announced. St. James paid the bill, and they all rushed to the gate.

Chapter 31

Wednesday morning, thick fog the colour of mushroom soup blanketed London. Pedestrians struggled to avoid the spray from passing vehicles as they plowed through puddles created by heavy overnight rain. Tiny slivers of sunlight struggled through the murky haze.

St. James and Smythe met in the hotel dining room for breakfast at the usual time. Dozer joined them five minutes later.

A young lady wearing a black hotel uniform and heavy makeup stopped to fill their coffee cups.

Smythe handed St. James a brown letter-size envelope containing his report on Taylor's computer systems.

"Thank you for this, Louis. I know it was a tough slog. I'm grateful for your tenacity. I'll read it as soon as we arrive at Scotland Yard."

Smythe nodded and drank coffee.

A short server with purple hair took their breakfast orders and disappeared. Smythe turned to St. James. "How'd the Zurich trip go?"

"Total and complete disaster."

"Understatement of the year," Dozer added and drank coffee.

Between Dozer and St. James, they recounted everything that happened in Zurich.

Smythe looked at them in disbelief. "Wow, you weren't kidding."

"Total waste of time, not to mention travel cost," Dozer said.

Smythe shook his head. "Why would Chamberlain send lawyers to Zurich just to deposit plain paper? Doesn't make sense."

"Remains to be seen," St. James said.

Breakfast arrived, and their attention turned to food.

"More coffee, gentlemen?" asked purple hair.

They held up cups simultaneously.

"I don't see any reason for me to stay now that I've struck out in Gundelsheim, and my man Louis here is safe. May as well go back to Toronto," Dozer said to St. James.

St. James plunged his fork into a blood pudding. "Let's see what Kingston and Joy have to say. Maybe they still need you for something. Remember we're doing penance for taking the law into our own hands," St. James said with a grin.

"Been trying to forget that," Dozer growled.

***

An hour later, Kingston, Joy, St. James, Dozer and Smythe were all sitting in the same meeting room they had previously occupied.

Joy looked at Smythe. "Herb Johnson heads up our technical group, and he's waiting to go through the contents of Chamberlain's cell and second computer with you."

Smythe nodded.

Joy texted Johnson, and a couple of minutes later, a tall boney man with a chalky complexion appeared in the door, clad in a threadbare grey button-down sweater. He asked for Smythe.

"Keep us posted, Louis," St. James said as Smythe and Johnson left for the technology department.

"Will do."

Kingston addressed the group.

"I spent a couple of hours yesterday with Harold Fernsby, a director at Revenue and Customs. He's the man responsible for Nigel Chamberlain's file."

"What did you learn, sir?" Joy said.

"Well, Hamilton was right. German authorities did ask Britain for help running down Chamberlain because of what they thought was a connection with Schneider and Fischer. The Germans opened a file on this Fischer guy a couple of years ago. They suspected him of running several illegal operations."

St. James perked up. "What kind of operations?"

"Fraud schemes, money laundering, drugs, you name it," Kingston said. "He operates out of Gundelsheim, just as we thought. His company is International Enterprises, IEI for short, and it's located on Gottlieb-Daimler Straße in Gundelsheim."

Dozer frowned. "Would have been nice to know that before I went. Might have been a more productive trip."

Joy's chin rested on interlocked fingers. She looked at Dozer and smiled. "Well, you have something to work with now when you go back."

Dozer turned to St. James with a grin. "Guess I won't be going home anytime soon."

Guess not, St. James's grin said. *More penance.*

He turned to Kingston and asked, "Did Revenue and Customs give you more background on Fischer or Schneider?"

Kingston smiled. "The most interesting thing about Fischer is that he's a … what is the term now? A little person."

"Oh," Joy said.

Dozer laughed aloud.

"What's so funny, Dozer," St. James said.

"When we captured those two in the Camden dump, you said, 'They're the little fish, we want the big fish, the one who ordered this.' It seems the big fish is smaller than the little fish," Dozer said.

St. James chuckled, but Kingston jumped in with a note of caution.

"The Germans say he's mean as a snake. Ruthless. Schneider's his hatchet man. Near as Revenue can tell from German counterparts, Fischer runs a tight operation. Everything's by his book. No exceptions. No employees or cars are allowed in the parking lot. It's almost as if the company doesn't exist."

"Any details on the operation?" Joy asked.

"Sketchy," said Kingston. "Germany guessed a small number of people work there, maybe twenty-five or so. They estimate the operation nets around $900 million a year. They're after the tax on that. Our Revenue guys will want a piece too, if Chamberlain was defrauding companies here in the UK."

"How did Germany make the connection between Fischer and Chamberlain enough to ask Britain for help?" St. James asked.

"Somehow, they accessed communication between the two. The Germans think Fischer disguises his criminal activity as international trade. East and Southeast Asian goods, antiquities, carvings, carpets, that sort of thing. Hence the name International Enterprises," Kingston recounted.

"Wait a minute," St. James said quickly, leaning forward. "Randall and Collins said Chamberlain was in international trade too. Could be another connection."

"Was Chamberlain working for Fischer?" Joy asked.

Kingston drummed a finger. "Revenue and Germany think they're partners."

"Remember Chamberlain's emails, talking about doing business with Schneider?" St. James said to Joy.

Joy nodded.

Dozer watched several people scurrying about on the other side of the meeting room's glass door. Rubbing his shiny shaved head, he said, "Do they know the name of Chamberlain's company?"

"Quantum," Kingston replied without hesitation. "They're digging into it as we speak."

"Another search for Anna, Hamilton," Dozer said.

St. James's cell buzzed.

"They won't let me in the room, Hamilton. Can you tell them it's okay?"

"Anna! Are you here?"

"I warned you what would happen if you didn't come home soon," she said with a chuckle.

"Just a second until I step out of a meeting," he said as he rose to move into the hallway, closing the door behind.

"I'm so glad you're here, babe. Put the hotel manager on, and I'll straighten things out."

St. James gave the manager personal information to prove he was, in fact, Hamilton St. James, and requested Anna have access to the room. The manager handed both a room key and the phone to Anna.

"Okay, dear. You get settled in, and I'll be back around five," St. James said.

"No hurry. Knee-deep in your searches. Lots to do."

They clicked off, and St. James returned to the meeting. "Sorry, folks. My girlfriend arrived unexpectedly and was trying to get into the hotel room."

Joy rolled her eyes impatiently. "I hope we won't lose your attention now you have other things on your mind," she said with mild sarcasm.

St. James ignored the comment.

Joy turned to Dozer. "Can you go back to Gundelsheim, stake out International Enterprises, see what you can find?"

"Yep," Dozer said quickly and left to make travel arrangements to Gundelsheim for the second time.

"I have to read Louis's report on Taylor's systems. Then see what Anna uncovered on Baker Sugars, Fischer and Chamberlain," St. James said.

Kingston smiled. "Let me know if you need more from Revenue and Customs. I consider myself on standby."

"Okay, sir. Thank you," Joy said. "I'll track down whoever's running the German investigation into Fischer's operation. See what that brings."

Chapter 32

St. James removed a grey flannel blazer, loosened his dark-blue tie and settled in behind the desk of his temporary Scotland Yard office. He pulled the contents from the brown envelope Smythe had given him that morning and began reading the twenty-seven-page Taylor systems report.

Smythe's reports were detailed, clearly written and offered a good account of his procedures, findings and conclusions. St. James expected nothing less from the one he was about to read. He made notes as he went, pausing periodically to reflect on what Smythe had written. When he finished, he made additional notes, and after considerable thought, concluded now was the time to interview Sauvé, Woods and Vanderbilt.

St. James called the hotel and asked for his room.

"Are you getting settled, Anna?"

"Yep. Already turned the room into my own," she said teasingly.

"I was afraid of that. You must be tired from the overnight flight."

"Barely keep my eyes open. Got to get some sleep soon to replenish my energy level."

"I won't keep you long. Can you tell me a bit about what you found?"

"Just a second till I grab my notes." Seconds later, Anna said, "A numbered company owns Baker Sugars. The number is long, so let's call it company one."

"Who owns that?"

"Partially owned by three other numbered companies; we'll call them two, three and four."

"Did you ever get to a real person?" St. James said impatiently.

"No. I got down to a London law firm. Goldstein & Stein. They incorporated all four numbered companies and held them in a trust that's worded in such a way to protect the identity of beneficial shareholders — anonymous companies. Lawyers are the nominee shareholders. Can't find a real beneficial owner."

"Damn! Who's the lawyer?"

"Harvey Goldstein."

"Okay. I'll contact him," St. James said. "What did you find on Harry Fischer?"

"Not much. He is, I believe the politically correct term is, a little person. Born in Bad Wimpfen, Germany. His father was a butcher; his mother was also a little person. He got through high school there but was badly abused psychologically and physically because of his size. I couldn't find anything on him after high school," Anna said.

"Did you come across a company called International Enterprises or IEI?"

"No. What's that have to do with Fischer?"

"According to UK Revenue and Customs, he owns it."

"I'll check it out," Anna said with a yawn.

"Oh, listen to you. Poor thing. Do you have enough in the tank to tell me what you found out about Nigel Chamberlain?"

"Think so," she said with a smile and another yawn. "Very wealthy. Made his money in international trade. Owns a hundred percent of a company called Quantum. It does the trading for him. Not much else. He appears to have been a very private person. Then, of course, there's his murder."

"Hmm. Nothing new to go on. Okay, babe, get some rest and I'll see you at five."

St. James Googled Goldstein & Stein and found the law firm in Strand Bridge House on Strand Street. He punched in the number, asked for Goldstein and was told he was in an all-day meeting. He left a message for Goldstein to call.

St. James called John Taylor, gave him an update on their progress and asked if he could arrange separate meetings with each of the three vice presidents. Taylor would set up appointments for the following morning.

***

Wednesday evening, St. James felt like Chinese food. Anna and Smythe agreed, and the three settled on Canton, a Chinese BBQ restaurant on Newport Place. They strolled up Wardour past Chinatown Gate and onto Newport Place. Lined with red and orange lanterns and bright lights from several establishments, Newport was full of people out for an evening of food and drink.

The Canton resembled a bowling alley: long and narrow with a small number of tables in single file along one wall. They were seated halfway between the door and a bar by a petite white-haired Asian lady dressed in a long brightly flowered traditional Chinese dress. She placed menus in front of them and said a server would be with them shortly.

A skinny waiter, who St. James thought was not much wider than a stick man, arrived within minutes. The young man wore thick green-rimmed glasses and a clip-on bow tie that looked like it had been trampled by a wild animal.

The server eyed Smythe's outfit with wonder. He took their drink order and rushed off.

"I'm hungry. We should decide on food," St. James said as he picked up a menu.

Anna looked at Smythe. "Louis, your face doesn't look so bad. The way Hamilton talked, I thought it would be a lot worse."

"A few days ago, it was. The stuff the doctor prescribed worked quickly."

Anna and Smythe looked at menus and settled on a mixed seafood platter, with a view to sharing. St. James ordered two bottles of Hermitage La Chapelle.

For the rest of the evening, they resolved to avoid talking about the case and stick to personal topics. Smythe was excited about an advanced fraud-detection course in New York City next February, while Anna was thrilled to be taking part in a panel at an upcoming conference on digital-research strategies in Toronto, where she also planned to do some shopping with a girlfriend. St. James, meanwhile, was eager to get back to teaching the university course in the fall.

After supper, they strolled back toward the hotel where Smythe opted for an early night, while St. James and Anna headed to the bar for a nightcap.

"I am so glad you came, Anna," St. James said, putting his arm around her and pulling her close. "I am hopeless without you."

"Me too," she said, smiling up at him. "Precisely why I am here."

"It's bothering me we can't find who's behind Baker Sugars. Someone's gone to an awful lot of trouble to be incognito," St. James said.

"I must say, I feel I've let you down on that one," Anna lamented.

"Nonsense. You didn't create the complicated share structure. And you know Goldstein isn't going to tell me who his real client is anyway. Solicitor-client privilege."

"Oh, I know all that intellectually, but emotionally I still feel bad."

St. James took her hand and kissed it. Anna smiled at the tenderness of his gesture.

"I do believe, though, we can get more on Lucas Vanderbilt."

"I'll put him back on the list tomorrow."

With that, they finished their drinks, St. James signed the bill to the room, and they called it a night.

Chapter 33

Thursday was a cloudless day in London. The forecast said sunny all day with a high of 22°C. Dozer had left for Gundelsheim the previous evening before dinner. So it was just St. James, Anna and Smythe for breakfast that morning.

After they'd had their fill at the hotel, St. James left for Taylor Supermarkets' head office to interview the three vice presidents. Smythe headed for Scotland Yard to resume his examination of Chamberlain's cell and second laptop, and Anna went back to the room to continue her research.

Three blocks from the hotel, a taxi turned left, lost control and struck an elderly lady, knocking her down and scattering the contents of her purse everywhere. St. James ran to the corner and found the woman lying face down on the pavement, crying in pain. He knelt to comfort her.

The cab pulled over to one side, and the driver jumped out and ran toward the injured woman. Shocked by what happened, the cabbie seemed incapable of helping St. James to care for her. St. James shouted for him to call an ambulance, and after fumbling with a cell, he eventually connected with 999.

A crowd began to form, so close that St. James asked people to stand back so the injured lady could have more breathing space. She mumbled something he couldn't understand. As far as he could tell, her arm was broken. Her face was also badly scraped, her eyeglasses were smashed to pieces, and her white dress was soiled and torn.

St. James put his sweater on top of her and stayed close until the ambulance and police arrived, comforting her as best he could. He didn't want to move her, for fear of doing more damage. While he knelt next to her and gently stroked her white hair and reassured her that help was coming, a young woman in the crowd gathered up the contents of the woman's purse and placed it next to her arm. When the rescue attendants carefully turned the old woman and strapped her onto a gurney and began sliding her into the ambulance with the purse safely tucked next to her, she reached for St. James's arm and drew him close. The attendants paused.

"I don't know who you are, but today you are my angel," she managed to squeak out with barely a smile.

"Only too happy to help, ma'am," he said as he gently kissed her bloodied forehead. "Get better soon."

By the time St. James gave his statement to police and walked the rest of the way to the supermarket, it was ten thirty.

He popped into Taylor's office first to provide an update and assure him the investigation was moving along as planned.

Taylor knew of Chamberlain's murder from the newspapers but nothing about his connection to Schneider, Fischer or IEI. When St. James began talking about them as though they were linked, Taylor interrupted him.

"I don't see what that has to do with my profit decline," he said.

St. James smiled a defusing smile at Taylor and spoke to him as gently and methodically as he could. "It was Schneider who arranged Louis's kidnapping. We think it was for Louis to unlock the data on Chamberlain's laptop, which Schneider had stolen. But we haven't completely ruled out the possibility Louis was getting close to something here, something Schneider didn't want him to uncover."

"Like what?" said Taylor with a distressed look.

"Like malware of some kind. A threat to your system."

Taylor's forehead furrowed. "How the hell could that happen?"

St. James relayed Smythe's description of external hacking complexities versus less complicated internal sabotage, diverting money and information for nefarious purposes.

Taylor grimaced. "I don't see how anyone could hack in from outside with all the extra security Lucas created."

St. James shrugged. "Could be internal help or suppliers that need to be here to carry out their work. They could have inserted a virus into the system when no one was looking."

"What are you insinuating?" Taylor said with a raised voice.

"I am not insinuating anything, John! You asked how it could happen. I'm telling you how it could happen," said St. James, with a bit more bite than he'd shown up to that point. "I'm not saying it did happen."

Taylor calmed. "Sorry, I'm quite stressed over all this."

"I know. It's okay, John."

"So what will you do now?"

"I'll do the three interviews you arranged this morning. Thank you for doing that, by the way. Then I'll work on the connection with Schneider and Fischer. I won't rest until I know for sure they're connected somehow, or not at all, with your profit issue."

Taylor nodded. "I don't understand how that could be. But if David Kingston has faith in you, you must know what you are doing. He's a hard marker."

St. James ignored the back-handed compliment. "Who am I interviewing first?"

"Cindy."

"Okay." St. James left to organize himself in the meeting room.

The ample Woods entered the room wearing a plain black pantsuit, gold earrings and matching necklace, her face heavily made up as if the interview were an evening out. She made herself comfortable in a chair opposite St. James, who was preoccupied with finding a restful position under the table for his long legs.

"Thank you for making time for me," St. James said with a smile.

"Pleasure."

St. James launched into business. "Tell me a bit about you, the person."

Woods recounted her personal history — upbringing, university years, time with the firm where she earned her Chartered Accountant designation, and family matters. She mentioned nothing about shoplifting, nor did St. James expect her to. Too embarrassing.

"What does your husband do for a living?"

"Right now, he's between jobs."

St. James let her answer hang, not wanting to broach the man's love of drinking. Some things were better left unsaid unless they gained importance later in a case.

"I spent time on the forecast analysis you forwarded to me. Did you pick up on the formula error before you finalized it?" — St. James's cautious way of approaching a potentially embarrassing question.

Woods was surprised. "What I sent was the final. What error are you referring to?"

St. James turned his laptop around so the screen faced Woods.

The analysis was already open. St. James pointed to the final profit calculation at the bottom right-hand side. "This one."

Woods leaned over for a closer look. "What's wrong with it?"

St. James double-clicked on the cell, and the mathematical formula popped up. "When you follow subtotals comprising the formula back to their source, you see some have been included twice, erroneously inflating the forecast by approximately £148,000 for the first six months of the year. Actual results will look lower than the forecast, by £148,000, even if they are not. And since John assumes the forecast is mathematically correct, he believes a discrepancy between the two lies within the actuals. He wouldn't find this discrepancy without checking every formula."

After Woods followed the formula for a minute or two, she went pale and covered her face with both hands. "Oh my God. When Mr. Taylor sees this, I'll be fired, for sure. He's paying you to find a reason for lower profit when there may not be lower profit at all. He looks at the forecast as being irrefutable. But he doesn't check formulas. He just satisfies himself that revenues and expenses are reasonable and achievable."

St. James swung the laptop around so the screen faced him again and waited for Woods to calm down. Tears were forming in her eyes but she stopped short of crying.

"What am I going to do, Mr. St. James?"

"My suggestion is — nothing."

"But you have to present your findings to him, don't you?" she asked, considerable stress in her voice.

A slight smile came over St. James's face. "Just what *I* consider relevant to the case."

"I should think this would be *very* relevant," she said frantically.

"Case isn't solved yet. I don't know what will be relevant in the end."

When Woods regained her composure, they talked for another hour and a half about accounting controls, procedures and weaknesses that she would fix if she had the budget to do so. St. James could see her mind never left the error.

As Woods was leaving, she turned to him. "Thank you for not making me feel stupid."

"Professional courtesy," he said with a smile and the wave of a hand. "Besides, I've done the same thing."

She forced a slight smile and headed back to her office.

St. James made notes and then invited Sauvé to the meeting room. The lanky VP operations looked paler than St. James remembered.

"When my associate researched you, she learned of your car accident years ago. Must have been incredibly stressful."

St. James observed Sauvé's tense body language.

Sauvé shook his head rapidly. "Nightmare, both emotionally and financially. Wiped me out. And I'm still paying."

"Must be difficult."

Sauvé nodded.

St. James asked him to describe his job and its challenges. Sauvé explained a typical day — maintaining quality customer service, keeping fresh produce flowing into the stores in the right quantities and ensuring economic order practices to meet customer demand while minimizing waste.

"Sounds like a huge logistics challenge."

"To some extent, it is, but we have programs that project when to order products that are based on their turnover history and the time it takes to deliver. Purchase orders pop out automatically based on that."

St. James nodded.

For the next hour, he asked about the competence of store managers, honesty, and reasons for firings, if and when there were any.

When the Sauvé meeting was over, St. James decided to break before meeting Vanderbilt.

It was 12:45 p.m. when he strolled over to Amorino. He ordered coffee and a waffle, grabbed a small table and reflected on what he'd learned from the first two interviews. At 1:15 p.m., he wandered back to Taylor's and prepared himself to interview Vanderbilt.

By 1:30 p.m., Vanderbilt was seated in the meeting room, looking his usual shabby self — old worn jeans and a sweatshirt, long black greasy hair in a ponytail. Gunmetal glasses slipped down on his square nose, revealing his green, almost cat-like eyes.

"Louis was very impressed with the security add-on you created."

Vanderbilt nodded, stone-faced. "He mentioned that."

St. James said, "I see you grew up in Utrecht. Beautiful city. Love its medieval centre, the belltower and Domplein Square."

"Favourite part of the city."

"What part did you grow up in?" said St. James, trying to loosen the man.

"Not far from the Museum Catharijneconvent on Lange Nieuwstraat."

"Nice area. Parents still live there?"

"Never knew them. Killed in a small plane crash when I was five," Vanderbilt said unemotionally.

John's right. No personality.

"Sorry to hear that. Who looked after you, brought you up?"

"Gramma Visser."

"She still living?"

"In a nursing home."

St. James wasn't getting anywhere warming Vanderbilt with chitchat, so he spent the next hour running through all his responsibilities and computer activities, looking for security holes and at the same time trying to assess the man's integrity. He knew he asked many of the same questions Smythe covered in his report, but he wanted to see if Vanderbilt's answers deviated in any way. They didn't.

When Vanderbilt left the meeting room, St. James concluded he had learned little from the three VPs.

Chapter 34

While St. James was interviewing Taylor's three vice presidents, Joy asked DS Billings to update her on Chamberlain's murder investigation.

In his blustery way the overweight Billings said, "We interviewed four people close to Chamberlain, presumably those who knew him best. Frank Keller worked with him in his import/export business. Told us he sourced East and Southeast Asian goods for Chamberlain to resell in the West," Billings said.

Joy knew the answer to her next question from her interview with Randall and Collins but asked it anyway. "What sort of goods?"

Billings rubbed his forehead as he checked notes. "Mostly carpets, carvings, pottery, that sort of thing."

"Any illegal substances? Stuff people don't mind killing for," Joy said with a smirk.

"Don't think so. Nothing he was willing to admit to, anyway."

"Did you see business records?"

"Yes. Keller was cooperative. He pulled records in his office, and the documents supported the purchase and sale of East and Southeast Asian goods for several years. I had one of my guys go through them in detail. Everything seemed in order — as much as we could tell, anyway, without actually witnessing transactions taking place."

"Did you see any merchandise firsthand?"

"No, the merchandise flowed through Chamberlain directly to customers. Keller only sourced pre-sold goods. Chamberlain didn't want to finance inventory. Said the margins were too thin."

Joy looked puzzled. "That doesn't make sense! I have two uncles in the same business. The mark-up for most of that stuff is anywhere from ten to twentyfold, sometimes more. Labour's dirt cheap. Figurines, carvings, goods crafted in those cultures sell for next to nothing."

Billings shrugged.

"Who else did you interview?"

Billings rechecked his notes. "His lawyer."

"Which one?"

"Daniel Scrivens. Sole practitioner. Checked him out with the law society. Member in good standing. No outstanding complaints."

"We've met with Chamberlain's lawyers," Joy said. "They're Randall and Collins over on Fleet Street. They said they did all Chamberlain's legal work."

"I'm aware of Randall and Collins and what they did for Chamberlain — contracts, safety deposit boxes in Zurich, movement of money, that sort of thing. But they don't do criminal work."

"So it was a criminal matter Scrivens handled for Chamberlain?"

"Yes."

Joy's eyebrows rose. "The plot thickens," she mumbled, then refocused. "Were you able to get any details?"

Billings's smile folded his double chin like an accordion. "Once I pushed."

Joy became impatient. "What's the story, Bert?"

"First of all, Chamberlain doesn't have a record."

"First thing we always check, you know that," she said gruffly.

Billings nodded. "Chamberlain owed Keller over a million pounds, and Keller was threatening to go to the authorities if he didn't pay. Chamberlain wanted to know what exposure to criminal charges he'd have if the police got any traction with a complaint."

Joy sighed. "Ah! It was to manage a potential incoming threat, not a real one."

"Correct. As far as we can tell, it was just that, a potential legal threat. No record of Keller ever reporting Chamberlain to police. Scrivens told him without proof of theft from Keller, police would likely say it was a commercial matter, one for the courts to decide. The debt arose from Keller's work, like unpaid wages. Scrivens was right."

"A million pounds is a lot of pay for sourcing cheap goods from East and Southeast Asia, don't you think?" Joy mused. "It would have to be one helluva volume to accumulate that amount of debt."

Billings shrugged.

Joy paused a beat. "What do you make of it?"

Billings removed a handkerchief from a suit pocket and wiped the sweat from his brow. "Don't know. It could be motive enough for Keller to kill him, I suppose. God knows people have killed for a lot less." Billings shook his head, emphasizing the point. "He'll remain a suspect, but it's not a slam dunk."

Joy wanted to move on. "Who else did you tackle?"

"Chamberlain's sister, Barbara. She lives in Cambridge."

"We searched for Chamberlain's relatives, living or dead. We found no one."

Billings cleared his throat. "Probably because they were estranged. According to her, they fell out ten years ago when their father died and left everything to her. Chamberlain wiped her out of his life, expunged every document he could get his hands on. Never acknowledged her existence again."

"But still," Joy argued, "there would be a record of the father's will, her birth certificate. Her life would appear somewhere."

"Not necessarily. The father's will was never probated. It doesn't exist anywhere other than in Barbara's home safe. And she's been married for thirty-three years to a man with the last name Evans. So Barbara Chamberlain would be almost impossible to track."

"That's all well and good, but her birth certificate must still exist. Chamberlain couldn't eradicate that."

"I can't explain it. Unless Scrivens found a way to seal it, I don't know, seems impossible to me."

"If she's buried that far down in the system, how did you come to find her?"

"Scrivens. Chamberlain engaged him to wipe out every record concerning her."

"Wow! Takes a lot of hate to go to that length to clear someone from your life. Sounds like he may have had motive to kill her because she got everything their father had, not the other way around."

"Possibly."

"Funny Chamberlain didn't ask Randall and Collins to do the cleansing. Seems more in line with their expertise than Scrivens's," Joy mused.

"Scrivens said Chamberlain wanted his dirty laundry all in one place, and Randall and Collins were busy doing other things for him."

"And the fourth interview was with whom?"

"Fellow by the name of Joe Stanley, university buddy of Chamberlain's, friends ever since. Managing director of a small technology company. Tachiai Inc. *Tachiai* is Japanese for 'fast movement.' Sumo wrestling lingo. Stanley was struggling to make a go of it. Chamberlain invested half a million pounds in helping him get the business off the ground."

"What about Chamberlain himself?"

Billings referred to his notes once again. "For the most part, he was a loner, but reasonably well-liked, successful with the business, so a half-million-pound investment was nothing to him."

"Did his buddy give you any details about Chamberlain's business?"

"Said Chamberlain refused to talk about business; only sports, world affairs and politics."

"Who benefits from his will?"

"Chamberlain left everything but the Wimbledon house to charity. A lot of cash when it's all liquidated."

"Who gets the house?"

"Jones, the butler."

"Wow! Nice reward for loyalty."

A huge grin parted Billings's chubby cheeks. "Maybe the butler did it!"

Joy rolled her eyes and said nothing.

Her focus drifted off for a moment. "So, when we boil all this down, Chamberlain was successful at a business no one knew anything about; a man with little social life, very few friends and a sister he hated enough to wipe out of existence. Yet he was reasonably well-liked, except for a business associate who chased him for a million-pound debt. Jesus, the man was a walking conundrum, a breathing oxymoron!"

Chapter 35

On Friday, Joy was having trouble locating the person in Germany responsible for Wilhelm Schneider's investigation. Eventually, she connected with Noah Weber, a senior investigator in Hamburg's Federal Criminal Police Office.

"Mr. Weber, we have confirmed Germany asked Britain to look into Nigel Chamberlain's possible connection to Wilhelm Schneider. I believe you are the officer investigating Schneider, is that correct?"

"Quite correct, Miss Joy," said Weber stoically, "but only as he relates to Harry Fischer. Fischer's our primary focus. He is, as you English would say, where the buck stops."

"I see. Did you know Chamberlain was murdered? Hands severed. Shot multiple times."

"*Mein Gott, nein!*" said Weber, clearly appalled. "*Wie schrecklich.*"

"Sorry, sir, I don't speak German."

"I am sorry. In English, it means — My God, no. How terrible. Sometimes I forget. I'll do my best to remain in English."

"Thank you."

"What can you tell me about Schneider and Fischer?" she asked.

"Schneider is Fischer's second in command, criminal talk for *hitman*. We've watched Fischer for some time but with limited success. He's rarely seen in public, if at all. His systems are as secure as any government-investigation agency. More firewall enhancements than the CIA. Well-financed, enough to create a steel-trap security protocol that our experts say is impossible to penetrate, which I find difficult to believe. Given enough time and resources, one can break into any system. If it was created by man, man can undo it. Fischer refers to the creation as Fischerlock. He thinks it's impregnable, like Fort Knox."

"What do you know about his activities?"

"We know he's into various computer frauds, diverting money from corporations for his benefit. Multiple countries."

"Why hasn't he been arrested?"

"Not enough evidence. Hell, we don't even see anyone coming from or going to the premises. Never any cars there. Looks like a vacant property."

"Customs and Revenue said the same. How did he come up on your radar in the first place?" Joy said, trying to make some sense of it all.

"We picked up bits of communication suggesting more than just hints of criminal activity. Some were exchanges with this Chamberlain fellow. Somehow our guys identified transmissions around Fischer's system but not into or out of it. Bizarre. We only know of Schneider because of his criminal past. By the way, how did you know about him?"

Joy told him about the emails and texts between Chamberlain and Schneider about working together and mentioned Anna's discovery of Schneider's assault and murder charge.

"Because Schneider handled all the communication with Chamberlain, we assumed he was the leader," Joy explained, "although we noted Fischer was copied on everything."

"Well, it was Schneider's texts that led us to ask Britain for help with Chamberlain. We saw much the same communication from this end. But Fischer pulls the strings."

"Could you make any sense of the communications, who was doing what, when and where?"

"Too vague. Schneider and Chamberlain used a code-like language."

"So you have no idea what they're doing?" Joy said.

"Not specifically."

"What about IEI's ownership?"

"There are numbered companies incorporated in the British Virgin Islands with interlocking ownerships held in trust by lawyers. Complicated structure. We know Fischer's behind it, but his name doesn't appear anywhere. Very frustrating."

"Frustrating, for sure. But clever if you don't want to be tied to anything," Joy said. "Why the British Virgin Islands?"

"Secrecy jurisdiction."

"I remember those from officer training but never had a case involving one."

"We get quite a few."

"Banking information, payroll, that sort of thing?"

"All run by numbered companies in trust with lawyers as nominee shareholders."

"Directors?"

"More lawyers."

"Man, these guys are either brilliant or they have the best advisers on the planet," Joy concluded.

"Or both," Weber said.

Chapter 36

Monday afternoon, Smythe, St. James, Joy, Kingston, and Herb Johnson were sitting around the now all too familiar meeting room with its wall of photographs of prime ministers.

St. James looked at Smythe and Johnson. "Gentlemen, what did you find on Chamberlain's second laptop?"

Johnson gestured to Smythe.

"The second laptop has a lot more detailed operational data and several pages of coded narrative," Smythe began. "Mostly about Quantum's business transactions, numbers, data, that sort of thing. Maybe the narrative code will offer more insight if we find a way to crack it."

"Is it a legitimate international trading company?" Joy asked.

"Don't know yet," Smythe said.

"What *do* you know?" Kingston said impatiently.

"Well, there are records buried in Quantum's books of goods imported from all over East and Southeast Asia and sold into the United States, Britain, Germany and France. This suggests an import/export business," Smythe said.

"Why the hesitation?" Joy pressed.

"I have no way of knowing whether the transactions actually took place or if they truly represent merchandise from what used to be called the Far East. Maybe the deciphered narrative will shed some light. Or maybe it won't."

Joy looked puzzled. "Has the term *Far East* actually been eliminated?"

"Pretty much. Some of the vendors still use it, but it's considered a relic of the colonial era," Smythe said. "Let's just say I wouldn't try using it on Twitter."

"What else did you find?" St. James interjected.

"Quantum does have a joint venture with IEI called ConQuest. We found evidence of that in the texts between Schneider and Chamberlain."

"That verifies the link between the two," St. James said with satisfaction. "Anything else on the cell?"

"Nothing of interest."

"ConQuest does what?" Kingston said quickly, finding Smythe's dissemination too slow.

"Quantum and IEI carved up parts of Europe. Quantum got Great Britain. IEI got Germany and other parts of Europe. Its East and Southeast Asian activity is transacted through ConQuest," Smythe explained. "And we're seeing some suggestion that there are other 'Quantums' out there — other organizations in other countries that also have joint ventures with IEI."

"What are they doing?" said a frustrated Joy.

Smythe shrugged. "Don't know."

Kingston rolled his eyes.

"Any other partners?" St. James asked.

"A fellow by the name of Frank Keller was responsible for conducting some of the joint venture business here in the UK."

St. James stroked his square chin. "I remember the name Frank Keller from Chamberlain's flat, going through his rolltop desk."

"And Billings interviewed him for Chamberlain's murder," Joy added.

Joy considered what Smythe reported. "None of this squares with what the Germans believe is happening. They say Fischer's running several frauds."

"I am just telling you what's on the laptop," Smythe said, slightly annoyed. "I'm not arguing it's right."

St. James butted in to avoid further awkwardness. "Any other names, Louis?"

"No, just the three — Fischer, Schneider and Keller."

Chapter 37

First thing Tuesday morning, St. James heard back from Harvey Goldstein, the lawyer who had been nominated as a shareholder for the numbered companies that directly or indirectly held an interest in Baker Sugars.

"Mr. Goldstein, thank you for returning my call," St. James said. "I am a Canadian private commercial investigator working with the Metropolitan Police in two capacities. I am looking into some business issues for Taylor Supermarkets and assisting Scotland Yard with their investigation into the murder of Nigel Chamberlain."

"I read about Chamberlain's horrible demise," Goldstein said in a voice that struck St. James as slightly feminine. "What are you doing for John Taylor?"

"You know John?"

"Not really. I met him once at a party. Know a couple of senior people over there."

"As you can appreciate, Taylor's business is a private matter I can't discuss."

"Very well. What can I do for you then, Mr. St. James?"

St. James explained his interest in Baker Sugars as best he could without divulging Taylor's business. He knew he hadn't a hope in hell of getting Baker Sugars information from Goldstein, but he had to try.

Goldstein chuckled when St. James asked for the names of the beneficial owners of the numbered companies. And he wasn't going to miss the opportunity to throw St. James's words back at him. "As you can appreciate, it's a private matter I can't discuss."

St. James laughed. "I had to try, sir."

Goldstein chuckled again. "I know. I've done the same thing with equal success. At least now you can check it off your to-do list."

They exchanged professional pleasantries and then clicked off.

St. James's cell vibrated. Anna.

"After you left this morning, I worked on Lucas Vanderbilt. You mentioned Vanderbilt's grandmother Visser raised him, and that she's in a nursing home in Utrecht."

"Right."

"Well, only three major Utrecht homes popped up in Google search. When I phoned each of them, I found only one Visser, a Hanna Visser in the Bartholomeus Gasthuis, a beautiful, highly rated nursing facility. Didn't find much more about Vanderbilt himself except he was awarded a prize for a brilliant paper he wrote at university."

"Excellent, Anna. I'll take it from here. How about you find us a nice place to eat tonight."

"Sounds wonderful, darling."

St. James's cell vibrated again.

"Hamilton, it's Dozer."

"Had you on my list to call today," St. James said in an upbeat tone.

"Yeah, missing you too," Dozer said sarcastically.

"Where are you staying?"

"Someplace I can't pronounce."

"Give it a shot."

Dozer butchered the words *NaturKulturHotel Stumpf*.

St. James laughed.

"Let me hear *you* say it!" Dozer fired back.

"Not a chance. Are you in Gundelsheim?"

"Hotel's about twenty-two kilometres outside Gundelsheim. Like the place. Near a beautiful nature park. Popular for business retreats, food is superb and the bar is well-stocked, as you would imagine."

"Find anything out?" St. James said in a more serious tone.

"Been staking out the International Enterprise building on Gottlieb-Daimler Straße."

"And?"

"It's odd, Hamilton. People are shuttled to and from the place in a brown Volkswagen van all day long. Yesterday, I followed the van to a large farmhouse south of town. Four people got out and went into the farmhouse. Five minutes later, four people came out and climbed into the van, but they weren't the same four people that went in. I followed the van all day, back and forth eight times. Each time the van took four people to the farm and brought four different people back to the office building."

"So there's a pattern here."

"Yes, but the odd thing is the van is a twelve passenger. Why make so many trips with only four people when you could cut travel time and expense by maybe two-thirds?"

"Weird. Have you seen Fischer?"

"No sign of him."

"So he's never in one of the groups of four shuttled?"

"Nope."

St. James was silent for a couple of seconds. "I don't know what to draw from that, Dozer. Keep watching. Maybe something will come of it."

"Okay," said Dozer and clicked off.

St. James considered Dozer's report.

Four people to the farm, four different people back to head office. Why? What's the point? Would there be four-person shifts? No. Doesn't make sense. And where's Fischer?

He put thoughts of Gundelsheim aside in favour of Frank Keller. He Googled the man he believed to be Chamberlain's partner and found him living on Queen Anne Street not far from Marylebone. He tapped Keller's number. Keller picked up on the third ring.

"Mr. Keller, I am a private detective assisting Scotland Yard with their investigation into Nigel Chamberlain's murder. I understand you worked with him in some capacity?"

"That is correct, sir." Keller's accent was a heavy Scottish brogue.

"Would you have time to meet?"

"Sure, if you can come to my home office. I have an opening at two."

"Perfect, I'll be there."

At one thirty, St. James climbed into the back of a traditional black London cab and gave the driver Keller's address.

Twenty minutes later, he stood in front of a four-storey stucco-and-brown-brick townhouse with a solid hardwood door and three French balconies attached to second-storey windows. Each window burst with colour from freshly watered flower boxes overflowing with petunias, geraniums and zinnias.

After a couple of knocks, the front door opened, and a plump middle-aged lady wearing a maid uniform greeted him with a smile.

"Mr. St. James, I presume?" she chirped.

"Yes. Good afternoon."

"Come in," she said, pulling the door wide open for him to enter. "Mr. Keller is expecting you."

Keller's home was elegant, with lofty ceilings, cove moulding and thick grey carpeting. The rooms were more significant than a typical British home and furnished with modern furniture.

The maid guided St. James up a wide staircase to the second floor, the location of two bedrooms and Keller's office.

Keller rose from behind a polished black walnut desk to introduce himself and shake St. James's hand. He motioned St. James to one of two uncomfortable-looking moulded European chairs.

Keller was tall and slim with a narrow face; he was well-dressed in a knitted brown sleeveless pullover sweater over a white dress shirt and light-brown slacks. His pitch-black hair was slicked straight back. St. James figured him for a young fifty.

"What is a Canadian detective doing assisting London's Metropolitan Police with a murder enquiry?" Keller said.

"Long story, Mr. Keller."

Keller nodded. "Please, call me Frank."

St. James reciprocated. "How were you and Chamberlain connected?"

Keller steepled his hands. "We were business partners. I sourced a lot of goods for Quantum to import from across East and Southeast Asia. Quantum is, or rather was, owned by Chamberlain."

St. James nodded and pulled a writing pad from his attaché case. "Did you source goods for International Enterprises as well?"

St. James eyed a picture on a credenza of Keller and a woman standing alongside a small yacht tied at an unknown wharf.

"No. I have no direct relationship with IEI. Chamberlain did, though, through Quantum. They were in a joint venture together. ConQuest. But I wasn't part of it."

St. James nodded. "What items did you source?"

"Antiquities, clothing, carvings, rugs, that sort of stuff."

"Where do you store the stuff?"

"Goods are shipped directly to Quantum."

St. James made a note.

Keller's accent made it difficult for St. James to understand, and he found himself guessing at some words.

St. James increased his questioning speed, allowing less time for Keller to fabricate answers, a technique he used frequently.

"Where does Quantum store its goods?"

"I don't know if Chamberlain ever stored anything, Hamilton."

"Why's that?"

"Didn't want to finance inventory or pay for storage. He pre-sold goods before asking me to source them. But for all I know, he may have had a holding space somewhere for goods in transit."

"So you never actually saw the goods you sourced?"

"No."

"Seems odd not to see the fruits of your labour."

Keller shrugged.

"Do you know Harry Fischer?"

"No."

"Wilhelm Schneider?"

"No."

St. James decided to launch a verbal grenade. "Were you aware Fischer and Chamberlain were running fraud schemes?"

Keller suddenly became animated. "My God! Where did you hear that?"

"German authorities." St. James changed the line of questioning. "Do you have any idea who would want to kill Chamberlain?"

Keller shrugged. "No, I don't. I can't imagine anyone. He was a nice man. Smart. Likeable. I am not aware of any enemies."

"How was your working relationship?"

"Reasonably good," said Keller slowly, wondering where St. James was going with all this.

"What do you mean by reasonably? Did you ever argue?"

"Not a lot. We were compatible business partners."

"Were you close?"

Keller looked puzzled. "We weren't drinking buddies, if that's what you mean."

"Did you share business ideas?"

"Occasionally, yes."

"You met frequently?"

"Couple of times a month, I think."

"Here or at Chamberlain's?"

Keller's forehead furrowed. "Why does that matter?"

"Shows a pattern of interaction between the two of you," St. James explained.

Keller nodded cautiously. "We always met at one of Chamberlain's residences."

"And you still didn't physically see any imported goods?" St. James challenged.

"No."

They talked for another half hour or so before ending the meeting.

"It was a pleasure meeting you, Frank. I may want a follow-up meeting if you don't mind, as I learn more about the case."

"Happy to assist, Hamilton," said Keller as he rose to shake St. James's hand.

Chapter 38

When St. James entered the hotel room, Anna ran to throw her arms around him.

"So glad you're back, Hamilton."

"I'm glad to be back," he said, holding her waist. "Also parched. Let's go downstairs for a drink."

"Good idea. I am tired of staring at the computer screen. Definitely in need of some excellent wine," Anna said enthusiastically.

"Me too. Have you heard anything from Louis?"

"No, nothing."

"Neither have I. Wonder if he's back in his room. I'm a little paranoid about his safety since the kidnapping."

"Understandable. We'll bang on the door on our way to the elevator."

St. James nodded.

Louis had just arrived from Scotland Yard and was freshening up when St. James pounded on the door.

"Anna and I will be in the bar. Come join us when you're ready," St. James shouted through the door.

"Give me fifteen," Smythe shouted back.

St. James and Anna grabbed a table in the bar downstairs. An attractive young woman rushed over, introduced herself as Prisha, and asked what they would like. They ordered the usual scotch and wine.

"What a pretty name," Anna said after the woman had already moved on to another table. While they waited, Anna, still in research mode, typed a phonetic version of the waitress's name into her phone, found what looked like the correct spelling and said, "Prisha. Hindi for 'Beloved. Loving. God's gift.'"

"Okay, Nancy Drew. You're off the clock," St. James said.

"Oh, all right."

A few minutes later, Prisha laid down drinks, smiled at the group, who all smiled back, then made herself scarce.

After the first sip of scotch, St. James said, "Any idea what products Taylor buys from Baker Sugars?"

"Louis is closer to that. I just focused on ownership. But I did have a chance to look at their website. As the company name implies, most of its products have a high sugar content — baked goods, cookies, cakes and pies."

St. James nodded.

Anna sipped wine. "What did you accomplish today?"

"Talked to Harvey Goldstein about Baker's shareholders."

"And?"

"Got nowhere, as I expected. As your search indicated, an anonymous numbered company owns Baker, and three other anonymous numbered companies partially own that numbered company; three layers of lawyer fog we're unable to lift. No way to get to beneficial human owners."

"Goldstein cooperative?" Anna asked.

"Cooperative as he could be. I liked him. He laughed when I asked who the owners were. I thought that was better than getting angry for asking, telling me to go to hell. Said he's tried the same thing with other lawyers and got as far as I got with him. Nowhere."

"Amusing response."

"After that, I interviewed Frank Keller."

"Learn much?"

"Not really."

Smythe showed up in a burst of plaid and pulled a chair in beside Anna.

"Hey, Louis. Feel refreshed?" St. James said.

Smythe smiled. "Yep. All set for wine."

Hamilton waved to Prisha, who materialized moments later.

"Louis, your face looks almost completely healed now. Hardly see any trace of kidnapper abuse," Anna said.

"Yeah, I feel back to normal."

"Whatever the hell normal is when it comes to Louis Smythe," St. James said.

Refraining from the usual "Up yours," Smythe nevertheless pulled a face in St. James's direction.

Prisha arrived and smiled through her puzzlement at Smythe's outfit but quickly righted herself. "Can I get you something to drink, sir?"

"I'll have a glass of Casillero del Diablo."

Prisha made a note and headed for the bar.

"Louis, Anna and I were just wondering what products Baker Sugars supplies Taylor."

Smythe nodded. "Different kinds of cakes and cookies mostly."

"Did your investigation lead you to Baker's website?" St. James asked.

Smythe shook his head. "No time for that, man," he said emphatically. "Consumed by the Pay Validation program."

"Then how did you know what products Baker supplied?" Anna wondered.

"Some of my system testing involved examining purchase orders for products Taylor ordered. Baker's purchase orders were among them."

Prisha placed a glass of red wine in front of Smythe. He immediately gulped a portion.

"I see," said Anna slowly. She noticed St. James staring off at nothing in particular. "What's wrong, Hamilton?"

"Baker Sugars' website. That's what's wrong," St. James said. "We haven't examined it." St. James turned to Smythe. "Louis, would you take a hard look at the site?"

Smythe's brow lined. "What possible bearing could that have on the case?"

"Don't know," St. James reflected. "But I'd like to be sure it doesn't."

St. James turned to Anna. "You were going to pick a restaurant for tonight."

"Yes, and I did," she said happily.

They finished the drinks.

"Great," said Smythe enthusiastically. "I'm starving."

"Where are we going?" St. James said.

"I made a reservation for seven at an Italian restaurant called Sergio's. According to the concierge, it's excellent, and only about a twenty-minute walk from here," Anna said.

Smythe checked the wall clock to the right of the bar. "Just enough time for another drink."

St. James caught Prisha's eye and drew an imaginary circle, the universal language for another round. Prisha acknowledged with a wave.

"So, Louis, what did you accomplish today?" St. James asked.

"Spent the entire day on Chamberlain's second laptop. I am still not satisfied I have the full story, and I won't be until I can crack the narrative code. Johnson and I are going to work on that tomorrow."

"David said Johnson submitted a report on the second laptop without your involvement. He was upset that Johnson left you out. Have you seen the report?"

"No, and I'm not interested in seeing it, either."

St. James was surprised by Smythe's attitude. "Why not?"

"Without the narrative deciphered, it would be useless, a waste of time."

Anna nodded.

"I asked Joy about the papers she found in the Wimbledon wall safe. They were copies of wills and third-party contracts with people and companies unrelated to the case. No help, I'm afraid," Smythe recounted with disappointment.

Anna noticed Smythe's attention evaporating. "Something else bothering you, Louis?"

Smythe's brow creased. "Hard to explain, Anna. It's a feeling more than anything."

Prisha placed the second round and left without a word.

"Can you be more specific, Louis?" St. James said.

"Everything looks too perfect."

Chapter 39

The following morning, St. James and Smythe taxied to Scotland Yard, where Smythe continued examining Chamberlain's second laptop with Herb Johnson. St. James settled into his temporary office and asked Joy to run Frank Keller through her databases. Anna stayed behind in the room to research more on Keller until Carolyn was scheduled to pick her up to go shopping at nine forty-five.

Smythe and Johnson huddled around Chamberlain's second laptop in Johnson's office, scrolling through mountains of data.

"I'll put this through a cryptanalysis program I've had some success with in the past. It's trial and error to find the right cipher translation," Smythe said. "Tedious work."

"Has to be by its very nature," Johnson said.

Smythe opened a file containing a list of code-breaking apps while Johnson looked on.

"What are you trying first?" Johnson said.

"Caesar Shift Cipher."

"I know about it but haven't personally used it. I usually outsource it to another group."

"It's not that complicated. It encrypts text by replacing each letter with another letter, a fixed number of alphabet spaces away. For example, if you replace the letter A with another letter, five alphabet places to the right, A becomes F, the fifth letter to the right of A," Smythe explained.

"I know that much from talking to colleagues."

"But we're trying to decipher an already enciphered code. In other words, reverse the process. I have a program to decipher text enciphered with Caesar Shift Cipher back to its original state. It's pretty straightforward. You just use trial and error to change the fixed number of spaces until one works. If no fixed spaces work, you try another cipher app."

"Makes sense," Johnson said.

Smythe copied and pasted a couple of paragraphs of Chamberlain's code into his decipher version of the Caesar Shift Cipher to demonstrate.

"You keep going with a grouping until it produces a real word. Then you move to another grouping to decode," Johnson said.

"Right."

"That could take a very long time."

"That's why code-breaking is such tedious work. You need the patience of Job."

"Then there's the substitution cipher. That's when you look at a group of letters and guess the actual word based on the order and frequency of code letters in a grouping. Much like a Cryptoquote puzzle. The more words you translate, the faster the rest of the translation goes because of letter repetition in the English language and the fact there are only twenty-six in the alphabet. The more letters you translate, the fewer code letters are left to replace, and the fewer unused ones are left to replace them with."

"Have you ever done Cryptoquotes, Herb?"

"Yes, love doing them."

"Then you are a natural," Smythe said. "I have research to do for Hamilton. It'd be a big help if you could do the substitution cipher on your own, using your Cryptoquote experience. It's the logical choice now."

"But, as I said, we outsource this stuff to people like you. I know what the cipher is, the theory and logic behind it, because of my training."

"Good," Smythe said. "We already have code letters deciphered by reversing Caesar Shift. Take those translated letters and carry them through the rest of the code. That will give you word clues, a head start. Just go from there."

When Johnson looked a bit concerned, Smythe said, "Just look at one grouping at a time. If you try to look at more than one, you'll get overwhelmed. The key is to keep a narrow focus."

Johnson chuckled. "Are you sure you want to trust me to do this right?"

"Absolutely! The whole decipher process is self-correcting. A code letter replaced by a wrong letter results in a word and sentence that doesn't make sense. In that case, you try different letters to replace coded ones until you arrive at a word that does make sense."

Smythe turned to leave. "Deciphering 101," he said as he rounded the door.

Chapter 40

As St. James requested, Smythe pulled up Baker Sugars' website and examined its construct. Staying on the home page for a time, he studied the URL at the top of the site, carefully looking at every letter and number. It certainly seemed to be a legitimate URL.

His eyes drifted to the left of the web address, searching for the level of security assigned to the site, and found it was not secure, meaning it wasn't a private connection.

Smythe made a note.

He looked for a valid trust certificate verifying its security. He pulled down the menu bar and made several clicks to discover the site didn't have one. He fixed his comb-over and made a note.

Smythe read through several pages of the site, noting nothing except colourful pictures of cakes, pies and cookies, as well as a few spelling errors. There was no way to purchase anything directly from the site.

The chief executive officer was a woman named Francis O'Ceileachair. Smythe dialled the company number and got a recording saying the office was temporarily closed and would reopen shortly.

I'll try again tomorrow, he thought, then summarized his observations and conclusions in a short written report for St. James.

***

St. James was reading some of Anna's research when Joy walked into his office looking quite pleased with herself.

"Got some initial results from our databases on Frank Keller," she said.

"What popped up?"

"Absolutely nothing!"

"What?" St. James exclaimed, sitting up straight. "My take was he would have priors of some sort."

"No. Guess you're not always right, Hamilton."

"Never said I was. You just assumed that I think I am always right! Not so. Assumptions are the mother of all screw-ups."

Joy just shook her head and walked away.

Minutes later, Smythe stuck his head in St. James's office.

"I have Johnson working on deciphering the second laptop," he reported.

"Does he know what he's doing?"

"No!" Smythe laughed.

"Hope this doesn't foul the investigation. Make us look stupid."

"You mean make *you* look stupid," Smythe poked.

"Whatever."

"It won't make us look stupid, Hamilton," Smythe assured with sincerity. "I'll review it closely."

"If it's screwed up, it will be on you, Louis."

"I know, I know."

"I reviewed Baker's website. Here is a summary of what I did, found and concluded." Smythe handed the report to St. James.

"And?"

"I'd prefer you read it for yourself."

St. James nodded as he took the document. "Where do we stand with the Taylor investigation?"

"I've gone as far as I can internally. Just waiting for you to tell me whether there's any outside interference."

"I'll call Taylor. He'll be anxious, and I don't want him complaining to David that we are too slow."

Smythe nodded.

"Just like Anna, you've earned a break," St. James said. "Take the afternoon off."

"Thank you," Smythe said and walked away.

St. James telephoned Taylor to give him an update. He told him Smythe had finished the systems review, and that he was now focusing on eliminating or confirming external interference in the supermarket chain. Taylor sounded impatient with the lack of progress and expressed concern about St. James's ever-mounting bill.

"I want to terminate the investigation, hold my breath and swallow the losses," Taylor said curtly.

"John, we can't terminate now. You'll have spent a lot of money and concluded nothing. Doesn't make sense," St. James argued.

"Well, have you found anything nefarious so far?"

"Nothing conclusive. Not until I can tie up the remaining loose ends."

Taylor was silent for a long moment, seemingly weighing the pros and cons of allowing St. James to continue.

"Okay," he said reluctantly. "But for God's sake, speed it up! I'm scared to death of your bill and losses that are probably mounting."

"I'll do my best, John. But these investigations take time. They involve eliminating suspects, events that may or may not have occurred, and an accurate take on those with both motive and opportunity to do wrong. And if there was wrongdoing, what was it? Investigations are never a straight line from beginning to end. They always have setbacks and trails that lead nowhere. If it were straightforward, your management team would have solved it long ago."

Taylor let out a long sigh. "Okay! Okay! Carry on then," he said with a weary tone.

When the Taylor call ended, St. James went down the hall to Kingston's office. Kingston was on the phone but waved St. James to a guest chair while he finished the call.

"What can I do for you, Hamilton?"

"I have a couple of things I'd like to talk about."

"Shoot."

St. James relayed his conversation with Taylor. "I wanted to give you a heads-up. Didn't want you ambushed by one of his calls."

"Appreciate that. Nothing worse than an ambush. I can't say I'm surprised, though. John's obsession with cost had to be thrown your way sooner or later. I'll sing the same song if he calls."

"Thanks, David."

"What's the second thing?" Kingston asked cautiously.

"DI Joy."

"I feel a problem coming on," Kingston said with a slight chuckle.

"No, not a problem. More like an ask for advice."

"What are we talking about here?"

"Well, like you said when we agreed to help, we have to work with Joy, and her requests are the same as coming from you."

"Yes."

St. James recounted all his interactions with Joy — his apology for circumventing her to rescue Louis, her jabs when they arrived at Chamberlain's flat, her anger at him when he settled in the Wimbledon study, and the flippant remark about his focus when Anna came.

"We've done everything she asked, when she asked. I can only apologize so many times, David."

Kingston stared out the window for a few seconds. A smile washed over his face.

"I've known Joy a long time," he said slowly. "She's a good person and a fabulous copper. She can carry a grudge a bit too long, but I don't get the sense that's the thing here."

"Okay. What then?"

"I think she's falling for you!"

Chapter 41

"Jesus, David! You're kidding."

"Afraid not, old boy," Kingston said with a huge grin.

St. James looked stunned. "How does ragging on me at every turn translate into a crush."

Kingston's grin widened. "She is attracted to worthy adversaries. I've seen this behaviour in her before. There was always a male who performs above average in the wings. And you, my friend, are an above-average-performing male. When she made the irreverent remark about your focus with Anna, that sealed my conclusion. Attractive women in your life would be competition in Joy's eyes."

"You're enjoying this, aren't you?" said an annoyed St. James.

Kingston laughed. "Not often I see the great detective squirm."

"What do I do now?"

"Ignore it," Kingston said quickly.

"Easy for you to say. I've been walking on eggshells even before this. What do you think I'll feel like now?"

"Like you're walking on bigger eggshells."

St. James shook his head and walked back to his office.

He made a few phone calls to take his mind off Joy. The first was to the University Hospital Rechts der Isar in Munich. When the switchboard answered, he asked for the chief administrator and was immediately transferred to Ms. Lina Meyer.

Without mentioning Taylor, St. James explained his role in the Chamberlain murder case, embellishing the latter, hoping Meyer believed he was on official police business. She'd be reluctant to give Gerda Wagner's information to a private investigator but maybe less so for a police detective.

"I don't understand what Miss Wagner's health care has to do with a murder in London," Meyer said with a raspy German accent.

Smoker, St. James thought. "Well, there're several persons of interest, some of whom may have connections with Miss Wagner."

"Who?"

St. James ignored the question. "Do you keep a log of patient visitors?"

"Well, of course, we do," she said, as if St. James had asked a stupid question. "Who are you looking for?"

Determined not to let her derail his questioning, St. James said, "I don't have a name, Ms. Meyer. I am looking for a lead to an unknown party," he lied.

"Why didn't you say that in the first place?"

St. James ignored the rebuke. "Would you kindly tell me who visited her?" he said politely, trying to conceal his annoyance.

"Give me a moment to pull up the list."

St. James heard the tapping of keys.

A moment later, she said, "She's had five visitors in the last six months. One visited several times."

"Names please?"

Meyer recited the five names.

"Any of them contribute to her health-care cost?" he asked timidly, fully expecting to be shut down.

"Yes, but I am not at liberty to say who."

He thanked Meyer and ended the call. St. James considered Wagner's five visitors and made a note.

He called the Bartholomeus Gasthuis long-term care home in Utrecht and once again asked for the chief administrator. He enquired about Hanna Visser, asking the same questions he asked Lina Meyer and receiving similar guarded answers. He made notes.

Suddenly St. James heard an ear-piercing scream down the hall. He ran to investigate and found several officers gathered around Joy's office. Standing motionless with her face buried in both hands was a stunned Joy, Kingston by her side.

St. James pushed his way into the office and eyed the contents of an open box. "Jesus," he exclaimed. "That takes a sick bastard."

Kingston passed St. James a note that came with the box. St. James studied it for a second. High-quality glossy letters from a magazine had been used to spell out a message: *I heard the Yard was short-staffed. I thought you could use a couple of extra hands.*

For a long moment, St. James stared at the severed hands in the box.

Kingston ordered another DS to Joy's office. "Take this to the lab," he said sharply. "I want them fingerprinted right away; let's see if the hands are Chamberlain's. I want every inch of the box and its wrapping paper tested. Don't forget the note. I strongly doubt it, but maybe the guy was careless enough to leave a print."

"Yes, sir," the DS said as he grabbed the box and paper and headed for the lab.

Kingston turned to Joy. "How did the box get to you?"

Joy gathered herself. "Someone left it on the steps outside. One of the assistants noticed it when she came to work. It had my name on it, so she brought it to me after security scanned it for explosives."

Kingston nodded. "Are you going to be all right, Phyllis?"

"Yes," she said, forcing a slight smile. Afraid of what her boss might think of her screaming, Joy said, "I'm a tough old copper. Don't confuse shock with weakness. I expect I'll see a lot worse before my career is over."

"Let's hope not," Kingston said with a frown and left.

St. James sat in one of Joy's guest chairs without being invited. Joy looked at him as if to say, what?

"What could be the significance of this, Phyllis?" he said, staring out the window, eying the Thames. "What message are they trying to send?"

Joy sat behind her desk, looking pale. "I honestly don't know," she said with a heavy sigh.

"Whoever it is, he's taunting us, but to what end?"

"Maybe he's saying, catch me if you can," she suggested.

"Could be. But maybe it's deeper than that."

"Like what?"

"I don't know."

Chapter 42

On Friday night in Gundelsheim, Dozer followed two guys from Fischer's farm to Engel57 MusicBar on Schloßstraße. At 7:00 p.m., they were dropped off by the brown twelve-passenger van. The two hopped out but stopped when the driver yelled something through the open passenger window. Both nodded, then made their way inside.

Dozer recognized them from shuttles between the farm and head office but had no idea who they were. He parked his rented Passat on a side street and walked back to the drinking establishment. Spotting the two leaning against the far end of the bar, he walked over, stood next to them and ordered a Beck's. Both men were of average height and dressed smart-casual. Dozer guessed midthirties. One spoke English with a French accent, and the other, Dozer figured, was Russian.

Dozer looked around the old public house, admiring the architecture, and realized he was the only Black man there. For a brief moment, he felt self-conscious but quickly shook it off as being stupid.

He turned to the Frenchman. "I am always in awe of European pubs," he said with a smile. "They have such character and hold so much history in their architecture."

The Frenchman nodded. "Where are you from?"

"Canada."

"What brings you to Gundelsheim?" the Russian said.

The Russian accent was intense and challenging for Dozer to understand. "Touring my way to Frankfurt to meet my girlfriend. She's flying in from Toronto tomorrow," Dozer said convincingly.

The Frenchmen nodded. "Where are you staying?"

Dozer drank some beer and grinned. "Some place I can't pronounce."

"That would be every place for me," the Russian said with a faint smile.

"How about you two?"

"Staying with a friend south of town," replied the Russian, arching his thumb to emphasize the direction.

Dozer extended a hand. "I'm Dozer."

The Frenchman shook Dozer's hand. "François."

"Dimitri," the Russian said.

"You are the first people I have met who speak English," Dozer lied. "Been sightseeing alone all day. Glad to have someone to talk with."

The two nodded.

Dozer drank the rest of the Beck's. He noticed François and Dimitri had finished their drinks too. "Can I buy you gentlemen a drink?" he said enthusiastically.

François smiled. "Thank you."

Dimitri nodded.

Dozer caught the bartender's attention and signalled a round. "What line of work are you fellas in?" Dozer asked innocently.

François and Dimitri looked at one another.

"Odd jobs," Dimitri said.

"Covers a wide range," Dozer observed. "Handymen, carpentry, technology?"

"Little of everything," François said.

"What about you?" Dimitri asked.

"Commercial real estate," replied Dozer.

The bartender placed the second round.

Dimitri took a couple of beats to enjoy the second beer.

"Lot of money to be made there," François said.

"Not bad. Where are you from?"

"St. Petersburg," said Dimitri. "Known for technology development."

"Beautiful City, St. Petersburg," Dozer said with a smile.

"I'm from Lyon," François said proudly.

"What's its major industry?" Dozer asked with genuine interest.

"Technology as well."

Dozer shook his head. "I'm hopeless when it comes to technology. You fellas any good at it?"

"Reasonably comfortable," replied François, beginning to look suspicious of Dozer's questions.

Dozer picked up on his change in demeanour, looked at his watch and said, "I must be going, fellas. I have some packing to do. Thanks for the chat."

Dozer paid the bar bill and left.

François and Dimitri nodded and wished Dozer safe travels. When Dozer left, they looked at one another, frowned and went back to their drinks.

Walking back to the rental, Dozer thought about the conversation. *Hamilton isn't going to be happy. He'll want more. But staying meant risking everything. François was getting close to catching on.*

Even though the next day was Saturday, Dozer resumed his post in front of a grey warehouse property three doors down from Fischer's head office to begin his watch. As usual, the Volkswagen van brought four people from the farm and took four back.

Dozer's fruitless weeklong surveillance established one thing: Fischer's operation functioned twenty-four seven. And the short, awkward conversation with François and Dimitri told him it was entirely about technology — they both mentioned this when asked about their hometowns. They could have said construction or manufacturing and been equally accurate. But when cities have several thriving industries, professionals tend to cite their own first. So François and Dimitri, citing technology first, told Dozer it was their profession.

Whatever the business, it transacted through the internet. Otherwise, there'd be a lot more activity around the property — trucks delivering or picking up, customers coming and going or waiting for service.

Then there was Harry Fischer. Dozer still hadn't seen the big fish. Either Fischer had personal quarters in the office building itself or a hidden compartment in the shuttle to conceal him when travelling to and from the farm.

Sitting in the rental for long hours with no results was beginning to wear on Dozer. He didn't have facts about IEI to go on, only plausible suppositions with no way of proving anything unless he walked in the front door, and that would be suicide. But whatever the company was doing had to be illegal. Otherwise, it would be more open for the world to see.

Just before noon, there was a tap on the driver's window. Dozer turned to see an athletic blond man standing by the car door. He lowered the window.

"I noticed you sitting here for the last several days. Can I help you?" said the man.

"No," said Dozer. "Just waiting for someone."

"It seems unlikely that someone would sit in a car for a week waiting for someone who doesn't show," said the German bluntly, raising a Glock 9 to Dozer's head. "I think you better come with me."

Dozer frowned. "Shit."

"Open the car door slowly and raise your hands where I can see them," the German said authoritatively.

Dozer did.

The man grabbed Dozer's gun and shoved it into his waistband.

"Now give me your cell."

"I don't have one."

"I find that hard to believe," the German said curtly.

He held the Glock tightly against Dozer's temple with one hand and checked Dozer's pockets with the other. Nothing.

"Now walk slowly toward the white building and don't try anything stupid," the German said gruffly.

Dozer opened the front door to IEI's head office. The German jabbed the Glock in his back as a reminder not to try anything.

Dozer studied the frantic activity of several people inside. There had to be twenty-five or more banging away on laptops and talking on cells simultaneously. The room was pure white, not another colour to be seen. Sitting side by side in the last row of computer screens were François and Dimitri, terror in their eyes when they spotted Dozer.

The German jabbed Dozer a second time and pointed to a set of stairs off to the right. They climbed to the second floor and entered the private office of Harry Fischer.

Chapter 43

Fischer looked up from a report and eyed Dozer. "Who the hell is this, Schneider?"

Knee-deep now; may as well go all the way, Dozer thought.

"This is the guy I told you about a couple of days ago, casing the place."

"Hmm," said Fischer. "Why are you running surveillance on us?"

"Wanted to meet you," Dozer lied.

"Is that right?" Fischer said, leaning back in his chair, forehead lined. He studied Dozer for a long minute. "What's your name?"

"Dozer."

"Dozer?" he said in a mocking tone.

"Yes."

"What kind of stupid name is that?" Fischer said.

Dozer said nothing.

Fischer surveyed Dozer with curiosity. "Why did you want to meet me?"

"I promised some friends of yours I'd say hello," Dozer said sarcastically.

Fischer arched his eyebrows.

Schneider poked Dozer with the gun once again. "What friends?"

"Gerhard Becker and Friedrich Schmidt."

Fischer gave Schneider a sharp look.

"What makes you think they're friends of mine?" Fischer said.

"I took three photographs before I left London." Dozer pulled the first from a pocket and placed it on Fischer's desk. "This is Louis Smythe just after your friends beat him. He's a friend of mine. And since you called the Glock man here Schneider, he would be the one who hired the two morons to steal Chamberlain's computer. When Louis wouldn't open the encrypted laptop, your dolts beat him within an inch of his life."

"How do you know that?" Schneider scowled.

Dozer's smile was wide. "Becker told me."

Dozer could see rage building in both men. Exactly what he wanted.

That's when bullies usually make mistakes.

"Because Smythe is a close friend, I felt compelled to act, to return the favour for Louis." He pulled the other two pictures from the same pocket and placed them on the desk next to Smythe's. "This is Becker and Schmidt after I beat them to a pulp."

Dozer watched Schneider grit his teeth.

Fischer rubbed his bald head. "You got a lot of nerve coming in here like this."

"I didn't come in here like this." Dozer pointed to Schneider. "He dragged me in here like this. You have only yourselves to blame."

Schneider hit Dozer with the butt of the Glock, knocking him to the floor. Slightly stunned, Dozer rubbed his shaved head and pulled himself up.

Without missing a beat, he said, "Oh, by the way, I had a drink with François and Dimitri last night. Nice guys."

Fischer smashed his fist on the desk and shouted, "What little chance you had of getting out of here alive just evaporated. Give me one good reason why Schneider shouldn't kill you right here, right now?"

"I'll give you two," Dozer said calmly. "First, Scotland Yard knows I am here. They're working with German intelligence to blow your operation wide open. Something happens to me, the authorities will swoop down on you quicker than you can say, NaturKulturHotel Stumpf."

Fischer's forehead crinkled. "What the hell's that?"

Dozer grinned. "I'm taking German lessons, can't you tell?"

"If I were you, I'd shoot my language coach," Fischer said sharply.

Not able to make up his mind what to do, Schneider said, "You're one cocky son of a bitch."

Fischer looked at Dozer, trying to contain his rage. "You said there were two reasons we shouldn't kill you. What's the second?"

"I have access to the laptop you had the two morons steal from Nigel Chamberlain. You kill me, and you'll never see what's on it. You blew your cover when Schneider forced me in here. I wasn't trying to, nor did I plan to come in here on my own. I was watching movements of your people to and from the farm, nothing more, nothing less."

Schneider looked at Fischer. "What do you want me to do with him, boss?"

Fischer stared at the ceiling for a long moment, weighing the risk of different options. Did Dozer have access to the laptop? Was he lying about the German authorities?

Finally, he said, "Lock him in the basement room until I figure out the best of our terrible options."

Schneider nodded and walked Dozer back down to the first floor and across the room to another set of stairs on the far side, leading to the basement. Along the way, Dozer eyed several large computer screens flashing data.

Computer operators briefly stopped typing to watch the two men heading for the basement.

Schneider shoved Dozer into the smallest of three basement rooms, the only one without a window, and locked the door. The space was barren except for a small table and a couple of chairs. The walls were white and bare; the floor, grey concrete. The room was dim, with only a small night-light. Dozer wondered why it was there. It didn't seem to serve a useful purpose.

He held his wrist to the night-light to check the time. Two thirty. Then he sat on a chair and waited.

As IEI was a twenty-four-hour operation, Dozer would never have an ideal time to make a move. So there had to be some distraction upstairs for him to have a decent chance of escaping, one that had Schneider focused elsewhere. He knew four o'clock was when the shuttle began moving the evening shift in from the farm. Because changeover only happened four people at a time, it took a while to complete. It wasn't great, but it was the only time there'd be enough confusion to camouflage an escape.

At four fifteen, Dozer pulled a small, thin lockpick from a concealed zippered pocket three-quarters of the way down his left pant leg and began working the lock. The lock was not a standard make, so it took longer than he expected to release. Eventually, the pick did its job, and the door creaked open. The small room was visible from the top stair, so Dozer immediately closed the door behind him. Schneider had to think he was still there should he check from the top stair.

He slowly crept along the right wall toward the foot of the stairs, stopped, waited and listened for sounds above. Minutes later, he heard the industrial metal door roll up in the back of the building, where the shuttle always parked for shift changes. Dozer figured most eyes would be on the shuttle, leaving the best of his poor escape options: the front door.

Dozer heard someone on the main floor opening the basement door. He took cover under the staircase. The door released, and through the risers, Dozer saw a pair of men's well-polished black shoes descending the steps. He grabbed a two-by-four from under the bottom step and waited until the man was almost at the door to the room where he had been held captive.

Dozer slowly crept from under the stairwell and hit the man he now realized was Schneider hard over the head with the two-by-four. Schneider collapsed to the floor, unconscious. Dozer quickly opened the door and dragged the limp body into the small room, took Schneider's Glock and key to the room and locked the door behind.

Dozer climbed the stairs and opened the door a crack, just wide enough to see what was happening. Several people were wandering toward the back of the building where the van would be parked. Others were firmly glued to computer screens. Neutralizing Fischer's most dangerous man gave him more confidence to pull off a successful escape. He exited the stairs, quietly crept along the right wall of the main floor and slipped out the front door.

The Passat was where he'd left it that morning. He climbed in, removed a cell from under the seat and cranked up the engine. Pulling the car into drive, he slammed the accelerator hard to the floor, tires squealing as the Passat serpentined away toward the hotel. Halfway there, Dozer put the car window down and threw the key to the basement room in a ditch.

Chapter 44

When St. James and Joy finished their impromptu meeting, following the shock of Chamberlain's hands showing up unannounced, he went back to the hotel.

Anna wasn't back from shopping with Carolyn Kingston yet, so he left a note and headed for the bar downstairs.

Prisha was on duty and greeted him with a warm smile that St. James attributed to his rather large tip the night before.

Prisha's jet-black hair was shoulder length, and her rich golden-brown complexion made her perfectly formed teeth seem whiter than white. Her genuine smile said she loved her job.

"Prisha … right?" he said as arrived at his table.

"That's right," she said, sounding almost surprised. "You have a good memory."

"Thank you. And *you* might remember I'm a scotch drinker."

"I remember," she said in a soft Indian accent.

"Tonight, I feel adventuresome. What do you recommend?"

"Old Pulteney's twelve-year-old malt whisky is popular in the UK. Have you tried it?"

"No, I haven't."

"Would you like a sample? I believe your name is Mr. St. James, if I remember correctly."

"Indeed it is. I'll try a taste."

Prisha went behind the bar, pulled a bottle from the shelf, poured a dribble in a shot glass and brought it to St. James.

He took a sip, savoured it for a few seconds and looked at her. "I like it, Prisha. Good suggestion. I'll have a double on ice."

"Very well, Mr. St. James. Just be a minute."

Shortly after, Anna breezed in, gave St. James a peck on the cheek and sat opposite. She was still buzzing from her shopping trip. "Carolyn and I had such a wonderful day, Hamilton," she said with glee.

"Is there any paint left on your credit card?"

"Not only is there no paint, but the numbers are down a millimetre or two."

"Where did you go?"

"We wore out the shopping end of Oxford Street. Spent time in Zara, where the Duchess of Cambridge shops. Topshop, Selfridges, Debenhams, and Marks & Spencer too. You name it, and we were there. And we had wonderful wat tan hor, a Malaysian hawker-stall classic with seafood served over noodles at a place called Laksamania on Newman Street. It's Malaysian but the chef does wonderful Thai food as well."

St. James grinned. "The day sounds delightful and exhausting all at the same time."

Prisha looked at Anna. "What would you like, miss?"

"I'll have an Armentano pinot, please."

"Right away," Prisha said, still grinning as she pivoted and headed toward the bar.

"Where's Louis?" Anna asked.

"It turns out he earned a break too."

"You didn't tease him because he pouted over me having time off, did you?"

"No. He was at a juncture with work, so I gave him the afternoon off. Besides, he's run out of plaid combinations and could stand to do a bit of shopping."

"Good. He looked exhausted last night. He's been working flat out since he got here. Being kidnapped and beaten wasn't much of a break either," she said.

St. James turned to the case. "Listen, I hate to be all business, but can you get back to researching Keller tomorrow?"

"Absolutely."

Prisha delivered white wine to Anna.

"I thought we'd have dinner at the Grosvenor Casino, The Rialto," he said with a devilish grin, knowing what Anna's reaction would be. "It's only a few steps down Coventry, close to Leicester Square."

Anna gave him a look that would melt a crowbar. "You know how much I hate your gambling. I had my fill of that at the casino in Quebec. It's a bad habit. May as well burn your money," she said, raising her voice to emphasize the point.

St. James continued the ruse. "Restaurant there is supposed to be excellent."

"I don't care if it has four Michelin stars."

"What if I promise not to gamble, just have dinner."

Anna downed half the wine in one gulp, unusual for a slow sipper, testimony to the height of her annoyance.

She wagged a finger. "I know you, Hamilton St. James. Once we're there, you'll say, 'Just one game of blackjack, Anna, that's all I want.' Three hours later, you'll be down a couple of thousand pounds, and I'll be out of my mind."

"If I'd known you felt that strongly, I wouldn't have suggested it."

"You know bloody well how I feel about it. And wipe that stupid grin off your face."

"Want to make love?"

"No! I don't want to make love," she said loud enough to turn heads two tables away.

St. James laughed when her outburst drew attention around the room.

Anna turned red, realizing now he was only winding her up.

"Next you'll say a kiss is totally out of the question."

Not able to hold back any longer, Anna burst into laughter.

"Why don't we just eat here and then go upstairs and have make-up sex," he said, laughing.

And that's exactly what they did.

Chapter 45

The following day Anna wanted an early start researching Keller, so she stayed in the room and ordered scrambled eggs from room service, pecking away on the keyboard with one hand and eating with the other. St. James and Smythe went to the dining room as usual.

Over toast and coffee, Smythe said, "I'd better check on Herb first thing. See how far he has gotten deciphering Chamberlain's code."

St. James drank coffee. "Best you don't let him go too far off track before checking."

Smythe nodded.

"I'm going to set up a second meeting with Keller, but I'd like to know what the deciphered document shows first in case there's something there I should ask him about."

"Makes sense," Smythe said, taking his time spreading peanut butter over a piece of toast. When he noticed St. James staring at him, he stopped.

"What?"

"Oh, nothing," St. James said. "Just hoping David hears something about the hands today."

***

Smythe and St. James got a massive surprise when they arrived at the Scotland Yard. Dozer was sitting in the meeting room, updating Joy.

St. James stopped in the doorway when he saw him, almost causing Smythe to walk into him from behind. Dozer stood up.

"Surprise!"

St. James was astonished. "What are you doing here?"

"My job!"

Dozer updated them on the events in Gundelsheim — the trips back and forth to the farm; drinks with François and Dimitri; being held at gunpoint by Schneider; meeting Fischer; the pictures he'd shown them of Becker, Schmidt and Smythe; being locked in the basement, and his escape.

"You took quite a chance, my friend," St. James said, shaking his head.

Smythe followed St. James into the room and leaned against a filing cabinet. He looked pale, worn down.

"You okay, Louis?" Dozer asked.

"I'm fine," Smythe said, shaking off the memory of his own captivity. "That could have gone very badly, Dozer."

Joy looked at Smythe and back at Dozer. "Tell them the best part," she said with enthusiasm.

Dozer nodded. "When Schneider walked me to the basement, I was close enough to several large computer screens to see data streaming in from multiple locations. It didn't look like transactions for Southeast Asian goods. In the short time I had, it looked like money transferring into numbered companies from around the world."

St. James looked over at a smiling Joy. "Why does this make you so happy?"

"When Dozer told me this, I immediately called Noah Weber, of the Hamburg feds. As far as he knows, Dozer's the only person other than an IEI employee ever to get inside headquarters. Weber thinks an affidavit from Dozer could generate a court order to search and seize IEI's computers. Don't you see? We have a chance to look inside IEI's operation, maybe view everyone and everything in Fischer's ecosystem. It's the break we've been waiting for," she said. "Weber's excited because his investigation was going nowhere without inside information."

Smythe looked on quietly.

"I see your point, Phyllis," St. James said slowly, considering the ramifications of such a move. "What do you think, Dozer?"

Dozer shrugged. "The quicker we crack this case, the quicker I get back to Toronto. I have a business to run, and this thing is sucking up all my management time!"

Joy suddenly stood. "Let's make your wish come true, Dozer. Let's go to Hamburg, give Weber what he needs for a court order. Get you back to Toronto sooner."

Dozer nodded.

"Makes sense," St. James concluded.

Joy and Dozer left immediately to catch a flight to Hamburg.

Smythe made his way down to Johnson's office and found him sitting in front of two computer screens: one opened to Chamberlain's coded narrative, and the other split between an online thesaurus and dictionary. Johnson looked totally focused on the task Smythe had assigned to him.

"How are you making out, Herb?"

"I've made better progress than I thought I would," he said proudly. "I'm on the last page. You're right, Louis, the more letters you replace, the less guesswork is left."

"I'm proud of you, Herb," Smythe said. "Let's see what you've got."

Johnson printed several pages and handed them to Smythe, who settled himself in a guest chair and read what Johnson deciphered. When he finished, he looked over at Johnson.

"Excellent work, Herb."

"Thank you."

"When you finish the last page, will you bring it to me? I'll be in the meeting room close to Kingston's office."

"Yes, of course," Johnson said, eyes rapidly alternating between the two screens.

***

St. James and Smythe were huddled in the meeting room, going over the deciphered code from Chamberlain's second laptop. St. James read each page carefully and passed them one by one to Smythe for further scrutiny.

"Looks like Chamberlain and Fischer were defrauding companies through ConQuest, Quantum and IEI's joint venture you discovered, Louis. Nothing to do with the sale of goods from Southeast Asia, as they would have us believe. They have to be extracting funds from companies around the world. Maybe that's what Dozer saw on IEI's computers."

Smythe nodded. "But it contradicts another file showing what looks like legitimate import/export transactions. Why is the narrative about frauds and the data about East and Southeast Asian transactions?"

"I don't have a satisfactory answer to that yet, Louis. Except, if someone did see what's on the second laptop, the data would reinforce what the crooks wanted the outside world to believe — that they were running a legitimate import/export business. The code could be just for communication among the fraudsters themselves, definitely a significant roadblock for anyone outside their circle to decipher. They'd have to have skills like yours. Not that common. It could be the code tells the real story known only to the crooks. Import/export data is there only in case the crooks were investigated; there for show. Cover to disguise the fraud operation."

Smythe nodded. "Plausible, I suppose," he said thoughtfully.

"For the time being, let's assume that's the case."

They read on.

"Here on page nine, Frank Keller is mentioned for the first time," St. James observed.

"I noticed that my first read-through," Smythe said, continuing to read as St. James passed the pages.

Johnson appeared and dropped off the last page.

"Good work, Herb," St. James said.

"Thank you, sir."

Johnson turned to Smythe. "Louis, let me know if you need help with anything else."

"Will do. Thanks again, Herb."

Johnson nodded and left.

"Looks like Keller was the one managing money defrauded from UK companies. Funds flowing into ConQuest. Quantum was to pay Keller for his work out of its share of ConQuest's profits," St. James said as he continued reading.

Smythe looked at St. James for a long moment. "Hamilton — this is huge."

St. James stared off. "Whatever this is!"

Chapter 46

"Lab report says prints taken from the severed hands are Chamberlain's," Kingston said.

"What about the box the hands came in and the note?" St. James asked.

"Partial one on the box. Smudged. Not enough to be useful. Nothing on the notepaper. He may be a sicko, but he's careful."

"Hmm."

St. James and Kingston were sitting in Kingston's office. St. James filled Kingston in on the deciphered narrative he and Smythe reviewed.

"What do you make of it?"

"Not a lot. The working relationship between Keller and Chamberlain is clearer but still a bit murky."

Kingston shook his head. "Breaks in this case are hard to come by."

St. James nodded.

"What now, Hamilton?"

St. James stared out over the River Thames, then turned to Kingston.

"The logical next step is a second interview with Keller. He acted shocked when I said Chamberlain and Fischer were running frauds. But we know now he was fraud-deep right along with them, at the same time swearing he only sourced goods from East and Southeast Asia for export to Western countries. He tripped over himself when I asked the location of inventories. Said he never saw goods he sourced for Chamberlain. They went straight to Quantum. But managing Chamberlain's criminal activity in the UK is really what he was doing."

St. James's cell buzzed.

Anna.

"Excuse me, David. I have to take this." St. James left Kingston's office for his own.

"Hey, babe. Where are you with Keller?"

"Reason for my call, handsome."

"Whatcha got?"

"Well, for starters, Keller has no priors," she said.

"That's what Joy said."

"He seems to operate under the radar."

"What do you mean?"

"I don't know what I mean," she said slowly. "Keller has a line of credit at an international bank for £2 million, and an account at a wealth management company worth about £25 million."

"What about relatives?"

"Nothing on genealogy that I could find."

"How much is he into the line of credit for?"

"Nothing! The total £2 million is available for him to draw."

"Hmm. Married?"

"No."

"Children from a previous marriage?"

"Never married."

"Girlfriends?"

"None noted anywhere."

"Boyfriends?"

"No."

St. James was quiet for several seconds.

"What is he, a bloody robot?" he said with a chuckle.

Anna laughed. "I guess that's what I mean by under the radar."

St. James paused again, then said, "I'll have to try another angle."

Chapter 47

The next day was the first of August. St. James and Smythe had been on the case full time for almost three weeks and were growing tired, both emotionally and physically. Headway was slow, and St. James was worried he wouldn't be able to keep John Taylor at bay much longer. The man could suffer a nervous breakdown if his current stress level continued.

They were no closer to finding who killed Chamberlain and why or where Chamberlain hid £50 million.

St. James called Frank Keller.

"Frank, is it possible to meet today?"

"Are you in Central London?" Keller asked. "I have a bank meeting that takes me there at ten o'clock. And a meeting with my lawyer at three. We could meet in between."

"Will your bank meeting be finished by noon?"

"Should be done by eleven thirty. Why?"

Keller's Scottish brogue was still making communication difficult, but St. James was understanding more words.

"Can I buy you lunch at the Westminster Arms, say at noon?"

"Sounds good. It's been a while since I enjoyed a pint at the Arms. Looking forward to it."

At eleven thirty, St. James left the Yard, walked to the Westminster, grabbed a booth and sat facing the door to spot Keller when he arrived. He waved a server over and ordered a Guinness.

Five after twelve, Keller strolled through the door. They shook hands, and Keller removed his coat and hat and hung them on a nearby coat hook.

Guinness arrived for St. James.

"Was your bank meeting successful?" St. James asked after Keller ordered a Tennant.

"Quite successful, thank you."

"You mentioned you have another meeting this afternoon — with a lawyer, I think you said?"

"Yes, that's right."

"I might require a good lawyer here, but I don't know anyone. Can you recommend someone?"

"Well, I've been a client of Goldstein & Stein for quite a few years now."

"Good service?"

"Always been satisfied. I always use Harvey Goldstein. He's the senior partner."

"Good to know," St. James said sincerely.

"I am assuming you didn't invite me to lunch just to talk about lawyers."

St. James smiled. "Quite true. I didn't. Since you were partners with Chamberlain, I thought you might appreciate an update on the case."

Keller's Tennant arrived, and the two ordered lunch.

"Thoughtful of you," Keller said as he downed Tennant. "Have you found the killer yet?"

"Not quite. But we have found some interesting things."

"Like what?"

"There was a laptop in Chamberlain's safe at his Wimbledon mansion," St. James said carefully. He studied Keller's expression closely and then drank Guinness.

"Anything interesting on it?" Keller said.

"There was data in one file referring to goods from East and Southeast Asia. It seemed to support what you said during our first meeting," St. James said.

Keller's slight smile suggested he was appreciative of the confirmation.

St. James flagged the server and ordered two more beers.

"A second file contained several pages of enciphered narrative, which I had my expert decipher. It contradicts the Asian import/export business you described and the import and export data in the first electronic file I just mentioned.

"The narrative suggests money flowed into a joint venture called ConQuest, owned by Quantum and IEI, for what appears to be questionable transactions," St. James said quietly, avoiding an accusatory tone. "Can you shed any light?"

"Strange," Keller said with raised eyebrows.

The beer and lunch plates arrived.

Keller forked french fries and drank beer, seemingly stalling to formulate an acceptable answer.

"I can't account for what may or may not be on Chamberlain's laptop. I've never received an enciphered or coded message of any kind from Chamberlain or anyone else for the matter."

Calm under pressure, St. James thought.

St. James's demeanour was relaxed and engaging, and his choice of words seemed benign enough.

"Chamberlain's narrative said you were responsible for certain of Quantum's UK operations. Can you tell me what the operations were and how it all went down?"

"I wasn't responsible for anything other than sourcing goods from East and Southeast Asia — what used to be called—"

"The Far East," St. James interjected.

"Right," Keller said as he cut away a piece of fish.

St. James paused to cut his steak. "So you're saying what Chamberlain enciphered isn't true."

Keller drank Tennant. "I don't know what Chamberlain wrote, but I do know what I was doing, and it wasn't running frauds."

"Were you paid up to date by Quantum?"

"No!" he said quickly. "The bastard died owning me over a million pounds."

"Back pay?"

Keller's voice rose. "Yes. No reason for it either. Chamberlain was almost a billionaire. A million pounds was pocket change to him."

Noting the agitation in Keller's voice, St. James decided to let the balance of his questions go for the time being.

Discussions turned to politics until one thirty when St. James paid the bill, and the two parted ways.

***

Three o'clock that afternoon, St. James received a call from Joy and Dozer. Dozer's affidavit covered everything he'd encountered, emphasizing the IEI computer screens that he'd been able to see when he was forced to the basement.

Weber's affidavit chronicled evidence gathered during his investigation and Fischer's roadblocks preventing access to IEI records. It was a detailed picture of an illegal business — secret operations, no access to information, employees suspiciously moved around four at a time, Dozer held at gunpoint and locked in the basement. All to support granting a search-and-seizure order at a hearing scheduled in two days.

Joy decided she didn't need to hang around for the hearing. So, when the lawyers were happy with preparation, she grabbed an early evening flight back to London.

Chapter 48

Joy came into St. James's office and invited him to lunch. Given Kingston's perception of her feelings for him, St. James was slow to respond. But she seemed to have gotten over his and Dozer's rescuing Smythe without her, and he didn't want to risk reversing that progress by refusing a luncheon invitation.

At 11:45 a.m., they walked over to The Lillie Langtry Pub on Lillie Road, a favourite of Joy's that offered vegan food. The blue bar area was warm and inviting, and they settled at a small table close to the bar itself.

Joy ordered the house white and St. James a Blue Moon.

"To what do I owe the honour of dining with DI Joy?" St. James said with a smile.

Joy was hesitant. "Well, we have been working together now for a couple of weeks. You and your team have been an immense help with moving the case along. Of course, we haven't solved it yet, but we're making progress. Hopefully, Dozer and Weber will be successful with the court order, and that will open a floodgate of new evidence."

"Does this mean you forgive us for taking the law into our own hands?" he said with a grin.

She smiled. "Let's just say it's less of an issue."

"Guess that's better than a no."

The server laid down drinks, then moved to another table.

They paused to enjoy a bit of libation.

"You and Anna been together a while?" Joy said innocently.

"Couple of years."

The server returned from the other table. "Are you ready to order lunch?" he asked.

They gave their choices. He made a note and rushed off toward the kitchen.

"Sounds like you two are serious," Joy said.

"Very!"

St. James hoped his response would be the end of it.

But it wasn't.

"I'd like to meet her."

St. James nodded. "I can arrange an after-work drink if you like."

"That would be wonderful."

Wants to meet the competition.

St. James stared off. "Phyllis, something's been bothering me, something we may have overlooked."

"What's that?"

"When we ruled out the Swiss banks and the Wimbledon safe as possible locations for money, I didn't have a clue where to look next. So I went back over everything we did, looking for holes in the investigation, procedures left out, those we might have done differently."

"What did you conclude?"

"When Jones toured us through Chamberlain's mansion, we saw every room, but only from the ground up. We never went to the basement."

Joy brightened. "That's right!"

Lunch arrived, and they paused to enjoy a few bites.

"Do you have Jones's cell?" St. James said.

"I do. Wonder if he's still there. He may have moved on."

"I doubt it. Did you see the look on his face when you asked what he'd do now Chamberlain was gone? It was the only time he showed any emotion. I think his ability to make decisions is frozen. I'll wager he's still there."

"Only one way to find out." Joy pulled a cell from her beige leather handbag, opened the contact file and searched for Jones's number. When she tapped on her cell, he answered right away. Joy explained what they wanted, and Jones was most welcoming, inviting them to return whenever convenient.

"I won't be leaving anytime soon," Jones said.

Will you be seeking another butler position?"

"Don't believe I have to, madam. You see, I've inherited the mansion."

"So I've heard. How wonderful for you."

"Not really, madam. I'd rather have Mr. Chamberlain back."

"I understand." Joy thanked him and said goodbye.

Joy told St. James about Jones's inheritance.

St. James stared off.

Joy drifted into thought and ate more lunch.

"Maybe we now have another suspect," St. James said finally.

Chapter 49

An hour after lunch, Joy's green Fiat rolled up the Chamberlain drive on Parkside Avenue in Wimbledon, this time without getting lost. Earl was outside trimming bushes.

They climbed out of the compact, made their way to the front door and rang the bell. Jones appeared and greeted them as warmly as a rigid butler could.

He led them down the wide hallway and past the study to a broad door that opened onto a set of rough stairs. When Jones left them, Joy and St. James carefully descended to a dimly lit cellar. They stood still for a moment, surveying the space, wondering how best to tackle the search.

"Not much of a basement," Joy mumbled.

"That's because it isn't a basement," St. James said lightly. "It's a cellar. A basement is a below-ground inhabitable floor, and this space certainly is not inhabitable. Basements didn't become popular until the 1950s."

"Well, aren't you a wealth of useless information," she said sarcastically.

St. James ignored the comment.

In the cellar, they could tell that the mansion had settled. The ceiling was low and uneven and the brick floor was rough and pitted. A few large cracks in the floor made the walking treacherous.

There were two cold rooms, one for food, another for wine; at the far end was a makeshift room for storing extra materials, tools, and yard equipment.

An open area at the bottom of the stairs was taken up by a vast decommissioned boiler. St. James thought it must have been installed before the house was roof-tight since it would have been too large to fit in afterward. A modern, efficient furnace had taken its place. The entire space was covered in a blanket of dust and reeked of mould.

St. James looked at Joy. "Lighting's dim."

They turned on their phone flashlights and moved forward.

"Phyllis, I suggest we stick together, so we do each room thoroughly with two sets of eyes at the same time."

Joy nodded. "I agree. It's about thoroughness, not speed."

"Let's start with the storage room, leave the cold rooms until last," he suggested.

Joy nodded, pointing her phone toward the room straight ahead. They walked the few steps with lights pointed down to avoid tripping over unseen obstacles.

"The mouldy smell is quite strong," Joy said, pulling the small pastel scarf around her neck up over her mouth and nose.

"Probably from hundred-year-old decayed bodies lying around here somewhere."

Joy didn't respond.

She flinched when St. James pulled open the creaking door and switched on the single bare lightbulb.

"Not afraid of ghosts, are you, Phyllis?"

"Shut up!"

Inside, he pulled a damaged extension leaf for a dining table away from the left wall and shone the light in behind, looking for openings or hidden doors.

"Phyllis, let's move all the junk to the centre and check the wall and floor around the perimeter."

"Makes sense, I guess," she said with little enthusiasm.

It took five minutes to shift everything to the centre so they could feel along the clay brick walls and floor around the circumference, looking for loose brick or markings that could lead to a compartment large enough to hide money.

Joy stood and worked out the kinks in her legs. She looked down at her clothes. "These slacks are ruined, not even dry-cleanable. I'll have to throw them away."

St. James looked at his pants. "Same here, they're shot." For a second, he eyed the pile of junk in the centre. "We have to put all this stuff back and feel our way along the centre of the floor too."

By the time they finished searching the entire room, an hour and a half had passed, and they were confident it didn't contain a hidden compartment.

"I need a bathroom break and a tea. My knees are killing me," Joy said, rubbing her legs.

They climbed the stairs to the main floor and found Jones sitting at the kitchen table enjoying a late-afternoon tea and scone. He immediately sat up straighter and seemed to go into butler mode.

"May I offer you something?" he said.

"I'd love a tea, Jones," Joy said.

"And you, sir?"

"I'm a coffee man, Jones, thank you."

"May I offer you a blueberry scone?"

They both declined, and Joy excused herself to head to the nearest bathroom, the location of which she remembered from their first tour of the house.

When she returned, Jones was carrying out a tray with tea for her and coffee for St. James. The three settled around the Victorian table.

"Jones," St. James said, sipping coffee, "did Chamberlain ever mention a secret room or compartment anywhere in the house?"

Jones bit into his scone and washed it down with tea. "No. Not that I recall. And I've been in every part of this house countless times over the years. I've never seen a door that didn't let you into or out of a regular room."

"What about the attic?" Joy pressed.

"Isn't one."

"Hmm," St. James said. "Did Chamberlain spend much time in the cellar?"

Jones considered this for a second. "I never saw him go to the cellar in all the years I worked for him. If he wanted wine, I fetched it. If we were out of foodstuffs, I fetched it. I put things in and took things out of the storage room too," he said. Jones ate the last of the scone and finished his tea.

St. James looked at his watch. "Best we get back to work, Phyllis, if we want to finish today."

Joy nodded.

When they thanked Jones and started heading back toward the cellar, Jones seemed surprised.

"Thought you were going back to work?"

"Ah, sorry, no, we have more to do downstairs," St. James explained.

"We'll be at least another hour, maybe longer," said Joy. "The tea break was just what I needed."

Chapter 50

Standing in the cellar's open space again, they decided to tackle the food cold room next.

"Remind me again why we're doing this," said a weary Joy.

"If we are to do our job properly, we have to exhaust every location where money could be hidden, if it exists to be hidden at all," St. James said.

"Right," she said, sounding unconvinced.

The food-laden floor-to-ceiling plank shelving that filled the room made Joy think of pictures of small shops from the 1800s. There were shelves for cheeses, root vegetables — beets, carrots, potatoes and rutabagas — oils, sugars, homemade jams and pickles, and herbs.

St. James was in awe. "There's enough here to feed a small country," he exaggerated.

"Got any bright ideas how we tackle this?" said Joy, hands on her hips.

St. James brought both palms to his face and sighed. "I have absolutely no idea where to begin. If we tried to move the shelving, I think the whole wall would collapse."

He stuck a hand behind a wall of shelving as far as possible and discovered the shelves were supported only by short pieces of timber.

"Nothing is holding it together; no screws, bolts or nails. Each shelf is held in place only by its weight."

Joy considered this for a moment. "That means Chamberlain couldn't have hidden anything behind. If he did, he couldn't access it without causing a food avalanche. And there's no space where shelving meets the ceiling and floor, so that rules out those places where someone could stuff money."

"I agree," he said slowly, eying the ceiling first and then the floor. He looked at Joy. "Want to dance?"

"Huh?" said a stunned Joy. "Have you gone nuts?"

He smiled and pointed to the other half of the floor. "You take that area, and I'll do this."

"What in God's name are you talking about?"

St. James said nothing. He began to step dance, making sure each time a foot came down, it landed on a different brick.

Joy giggled. "Do you have any idea how silly you look?"

"Not nearly as silly as I feel. Don't just stand there admiring my moves. Half the floor is your responsibility."

Joy moved to the other side of the room and began dancing like St. James. "Why didn't you think of this when we did the junk room? I wouldn't have ruined a perfect pair of slacks and ended up with sore knees."

"Life is a spectrum of continuous learning."

Joy just rolled her eyes.

All the floor bricks were tight, only minimal movement.

"Doesn't appear to be any false section in the floor," St. James said as he grabbed a broken broom handle to poke the ceiling. That got him nothing but a head full of plaster dust.

St. James looked at his watch. "I think we did this thing ass-backwards, Phyllis."

"What do you mean?"

"It's quarter after four, roughly the time I begin to think about a five-o'clock drink."

"What's that got to do with what we're doing?"

"We're headed for a cold room full of wine."

Joy just shook her head as they entered the last room. "Why do I always feel like I'm one step behind you?"

"Because you are."

"Cretin."

Chapter 51

The wine racks extended from the floor to the ceiling just like the food shelving, except they were metal and attached to the wall behind with bolts and screws — a far more solid arrangement than planking.

Joy and St. James walked back and forth in front of the walls of racks filled with wine, studying the structure, hoping to see a hinge or something that smacked of an entrance to a secret compartment. They jiggled the racks, gently pushing and pulling different sections in different directions. Nothing.

"Must be two thousand bottles here," St. James mused.

"I'm tired, Hamilton, and I hurt," Joy said as she sat on an empty wooden wine crate, rubbing her knees.

St. James pulled a second crate beside her. "Got a corkscrew?"

Joy playfully slapped his arm. "Don't even think about it, you beggar."

"A man can dream."

Joy feigned admonishment. "Yeah, well, dream about something else."

"I'd be afraid it would be something naughty, and I'd be embarrassed," he teased.

Joy gave him a look. "You're a piece of work. You know that?"

St. James smiled. "I am intellectually and emotionally comfortable with myself. Up to you to be equally mature."

Joy just shook her head.

They sat quietly for a few minutes, leaning gently against a wall of wine behind, staring at another across the room.

When St. James peered at rack straight across from where he sat, something caught his eye. He stood, walked over and ran a finger over that section. Then he felt the rack three feet to the left. The rack on the left seemed slightly smaller than on the right, the difference negligible to the naked eye but pronounced to human touch.

All the racks looked the same, standard round silver metal, a centimetre in diameter, except for the one section that felt slightly larger.

He went back to the more significant section he estimated to be six feet high and four feet wide. Arms fully extended, he grabbed either side and pulled the segment toward him.

Joy looked on with hopeful eyes.

St. James pulled harder. No movement. He jiggled the section from side to side, hoping to dislodge something. Nothing. He stood back and studied the area for a time.

He lay on his back in front of the larger rack and placed his feet against the middle of the rack in that section, two feet apart, then slid his torso forward to create maximum leverage and pushed equally hard with both feet. No movement. He gradually increased the pressure with more leg power. No movement. Not wanting to break expensive bottles of wine, he paused and just lay there.

Anxiety in her voice, Joy said, "No sense of movement at all?"

"No," he said with a huge sigh.

"What do we do now?"

"I just want to lie here and think."

Knowing that interrupting him would be counterproductive, Joy remained silent.

St. James's eye wandered back and forth along the rows of bottles as he thought about what to do next.

Three rows above where he lay were two bottles stored in hexagonal slots, ten bottles apart. He scanned the entire wall of wine from left to right. Suddenly he realized they were the only two hexagonal slots along the whole wall. Every other wine slot was round. When standing, it was impossible to see that only two slots in the section were hexagonal. It was only noticeable looking up from the floor where St. James lay.

He jumped from the floor so quickly it startled Joy into a yelp.

"You frightened me half to death," she said with one hand over her heart.

St. James didn't respond. He grabbed the necks of the bottles in the two hexagonal slots and simultaneously pulled them outward, then waited. Nothing. He yanked harder and waited. Nothing. Then he pushed the two bottles inward and waited. Nothing. He pushed harder. Seconds later, they heard a slow, low grinding sound — metal on metal. The brick floor began to shake and shift under the weight of a moving wall. Grinding turned into an ear-piercing screeching sound as the wall slowly receded along rusted tracks into darkness.

Palms glued to her face, Joy squealed and jumped from the wine crate. "My God, Hamilton, you did it! You found the hidden room. You're a genius," she said, throwing her arms around him.

St. James gently pulled her arms away. "We may have found a room, but we haven't found money, at least not yet anyway," he said. "Let's see what's in there."

Slightly put off by St. James's rebuff, Joy followed him into the newly discovered space.

Inside was blacker than black. Phone lights revealed a door less than two feet in. St. James carefully stepped in to examine it. He didn't see a hole that would demand a key to open the door. He knelt to wipe away dust and soot, revealing what looked like a sensor of some sort, an inch square. It didn't appear to be an electric eye. He moved closer for a micro look, rubbed a forefinger over the square and quickly turned to Joy.

"Phyllis!" he yelled. "Call Kingston! Get him to send someone out here with Chamberlain's hands — now!"

Chapter 52

DS Yvonne Davies arrived at the Wimbledon mansion two hours later carrying a medium-size brown box containing Chamberlain's severed hands.

While waiting for Davies, St. James texted Anna that it would be a late night, and she should order room service rather than wait for him.

Kingston insisted Davies be accompanied by four men from the Specialist Firearms Command in case protection was necessary.

The four specialists fanned out in an arc just outside the wine room entranceway while Davies passed the box to Joy inside the space.

St. James knelt in front of the door, and Joy crouched a foot behind, with Davies a foot behind her. They looked like a fire brigade ready to pass buckets of water.

Joy handed the box to St. James. "I'd rather you do this, Hamilton."

Hamilton took the box. "Do you have a pair of nitrile gloves?"

Joy nodded, pulled a pair from a pant pocket and handed them over. St. James quickly slipped them on and pulled the top from the box. Chamberlain's hands had begun to decompose even with HQ's refrigeration and gave off a very pungent odour. Joy wrestled with her stomach. St. James pulled back and choked from the rancidness.

Davies quietly looked on with amusement.

"I hope they haven't deteriorated to a point the prints are skewed and useless," St. James said as he pressed the thumb of Chamberlain's left hand over the square patch on the door, rolling it from side to side to ensure the full print made contact with the patch. He repeated the process for the remaining fingers on the left hand, each time waiting a couple of beats, hoping to hear a sound of some sort, like the retracting wall, before going on to the next finger.

Davies broke her silence. "I read somewhere that most people who secure valuables with fingerprints use their index finger."

Joy turned to her. "That would make me choose any finger but the index one," she said with a nervous smile.

St. James paused a minute and turned to Joy before moving to the right hand.

"You know I've been waiting for a click or some other sound caused by a successful finger. It just dawned on me there may not be any sound at all. I should be pushing or pulling the door after each print," St. James said, slightly annoyed with himself. "I'll do that for the right hand now. If there's no success, I'll redo the left."

"All right," Joy said.

St. James pressed the right hand's thumb over the patch, waited for a second and pushed and pulled the door. Nothing. He pressed the forefinger, waited and pushed and pulled the door. Nothing. Then the middle finger. Nothing. Then the next. Nothing. Then the smallest finger. Nothing.

"The suspense is killing me," Joy mumbled.

St. James went back to the left hand, repeated all the procedures he'd conducted the first time, pushing and pulling the door after each print.

They looked defeated when St. James finished with the fourth finger on the left hand. It had all been for nothing, a waste of time. Then he applied the smallest finger and pushed the door open.

Chapter 53

It was ten o'clock at night, and St. James and Joy had been searching, pushing, pulling or dancing for almost eight hours. They were exhausted both physically and mentally. On top of that, they hadn't eaten since noon. But that wasn't enough to dampen the jubilant spirit created by what they found in Chamberlain's cellar that night.

On the other side of the door was a rectangular small-scale vault, scarcely large enough to accommodate St. James's height, crammed with boxes containing hundreds of blocks of well-wrapped currency. St. James counted over three hundred fifty boxes.

They opened a sample of four boxes from different vault locations to find a mixture of £20 and £50 notes. Standard denominations, easy to spend without attracting attention.

"What a breakthrough!" Joy said with a huge smile. "Thank you, Hamilton. You *are* a genius."

They stood in the open area of the cellar where the Specialist Firearms Command men and DS Davies had gathered.

"We have some decisions to make, Phyllis," St. James said, rubbing his aching neck.

"Just thinking the same thing."

St. James nodded in the direction of the firearms crew. "These fellas will have to stand guard over the evidence the rest of the night."

"Agreed. I'll clear it with DCI Kingston," she said quickly. "They'll need food, water and replacements in the morning."

"Yes. The money has to be moved to a secure location as soon as possible. For that, we'll need an armoured truck and several men to load and guard it as the truck moves to wherever the money's to be stored."

Davies watched as the firearm specialists moved around the cellar to assess risk.

"Phyllis, we have to remember, whoever severed Chamberlain's hands was looking for what we just found. When they find out we have it, they'll come after it," St. James cautioned.

"I know, Hamilton. But why did they send the hands to me?"

"My guess is they decided it was smarter to let us do the hard work. Find the money for them. Even though it would be very difficult to take it from the police later, they'd at least know where it was."

Joy nodded slowly. "I'll have someone at the Yard arrange an armoured truck service to move the money tomorrow. Kingston will have to authorize it and figure out where to store it. He'll arrange something with the Bank of England. He has a mate in the senior ranks over there."

St. James stared off.

"What's wrong?" she asked.

"Just thinking about what to tell Jones."

"I have crime scene tape in my car," Davies offered. "You could tell him it's off-limits because there's evidence here related to a crime that can't be disturbed. And four armed guards are standing over it below him. Put the tape across the cellar door as a reminder. But I wouldn't tell him the evidence is money."

St. James smiled. "Excellent suggestion, Davies. Thank you. Go ahead with the tape, and I'll talk to Jones."

St. James went upstairs to meet with Jones and returned to the cellar ten minutes later.

"The talk with Jones went better than well," he said to Joy. "He offered to leave food and water for the men on the top stair and promised to respect the yellow tape. I think he's simply happy to have someone to look after."

"Wish I could afford him," she said with a smile.

She and Davies gave instructions to the firearms specialists before climbing the stairs for the last time that night. Davies placed the yellow tape across the door to the cellar, high enough for Jones to deliver provisions without interfering with it. Then they climbed into their vehicles and headed home.

"Well, Hamilton, I wouldn't want to put too many days in like this. I'd get very old, very fast," she said as she pulled the green Fiat into gear and rolled out the mansion's drive.

Chapter 54

Anna was asleep when St. James entered the hotel room shortly after three. He slipped off his shoes and walked softly, so as not to wake her. In dire need of a shower, he headed straight for the bathroom, turned on the light, looked in the mirror and was immediately disgusted by the filth.

Anna's sleepy voice drifted in from the bedroom. "There's a sandwich and a triple scotch in the fridge."

"I was trying hard not to wake you."

"It's okay. I was sleeping light. Been worried about you."

"Other than hunger, exhaustion and filth, I am terrific," he said lightly. "Thanks for thinking of food and the scotch. After you, it's the most welcome sight I can think of."

"You silver-tongued devil, you," she mumbled and drifted back to sleep.

St. James spent a good twenty minutes under a hot shower, as much to soothe aches and pains as to clean.

He sat in the dark at the small table, eating a chicken sandwich and sipping scotch, wondering what his next move would be in this complicated mess. Too exhausted to do it justice, he finished the food and drink and collapsed into bed.

He woke at eleven feeling much better. A sticky note on the bathroom mirror said Anna had gone for coffee and a walk so as not to disturb him, and DI Joy left a message for him on the hotel message system.

He made coffee with the room's small Keurig, sat on the edge of the bed and listened to Joy's message.

Joy started by poking him for not being at work on time. Her message was lengthy. Kingston had been very complimentary about their tenacity in finding the money. He'd approved the specialists' overtime for their commander, an armoured truck, and extra protection to move the funds to the Bank of England that afternoon. Joy organized replacements for the specialists until the armoured truck could arrive.

She reminded him today was Weber's day to seek a court order for seizing IEI's computers. "Should open a whole new can of worms," her message said. Her sign-off was, "Get your ass in here, genius."

Maybe I didn't make it clear I wasn't interested, he thought, cradling the phone. *May have to bring out Anna, the heavy artillery.*

***

Five o'clock that afternoon, St. James, Kingston and Joy were sitting in the meeting room once again. Dozer and Weber were on Zoom recounting the day in a Hamburg courtroom.

"Dozer was fabulous!" said a euphoric Weber. "Lot of abuse lately when it comes to seeking orders without giving notice to defendants. Some judges are reluctant to grant them. It looked like we would be unsuccessful. Then our lawyer had Dozer sworn in to testify that he'd been taken at gunpoint, struck down with the butt of a Glock and locked in a basement. When the judge heard all this, she concluded advance notice would give the defendant time to destroy evidence. Icing on the cake was the data Dozer witnessed streaming on IEI's computers. That tied nicely into our affidavit. The judge granted the order twenty minutes ago."

"Great work, Dozer," St. James said proudly.

Kingston and Joy took turns thanking Dozer.

Joy turned to St. James. "I guess Dozer's a genius too," she said with a grin.

"I only hire geniuses," he said stone-faced.

"Bullshit."

***

St. James invited Joy for dinner that evening to introduce her to Anna and asked Smythe to come along.

The four met at Temper Soho on Broadwick Street. St. James requested a booth close to the large open clay oven where patrons watched chefs cook vast cuts of meat.

"Definitely the mother of all steak houses," Anna said to Joy as they were seated.

Joy nodded. "I've lived in London all my life, and this is my first time in a Temper restaurant."

A tall, gangly server wearing the name tag Alan approached for orders.

"Ladies first," St. James said, gesturing to Anna and Joy.

"Phyllis, are you a white-wine person?" Anna asked.

"Good guess."

"Hamilton, why don't you order a nice bottle of white for Phyllis and me to share?"

"Okay, ladies. What do you prefer? Chardonnay? Pinot Grigio?"

"Pinot," they said in unison.

St. James looked at Alan. "A bottle of Santa Margherita for the ladies, please."

"Of course, sir." Alan eyed Smythe's purple sports jacket.

"A large Casillero del Diablo for me," Smythe said.

Alan nodded and looked at St. James. "And you?"

"For a change, I'll have a double Speyburn on the rocks."

Alan moved on.

Anna and Joy fell into a deep conversation about shopping.

St. James turned to Smythe. "Where did you go today, Louis?"

"Went back to Taylor's to double-check some things. I think you should see him tomorrow, Hamilton. He's anxious as hell to wrap this up. You need to do some public relations work there."

"I know, Louis," St. James said with a heavy sigh.

Anna and Joy took a break from their discussion.

"We haven't had a chance to discuss your long night," Anna said to St. James.

Between St. James and Joy, they told Anna and Smythe about their adventure in Chamberlain's cellar and efforts to obtain the court order to seize IEI's assets.

"My God," Anna said. "That's one helluva twenty-four hours on a case that up to now has been slow to bear fruit."

"I agree, Anna," Joy said, as if she hadn't been there when it happened. "I've gone from smelling rancid from Chamberlain's decaying hands to smelling of woodsmoke tonight. My skin may never be the same."

Smythe just shook his head at St. James. "Every time I see you do the impossible, I think it has to be the last. Then you do something like this and push the impossible out another notch."

"So true, Louis," Joy said, looking at St. James with admiration.

Alan appeared with drinks. "Are you ready to order food, folks?" he said.

They gave their choices. Before he left the table, Alan topped up the ladies' wine.

Anna and Joy recounted their early years to one another, swapping stories about their upbringing, education, and old boyfriends.

St. James saw they enjoyed each other's company and shared many common interests.

Heavy artillery's working.

"Louis, as you suggest, I'll see Taylor in the morning."

"Can I go home now?" Smythe said, as if he hadn't heard St. James.

"What about your feeling that everything's too perfect?"

"I knew you'd mention that again. So, when I was over at Taylor's today, I reviewed my notes and made a list of things that have been bothering me. Things I thought were too perfect and what I drew from them. I'll give that to you in the morning at breakfast."

St. James nodded and waited a couple of beats. "Tell you what, Louis, if your list gives me everything I need, you can go home."

Smythe's face lit up. "That's wonderful, Hamilton!"

"On one condition."

Smythe felt his smile fade. "What?"

"If something demanding your skills comes up, you agree to come back. No argument. No fuss."

"Fine by me, Hamilton. At least I'd feel useful. Right now, I don't. I'm just running up unproductive hours you won't collect from Taylor."

St. James nodded.

"Look at the bright side," Smythe said. "You can tell Taylor the fee will taper off with me gone."

Their food arrived, and St. James ordered another bottle of pinot grigio for the ladies and a bottle of 2016 Chateau Montelena Estate Cabernet Sauvignon for Smythe and himself.

At ten o'clock, Joy thanked them for a wonderful evening and made her way home. St. James, Anna and Smythe strolled back to the hotel. Smythe said good night and headed off to bed. Anna and St. James went to the bar for a nightcap.

"Phyllis is a very nice person," Anna said as Prisha placed liqueurs in front of them.

"Yes, Anna. Joy is a genuinely nice person and an excellent detective too," St. James said, taking a sip of cognac from a snifter.

Anna's forehead furrowed. "I think she likes you, maybe a little too much."

"What makes you say that?" he said.

"Women sense these things in other women."

"I don't sense it," he said, trying to maintain a straight face.

"That's because you're a man, and men don't have any sense," she said, laughing.

Chapter 55

Weber wanted Dozer to come to Stuttgart with him, where the SWAT team selected to execute the court order against IEI was assembling.

Dozer stood next to fifty well-armed, well-built police officers, lined up near the Stuttgart airport to receive mission instructions. He had already provided the mission commander with the intelligence he had gathered as the only man outside IEI's organization to make it inside headquarters. Weber had more than enough men and didn't need Dozer for the takedown itself. But he thought Dozer's knowledge of the premises could be insurance if something went wrong. So Dozer had agreed to go, if for no other reason than to see the mission through and maybe learn some strategy and tactical techniques he could deploy in future contracts.

Weber's superior made arrangements with the president of the Federal Criminal Police for Stuttgart officers to facilitate the team assembly and provide transportation to Gundelsheim. Several qualified team members already worked out of Stuttgart. But the mission demanded skills that were not available at every federal police location. Stuttgart had to transport certain specialists from Hamburg, Dusseldorf and Frankfurt.

The team gathered two days before execution day to practise and perfect their moves. Ten of the fifty officers were computer experts, handpicked by the mission commander for their training and ability to disassemble and pack computer equipment safely.

Ten o'clock, mission-day morning, four trucks carrying the SWAT team rolled into Gundelsheim followed by a much larger empty truck for IEI's equipment extraction. Two trucks parked in a lot on the north side of Gottlieb-Daimler Straße, perpendicular to Heilbronner Straße. Several officers jumped from the back of each vehicle and, under the cover of buildings, they slowly crept in U-formation toward IEI headquarters. The commander insisted they be well spaced to minimize the chance of being spotted by Fischer's men.

The remaining two trucks crawled up Highway 27, on the opposite side of Gottlieb-Daimler, until they reached a set of railroad tracks. Another group of men piled out of the trucks and began making their way across the tracks and up a grassy knoll to the back of the IEI building. The empty truck parked in front of Harry's Coffee Roastery down the street from IEI. The driver bought a coffee and sat at a window table waiting for a signal from mission commander Elias Kohl.

Kohl referred to the men from the north side of Gottlieb-Daimler as the Heilbronner group to distinguish them from other activities on Gottlieb-Daimler.

From their positions surrounding the IEI building, the Heilbronner and Highway 27 groups waited for the go-ahead from Kohl.

Each group knew their role, where and how they'd enter the building and how they'd take control of computers, including ushering the employees to one side before anyone had a chance to damage equipment. It was split-second timing, made possible by Dozer's intelligence. He drew the layout as best he could remember, giving the team a significant advantage in addition to surprise. He knew roughly how many employees were there, where Schneider's office was on the first floor and the size and location of Fischer's office on the second.

The only question in Dozer's mind was how Schneider and Fischer would react when the mission went down. Schneider was known to police as a violent man, capable of killing with little or no provocation. The only reason Dozer wasn't dead already was that Fischer wouldn't give Schneider the order until he could decide what to do with him.

Dozer didn't know what nefarious behaviour Fischer was capable of, only that he would do anything to succeed. So Dozer had to stay vigilant and loose, ready for anything.

Kohl had planned a two-phase execution. The Heilbronner team would move in first from the front of the building at exactly 11:01 a.m. Then, at precisely 11:02 a.m., the Highway 27 team would enter the building from the rear.

Combined with staggered lunch breaks and partial shift changes, Kohl hoped that this one-two punch would afford sufficient distraction to maximize the surprise and leave little time for a violent reprisal.

Intelligence on Schneider's brutal behaviour told Kohl the team had to wear riot gear and Kevlar vests. The four forward men carried large protective shields. Kohl followed police protocol — plan for the worst, hope for the best.

It was 10:55 a.m. when Kohl time-checked everyone through earbuds. At eleven sharp, he began counting off seconds.

Dozer stood off to one side of the Heilbronner team, watching and waiting. Kohl suddenly yelled "Go!" and five members of the team pounded the wooden front door with a steel ram. The door gave way without a fight and the team burst through to an open space. Two computer programmers on their way for coffee screamed when they found themselves facing a dozen guns two feet away. Police frisked and pushed them to one side. The rest of Kohl's team ran with guns trained on the working computer operators ahead. Everyone jumped in horror, surrendering with hands automatically raised.

Dozer's intel said there were seven rows of computers and five operators to a row. Kohl had assigned an officer to the left side of each row and ordered them to push the five operators through the rows and hold them up against a far wall, several feet from the computers, leaving no chance for equipment sabotage. With the computer operators quickly neutralized, team 27 broke through the metal back door using a second ram, and specialists swarmed equipment to begin disassembling and boxing. Several officers in the rear carried flattened boxes and bubble wrap to keep the equipment safe.

Weber remained an observer on the sidelines throughout the entire takedown.

Kohl grabbed Dozer by the arm and yelled, "Schneider's not in his office!"

Dozer nodded, pointing to the narrow staircase leading to the second floor. "Let's check Fischer's," he shouted for Kohl to hear above the fray.

Kohl nodded, and they hit the steps with weapons drawn.

At the top stair, they suddenly came face to face with Schneider, his Glock 9 aimed straight at Dozer's head.

"Seems to me I owe you for a lump on the back of my head," Schneider snarled. "Drop your weapons."

Kohl and Dozer complied.

"I should have killed you when I had the chance," Schneider growled.

"You should have tried!" Dozer said.

"I have something for you, but you need to let me go into my right front pocket," Kohl said to Schneider, who squinted back at him by way of permission.

With his eyes trained on Schneider, Kohl retrieved the court order authorizing the seizure and handed it over. "In case you're wondering what this is all about," he said in a stern voice.

Schneider took the order, his eyes shifting rapidly back and forth between the document and Dozer's Glock.

"Doesn't say anything about arresting our people, so I assume we're free to go," Schneider said with an evil smile.

"Not so sure," Kohl said tersely. "My men are packing the computers right now. We'll see what they show you've been up to before we make that decision."

"Where's Fischer?" Dozer demanded.

"Right here, puss-head," Fischer shouted as he entered the upstairs hall from his office to where the others were standing. "Did I hear you say we're free to go?"

"No," Dozer said and turned to Schneider. "Put that gun down before I shove it down your throat."

Schneider laughed. "You must think I'm stupid."

Dozer smiled. "As a matter of fact, I do."

Schneider's face reddened. "You're not in a very good position to be giving orders."

Just at that moment, a woman exited the bathroom a little farther down the hall, still wiping her hands on a paper towel. She screamed when she saw the unfolding scene, and when Schneider briefly looked at her, Dozer lunged forward and grabbed Schneider's gun hand by the wrist, forcing it down hard and to the right and snapping a finger caught in the trigger. In one fluid movement, Dozer twisted the gun loose and tossed it underhand to Kohl. Then he grabbed Schneider's shirt, pushed him backward off balance and swiftly yanked him forward, delivering a solid head-butt that knocked Schneider further off balance. Dozer followed with a rapid kick to the solar plexus and a roundhouse kick that connected below Schneider's left ear, dropping him to the floor. Unconscious.

"I'd say I'm in an excellent position to give orders, wouldn't you, Commander?" Dozer said with one of his patented smiles.

Kohl nodded. "Nice work, Dozer," he said as they picked up their weapons and retrieved Schneider's Glock.

Kohl turned to Fischer, who was standing perfectly still, doing his best to appear unfazed. "We're taking you and Schneider in."

"You can't do that," Fischer said coolly.

"Watch me," Kohl said.

Kohl summoned one of the officers to the second floor and ordered him to guard Fischer until they moved out.

"If he moves, shoot him — in the leg," Kohl said with a wink in Dozer's direction.

The officer nodded and stood beside Fischer, pistol at the ready.

For the first time, Fischer's expression melted a degree from domineering to concern, though he was still trying hard not to show fear.

By 4:50 p.m., the trucks were loaded with men and equipment, ready to return to Stuttgart. Fischer and Schneider were handcuffed, sitting in the back of one truck next to the police officer Kohl assigned to guard Fischer. Schneider winced with pain from a broken nose and finger.

Kohl had his men interview all the other employees, take their statements and note contact information for further follow-up, if necessary. Then they were let go.

Dozer suggested to Kohl that they check the farm. Four trucks carrying the rest of Kohl's men remained in IEI's parking lot, while he and Dozer rode to the farm in the truck full of equipment. When the truck pulled in the drive, they piled out with weapons drawn. Dozer went around back, and Kohl went through the front door. Inside they found two house cleaners and an elderly cook. There was no sign of computer equipment. They were in and out in less than five minutes.

When all the trucks arrived back at the Stuttgart airport, Kohl and Weber turned to Dozer.

"You know we couldn't have done any of this without you, Dozer," Kohl said with a grateful smile. "Though I doubt you'll be getting a Christmas card from Schneider or Fischer this year."

Dozer laughed. "I'll just have to suck it up."

They shook hands, and Kohl went to his truck.

As Dozer and Weber shook hands, Weber said, "I'll make sure Joy and Kingston know what you did here today. I believe in giving credit where it is due," Weber said.

"Thanks, Noah. Appreciate it."

Dozer walked into the terminal, pulled a carry-on from the locker where he'd stowed it a couple of days before and headed for the Lufthansa check-in counter to catch a flight to London.

Chapter 56

While Dozer and the team in Germany were raiding IEI's head office, St. James met with John Taylor.

"I know you're frustrated with the speed of the investigation, John. But considerable progress has been made since we last spoke."

"And what progress would that be?" Taylor said in a surprisingly calm voice.

St. James recounted everything he and Joy went through to find the hidden room in Chamberlain's cellar and the millions of pounds seized by the Metropolitan Police, now in safekeeping at the Bank of England. He described the work to obtain a German court order for seizing IEI's computer equipment.

"German police are poring over the computers now. I expect to have an initial verbal report in a couple of days," St. James explained.

Taylor listened quietly without interrupting.

St. James continued: "We'll have a trail of fraud schemes perpetrated by IEI very soon, including those here in the UK. IEI pilfered hundreds of millions of pounds from businesses around the globe. Harry Fischer had local lieutenants running operations in several countries in return for a piece of the action. We are certain Chamberlain was Fischer's UK lieutenant. We found enough evidence on Chamberlain's laptops and cell phone to support that preliminary conclusion. I need confirmation from the German police before I'm one hundred percent certain."

Taylor nodded stiffly. "Remind me again, Hamilton, what this has to do with my problem."

"I believe the evidence will show that some of the money we found in Chamberlain's cellar came from Taylor Supermarkets."

Taylor's emotional pain exploded. "But how?" he yelled, fist pounding the desk. "How — how — how!"

St. James was taken aback by the outburst but remained calm and spoke slowly. "The answer to that lies with the connection between Chamberlain's holding company, Quantum, and you. Still work to be done."

Taylor shook his head. "I don't think I can take much more of this, Hamilton."

St. James thought the man was about to cry and waited a moment for him to collect himself.

"Let me share my plan, John, at least as I see it at the moment. I detest doing this before I am ready to unfold the case to everyone at once. But you're so distraught, I have to make an exception."

Surprised by St. James's conclusion, Taylor calmed and lifted his head.

"First of all, I am sending Louis home today, so he'll not be charging more time to you unless something unforeseen happens. I believe Dozer will follow tomorrow or the next day, reducing your ongoing professional obligation to me by another team member. That leaves me and my researcher, Anna Strauss, who you have not met, because she's set up an office in the hotel room. You will only pay for the time she spends working. Because she's my significant other, I will absorb her travel and accommodation expenses."

St. James could see Taylor's anxiety lightening a notch.

"My guess is it will be impossible to return every penny to its rightful owner. Crooks are not meticulous recordkeepers except when it comes to falsifying information. Then they're downright scrupulous. Some of the money is probably already spent."

Taylor sank into his chair as he listened.

"In a situation like this," St. James continued, "money is usually paid into court. A custodian is appointed with powers to develop and administer a fair and equitable distribution process to return whatever funds are found to defrauded companies. The custodian is a disinterested party, independent, and the court approves all accounting and decision-making. Once cheated, a victim never trusts another individual again without such significant oversight."

Taylor was quiet for a long moment. "I see," he said thoughtfully. For a moment, his pain seemed to return. "Why didn't you tell me this before?"

"Because up until a day and a half ago, there was no money to claim. No sense raising your hopes without a reasonable chance of financial success, and without money to fight over, there is no reasonable chance."

Taylor brightened. "And there was a large sum of money in that basement?"

"Boxes and boxes of it." St. James wasn't sure Taylor understood everything he was saying, but he kept going anyway. "In certain situations, courts will allow reasonable expenses to establish a claim to be added to the principal claim for defrauded funds. That may include my costs if acceptable to the court."

Taylor's face brightened further.

"Now before you emotionally grab on to success as a lifeline, there are a hundred things that can go wrong. I hate laying out a story when not everything is known, for that very reason. It gives you hope when reasonable hope hasn't been established."

Taylor's face clouded over. "What can go wrong?"

"Just about everything. Parties with legal standing often dispute the claims of others. Money can be tied up in litigation for years. There could even be an argument over an acceptable custodian, holding everything up before the process begins. And you may not be able to substantiate your claim to the court's satisfaction. The list goes on and on."

For a few moments, Taylor stared at the water-stained ceiling. "I don't know whether to be encouraged or discouraged," he said finally.

St. James lightly drummed Taylor's desk. "Good!" he said quickly. "Partially encouraged and partially discouraged is where I wanted you to be all along. Cautious optimism is a healthy state of mind in these situations." St. James stood. "Now I'm leaving to get on with my job."

Chapter 57

The following day, Dozer debriefed Kingston, Joy and St. James on the details of the IEI takedown.

When Dozer finished, Joy said with a radiant smile, "Between us and Germany, you could get elected pope, Dozer."

Kingston nodded.

"I agree. Before you were careless enough to be caught, case progress was slow," Kingston said with a wide grin. "The way I see it, they brought their own house down by forcing you into IEI's head office. So hell-bent on capturing you, they didn't realize the impact it could have on the whole operation. All the money spent on next-generation cybersecurity, obsessive-compulsive secrecy policies, and insane employee restrictions blown up by their stupidity."

"Come to think of it, it's weird that anyone running such a tight operation would let their guard down at all," Joy said.

"Risk never crossed their minds, because all along, they planned to kill me. They were confident I couldn't escape," Dozer said, shaking his head.

St. James nodded. "They didn't know how resourceful you could be, Dozer."

"Can I go back home now?" Dozer said hopefully.

"Okay by me," St. James said quickly, hoping Kingston and Joy would agree.

"I don't see why not," said Joy. "You've certainly earned both your keep and your freedom."

"I agree," Kingston said.

"Dozer, I'll say the same thing to you I said to Louis. You can go home on the condition that if I need you back here, you come back, no argument."

"Agreed," Dozer said.

After the meeting, Dozer packed up and made reservations to return to Toronto.

St. James went back to his assigned office and phoned Anna at the hotel.

"Just you and me, babe. Both Louis and Dozer have headed home."

"You sure about letting Dozer go?"

"Well, he's done everything we asked him to do, and I couldn't think of anything else worthwhile. It would just be make-work, useless, not very profitable."

"What if something urgent comes up?"

"They both agreed to come back if I need them."

"What are we doing?"

"Well, I want to spend more time thinking about Louis's findings. It would be great if you'd continue your searches on everyone. I want to make sure we've got everything on everybody we possibly can. More importantly, find us a delightful place for dinner."

Before Smythe left, he talked to St. James about his concerns that everything was just too perfect. St. James spent the afternoon reviewing everything in greater detail, assembling and sorting his thoughts in the order that made the most sense. By four thirty, he had taken everything as far as he could, but there was still a lot to learn.

Hopefully, the Germans will have preliminary observations from IEI's system by tomorrow, he thought as he packed up and headed for the Thistle Hotel.

That evening Anna and St. James went back to Sergio's for dinner. With St. James nursing a Glenfiddich and Anna a pinot, she said, "When I went back over my searches today, I found nothing more on IEI."

"Okay," he said, rimming his glass with a forefinger. "I don't think it's worth you spending more time on it. What about the others?"

"Fischer and Schneider are dead ends too. I've gotten everything I can on them."

"Chamberlain?"

"Nothing."

"Keller?"

"Just that he has a sister. Mary Louise Keller."

St. James's forehead puckered. "You said you couldn't find any relatives for Keller. How come we're just finding out about her now?" St. James said, sounding bowled over.

"Couple of reasons. Mary Louise changed her last name from Kell*er* to Kell*ar* — spelled with an *a* instead of an *e*. So when I searched for every connection to Keller, she didn't appear anywhere."

St. James nodded. "If that's true, how *did* you find her?"

"You wanted me to make sure we knew everything possible about everyone. So I Googled diverse ways to spell everyone's surname and then did a Boolean search on each. That's how I found Mary Louise Kell*ar*, who turned out to be Mary Louise Kell*er*. She's three years younger than Frank."

"Wow! Interesting."

"This stuff is all judgmental, not a science. Guess you have to trust my instincts," she said with a radiant smile.

He leaned across the table and kissed her. "I'm lucky to have the best researcher in the world both on my team and in my life," he said.

"Aw, that's sweet," Anna said, blushing a little.

St. James thought for a moment. "Having said that, I'm not sure there is anything more for you to do at the moment."

The server arrived with their meal, and St. James ordered wine.

They took time to have a few bites of pasta.

St. James broke the silence. "I'll talk with Joy in the morning about how we liaise with the Germans as they search Fischer's system. I want to see IEI's transactions with UK companies."

"I'm surprised you let Louis go if you were thinking that. Wouldn't he be essential for that role? He knows how you think, what's important and what's not. German police may consider different things important. You could miss something just because they didn't think it important enough to tell you."

"Quite possible. I might need Louis," St. James said thoughtfully. "I didn't mention it to him because the Germans have a potent team going at this thing full bore. But, as I said, both Louis and Dozer are on standby. We'll see what resources are needed as the Germans get further along."

***

Anna went to Scotland Yard with St. James the following day. Sitting in Joy's office drinking coffee, they discussed what to do with the Germans and who, if anyone, should go to Hamburg to meet with Weber and his team.

"It makes sense for you to go, Hamilton," Joy said, brushing lint from her pantsuit. "You know Taylor's situation, and it's you that's looking for a thread between the supermarket chain, Chamberlain, and Fischer. I only know half the story. You're the one with the whole picture."

St. James nodded. "The whole picture as we know it *now*, you mean. No one, including me, has the complete picture."

"Agreed," Joy said, "but you'll know what you're looking for when you see it. Without knowledge of Taylor's issues, I wouldn't. And because John Taylor is a close friend of my DCI, I can't afford to overlook anything, screw up his end of the case. It's all about knowing the pieces of this bizarre puzzle and what, if anything, might be missing."

"Okay, Phyllis. Anna and I will go to Hamburg."

"Thank you." Joy turned to Anna. "I enjoyed our conversation at dinner the other night. We have a lot in common. Hamilton's lucky to have you."

Anna blushed slightly. "Thank you, Phyllis. I enjoyed the evening as well. I believe we could become good friends."

Joy smiled. "I think so too."

St. James did his best to hide his relief.

"Hamilton, I want you to keep me posted at every turn. We should have a Zoom meeting every couple of days," Joy said. "More often if things heat up."

St. James nodded. "Can you tee it up with Weber? Better coming from you. More official."

"I will as soon as you leave."

St. James turned to Anna. "We've got some organizing to do, my dear. So we better get going."

"You mean *I* have some organizing to do!" Anna said, grinning.

Joy laughed for a brief moment, then became serious. "Hamilton, we're counting on you to crack this thing."

Chapter 58

James and Anna packed up that afternoon, checked out of the Thistle Piccadilly, and rode the Tube to Heathrow. Anna booked them on a British Airways flight and requested a standard room at the NH Hamburg Horner Rennbahn, a short walk and quick bus ride from the Federal Criminal Police Office.

It was a beautiful, clear evening, and the full moon was visible in a cloudless sky when they checked into the hotel a few minutes past eleven. The beige room was basic but comfortable and overlooked a well-kept park area with what looked like a grassy racetrack below the restaurant patio.

St. James was pleased to see a small desk between the king-size bed and a door that slid open to an iron railing.

***

The following morning, they enjoyed a light breakfast in the hotel dining area, grabbed their laptops and files from the room and walked to Tribünenweg terminal to take the brief bus ride to the Federal Criminal Police Office.

Noah Weber met them at the front desk, and the three agreed to a first-name basis. Weber escorted them down a long white brightly lit hallway, bearing pictures of castles along the Rhine, to a large green room where four people had already begun their daily probe into IEI's computer systems.

The short and wiry Weber, with broad shoulders and military-style blond hair, radiated a pleasant but no-nonsense energy. He introduced them to the four computer experts.

All four faces were square, expressionless and emotionally unavailable, reminding St. James of the *Transformers* toys he played with as a boy.

The four Transformers had no time for pleasantries. They shook St. James's and Anna's hands with a single abrupt shake, as if trying to snap their wrists, and returned to work without a word.

The room resembled a high-tech assembly line, with IEI's computers spread over ten long grey metal tables, spaced just far enough apart for a single person to work on each computer.

Taped along one wall was a massive sheet of white bristol board, approximately eight feet square, stretching floor to ceiling and covering maybe twenty percent of the wall's width.

St. James guessed it to be a summary of what they'd uncovered so far. Across the top, different sectors of the world were named, printed in the neatest penmanship he had ever seen — East and Southeast Asia, Pacific Rim, North America, United Kingdom, Western Europe and Central Europe, horizontally from left to right. To the right of each sector name was the name of a sector chief. Below it was a list of countries within that sector, and to the right of each country, a country leader's name appeared.

St. James looked at Anna, who was staring at the chart in awe. Hamilton studied the chart closely and shook his head. "You're very well-organized, Noah."

Weber smiled. "It was the only way we could manage it, Hamilton. Too easy to get lost in detail with such a complicated structure. Maybe miss something important, something so significant we'd draw the wrong conclusion. Without a chart like this, there'd be no way to identify a trail, and even if we could, no way to follow it to any logical conclusion."

Anna stepped closer to the board and peered at some of the smaller writing, then looked at Weber with admiration.

"Mind taking us through it?" St. James said.

"Happy to." Weber grabbed a telescopic metal pointer from a nearby table, pulled it to its full length and made a broad sweeping motion over the entire sheet of bristol board. Anna stepped back to give him room.

"Think of all this as a pyramid," Weber said, running the pointer from left to right over the six sector names across the top. "Each sector reports directly to IEI at the very top of the pyramid. People named on the right of each sector are sector chiefs, responsible for making countries within their sector perform profitably, under strict rules set by Fischer."

Weber ran the pointer down the Western Europe sector.

"By way of illustration, this sector is composed of countries commonly referred to as Western Europe: Austria, Belgium, France, Germany, Liechtenstein, Luxemburg, Monaco, Netherlands and Switzerland. Each country has a leader whose name appears to the right of the country name. You can visualize the pyramid widening as I move the pointer closer to the bottom of the chart." Weber pointed to each name down the list. "Country leaders are responsible for identifying and recruiting companies within their countries, developing strategies to bring them into the IEI fraud fold, and once in, making sure they meet Fischer's fraud projections."

St. James interjected, "What are the criteria for companies to be selected?"

"We're still working on an answer to that. Initial findings suggest the target is up to a hundred million in revenue, regardless of the currency used to report financial results. So €100 million for Western Europe, £100 million for a United Kingdom company. The constant seems to be the hundred million number. Every company so far is private, not public, presumably to avoid the extra oversight of public reporting, which would mean a greater risk of Fischer being caught."

St. James nodded thoughtfully.

"How many companies did Fischer expect each country leader to recruit?" Anna asked.

"From what we can tell so far, a minimum of twenty-five," Weber said.

"And what happens if they don't meet that minimum?" St. James said.

"We don't know. But from what we know about Schneider, the sector chief would likely be given a short time to rectify the situation or replace the underperforming country leader."

"Suppose the sector chief couldn't fix the problem within the time dictated by Schneider?" St. James said.

"In that case, our guess, the next time he went to the bathroom, the likelihood of coming out would be somewhere between zero and nil. This would not only serve as punishment for his failure but a deterrent to other leaders … encourage them to walk the straight and narrow, so to speak."

St. James and Anna both smiled.

"This, of course, is just the beginning. Below, the bottom row is not shown due to the chart's space restriction. It would be the widest part of the pyramid," Weber explained. "If we had room, there'd be a minimum of twenty-five companies for each country, all streaming cash up the chain, first to country leaders, then to sector chiefs and finally to IEI and Fischer. We'll add more space to accommodate that. If it all worked correctly, it represents a tremendous, continuous, upward flow of cash."

"UK Customs and Revenue mentioned Fischer was into money laundering, prostitution and maybe a few other things," St. James said.

Weber shook his head. "We've seen no evidence of those activities. That doesn't mean they don't exist on some other system. But IEI only runs international fraud schemes."

"Hmm," St. James said, watching the four Transformers beavering away on Fischerlock.

"How is money extracted from each company?" St. James asked.

"We're not far enough along yet to answer that. It's a long, tedious process to get into the minutiae that far down. And, as you can see, I only have four experts. I estimate three weeks with the resources I have," Weber said grimly.

"How long would it take if you had another body?" St. James countered.

Weber squinted, trying to estimate time saved from an additional resource. "Hard to guess. Depends on what technical problems we run into. These investigations never run smoothly. Always cyber roadblocks to work around. And it depends on the skill of the resource."

St. James nodded. "Hmm, let me see what Anna and I can do."

"What about Louis?" Anna suggested.

"That's what I was thinking."

Weber looked puzzled. "Louis?"

"An expert on my team. Brilliant fellow."

"We could sure use the help," Weber said.

"Let me see what's possible."

Weber nodded. "Thanks."

St. James paused for a long moment, trying to decide the next steps.

Finally, he said, "Where are Fischer and Schneider now?"

"Holding cells downstairs."

St. James nodded. "Have you questioned them?"

"Several times."

"Anything worthwhile?"

Weber's face looked pained. "Absolutely nothing! Unless you count abuse and attitude as worthwhile."

St. James shook his head. "Mind if I have a go?"

"Be my guest," Weber said with the sweep of a hand.

Chapter 59

Weber invited St. James and Anna to lunch at the Schifferbörse, fifteen minutes from the station by car. Weber parked his black Audi A6 on a side street a block and a half away, and the three walked to the restaurant, where, amazed by the multitude of ship models, St. James and Anna stood for a couple of minutes taking it all in, slowly turning to eye original ship parts sourced from around the world and magically turned into a unique nautical theme. Some pieces were over three hundred years old — paintings of clipper ships in full sail, original ship wheels, engine throttles for prop rotation, nautical chandeliers, diving suits, stained glass, and barrels made from staves everywhere.

"You can see why the restaurant is called Schifferbörse, which is *shipping exchange* in English," Weber explained.

"Noah, I have never seen anything quite like this, and I have eaten in a good many places around the world," St. James said.

"Unbelievable!" Anna added.

Weber smiled. "Thought you'd like it. I love bringing first-time visitors here, just to watch the amazement on their faces." He pointed to one of the barrels that looked at least a century old. "In those days, the average barrel took thirty-two staves to make it watertight."

"Wow!" Anna said.

A tall, heavy-set waiter with white hair appeared, seated them at a bench and table replicating a ship's galley and took refreshment requests.

Anna perused the menu while St. James and Weber discussed the case.

"I'll call Louis later today and arrange for him to fly over to help," St. James offered.

"Have you collaborated with him long?"

The waiter placed two Becks in front of the guys and a glass of pinot before Anna. "Are you ready for food?" he asked.

Weber looked up at the large man. "Can you give us a minute to look at the menu?"

The waiter nodded and moved on.

"Louis and I have worked together for five or six years. Solved a dozen or so cases. The man's a genius when it comes to chasing fraud through a computer system and deciphering codes," St. James explained.

"Excellent."

"Have you made arrangements for me to interview Fischer and Schneider?"

Weber nodded. "Yes, I booked an interview room for this afternoon and an armed officer to chaperon. You want both at the same time?"

"God, no!" St. James said emphatically.

Weber smiled. "Thought so."

"I'll take Fischer first. Please make sure he doesn't meet Schneider in between interviews. Don't want Schneider regurgitating whatever Fischer says."

"Always use separate corridors for situations like this. They won't even have eye contact."

St. James nodded. "Let's have a look at the menu," he suggested.

When they had ordered food, Weber said, "I didn't tell you we charged the two with massive fraud, theft of Chamberlain's computer, and illegal confinement of Dozer," Weber advised.

"DCI Kingston and I are working on the paperwork. Probably one of many reciprocal inter-country arrangements we'll have to negotiate going forward. A lot of countries involved. Has the potential of being the largest fraud scheme in the world, geographically if not moneywise," Weber said.

St. James nodded.

"Since the UK and ourselves are benefiting from your work, I've spoken to Kingston about costs. He's talked with this Taylor person, who I believe is a friend. The three of us have come to an arrangement. To start with, we'll each pay a third of your fees."

"How can you afford to do that?" St. James said incredulously.

"Both Kingston and I are short two inspectors, budgeted for but not hired," Weber explained. "Since you are doing work that those inspectors would have conducted, we have budgetary room. My superiors have blessed the arrangement."

St. James said, "I knew David was trying to broker a deal but he didn't mention he'd made one."

"That's because we only got final approval from all parties last night. Kingston gave me the go-ahead to tell you."

"Wonderful!" St. James said. "Thanks for the initiative."

"Only fair," Weber offered with a smile.

Weber explained the distribution process he had in mind. "If other countries want to share in recovered funds, they'll have to share the fee obligation too. We may have an opportunity to recoup money if there are pools of defrauded funds in other countries."

"How would that work?" Anna said.

"On another case we had a few years back, a much smaller one, three countries shared costs pro rata, based on amounts stolen from the victims in each country," Weber explained.

St. James stared off as the whited-haired waiter laid down food. "You're taking quite a chance charging Fischer and Schneider before having the complete system analysis."

"Yes and no," Weber said, pausing to eat fries. "There is enough evidence so far to give us the confidence to charge. Besides, we were getting close to the forty-eight-hour holding limit. We have to charge them, ask the court for an extension of holding time or let them go. And I wasn't about to let them go. Major flight risks. As it is, their lawyers are in court today trying to get them released on bail."

Anna looked alarmed. "What's the likelihood of that happening?"

"Our lawyers are confident we can prevent that," Weber said. "Coincidentally, it's the same judge who issued the seizure order for IEI's assets. She's going to be incredibly happy to see our affidavit. Means her decision to grant the original order was the right one. It makes her look good, and it makes us look more credible than the other side."

"Noah, I don't want Anna attending this afternoon's interviews," St. James said with a concerned look. "Fischer and Schneider may decide to get to me by kidnapping her. Even in prison, they can organize that. I'd rather they don't know she exists."

"Don't blame you."

"She's an excellent researcher, if you need anything done," St. James offered.

Anna spoke up. "Yes, Noah, I'd love something to do. I don't have the skills you need for the system investigation, but I'm a good researcher and administrator."

"I'm sure we could use your help somewhere," Weber said. "We never seem to catch up. Your offer is a welcome one."

They finished lunch at one thirty. Weber paid the bill, and at one forty-five, they walked into the Federal Police Office on Rennbahnstraße.

Anna went with Weber to his office, where she met the chief administrative officer.

St. James grabbed a table in the computer room, where the Transformers were still hammering away at IEI's systems, and he prepared himself for a challenging interview with Harry Fischer at two thirty.

Chapter 60

"Dozer sends his regards, Harry," St. James announced when Fischer sat in the chair opposite.

Fischer, handcuffed and wearing a white military-style suit, glared at St. James from across the black metal table.

St. James thought he detected a smirk from the tall, thin officer in uniform who leaned against one wall, monitoring the interrogation.

Fischer scowled as he adjusted his rimless glasses.

"I am recording this interview, Harry."

"I object!" Fischer bellowed.

"Don't care," St. James said and hit the record button.

Fischer studied St. James for several beats. "Who the hell are you, anyway?"

St. James bluntly described who he was, what he did and why he was in Germany. "And Dozer works for me," he added.

"What he did was entrapment."

"No. What you and Schneider did was stupid."

"What do you mean by that?" Fischer snapped.

"Schneider yanked Dozer out of a rental car at gunpoint and marched him into your office. That allowed Dozer to see everything, including the computer screens showing money streaming in. You blew it, Harry. If you hadn't done that, we still wouldn't know what you were up to."

"Who are you to judge me?" Fischer shouted.

"Get used to it," St. James said aggressively. "I'm not one of your flunkies. To me, you are as intimidating as a housefly."

Fischer gazed down, smiling bitterly. "I should have fired that son of a bitch, Schneider, long ago. He's just a ready-shoot-aim thug."

"What do you mean?"

"Acts before he thinks! Why did you have me brought here?"

"I wanted to see if you were smart enough to cooperate or stupid enough to try to bully your way through."

Fischer's wily smile was starting to irritate St. James.

"The boys in prison will fight over who will be your new boyfriend. Petite thing like you would be considered a trophy wife, Harry. Just think of all the fun you'll have."

Fischer's frown was childish. "Don't try to scare me, St. James. It won't work."

St. James grinned. "Not trying to scare you, Harry. Just telling you how exciting your life is going to be."

Fischer shook his head. "I assume you didn't bring me here just to trade insults. What do you want?" he said in a tone St. James thought as civilized as Fischer could ever be.

"Your cooperation," St. James said quickly.

Fischer forced a laugh. "Ha! Why the hell should I cooperate with *you*?"

"If you do, it might go a long way to minimizing whatever punishment you could be facing. If you don't, I doubt you'll have an easy time with the authorities."

Fischer considered this for a long moment. "What do you want to know?" he said deviously.

"Were you siphoning cash from companies in several countries?"

Fischer knew that, if the police cracked Fischerlock, it would show what he had been doing, all the companies he was defrauding in many countries. But he wasn't about to confess anything to St. James.

"Absolutely not," he said abruptly.

"We know you were. How many companies did you bilk?"

Fischer shrugged, his smile beguiling.

"How many countries?"

Fischer stared off. "I have no idea what you are talking about."

St. James looked disgusted.

Restricted by the handcuffs, Fischer had to grab the bottle of water from the centre of the table with both hands. He took a moment to drink.

"An organization like yours would take a long time to set up," St. James said, sounding almost impressed. "By the time you found sector chiefs you could trust, country leaders they could trust, and vulnerable companies to swindle, years would have passed."

Fischer's sneered but said nothing.

St. James's eyebrows rose as he leaned forward. "How did country leaders access new companies without getting caught?"

Fischer drank water and shrugged.

Not going to cooperate, St. James thought as he made a note.

"Why did you have Nigel Chamberlain's laptop stolen?"

"I don't know any Nigel Chamberlain," Fischer said abruptly.

St. James ignored the answer. "My guess is he was cheating you somehow. Withholding money in some way."

"Like I said, I don't know the man."

"Here's what I think, Harry. When you assess a fraud target, you estimate its revenue and expenses and profitability based on whatever information you can find — financial ratios, company size, number of employees, revenue size, ranking within the industry, that sort of thing." St. James smiled. "How am I doing so far, Harry?"

St. James detected a slight look of surprise. "Thought so," he said and continued. "You used that information to determine what could be safely scooped from the target without setting off alarm bells with management. You probably consider normal industry fluctuations, so money extracted can be adjusted for the usual ups and downs to avoid alerting management during downturns. I'll bet Chamberlain's actual cash flow was out of whack from estimates. Substantially lower. So you thought he had to be siphoning money from you — likely off the top."

Fischer was becoming more tense. St. James liked that. It often weakened the guard of an accused, oftentimes causing them to make a mistake, let something incriminating slip.

"Nice story St. James, but it's just that — a story. You're fishing. You have no proof of anything," Fischer blurted.

St. James smiled. "Thank you for agreeing with me."

Fischer snarled. "I agree with nothing."

St. James considered Chamberlain's laptop. "So us taking the laptop from the two morons you hired to steal it meant you never actually proved Chamberlain was stealing — one way or another."

Fischer stared blankly at St. James.

St. James waited several beats, letting everything sink in, then he banged the table hard. "Why did you kill Nigel Chamberlain?" he barked in a raised voice.

Not expecting St. James's loud theatrics, Fischer jumped. "I didn't! I barely knew him!"

Chapter 61

Even though St. James was pleased with the result of the interview so far, it was nowhere near what he needed to advance the case. So he trudged on.

"Now that we've established you knew Chamberlain, if you thought he was cheating you would have had Schneider confront him immediately. Schneider beating the truth out of Chamberlain would have been the next step if he didn't confess right away."

"I have said too much already."

St. James smiled and changed course. "Do you know Frank Keller?"

Fischer frowned. "Never heard of him."

"He is, or rather was, a colleague of Chamberlain."

Fischer just shook his head. "I want you to tell Weber I've cooperated," he demanded.

"You did no such thing. I'll tell Noah what I want when I want," St. James said bluntly.

"Son of a bitch."

St. James nodded to the uniform to escort Fischer back to his cell.

When Fischer left, St. James walked down the hall, poured a coffee and went outside for a short stroll to clear his head. A gentle breeze greeted him as he gazed up at an overcast sky. He watched the cars go by for a couple of minutes, thinking the traffic was light for a central transportation hub.

He ran a free hand through his black hair, rubbed the kinks from his stiff neck and flexed his knees before he strolled down Washingtonallee, past a long four-storey red-brick building he thought housed apartments. Mature trees provided a pleasant cover along the street. He stopped to sip coffee and considered Fischer's interview.

Certainly had motivation to kill Chamberlain. A ready-shoot-aim thug was a good reason to hire Schneider.

It was three thirty when the same uniform escorted the rugged, square-faced Schneider into the stark interview room. Schneider sat in the same chair Fischer had occupied not long before. He watched as St. James pushed the record button. "Who the hell are you?" he snarled.

"What a coincidence, Wilhelm," St. James said. "That's what Harry said."

St. James gave Schneider the same description of his role that he had given Fischer.

"What does any of that have to do with me?"

"Given you were Fischer's operations man, primary security and fixer it has everything to do with you!"

Schneider's face hardened. He shrugged as if to say, so what.

"Fischer said Chamberlain was skimming off the top," St. James lied. "Is that right?"

Schneider sat quietly, glaring at St. James.

"Well, are you going to answer?" St. James demanded.

Schneider shrugged but said nothing.

St. James moved on. "Did you kill Chamberlain?"

"Maybe. Maybe not."

"If you refuse to answer, you do nothing to help yourself."

"Bullshit," Schneider blurted. "It means I do nothing to help you."

St. James let a pen fall on his notes, leaned back in the chair and folded his arms across his chest. "What do you hope to achieve by this tactic?"

"I think that's pretty obvious," Schneider said tersely.

"Indulge me."

"Give you nothing to use against me."

St. James turned off the recorder. "This interview's over," he said with a stern face.

When the recorder clicked off, Schneider leaned forward and whispered, so the uniform couldn't hear, "You know, even inside, I have strong connections to take you out whenever I snap my fingers."

St. James leaned closer still. "You know Dozer has strong connections within the prison system in North America — people he trusts and who trust him because he's helped them in one way or another. They have connections in European prison systems. From the moment you walk past the prison gates, no matter where, his network will activate a missile lock on your head. Any attempt made on my life or any member of my team, and you'll automatically meet with an unfortunate accident. You will never have a peaceful night's sleep again."

Chapter 62

At 4:00 p.m., Weber brought Anna to the interview room where St. James remained after Schneider was escorted back to confinement.

"Hamilton, you certainly have someone exceptional here," he said warmly, pointing to Anna. "She did a fabulous job helping to organize my admin people today."

Anna blushed.

"I know it," St. James said quickly. "And believe me, I don't take her for granted, not for a minute. Best thing that ever happened to me."

When Weber left, St. James said, "I promised Joy we'd stay in touch by Zoom, so I'd better send her an invitation."

"Good idea."

St. James invited Smythe and Dozer to the meeting. Joy thought Kingston should attend too.

An hour later, the six were face to face electronically.

"So where do we stand, Hamilton?" Joy asked.

St. James took the team through what he and Anna had learned since arriving in Hamburg — the number-crunching Transformers, the wall chart, Weber's process tutorial, and the interviews with Fischer and Schneider.

"The wall chart is an excellent idea," Joy said. "I want to see what countries are involved and how IEI structured itself. The chart concept could be helpful in future cases. "

"I'll send you a picture, Phyllis."

Smythe looked pensive. "They'd have put a lot of hours in to glean that much information and assemble it in an order logical enough to chart."

"It's not progressing as quickly as Weber would like. They're short of resources," St. James said. "That brings me to my next point."

"Don't say it!" Smythe blurted. "I almost turned down this meeting because of what you're about to say."

"Louis, don't be like that," St. James said as if talking to a child. "You don't even know what I was going to say."

"Yes, I do. I know you. You love doing this to me. Email me your hotel information so I can book. I'll be there when I can."

"You sound like an old married couple," Kingston said with a grin.

"In many ways, we are," St. James added.

Everyone laughed.

Dozer ignored the banter. "So you were threatened by Schneider?" said a concerned Dozer. "You want me there?"

"Not just yet, Dozer, but I would like you to beat the jungle drums with your prison connections, assuming that's where Schneider's headed. Because your connections are mostly North American, it will take time for you to work the United Kingdom and Germany penitentiary networks."

"Will do, Hamilton."

"So you got nothing out of Fischer," Kingston said.

"No. He was sly, tight lipped."

"If I heard correctly, he didn't argue with you when you laid out the scamming system you believed he'd set up."

"No, he didn't," St. James confirmed. "Hopefully Fischerlock will provide useful evidence, if we can get to the bottom of it."

"He denies killing Chamberlain?" Kingston said.

"Absolutely," St. James replied.

"If Chamberlain was skimming from Fischer, that's motive enough for murder," Joy concluded.

Chapter 63

When the Zoom meeting concluded, it was shortly after six. St. James asked Anna to send a picture of the case chart to Joy. She did and returned to her research to clear notes she'd made the day before.

St. James made his way back to the Transformers and found them still toiling away over Fischer's system, adding to the wall chart as they went. He stood by for fifteen minutes, observing, studying their method and procedures. He had to be sure they were on solid ground and headed for a reliable conclusion.

He returned to the room where Anna was working. "Five thirty in London," he said, looking at his watch. "I have to brief Taylor before he leaves the office. Why don't you find us a nice place for dinner, love?"

"Okay." Anna began Googling restaurants close to the hotel.

St. James tapped Taylor's cell phone number. Taylor answered right away.

"John, I just wanted to bring you up to date. As you know, we seized all of IEI's computer equipment. The German police are wading through the contents here in Hamburg. Fischer and Schneider have been arrested and interviewed by both police and myself."

"Have you found the link to me yet?" he said anxiously.

"No. Unravelling Fischerlock is slow going. The police are short of resources, so I've asked Louis to come to Hamburg to help speed up the analysis of Fischer's system. Otherwise, it'll take too long to get through all of the details. It's the details that should tell us who was defrauded. John, finding a link to your company is key for you to have a claim against the money we exhumed from Chamberlain's cellar."

Taylor broke his silence. "I think I'm finally getting the gist of all this, Hamilton. As it relates to my business, I mean," he said slowly. "I'm feeling a bit better since David and I and the German government agreed to split the cost three ways. And if I understand correctly, other countries opting for a share of the spoils have to share the cost from the first day you landed on United Kingdom soil. And as you've explained, I have a claim for my loss plus a share of your costs. Rightly or wrongly, I'm feeling some light of day."

"Good," said St. James. "But remember the risks I told you about and the things that can go wrong."

"You have a way of describing things so it's hard to forget."

For the first time since they met, St. James heard Taylor speak without a half pound of anxiety attached to every word. "I'm supposed to see the strategy path one step at a time, knowing full well there could be battles and delays somewhere ahead. Right?"

"Right, John," St. James said, a smile in his voice. "I'll keep you informed as we go along."

They clicked off.

"Successful call?" Anna asked.

"Very. Taylor's finally in a place of cautious optimism, where I wanted him from day one. Up to now, he's been harder to regulate than the Hoover Dam. His emotions run back and forth on an imaginary track, between doom and gloom and a guaranteed positive outcome — from black to white and back to black again," St. James explained.

"I guess I'm naïve. Taylor has to be very smart to be an Oxford business graduate. So why has it taken so long for you to reach him?"

"First of all, the man is very smart. But all he's ever known is the food industry. He's never faced the level of uncertainty I do, ferreting out facts that may or may not exist, separating truth from the other stuff that pours out of people's mouths, not to mention the occasional life threat. Taylor is anxious by nature, and the only thing that appeases him is a steady progression toward certainty. High IQ and high anxiety levels can go hand in hand. It's not necessarily one or the other."

"Excellent explanation," Anna said. "I found an interesting restaurant for dinner, called Das Dorf. It's supposed to be a romantic little German restaurant about a fifteen-minute cab ride, over on Lange Reihe."

"Wonderful! I'm hungry. Let's pack up and head back to freshen up."

Armed with computers and files, they walked to the closest bus stop and rode the five minutes back to the terminal nearest to the hotel. It was seven thirty by the time they'd showered, changed and finished a kick-start drink in the hotel bar. A young lady at the front desk arranged a taxi, and by eight fifteen, they were seated in Das Dorf.

The restaurant's tables were impressive, large and sturdy with oversize spindle legs that supported formidable tops. Rustic but nicely finished. A black ornate wood-burning fireplace circa 1925 stood to their right; walls, a warm orangey brown, were soothing to the eye. A tall sandwich board displayed handwritten selections and specials for the day.

Shortly after settling at a table, they were approached by a young server whose name tag said Ursula. Oddly, she stood next to their table without speaking until Anna broke the silence.

"Hello ... Ursula?"

The waitress nodded with the smallest of smiles and kept her pen poised over a notebook.

"I feel like a change," Anna said to St. James. Then to Ursula she said, "I'd like a vodka martini, please."

Without a word, Ursula noted Anna's request.

St. James said, "I am a scotch drinker. Can you recommend one?"

Ursula reached across to the drinks menu he was holding and ran the top of her pen down a list of scotch brands, without a word.

St. James grimaced at her standoffishness.

"Double Glenmorangie on ice," he said coolly.

Ursula left.

"I don't think she's suited for this work," Anna said.

"Not hardly," St. James said bluntly.

"I think Prisha spoiled us."

"Prisha's personality earns huge tips. With an attitude like Ursula's, she's probably starving to death."

A few minutes later, Ursula plunked down drinks and left.

Anna rolled her eyes. "Maybe she has a speech impairment. Tough career choice, if that's the case."

St. James sampled the scotch with satisfaction, and Anna sipped her drink. "How's the martini?"

"Bit heavy on the vermouth," she said with a slight face-scrunch brought on by the extra sweetness.

"Want me to send it back?"

"No. It's not worth the fuss. I'll be okay."

Anna fingered the rim of the glass and smiled across at St. James. "So how do you see the case playing out from here?" she said slowly.

"Could end in different ways. The worst would be if I were completely wrong about the link between Fischer's frauds and Taylor's profit problem. A few days ago, I was feeling exposed and vulnerable with the theory."

"You didn't say anything," Anna interjected, disappointment in her voice.

"Didn't want to worry you."

Anna's irritation was without anger. "Listen, buster. We're a team. And teams share everything, good or bad. So let's get the ground rules straight."

St. James smiled. "As I've always said, you're more beautiful when you're angry."

"Don't give me that deflection crap. It won't work, not this time."

"Well, if that's not going to work, why don't I just apologize?"

"Should have done that in the first place," Anna mumbled as she drank.

"No," he countered, "I should have told you about my doubts when I had them."

"Can we get back to the case before this conversation deteriorates into something we'll both regret?" Anna said.

"Agreed. The way I'm hoping it will end is that Taylor Supermarkets was one of the companies Fischer swindled, and his computer system proves it. That would make my theory credible."

"But that could be only part of it," Anna argued. "Fischer's system could show Taylor was a target, but not necessarily a successful one. Maybe not all frauds worked. We still wouldn't know if Taylor was defrauded."

Ursula arrived looking for a food order. She held her pen up and communicated solely with her eyes.

They gave her their selections, and when she issued a terse nod, St. James passed their menus back to her.

St. James cleared his throat. "You make an excellent point, Anna. Fischer's system may not provide enough cradle-to-grave detail to completely unfold Taylor's case. But we'll just have to be patient, persistent, and plug away at it."

Anna nodded. "When's Louis arriving?"

"Hopefully, tomorrow."

Ursula arrived with second drinks and salads.

"What's your best guess for wrapping everything up enough for us to go home?" Anna asked, enjoying another sip.

St. James peered at a large group three tables over, who seemed to be celebrating some sort of sporting win, from the look of their matching jerseys. "Probably less than a month for you."

"Me? Alone?" Anna said, concern in her voice. "What about you?"

"For me? About five years!" he said as if casually guessing kilometres left on a drive.

Chapter 64

"What do you mean five years?" Anna said, her voice loud enough to draw attention from surrounding tables.

"That's only an estimate, mind you. Could be seven or eight," St. James teased.

"I don't want to hear any of your nonsense!" Anna said sharply. "What are you saying?"

St. James suppressed a smile and answered her in earnest. "I'm saying, there will be other joint ventures around the world. It's a huge job to separate the money by country and then ask each court to approve the same allocation process in as many jurisdictions. A fair and equitable process could take a year to negotiate, maybe longer to reach a consensus. We'd manage it all out of Germany — fraud Ground Zero. Fischer's home base. I've had preliminary discussions with Noah about this, and he agrees with the general approach."

Anna was quiet, in awe of the magnitude of it all.

They finished the salads, and minutes later, Ursula arrived with main courses and a bottle of Dornfelder. She uncorked the wine in silence and poured a dribble for St. James to sample. He nodded approval, and Ursula filled each goblet and left. St. James and Anna exchanged amused looks and then shared a toast.

"To world-class service," St. James joked, and Anna laughed.

Over dinner, St. James explained how the process would work, how it could manage such vast geography with so many different governments and laws from one location.

"Weber wants me to head it up."

"Why you?" she asked, forking bits of ox cheek.

"Two reasons. Coming from Canada, I don't have a significant conflict of interest. Canada will likely have a claim, but not likely substantial enough for another country to object to a Canadian sorting out the mess. The larger a country's claim, the less trust other countries will have; they'll be worried that a country with a big claim might tilt the distribution scales in their favour. The courts have to pick someone. Every candidate will have some conflict because most claims will come from developed countries where wealth existed for Fischer to target."

Anna nodded. "Second reason?"

"I've set up the process before, albeit on a much smaller scale. But Weber thinks the experience would make me credible enough in the eyes of a court."

He drank wine.

Anna considered this for a moment. "Quite a feather in your cap."

"A lot can happen between now and the approvals stage. The initiative could die at any turn. A lot of politics among countries. I'd get a rough ride from some."

"That worry you?"

St. James smiled. "Huge fees every year would dull the pain."

Suddenly fearful, Anna said, "What will this do to us, our relationship, I mean?"

"Make it stronger," he said without hesitation.

Anna cocked her head. "How the hell do you figure that?"

"I'll need a shitload of research for every country. We'll travel together to places we've never been. And many times, I'll work from home, waiting on others to complete their responsibilities. You might get sick of me."

"Oh, I never thought of all that," she said slowly.

Chapter 65

The following morning when they went to breakfast, Anna spotted Smythe sitting at a window table for four, staring out at a young girl trying to bridle a thoroughbred next to the track.

"Hey man, good to see you made it," St. James said.

Smythe turned from the window, acknowledging St. James with a royal wave.

Anna rushed to give Smythe a warm hug. "When did you get in?" she said.

"Late, almost midnight when I laid my head down," he said, fixing his comb-over.

"Must have had flight problems," St. James guessed as he and Anna sat.

The dining area was beginning to fill. Anna smiled at two couples seating themselves at a nearby table.

"Yes. I couldn't get into Frankfurt until late yesterday afternoon. Had to wait a couple of hours to catch a nine-thirty flight here. Long day."

A tall, slim brunette with broad, muscular shoulders stopped to fill coffee cups and asked for breakfast choices.

St. James brought Smythe up to speed on their Hamburg experience. Smythe listened intently, sporting the occasional surprised look and asking questions as St. James recounted events.

Smythe held his coffee up to his face as he tried to shake off the jetlag. "Transformers, eh? Haven't heard that word for a long time. I take it from your description I shouldn't expect a lot of laughs from these guys."

"You'll be lucky if you hear them speak," St. James said.

"Should add to the pleasure of being yanked back here."

St. James let the dig go.

Anna looked on with her eye-catching smile.

After breakfast, the three made their way to police headquarters. Smythe's laptop and extra files made a taxi necessary to accommodate the short jaunt.

They pulled into the police parking area minutes later, and the three crawled out of the vehicle. St. James paid the driver, and they loaded themselves down with laptops and files and juggled their way inside.

Weber had arranged passes for St. James and Anna to move freely about the office the previous day, so they led Smythe to the computer room unescorted, where St. James introduced Smythe to Weber, who in turn introduced him to the four Transformers.

They allocated the remaining workload in a way that seemed to make the most sense, and when they rechecked, they concluded that, by onboarding Smythe, they had shortened the investigation by about a week.

Weber assigned St. James a different meeting room for the day. It was scantly furnished with a small wooden table that had seating for four, and large brightly coloured oil paintings of the German countryside on the walls.

With Smythe overseeing the German experts, St. James could now resume Taylor's end of the inquiry. He flipped open his laptop and double-clicked the icon Taylor Files so he could spend the next hour refreshing his memory of what happened and assessing the remaining steps to solve the case. He knew the questions that had to be answered and what was needed to answer them.

Chapter 66

It was 2:00 p.m., and Joy was sitting at her desk reading emails and texts when the phone rang.

"Phyllis, it's Hamilton."

"Nice to hear from you. What can I do for you?"

"Just wanted to report that I'm back into Taylor's end of things now that Louis is here to mind the Transformers."

"Wait a minute!" Joy said quickly. "You keep using that word, but I don't know what you're talking about."

"Kids' cartoon show. You can get the picture with a Google search," he said with a chuckle. "They're robots that transform themselves into cars and other things. The four here move like robots, talk as much as a headstone and have names I can't pronounce. *Transformers* is a term of convenience to reference them, that's all."

Joy laughed. "Whatever! So what will you do with Taylor's end of this worldwide mess?"

"Narrow the field, knock off some unanswered questions."

Joy repeated herself. "Then what can I do for you?"

"I need an update from Billings on Chamberlain's murder. Can you conference him in?"

"I might be able to do better. Billings just walked past my door. Hold on." Joy laid the receiver down and ran into the hall. Seconds later, she was back, Bert Billings in tow.

Joy hit the speaker button.

"What do you want to know, Hamilton?" Billings said gruffly, unhappy at having his schedule interrupted.

"Phyllis said you were checking into purchases of Ruger SR22 firearms. Did you find anything?"

Billings pulled a notebook from an inside suit pocket. "Three SR22s were purchased in London during the last couple of months."

"Names?" St. James said.

"Harold Jenkins, a retired banker living in Worcester. He said he purchased the firearm solely for target practice. Has a grandson he wants to teach gun safety to. He showed us his secure cabinet where he keeps the Ruger under lock and key, twenty-four seven. No one else has access to it. We visited a private range where we watched Jacob practise with Jenkins coaching. Jenkins seems like a straight shooter."

Billings grinned at his own joke, and Joy rolled her eyes. When St. James ignored the quip, Billings cleared his throat and went back to his notes.

"Nancy Sweet, an elderly lady living in Nottingham, hates the sight of a gun. But she had a burglary two months ago and bought the SR22 for protection. She chose that model because it's light, easy to handle and least likely to kill with one shot if she doesn't aim for the head or heart. Struck me as a woman who didn't aim at all, so that shouldn't be a problem. So afraid of the gun, she probably closes her eyes before squeezing the trigger. We checked out her story. Local police confirmed the robbery and that they knew about her weapon. Everything's above board."

"And the third?" St. James prodded.

"Bob Harman," Billings said. "Gun collector living in Oxford. Doesn't shoot. Hobby's just for show. Has about fifty firearms in display cases in a double-locked windowless room. Secure enough. Checked him out with a collectors' club he belongs to. Member in good standing. Oxford police said he provided a complete inventory of the weapons — models, serial numbers, origin and pictures. Oddly enough, they regard him as a resource. Call upon him for information from time to time."

"Any of the three have records?" St. James interjected.

"Not so much as a parking ticket."

Joy spoke up. "What about connections to Chamberlain?"

"Say they never heard of him. We interviewed neighbours, friends and acquaintances as best we could. No one ever heard of Chamberlain."

"They could have left names out, kept them from you on purpose," St. James said.

"I suppose," Billings said quickly and went back to his notes. "I had our tech people search every angle on the web, looking for a link between the three and Chamberlain."

"And?" said St. James.

"Nothing."

"Hmm. Seems thorough enough," St. James said. "Be nice to know what's on their cells and computers, whether any texts or emails offered a clue. Probably not worth the trouble of a warrant, I suppose."

"No need for warrants," Billings said. "When I told them the dreadful way Chamberlain died, they offered up their phones and computers without a warrant. Said they wanted to help in any way they could."

"Wow!" Joy chirped. "How many times has that happened?"

"Never!" St. James said.

"Last question, Bert," St. James said quickly. "Did the three ever report their Ruger stolen?"

"No," Billings said abruptly.

Joy thought for a second. "Where does this leave us, Bert?"

"Nowhere!"

Chapter 67

St. James sat in the small meeting room peering out the window, thinking about Billings's verbal report on the Ruger purchasers. He smiled when a miniature white poodle poked its head from a stroller that a woman pushed along the sidewalk, then returned to his thoughts.

Although Billings's investigation *seemed* thorough, it didn't answer all of St. James's questions. The new Ruger owners could have lent the gun to someone, providing a third party with the means to kill Chamberlain. Other than Jenkins, had the other two fired their Rugers? Even if the three didn't know Chamberlain, they might know someone connected to him, maybe someone not on the contact lists provided to Billings. There were holes in Billings's work that bothered him.

St. James considered talking to the Ruger owners directly. Going around Billings would piss him off for sure, but so would asking if his investigation was complete. Either way, Billings would be riled. St. James decided to run it by Joy.

Joy laughed when St. James described his dilemma.

"You're not going to take the law into your own hands again, are you Hamilton?" she said, still laughing.

"I can always count on you for help, Phyllis," he said sarcastically.

Joy dialled back the laughter. "In case you hadn't noticed, Billings can be prickly. Has a burr in his pants most of the time."

"That's why I'm talking to *you*."

Joy became serious. "Look, Hamilton, do what you think is best for the case. Not a week goes by Billings isn't mad at me for one thing or another. He keeps getting passed over for promotion because of his attitude."

"Okay. In case David becomes the target of a Billings rage, you might want to alert him."

"Oh, I fully intend to," she said lightheartedly. "Any day I can get a laugh out of my boss is a good day."

Before they ended the call, St. James obtained contact information for the Ruger purchasers.

He emailed each gun owner explaining who he was and that Billings wanted him to ask a couple of additional questions. A lie, to be sure, but necessary to validate himself. They'd be more willing to respond to him if they thought he was on Billings's team.

St. James strolled down the hall to the computer room to see how Smythe made out with the Transformers. Smythe left the line when he saw St. James and walked over, looking incredibly happy.

"Boy, am I glad to see you. The only difference between these guys and a post is that the post doesn't move. I've had better conversations with store mannequins." Smythe smiled. "Mind you, they were female mannequins."

St. James laughed.

"Aside from that, how is it going?" St. James asked, attempting to put Smythe back on point.

"Took me a while to get in the groove, but it's going fairly well now. We are down to transaction levels in a bunch of East and Southeast Asian countries. We'll move west, one country at a time. It will take five days to complete fifteen to twenty-five countries. It's repetitive work, so it should pick up, take less time per country as we go."

"Great. I'll leave you to it." St. James returned to the small meeting room.

An email from Harold Jenkins said St. James could phone him anytime that morning. So St. James did so right away.

A raspy voice answered, and St. James said, "Thanks for getting back to me so quickly, Mr. Jenkins."

"Call me Harold," Jenkins said gruffly. "I hate formality. Had to put up with it my forty years with the bank. Don't want it in retirement."

"Very well, Harold," St. James said. "You can call me Hamilton. Just a couple of questions, if you don't mind."

"Fire away," Jenkins said.

"What made you choose the Ruger SR22?"

"Well, as I told that Billings fellow, I wanted to teach my grandson Jacob gun safety. He's a little on the small side, couldn't withstand much recoil. That ruled out a higher-powered firearm. Ruger seemed exactly right, and I'm pleased with it."

"That's great. Jacob's lucky to have you."

"That's what I keep telling him."

"Billings told you about Nigel Chamberlain's ghastly murder?"

"Yes. Couldn't believe my ears, appalling way to go, hands cut off and all."

"It is appalling," St. James said. "Where'd you spend your career?"

"London, mostly. Thirty years. The rest in Oxford."

"Now you're retired, can you tell me the city where those clients banked?" St. James asked cautiously.

"Can't tell you who they were, but I suppose telling the city wouldn't hurt, although I don't see what good it will do you."

"If you don't mind, Harold, it will narrow the field I have to search."

"London."

St. James made a note.

"Coming back to Chamberlain for a moment. You told Billings you had no idea who he was."

"That's right. Billings made a snide remark about it. Seems to think he's funny."

St. James nodded to himself. "You know anyone who might have known Chamberlain, a friend of a friend, perhaps?"

"No."

"Okay. You gave Billings a list of people to check for possible connections to Chamberlain."

"Correct."

"Can you think of anyone you may have missed, left out by mistake, overlooked?"

"No, no one I can think of at the moment," he said.

"That's okay, Harold. You have my email if a name comes to mind later."

"Yep, I'll let you know."

"One final question, Harold. Have you ever lent the gun to a friend or family member?"

"That would be the worst thing a gun owner could do, short of killing somebody with it himself," Jenkins said defensively. "What kind of grandfather would I be if Jacob thought it was okay to lend a weapon, provide an opportunity for someone to commit a crime with your gun, suck you into a mess with the law?"

"I'm sorry, Harold. I didn't mean to offend, but it's a question I had to ask to do my job properly."

Jenkins was silent for a moment. "Well — maybe I overreacted."

"Let me know if anything comes to mind, questions you thought I should have asked but didn't," St. James said.

"I will."

St. James closed the call and made notes.

Chapter 68

While St. James was interviewing Harold Jenkins, emails consenting to interviews bounced in from Nancy Sweet and Bob Harman. They'd make themselves available anytime convenient for St. James.

At 5:45 p.m., he packed up his laptop and files, then left to round up Anna and Smythe.

Rather than lug everything back and forth from the hotel, St. James asked Weber if a secure lockup was available to store their things overnight. Weber escorted them to a small windowless storage room behind second-floor investigator offices and handed St. James the key.

Laptops and files safely stored, St. James locked the door to the otherwise empty room, testing it twice to ensure things were secure. Anna looked on.

"Do we really have to do this in a police station?" she asked.

"Yes!" St. James said emphatically. "Nosiness knows no boundaries."

Anna just shrugged as the three left for the hotel.

The temperature outside had dropped since the morning commute. The rain had come and gone as the forecast predicted, but the sky continued to be slightly overcast.

St. James wondered why traffic was almost nonexistent on Rennbahnstraße. But they didn't have to walk far to find out why.

A massive truck with heavy drilling equipment mounted on the back burrowed down through the sidewalk on their side of the street, forcing them to cross over to the other side. Water pushed its way through broken pavement, flooding the street. Three men frantically worked the drilling equipment to locate the broken water main.

When they arrived at the hotel, Anna and St. James took turns in the shower. Smythe went to his room to do the same thing.

Thirty minutes later, the three gathered in the bar downstairs.

A portly twenty-something server approached the table, identifying himself as Lucas, and the three ordered their usual preferences. Lucas sauntered in the direction of the bar, returning minutes later to place drinks.

"Where are we eating tonight, Anna?" St. James said.

Anna held the wine glass gently between fingertips on both hands. "Were we happy enough with Das Dorf to go back a second time?"

"Except for our jolly Ursula, it was perfect," St. James said, nursing scotch.

"Who's Ursula?" Smythe interjected, placing his glass on the table.

"Our server last time," St. James said. "Hated her job, showed it by not speaking. Very rude."

Smythe smiled in Anna's direction and pointed to St. James. "Let me guess. I bet he gave her the old St. James tip punishment to teach her a lesson."

"Yes," Anna said, smiling back.

St. James looked on.

"That's my man!" Smythe said, laughing, slapping his knee.

"I suppose you think that's funny, Louis," St. James said.

"Yes, I do. You always think you're teaching the server a lesson when all you're doing is reinforcing a bad attitude. To them, you're just another cheap bastard."

Anna laughed.

St. James shrugged. "Let's finish the drinks and catch a cab to the restaurant."

Twenty minutes later, they were seated at one of Das Dorf's heavy wooden tables, close to the antique fireplace St. James and Anna had admired on their first visit.

"What does Das Dorf mean?" Smythe asked.

"The village," Anna said.

"How do you know that?"

"Looked it up before Hamilton and I came the first time."

St. James was happy there was no sign of Ursula. "Probably fired," he mumbled.

"I enjoyed the ox cheeks so much last time I think I'll have them again," Anna said, hoping to avoid a second Ursula rant from St. James.

A goofy-looking waiter with a shaved head, bulging deep-blue eyes and a long skinny neck dropped menus off. He introduced himself as Leon.

In addition to drinks, St. James ordered two bottles of Dornfelder, medium dry, for the table. Leon nodded.

"What did Weber's people have you doing, Anna?" Smythe asked.

"Researching suspects in a Berlin fraud case involving COVID aid. Twenty-five thousand cases have been reported all over Germany."

St. James whistled. "That's a heap of investigating. How come Berlin police aren't working it?"

"Weber's team are known as *the* experts to work this type of fraud."

Turning to Smythe, St. James said, "What about you? Where are you and the Transformers with uncovering the weeds of Fischer's worldwide flimflam?"

"Information repetitiveness allowed us to pick up speed."

Leon placed before-dinner drinks and took their meal requests.

Smythe sipped cabernet. "We've updated the wall chart now to include thirty-nine countries."

Anna took a small sip of pinot and eyed four teenage girls seating themselves at the next table. "How many companies would thirty-nine countries represent?" she asked.

Smythe squinted, trying to formulate an estimate. "I'd say about nine hundred, maybe a thousand. It's hard slugging but we'll get there," he said confidently. "The thing that's bothering me is that nowhere does Fischer explain how any of the companies in any country were actually tricked into being scammed."

Chapter 69

The following morning St. James went back to the small meeting room to resume interviews with the Ruger purchasers. Anna returned to research the COVID subsidy frauds for Weber. And Smythe grudgingly went to spend another silent day with the Transformers.

Considering the remaining Ruger people, St. James decided to take on Nancy Sweet first.

Sweet took control of the interview before St. James could ask a single question, diving into the burglary experience she had encountered two months before.

"Hamilton, I was sitting in my chair in front of the telly, watching *EastEnders* as I do every day, working away at my knitting, when suddenly I heard a noise that sounded like wood splitting. I jumped to see what happened and discovered the front door had been forced open, and the doorjamb shattered into splinters. Then I came face to face with a six-foot gorilla wearing a ski mask, with a huge gun in my face. He demanded all my jewellery, any cash I had, silver, gold, investment certificates, that sort of thing." Sweet began to laugh.

"I'm surprised you find this funny. You must have been terrified," said a puzzled St. James.

"Oh, I was scared, all right. Shitless! I don't know who he thought he was robbing, but it had to have been someone else because my husband and I, God rest his soul, barely made a living. I have nothing of any value. The few pieces of jewellery I have are cheap costume junk. No investments, whatsoever." Sweet continued laughing between sentences. "So I gave him my junk jewellery and then made a big fuss about the junk being a family heirloom handed down generations and how it was supposed to pay for my retirement. I must say I found it difficult to pretend to be in tears over these losses."

St. James enjoyed the story almost as much as Sweet obviously enjoyed telling it.

She didn't sound elderly. Her voice was robust, and her explanations were as clear as a twenty-five-year-old's.

"I can just imagine the look on the stupid bastard's face when he tried to flog that trash, expecting to get several hundred pounds and offered maybe five, or even less."

"No matter what, Nancy, I hope this never happens to you again," St. James said sincerely.

Sweet burst into laughter again. "If it does, I'll tell the piss-ant I've already been robbed of the good stuff, and he's shit out of luck. It's Halloween night, baby, and I'm out of candy. When he turns around, he'll get a bullet in each cheek. Might not stop him, but he won't sit down for a while."

Even though St. James found himself laughing with her, he had to wrestle the interview back to its original purpose.

"Well, I guess you answered my first question," he said with a chuckle.

"What was that?"

"Why you bought the gun."

"Guess maybe I did. What else you want to know?"

"You taking shooting lessons?"

"Took two from a young fellow out in the country. Said I'd never hit anything and didn't want to teach me anymore. Thought I was hopeless."

St. James didn't try to restrain his humour. "You'd better hope the next burglar has one huge monstrous ass, one you *can* hit."

She broke into laughter again.

"You ever lend the gun to anyone?"

"No sir!" Sweet said swiftly. "When I told the police I had a gun, they warned me never to do that, took down the model and serial number in case they ever had to trace it."

"Good. Now DI Billings asked you for the names of people who might know Nigel Chamberlain?"

"That's right. I told him I never heard tell of the man, and I don't know anyone who does."

"The next question is critical, Nancy."

"I thought they all were critical," she said with a giggle.

St. James smiled at her quick wit. "Yes, they're all important, but this one requires a bit more thought."

"Shoot. Pardon my choice of words."

"By chance, did you miss any names on the list you gave DS Billings, perhaps by accident or oversight?"

"That guy reminded me of Elmer Fudd. Thought of two people after Elmer left."

St. James smiled. *Not a bad likeness*, he thought.

"Remember their names?"

"Of course."

St. James noted the names and thanked Sweet.

Chapter 70

St. James was anxious to see how far Smythe and the robot crew had gotten listing UK companies Chamberlain had been milking for Fischer. So after Nancy Sweet's interview, he wandered down to the computer room.

Smythe looked up from his work with a grin that rivalled the Cheshire Cat's. The Transformers remained expressionless. Several more companies falling victim to Fischer's deceit had been identified and neatly entered on the wall chart, which now covered three of the four walls.

"Louis, your face is going to split from grinning," St. James blurted.

Smythe could barely contain himself. "Can't help it, Hamilton. The fifteenth company we uncovered in the UK electronic file is Taylor Supermarkets."

St. James's sigh was huge, his relief overwhelming, his smile almost the size of Smythe's. He bent over, both palms resting on his knees, eyes closed, and stayed there for twenty long seconds. "Thank God! The connection I've been hoping for," he said jubilantly. Straightening, he clapped his hands together. "I bet heavily on finding this, Louis. More than I should have."

"I know, Hamilton!"

Smythe and St. James high-fived.

"If Taylor Supermarkets hadn't been there, I would have blown the whole case. Wasted a lot of time and money chasing something that didn't exist. Would have destroyed my credibility forever." St. James took a moment to gather himself. "I'll never do that again."

A young lady wearing a blue pantsuit struggled to hang additional bristol board on the wall.

One of Weber's recruits, Smythe thought as he soaked up his boss's relief, happy to be the one who created it.

St. James drifted off for several seconds, trying to decide what should be next. First and foremost, he had to call Joy and Taylor, the two who doubted him the most for spending so much time trying to link Fischer's operation to Taylor's losses. Vindication time.

St. James returned to the present. "Show me the details, Louis, before I call London."

Smythe led St. James over to the third wall and pointed to Taylor Supermarkets halfway down the chart.

"Taylor's company was brought on by Chamberlain only a few months ago," Smythe said.

"That's about when Taylor first noticed the discrepancy," St. James said, relief now giving way to excitement.

Smythe nodded. "They diddled Taylor for insignificant amounts at first. Hardly seemed worthwhile. Maybe they do that with every new company — test the waters for financial sensitivity. I don't know. Clever system, though."

"How were they doing it?"

"As I said at dinner, the files don't say. No explanation for how any company was debunked, at least so far."

"Hmm. Fischer said every company was tapped a separate way depending on the circumstances. He must have left it to the sector chiefs to decide the best way to do it."

The recruit yelped as bristol board fell to the floor.

St. James and Smythe looked without missing a beat.

"Probably," Smythe agreed.

"Beside amounts rooked, does it show anything else?"

"No. And that's consistent with every company."

"That means to solve this case, I'll have to do it from Taylor's end of things," St. James concluded with a frown. "Determine how Chamberlain set up the bilking system from there."

They discussed what work remained. Then St. James went back to the small meeting room to phone Bob Harman, the third Ruger purchaser.

Before phoning Harman, St. James paused and stared out the window. The sunlight screened the view.

Although connecting Fischer with Taylor was a relief, it didn't solve the case. Validating his theory was huge, but, to some extent, it raised more questions than it answered.

How did Chamberlain extract money from Taylor? Smythe's report didn't provide precise answers. He knew for sure Vanderbilt's add-on program hadn't diverted money. Then there was Pay Validation and Baker Sugars. He never found out who owned the four numbered companies connected to Baker, incorporated by Goldstein. And who killed Nigel Chamberlain? He was quite sure Harry Fischer would have ordered Schneider to make the hit. Fischer denied it during the interview, but Schneider didn't. *Maybe, maybe not,* Schneider had said.

The more St. James thought, the more he realized how little he knew.

Chapter 71

When St. James came back to the present, he decided not to call Joy and Taylor until he'd interviewed Harman. Then he could report on everything at once.

Harman turned out to be more formal than the first two Ruger owners. A strong accent said he was well schooled in British decorum. Stiffness in his voice suggested he might be more challenging to engage.

St. James explained his role and background.

"Why did you purchase the Ruger, Mr. Harman?"

Harman cleared his throat. "I bought the gun because I've been getting death threats. My collection is registered entirely with the police. If I had to use a weapon to defend myself and my family, I didn't want it traced to me."

"Mr. Harman, that's huge! Did you report the threats to the police?"

"No," he said sheepishly.

"Why?"

Harman's voice began to crack. "The note said if I did, my family would die first with me forced to watch."

"Mr. Harman, you have to go to the police," St. James insisted. "If you don't, you'll be under this cloud for as long as you live. The police will protect you and your family. You must trust them. How many threats have you received?"

"Five."

"In what form?"

"Plain white paper inscribed with letters cut from newspapers. Left on my doorstep during the night."

"Do all five say the same thing?"

"Yes. I have one here on my desk. It's short. I'll read it."

"Go ahead."

"*Time is running out, Harman. You'll be dead soon. If you go to the police, we'll kill your family before your very eyes.*"

"Jesus!" St. James blurted. "Are all five notes worded the same?"

"Yes."

"Do you have any idea who would want to kill you?"

Harman paused a moment. "Several people lost a lot of money investing in a project I promoted. They want their money back. That's what the notes are for. Pay me back or your family dies."

"That would give you a promising idea who is sending the notes then."

"Not really. There were seventy-nine investors."

"Were they well-to-do, knowledgeable investors?"

"No. Some mortgaged their homes to buy in. Unsophisticated people, chasing the dream. I warned them of the risk and advised them to seek independent advice. But they were determined to go ahead on their own. Afraid of missing out, I guess. Of course, all of my warnings were forgotten as soon as they lost their money. They're looking for a scapegoat, and you're talking to him."

Both men were silent for several seconds.

St. James spoke first. "DCI Kingston is a friend of mine. He heads Scotland Yard's fraud division. But this sort of situation would likely be handled by another division. Kingston's worked them all at one time or another and knows the senior people in every division. He'll find the right detective to track down those responsible for the threats and provide protection for your family."

St. James didn't bother asking his prepared questions. Instead, he spent the next half hour persuading Harman the only way out of this was with the aid of the Metropolitan Police. Finally convinced, Harman allowed himself to be connected with DCI Kingston.

Chapter 72

When St. James finished the marathon phone meeting with Robert Harman and delivered him into the capable hands of DCI Kingston, he arranged a Zoom meeting with Joy and Taylor.

He relayed Smythe's progress unveiling companies Fischer was bilking in the several countries. Smythe only needed a couple more days to finish the job.

Saving the best for the last, St. James said, "Smythe was able to confirm Taylor Supermarkets was one of the UK companies Fischer swindled. So you do have losses caused by an outside party, John, even though you thought it impossible."

Taylor winced. "I don't know whether to be happy you were right or upset that I was one of the companies defrauded," he said, anxiety level bubbling.

"Both," St. James said. "Remember our conversation: one step at a time, with cautious optimism."

"I remember."

Joy leaned forward and smiled. "You know, I doubted your theory from the beginning, Hamilton. But I have to hand it to you. It was brilliant."

"How did they do it?" Taylor asked.

"The answer to that will come from the next leg of the journey," St. James said. "We know someone swindled you, just not how."

Taylor was silent.

"What about the other countries? There must be lots of cash stashed somewhere in each one, as we found in Chamberlain's cellar," Joy said, trying to grasp the total picture.

"Not necessarily. Most of it would have been transferred to IEI electronically. But there's bound to be some cash in transit. As for money found in Chamberlain's cellar, remember that's cash Chamberlain skimmed from IEI, not the total pilfered from UK companies," St. James explained.

Joy nodded. "How is all this going to unfold?"

"Weber plans to develop a cash-distribution process for legitimate claimants around the world to share in whatever funds are available from IEI. Once the German courts approve a distribution order, it'll come before every country's court system for approval."

"And if a country doesn't approve?" Taylor asked.

"That country won't receive a share of the cash distributions, and no funds would be available for its wronged companies to share."

"What happens to money otherwise available to a dissenting country?" Joy said, folding her arms.

"Their share would sit in trust."

"Would a holdout country affect my payout in any way?" Taylor asked.

"No. Distributions are usually stand-alone for each country. That's so dissenting countries don't have the power to hold other countries hostage, to negotiate a greater share of the pot. By holding out, they're only hurting themselves. It's a lot more complicated than I have described, but that's the gist."

"Wow!" said Joy, impressed by St. James's explanation.

"Clear enough for me, Hamilton," Taylor said thoughtfully.

When the conversation turned to Chamberlain's murder, Taylor dropped off the call.

"What did you learn from the three Ruger purchasers?" Joy asked.

St. James recounted his conversation with Harold Jenkins.

"Teaching his grandson gun safety. Nothing suspicious."

Joy laughed when he told Nancy Sweet's break-in story.

"She bought the gun for defence reasons," St. James concluded.

"Sound like quite the character," Joy said with a chuckle.

"Entertaining."

"Anything else?" Joy said.

"Yeah," said St. James said with a chortle. "Nancy Sweet thinks DS Billings looks like Elmer Fudd."

Coffee spewed from Joy's mouth across her computer screen, followed by choking, then laughter. "You all right, Phyllis?"

"You caught me off guard with a mouthful of coffee. That's hilarious! And now that you mention it, I do see a resemblance."

Joy regained her composure.

"Would you mind wiping the coffee from your screen? I can't see you."

Joy chuckled as she wiped her computer with a tissue.

Kingston had already filled Joy in on the threat against Bob Harman.

"The three had no idea who Chamberlain was, nor anyone who might, and they didn't lend their gun to anyone. Dead end, Phyllis."

Chapter 73

After the Zoom call with Taylor and Joy, St. James went back to the computer room to see Smythe.

"Louis, I've covered everything I can here in Germany. Somehow I have to take what we've learned and piece it together with whatever happened to Taylor from that end."

"What do you want me to do when we finish the chart?"

"Have the force's photographer take pictures of every part of the chart in an order that we can follow and use for affidavits. Multiple copies for Weber, Joy, myself and court appearances in however many countries you can confirm when you are finished. Let's say a hundred and fifty prints to start."

St. James watched the four Transformers glaring at nothing and wondered what kind of life they had. Whether they ever went out and had fun. Whether they had any little Transformers at home.

Smythe nodded. "Then what?"

See if Weber needs you for anything else. If not, I guess you can go home."

Smythe's face brightened. "That's great! Excellent."

St. James smiled. "I will let Weber know we have gone as far as we can here in Hamburg, and Anna and I will be leaving for London."

***

Weber seemed more upset about losing Anna than about losing St. James.

"Can't she stay for a couple more days?" he pleaded.

"Afraid not, Noah," St. James said with a smile. "Need her with me."

Weber sighed. "Suppose I should be grateful I had her this long," he said, consoling himself. Then he brightened suddenly at a new thought. "When we work on the distribution process, will she come back with you?"

"Yes. She'll have to conduct considerable research to make a distribution system work," St. James said, knowing full well what Weber had in mind.

"Think you might be able to spare her a day here and there, Hamilton?"

"We'll see Noah; we'll see."

Anna and St. James left Weber standing at the reception desk, staring until they were out of sight.

"Why do I feel like I just broke up with a boyfriend?" Anna said with a giggle when they were a block away.

St. James smiled. "And I feel I'm letting down a friend."

"He's a nice man, extremely hard-working. If you don't need me full time during the distribution process, I'm okay giving him a day here and there."

When they arrived at the hotel, Anna booked a flight into London City Centre and another room at the Thistle Piccadilly Hotel.

They packed up the Horner hotel room, checked out and hightailed it to the Hamburg airport to catch a London flight that boarded in three hours.

It was 8:30 p.m. when they checked into the Thistle Piccadilly. Anna and St. James worked together to organize the room, then St. James called housekeeping to see about laundry service and dry cleaning. Housekeeping agreed to collect everything in the morning.

Finally settled, they went down to the bar and were delighted to see Prisha working.

"Welcome back, you two," she said, approaching the table. "I wondered what happened to you."

"Had some business to take care of in Germany, Prisha," St. James said. "And boy are we ever glad to see you."

Anna caught Prisha's look of curiosity. "We had an unpleasant server in a Hamburg restaurant who never spoke or smiled," she explained. "Hamilton took particular offence. He didn't leave much of a tip. You were so wonderful. You spoiled us."

"Thank you for the compliment. The job isn't for everyone. You have to be pleasant with everyone, even when they're not so pleasant with you. Unpleasant servers don't get it that you make more tips projecting warmth. The irony is, making less reinforces the undesirable behaviour. Vicious circle. Stupid, when you think of it. Their own worst enemy," Prisha observed.

St. James and Anna both nodded.

"Sorry, that's probably more than I should have said. You two must be thirsty. What kind of scotch would you like, Mr. St. James?"

"What was the one you suggested last time?"

"I believe it was Old Pulteney."

"I'll have a double on the rocks."

"Very well," she said and turned to Anna. "And you, miss?"

"We're going to be here for a couple of days, Prisha, maybe longer. Please call me Anna." Anna pointed to St. James. "Hamilton."

"Yes, Prisha, we are not formal people."

"Very well," Prisha said happily.

Anna looked at the wine list, then up at Prisha. "I'll have the Farinelli pinot grigio."

"Excellent choice, Anna. Best white we have."

When Prisha turned and left, Anna said, "She's so lovely. If I ever had a daughter, I'd like her to be just like her."

St. James said nothing.

Anna thought for a moment. "How are you going to tackle Taylor?"

"I was thinking about that very question on the flight," he said vacantly. "I'll review everything we did before Hamburg: your research, Louis's systems analysis, interviews and notes. From there, I'll try to map a road of some sort — hopefully, one that leads to a satisfactory conclusion."

Prisha returned and placed drinks. St. James and Anna took a moment to sample.

"Excellent wine," Anna murmured, and then looked at St. James. "So there's not much for me to do at the moment?"

"There'll be lots for you to do before this case is finished."

"I know the chart in Hamburg tells enough of a story to put Fischer and Schneider away for a while, but I didn't grasp much about Taylor's situation from the Germany side to help in London, other than someone defrauded him. Nothing that I think would help on this end," she said quizzically.

"That's because there wasn't anything to learn," St. James said with disappointment. "The biggest takeaway was that outside crooks defrauded Taylor. Before Hamburg, I only suspected it. Then, everyone thought I was wasting their time and money. Now we know it actually happened."

"Knowing you, you have the road already mapped out in your head. Reviewing notes will only confirm that road is the right road, correct?" Anna said with a wide grin.

St. James's smile was devilish.

Chapter 74

The following day, Anna went to the hotel gym for a workout, and St. James made the trek to Taylor Supermarkets' head office. As usual, he was met at the top stair by Taylor's executive assistant, Deborah Singent-Smythe, and was immediately taken to Taylor's paltry office. Taylor rose to shake hands.

"Wasn't expecting you until tomorrow," he said, no trace of anxiety in his voice.

Taylor's black sports coat rested on the back of a swivel chair that looked like it might pre-date World War II. He'd just finished writing something and still had his light-blue tie flipped over his shoulder to avoid touching it with his fountain pen. Taylor righted his tie and motioned for St. James to sit.

"Well, I did everything I had to do there, and Louis is close to finishing IEI's Fischerlock system," St. James said, once he was seated. "I need to find the connection between you, Chamberlain and IEI, who defrauded you."

Taylor nodded. "Do you need time with me now?"

"Not right now. Is the meeting room free?"

"I'll ask Deborah to make sure it's yours for as long as you need it and that no one disturbs you in the meantime."

"Thank you, John."

"Just out of curiosity, what will happen to Fischer and Schneider?" Taylor asked.

"I think it's the largest fraud case to date. Those two will be lucky to get out in twenty-five."

"Good!" Taylor said with a grin. For a brief moment, he searched for words. "I owe you an apology, Hamilton," he said finally, sounding somewhat embarrassed.

St. James looked surprised. "For what?"

"For being so rough on you, doubting your judgment and competence. Threatening to kill the investigation," he said humbly.

St. James's smile was generous. "John, you're not the first person to doubt my direction, and you certainly won't be the last."

Taylor nodded.

St. James went down the hall to the modest meeting room where he and Smythe had begun the investigation weeks earlier. He set up his laptop, pulled Taylor's files from a mobile office case he'd purchased to accommodate the ever-mounting pile of documents, and began reviewing what he and the team had accomplished to date.

He noticed the Baker Sugars report didn't say whether Smythe ever talked to a live person in the company. St. James tapped Smythe's number on his cell.

"See you made it, boss," Smythe said when he accepted the call.

"Safe and sound. You ever talk to anyone at Baker Sugars?"

"Nope," Smythe said quickly. "Tried a bunch of times, maybe ten or twelve on different days."

"Hmm," St. James said and abruptly clicked off without a word. He stared off. "Think it's time to stir the pot."

St. James phoned Harvey Goldstein, the lawyer for the four numbered companies with an interest in Baker Sugars.

After mutual greetings, Goldstein said, "Solved Chamberlain's murder yet?"

"Getting close," St. James lied.

Goldstein was silent for a second, then said, "What can I do for you?"

"I don't know for sure, Harvey, but I may need a lawyer to do some work. I had lunch with Frank Keller a week ago, and he strongly recommended you. Said you always gave good advice and service."

"Frank is a great client," Goldstein said happily. "Sharp mind. He pays his legal bills on time too. That's the part I like most about him," he said with a high-pitched chuckle.

"Wonderful."

"What kind of work is this likely to be?"

"Corporate searches, contracts, that sort of thing. Some of it may involve Chamberlain's business."

"How urgent is it?"

"Well, I am reviewing the files right now. If I find what I think I'm going to find, my need will be urgent. This call is to give you a heads-up and to see if you're willing to work with me."

"Oh, I am more than happy to work with you, Hamilton, but I'm conducting a trial right now that's taking most of my time."

"How long is it likely to last, do you think?"

"Scheduled for another thirty days at the moment. But that's only a guess. If we get into an argument over legal interpretations or there's protracted testimony, it could be longer."

"Then probably this isn't going to work. I'm sorry. I was looking forward to collaborating with you. Maybe next time."

"Well, thanks for thinking of me, Hamilton. Good luck with whatever you're doing."

They clicked off.

St. James made a note.

He reviewed several areas of the investigation — *Gerda Wagner's five visitors, Vanderbilt's grandma Visser*. Then he rifled through pages of notes —

Smythe's rescue, Chamberlain's death, property searches, size 39 women's clothes, Chamberlain and Schneider texts, Randall & Collins meetings, Zurich, and Lisa's recollection of the man in the long grey coat.

He took a short coffee break to consider what he'd covered. Then went back at it — *Chamberlain's cellar, Nigel Chamberlain's sister (Barbara Evans), Daniel Scrivens, Billings's investigation, Chamberlain's will, Mary Louise Kellar, Woods's forecasting error, Pay Validation, vice-president interviews, Keller, and the Ruger purchasers.*

All this ricocheted around every corner of St. James's mind like balls in a bingo blower. And just as bingo balls had to dispense in a certain order to have a winner, St. James's information had to dispense in a certain order to solve the case.

Chapter 75

By four o'clock, St. James had had enough. He packed up the laptop and files, carefully stowed them in the mobile office case and left for the hotel. He strolled along Shaftesbury, mind focused on the case, oblivious to his surroundings.

Suddenly, St. James was yanked past a rolled-up metal door into a loading bay for delivery trucks and shoved against a cement wall. Two poorly dressed men pinned him there. One man's face was heavily scarred, and his neck was the size of a drainpipe. That one must have weighed three hundred pounds. The other one was slightly smaller and rugged, with broad shoulders and short brown hair.

"Who the hell are you?" St. James shouted.

"We'll do the talking," Drainpipe scowled.

St. James struggled to break free but was pinned too tightly to succeed.

"What do you want?" St. James said aggressively, more angry than frightened.

"You to stop investigating Taylor!" yelled the more diminutive guy.

"Not a chance!"

Drainpipe drew back his huge fist and punched St. James hard in the stomach, doubling him over and sending his case onto the concrete floor.

Two well-dressed middle-aged women screamed as they passed.

"This is a warning. Go back to Canada, where you belong. You won't get off so easy next time," bellowed Brown-Hair.

The two thugs disappeared, leaving St. James working hard to catch his breath.

Partially recovered, he righted the case and checked its contents. Satisfied everything had survived intact, he slowly walked down Shaftesbury toward the Thistle Hotel.

When he entered the room, he found Anna lying on the bed reading a book, wearing her favourite blue track suit. She stared at him. "Hamilton, you're as white as a sheet. What's wrong?" She laid the book on the bed.

Without a word, he made his way over to an armchair and sat. When he'd collected himself, he explained what happened when he left Taylor's.

Anna listened without interrupting, perched on the end of the bed, staring at him. Fear began to cloud her features. She hesitated for a few seconds until her anxiety turned to anger. She climbed off the bed and stood in the middle of the room with fists clenched. "This is why I didn't want Dozer sent home!" she said aggressively, stomping her foot. "I want Dozer back here!"

St. James had no comeback. He pulled his cell from his pants pocket and tapped Dozer's Toronto number. At first there was no reaction when St. James explained everything. He pictured Dozer playing out scenarios in his head, trying to choose the optimal course of action.

Finally, Dozer said, "Book me into the same hotel. I'll be on the next available flight." Dozer hung up without another word.

St. James stared at the cell as if the phone itself had cut him off.

"Well?" Anna asked impatiently.

"On the next available flight."

"Good!"

St. James moved to the small desk and pulled a fresh notepad from the case.

"What are you doing?"

"Writing a description of the hoodlums for Dozer while it's fresh in my mind." St. James sounded more determined than ever. "Damn the threats."

"Let's go for a drink," Anna said with a huge sigh. "Can you manage? I think we both need one after all this."

"Oh, I can manage."

When he finished describing his abusers, he texted Dozer. Dozer replied by email a few minutes later, giving strict orders to St. James — the kind only Dozer could issue. Anyone else who tried to boss Hamilton around did so at their peril.

He and Anna were to stay in the hotel until he arrived. They were to have meals only in the Thistle dining room, nowhere outside. If Dozer couldn't get there until the day after, they were to work from the hotel room. Chances are the hooligans wouldn't try anything in the hotel, Dozer's email said.

Feeling better with Dozer's imminent arrival, they headed to the bar and seated themselves at a table by the window.

Prisha popped around immediately. "How are my two favourite guests today?" she said.

"Little worse for wear, Prisha," Anna said with less enthusiasm than usual.

Prisha took in Anna's unspoken language but decided not to ask.

"What can I get for you, Anna?"

Anna looked up at Prisha. "Don't think white wine will cut it tonight, Prisha. Better make it a very dry vodka martini, straight up with an olive, please."

"Very well. Hamilton?"

"Double Macallan on the rocks."

Prisha nodded and headed off to the bar.

"Poor Prisha," Anna said, shaking her head. "She has to be wondering what's wrong."

St. James nodded. "I have to determine how this is going to work with Dozer."

"What's to work? Dozer's protected you many times."

"Quite true. The concern is how I introduce his role to Taylor. Taylor's temperamental personality means I have to be careful how I handle it."

"You'll figure it out."

St. James nodded.

Prisha arrived with drinks.

"Prisha," St. James began as she placed glasses, "we owe you an explanation for why we seem a little off tonight."

"No, no, Hamilton. Your business is your own, not mine. It's just that you both treat me so much better than most. It makes me feel special. So if things don't seem right with you, I — well, you know — feel it. Anyone else, I wouldn't care."

Anna smiled. "You are special, Prisha. Hamilton had an unpleasant experience this afternoon walking back from a client. He was attacked by two men, roughed up a bit and threatened."

Covering her mouth with one free hand, Prisha looked at St. James. "Oh my God! Are you all right?"

St. James smiled inwardly at her concern. "I'm fine. It was a little off-putting, as you British would say."

"I should say so." Prisha's concern lingered as she drifted back to the bar.

"I see you ordered Macallan scotch," Anna said with a slight smile. "I didn't think a punch in the stomach qualified as life threatening."

"It does now," he said, looking out the window.

"Why?"

"See the two standing on the other side of the street?" he said slowly.

Anna looked out. "What about them?"

"They're the ones."

Chapter 76

Dozer managed to catch the Lufthansa 8:45 p.m. flight to Heathrow the same day St. James called. After checking into the Thistle Hotel the following morning, he banged on St. James's door.

Anna greeted him. "Boy, am I ever glad to see you."

Dozer hugged her gently and grinned. "Aren't you always glad to see me?"

"You know what I mean, ya big lug," she said, swatting his arm.

Dozer quickly eyed the room. "Where's the target?"

"In the shower. Want some coffee?" Anna pointed to a carafe delivered by room service shortly before Dozer arrived.

Dozer shook his head. "Coffeed out. I must have had two pots on the plane. I could use a bit of breakfast, though. Airplane food upsets my stomach."

"You're in luck. We haven't had breakfast. Soon as Hamilton's ready, we'll go to the dining room."

"I'll go now," Dozer said. "Get us a table and a start on food. Stomach's yelling like a banshee."

Anna smiled. "Okay. We'll be down in a few minutes."

Ten minutes later, the three were sitting together in the dining room, and Dozer was finishing toast and jam.

"That all you're going to have, Dozer?" Anna said.

St. James smiled. "That's just a warm-up. A Dozer kick-start. The big fellow needs more than that to protect the world's greatest commercial detective," St. James said.

"Huh! Some detective! Let two fat guys take you," Dozer said and drank water.

St. James squinted at him but let it go.

"Spotted them standing on the other side of the street last night when we were having a drink in the bar."

"Watching to see if you go like they told you to," Dozer speculated.

The server dropped by to pour coffee and to see about breakfast.

"Scrambled eggs and dry whole-wheat toast," Anna said.

The server glanced at Dozer. "Full English breakfast."

"Same for me," St. James said quickly.

St. James looked at Dozer. "So what's the plan?"

"Well, if they're watching to see if you go, we'll make it easy for them to see you haven't."

"Live bait?" Anna said with a worried look.

"Live bait," Dozer confirmed. He turned to St. James. "You said you were walking back from Taylor's when they grabbed you?"

"That's right."

"Then we'll take the same route after breakfast, just as if nothing happened. See if we can flush the villains out."

"When they see you, they probably won't show," Anna said to Dozer.

"They won't see me," Dozer said, grinning. "Don't you remember Ottawa? When I shadowed you from home to work and back when you worked at the pub?"

"Now that you mention it. I was amazed how your surroundings could absorb such a big guy."

"The problem is when you want him to be absorbed, he's in your face," St. James said with a chuckle.

"I was hoping to get through breakfast without one of your stupid remarks," Dozer said lightly. "Guess I couldn't be that lucky."

"And so it begins," Anna said, shaking her head.

"And so it begins," St. James repeated.

Breakfast arrived, diverting their attention.

St. James explained Taylor's sensitivities.

"You'll have to let me do the talking — and be on your best behaviour."

"I'm always on my best behaviour."

Anna smirked.

When they finished breakfast, Anna went back to the room to read.

St. James and Dozer left the hotel and walked down Great Windmill Street, Dozer on the left sidewalk a few paces back, St. James on the right. Dozer's head was on a swivel, taking in every movement, in every direction, of everyone. Partway down Great Windmill, he spotted two guys leaning against a building, smoking, watching pedestrians. For a moment, he considered them. *Too thin.*

St. James strolled along at his usual gait, pulling the mobile office case. They turned onto Shaftesbury Avenue without incident. Partway down Shaftesbury, he noticed the garage door, where his attackers had hidden, rolled up again. Approaching cautiously, he tensed when he saw two men inside. A second look said they were not his attackers.

A few minutes later, he and Dozer climbed the stairs to Taylor's head office, and Singent-Smythe escorted them into Taylor's office where St. James carefully explained Dozer's presence.

"Someone attacked you for investigating my business?" said a shocked Taylor.

"Yes. That's why I asked Dozer to come back to be my bodyguard."

Taylor reflected on this for a second. "Am I in danger?" he said anxiously.

"No," St. James said quickly to reassure Taylor. "Just me. I'm getting too close to something here, and that's making someone nervous. So Dozer will be with me everywhere I go until the case is solved."

"Mr. Taylor," Dozer said quietly, gentling his deep baritone voice. "Is there another way into the premises besides the front door to the store?"

"There's a loading dock at the rear. Why?"

"I have to assess potential risks to Hamilton while he's here."

Taylor considered this for a moment. "I'll introduce you to our VP operations, Daniel Sauvé. He'll show you around."

"Thank you."

Taylor paused for a moment. "I'm not sure how to explain Dozer's presence here. I don't want to spook my people, make them unnecessarily afraid."

"Say he's a member of my team. That's true. And he's my security adviser, also true. No need for them to know what happened yesterday," St. James suggested.

"Okay."

Taylor escorted Dozer down the hall and introduced him to Daniel Sauvé, Lucas Vanderbilt and Cindy Woods the way St. James suggested. St. James went to the meeting room and set up his mobile office.

Almost a full hour passed before Dozer arrived in the meeting room to report his observations.

St. James looked up from notes. "How'd you make out?"

"Three VPs were a little intimidated when they saw me."

"Can't imagine why. You're so small, meek and mild. Bet if I said, 'boo,' you'd run."

Dozer feigned annoyance. "Okay, okay! I get the point."

St. James became serious. "How vulnerable is the place?"

"Very. The loading-dock door has a lock older than the furniture in this room."

"Tell Taylor. I'm sure he'll gladly replace it."

"Has to now," Dozer said as he pulled a badly rusted lock from a jacket pocket. "I tugged on it, and this is how it turned out. Proof of my conclusion."

St. James shook his head. "What else did you find?"

"Windows are wooden, ancient, some rot. Definitely should be replaced. Easy to break in, steal inventory or burn the place down. And the cellar window has no latch."

St. James considered Dozer's findings. "You'd better report this to Taylor right away. He'll want the lock replaced today, for sure. The windows he'll probably mull over for a bit. Just the way he is."

"Even though it's just as easy to get in through the windows as a poorly locked door?"

St. James frowned. "Even though. Cost is everything to him."

Dozer shook his head and left the room to find Taylor.

St. James went back to his notes. He considered several ways events could have happened and by whom, playing each scenario out in detail in his head and then documenting it on paper, weighing the plausibility of each as he went. If he considered a scenario plausible, it didn't mean it happened. It just meant it could — and if it did, who would have a motive and opportunity to bring it about?

Billings had growled when he found out St. James went around him to interview the three Ruger owners. Now he was about to make Elmer Fudd mad a second time.

St. James concluded he had to interview Barbara Evans. He didn't know why, but it bothered him that Chamberlain had a criminal lawyer eliminate every trace of Evan's existence, just for inheriting their father's estate. Chamberlain was a wealthy man. He didn't need half his father's estate to live. It didn't seem reasonable that he'd go to all that trouble because his father favoured Barbara over him.

He called Barbara and used the same explanation he had with the Ruger owners; he worked with Billings and had more questions. She agreed to meet the next afternoon at her home in Cambridge.

When Dozer finished updating Taylor, he made several calls back to North America. So as not to disturb St. James, Taylor set him up in an empty office across the hall.

At twelve thirty, Singent-Smythe brought in lunch. She kept them topped up with coffee throughout the day.

At four thirty, they left Taylor's for the hotel, taking the same route back they'd taken that morning. Dozer walked on the side opposite St. James, a few paces behind, studying faces and assessing potential threats as they went.

Walking Shaftesbury toward Great Windmill, St. James cautiously approached the open garage. He could see no one inside.

Suddenly, he heard a man's voice from behind. "I thought I told you to go home."

The man grabbed St. James's arms, twisting them behind him, and shoved him into the garage, where he came face to face with the smaller, brown-haired ruffian. St. James turned to face the man holding him. It was Drainpipe.

"Now you're going to be sorry," Drainpipe said, spittle spraying with every word.

As he was about to grab St. James, Drainpipe heard a voice from behind. "May I be of some assistance, gentlemen?"

Drainpipe turned to face Dozer and made a disgusted face. "This is a private matter, none of your business. Piss off," he snarled.

Dozer remained polite. "The British government has asked me to randomly select people on the street and ask which hand is their dominant hand," he said convincingly. "It's a study they wanted conducted."

St. James tried not to laugh.

"Why?" Drainpipe said idiotically.

"Bureaucracy," Dozer said with a straight face.

Drainpipe looked at Dozer dumbfoundedly, his head cocked sideways like an animal hearing a strange noise. "Right-handed," he said stupidly.

"Excellent. Thank you, sir," Dozer said and gently took Drainpipe's right arm, twisted it around his back and shoved it slowly upward until it snapped.

Drainpipe howled in pain and held his broken arm tightly against his torso as he swore and backed away, wounded and in shock.

Pointing to St. James, Dozer said, "Guess you won't be punching my friend again anytime soon."

St. James chuckled.

Dozer looked at the other man. "Who are you working for?" he snapped.

"Don't know," Brown-Hair said, eying his suffering friend, frightened he was in for the same treatment.

Dozer eyed him and pointed to Drainpipe. "You want the same?"

"No. No. Please—"

Dozer followed him as he backed away. "Then who are you working for?"

Shaking, Brown-Hair said, "We're only told his first name. Percy. No last name. We don't even know if Percy's his real first name."

Dozer reckoned he was telling the truth because he wouldn't permit real names if he ran the thug operation.

"Okay," Dozer said. "Get your sissy partner here to the hospital and tell Percy, or whoever he is, if he sends anyone else, they'll get the same treatment, and I'll hunt him down, no matter how long it takes."

Chapter 77

St. James, Anna and Dozer were sitting in the hotel bar ordering a second round from Prisha. Dozer finished the dregs of his first Guinness and was watching Prisha. She wore a light-grey pantsuit, gold earrings the shape of bird's wings and a long matching necklace. *Beautiful*, he thought.

The bar's lighting dimmed gently, creating an inviting atmosphere, though late afternoon sun stubbornly made itself known through a slightly sullied window.

Four well-dressed businessmen stood at the bar discussing meetings over a pint. The room filled as more people drifted in.

Prisha was having trouble adjusting to Dozer's intimidating presence, even though he wasn't trying to frighten her. She took his order but moved away quickly.

Dozer had what St. James called "an air of quiet intimidation." He looked scary, even when he was relaxed. Once you knew him, it was easy to see through this demeanour to the naturally kind and gentle person underneath — the real Dozer. Intentional intimidation only shone when innocent people were bullied, taken advantage of or physically harmed.

"You should have seen this guy's act today, Anna," St. James said, pointing to Dozer. "He played this calm bureaucrat, out randomly interviewing people, asking if they were right- or left-handed, dumbfounding the guy I call Drainpipe."

Anna smiled. "What happened?"

"Believe it or not, the guy answered, 'Right-handed.' Dozer completed the survey by gently twisting the rogue's right hand up behind his back until it broke. No aggressive language. No threats or punches. Just slow movement until he heard the snap."

Not sure of her approval, Anna stared at them both neutrally. "Clever way to determine which arm to break, I suppose."

Dozer nodded as Prisha laid down the second round.

"He won't be going near Hamilton anymore," Dozer said, sipping Guinness.

"Don't think so," St. James interjected. "But this guy Percy, or whatever his name is, could sic another thug on me."

Anna drank wine.

"There's always that," Dozer mused thoughtfully.

Anna's eyes suddenly became moist as she looked at Dozer and took another sip of wine. "I'm glad you're here to look after him."

"Somebody has to. I'm surprised he can tie his own shoes."

St. James rolled his eyes at Dozer.

"What do you two have planned for tomorrow?" Anna asked.

"Dozer and I are driving up to Cambridge to talk to some folks there," St. James said casually, sipping scotch.

Dozer gave St. James a look. "I didn't know we were going to Cambridge."

"Like to keep you in suspense."

"Yeah — right!"

"Who are you interviewing?" Anna asked.

"Wish I could tell you."

Dozer looked at Anna. "Jesus! Shutting us out already. Must be getting close to something. Hoarding information for the big show."

"I was afraid of that," Anna said. "I hate it when you do this, Hamilton."

St. James refused to compromise. "You know very well why I do it. Whatever the story is, it will be long and complicated, and I only want to tell it once."

Dozer and Anna shook their heads.

St. James briskly changed the subject. "Want to go to Sergio's for dinner?"

"Sergio's?" Dozer said.

Anna described the restaurant to Dozer, and the three agreed to dine there that evening. St. James signed the bill to their room, and they strolled over to Great Titchfield.

Chapter 78

It was Antonio's night off. A tall strawberry-blond server named Camilla — a beauty with broad shoulders, thin lips and heavily made-up green eyes — looked after them for the evening.

They agreed to pass on drinks and go straight to wine.

Dozer asked for rigatoni and meatballs.

"Spaghetti alla Bolognese, please," Anna said.

Camilla looked at St. James. "Tagliatelle salmon for me."

Camilla noted their requests and trotted off.

St. James's cell buzzed. He excused himself and went outside to answer.

"St. James," he said when he accepted the call.

"It's Louis."

"What's up?"

"Finally wrapped up Hamburg." There was relief in Smythe's voice. "We got through every country, all Fischer's leaders, the companies he defrauded, listing every piece of data on the wall chart. The chart now covers all four walls in the examination room."

"In the end, how many companies were there?"

"Seventeen hundred and twenty-nine!"

St. James whistled. "Wow! How many countries did you confirm?"

"Fifty-seven."

Smythe sounded quite pleased with himself. "I had the charts photographed and made a hundred and fifty copies, as you asked."

"Did you send copies to Kingston and Joy?"

"Yes, and one should be in your inbox shortly."

"Good. Thank you. Does Weber need you for anything else?"

"No, he said I could go if it were all right with you."

"Okay, with me. You've done a marvellous job on a very tedious assignment, my friend. Yeoman service. Thank you!"

"You're most welcome," Smythe said, buoyed by the praise.

"One last thing."

"What's that?"

"You should take the Transformers out for a night on the town. Whoop it up a bit. Thank them for their arduous work and camaraderie."

Smythe abruptly hung up.

St. James laughed his way back to the table where Dozer poured him and Anna a second glass of wine.

"That was Louis."

"Thought it might be," Dozer said, wiping wine from the table with a napkin.

St. James told them what Smythe reported.

"So what happens now?" Anna asked, showing greater interest.

"Noah will contact his counterparts in the fifty-seven countries, tell the story and forward copies of the charts full of data gathered from Fischer's computer. Officials will formally interview Fischer's sector chiefs and country leaders. That'll likely lead to arrests and court applications to approve whatever distribution procedures Weber's team develops. That's when all hell will break loose in all the countries. Should be fun," St. James said with a huge grin.

Anna's look was strange. "It's times like this I feel like I fell in love with a psychopath."

Dozer laughed. "You did."

"Anyone who gets off causing world chaos has got something wrong with them," she said.

Camilla arrived with food and placed plates around the table.

"Can I get anyone anything else at the moment?" she said with a smile.

"Good for now, Camilla. Thank you," St. James said.

Camilla topped up wine glasses and moved on.

Dozer ate a meatball. "Have we got enough to hang Chamberlain's murder on Fischer?"

"I think so," St. James said, cutting salmon into smaller bites. "The millions skimmed from Fischer is a pretty strong motive. And he didn't deny having Chamberlain's laptop stolen to prove it."

Chapter 79

When they returned to the hotel, Anna phoned Carolyn Kingston to see if she would like to do something the next day.

"Hamilton and Dozer are driving up to Cambridge tomorrow to interview some people, and I'm left to fend for myself," Anna said, hoping Carolyn would suggest an outing of some sort.

"I'm okay to do something if you like. What would appeal to you?"

"Well, I haven't had a good tour of London, even though we were here on holiday last year. So that would be nice. Maybe lunch somewhere. And you wouldn't get a huge argument from me if you wanted to stick your head in a shop or two." Anna laughed.

"Let's do it all!" Carolyn said enthusiastically. "It's been two years since I toured the city myself, and that was with David's aunt and uncle visiting from Edinburgh. I didn't see much because she never shut her mouth the whole tour."

Anna chuckled. "I promise to be a better tour mate."

"I'm busy at home until ten, so it will be almost eleven before I get to your hotel."

"Perfect," Anna said happily. "I'll make the tour arrangements."

***

"How far is it to Cambridge?" Dozer said as they climbed into the rented blue Hyundai Tucson arranged by the hotel concierge.

"Google says sixty-five miles if we go the M11. An hour and a half, give or take," St. James said as he cranked up the engine and put the Hyundai into gear.

They were quiet until St. James manoeuvred the Tucson out of London. When they reached the open countryside, Dozer said, "Who do you plan to interview up here?"

St. James monitored the rear and side mirrors, checking for traffic closing in behind. A stream of vehicles far back posed no tailgating threat.

"Barbara Evans, Chamberlain's more-than-estranged sister," St. James said, scanning the countryside.

"You believe Chamberlain *actually* wiped her out of existence without a trace?" Dozer said doubtfully.

"That's what Scrivens said."

Dozer was skeptical. "Hardly seems possible."

"Don't disagree." St. James checked miles remaining to Cambridge.

"Be an awkward thing to do. Almost impossible."

Miles drifted by.

"Anyone else you plan to see?"

"I talked with a Detective Sergeant Harris of the Cambridge police yesterday. Mostly a courtesy call to let him know we'd be in his playground for the day. I filled him in on the investigation. He offered help if we need it."

Dozer gazed at a herd of cows as they passed a large farm. "What'd ya tell him?"

"Said I didn't know, but something might come out of the Evans interview."

"What am I supposed to do while you interview her?"

St. James slowed for a truck to pass.

"Find a coffee shop somewhere and give orders to your people in Toronto, same as you always do."

"And if someone attacks you?"

"I'll be in Evans's home, not walking the streets. You'll only be gone for an hour. When you come back, park in front of her house until I come out. Chances are I won't be longer than an hour, anyway."

Dozer nodded. "Okay."

It was one thirty when they pulled in front of Evans's home. St. James crawled out from behind the wheel, and Dozer slid in to replace him.

"I have a little after one thirty," St. James said, standing by the open driver's door, looking at his watch.

"Me too," Dozer said. "I'll be back no later than two forty."

"Good enough."

Dozer closed the car door and pulled away.

Barbara Evans lived in a brown brick row house off Saxon Street in Cambridge. St. James made his way up the cracked, weedy walkway, knocked on a slightly faded brown door and was greeted with a warm smile from Evans when it opened. Evans's shoulder-length black hair was nicely coiffed, her purple pinstripe trouser suit immaculate. She was an attractive woman. *Probably in her midfifties*, St. James thought.

Evans showed St. James into a small grey sitting room, crowded with furniture, that was situated off a narrow hallway. She gestured him to a green sofa in front of the only window and gracefully seated herself in a chair opposite. The two black cats sleeping on the floor didn't stir.

Resting on a perfectly restored coffee table was a carafe of tea and a plate of scones.

"Help yourself to a scone, Mr. St. James, while I pour some tea," she said, reaching for the carafe.

"Thanks, Barbara," he said with a smile, placing a scone spread with butter and strawberry jam on a small side plate from the table in front. "Delicious," he said after a bite.

Evans nodded and smiled.

"Cream and sugar?"

"Black, please," he said as he finished the calorie-ladened pastry.

"Very well … ah … may I call you Hamilton?"

"Yes, of course."

Pleasantries behind, Evans said, "How can I help?"

"I was shocked to hear the extent Nigel went to eradicate you from his life."

Evans shook her head. "Nigel was a very vindictive man and would go to any length to get even with anyone who wronged him."

"Was it because you were the sole beneficiary of your father's will, or was there something else?"

Evans gazed off for a second, looking vacant. "I can think of no other reason than the inheritance," she said slowly.

"But it was your father's wish, not your doing. Nigel couldn't possibly blame you."

Evans shrugged as if to say that was Nigel's way.

"What did you inherit?"

Evans waved a hand. "This place for one thing."

"And…?"

"About a million pounds," she said as if it was a small amount. "And a box of junk."

"Your brother was quite wealthy. He didn't need anything from your father."

Evans poured more tea and offered St. James another scone. He declined.

"It wouldn't matter how much money Nigel had." Evans placed the carafe on the coffee table. "He saw the world in black and white. In his mind, if he was entitled to more, he was entitled to more, no matter what. And that was that. I showed the will to DS Billings when he was here. Would you like to see it as well?"

"Yes, I would, thank you."

Evans rose and went into an adjacent room. St. James heard the clicking of a safe dial. Seconds later, she returned and handed him a document. St. James took time to read and then passed it back.

"Straightforward enough. Was it probated?"

"No."

"Drafted by a solicitor?"

"No. My father made it himself."

"When was the last time you saw your brother?"

Evans squinted, trying to remember. "Ten or twelve years ago, I believe. Long enough, I probably wouldn't recognize him if he were alive and walking by."

St. James pulled a small notebook from an inside coat pocket and noted her response. He took a picture of Chamberlain from another pocket and handed it to her. She studied the photo for a long moment.

"Someone took that about a week before his murder," St. James added, pointing to the photo.

She passed it back. "He aged a lot. I wouldn't have recognized him."

St. James scribbled a few words in the notebook.

"What did you do with the million pounds?"

"I made a few repairs around the house and invested the rest for living expenses. My husband left me pretty well off with investments. I just added the remainder of Father's money to that."

"What was in the 'box of junk,' as you describe it?"

"Nothing of value." She raised the carafe in his direction. "More tea?"

"No thanks."

Evans pointed to the plate. "Scone?"

St. James shook his head. "I'd like to see the box, if I may."

"I can assure you it would be a waste of your valuable time."

St. James gave her a look that said he would persist.

Noticing his body language, Evans said, "Very well. Don't say I didn't warn you. Follow me."

Evans led St. James down a narrow green hallway, packed with boxes, to a dated yellow kitchen where she opened a cupboard drawer that held, among other things, a flashlight and an assortment of bolts, screws and other pieces of hardware.

She removed the flashlight and flicked it on to check if it still functioned. Satisfied it would serve her purpose, they moved to a white door off the kitchen that opened to narrow steps down to a dark, cold, musty cellar.

Sitting on the concrete floor to the right of the stairs was a box, slightly larger than a mover's box, made of rough, unfinished wood.

Evans flipped off the lid and stood back, gesturing for St. James to see for himself. There were assorted sizes and types of wrenches, screwdrivers, chisels, hammers and several other small tools.

"I take it your father was quite handy," he said, wiping the dirt off his hands.

Two mice scurried along a far wall.

Evans nodded. "He was a fairly good carpenter and knew his way around an engine, I guess. Have you seen enough? I'm anxious to get out of here. This place gives me the creeps, the smell is unpleasant, and I hate mice."

St. James looked up.

"Not yet," he said quickly. "Have to work my way to the bottom."

Evans stiffened slightly. "Very well."

St. James began removing the contents of the box a piece at a time, lining them neatly on the cellar floor. He lifted a set of wrenches. "This stuff may be dirty, but the tools are not junk, Barbara."

Focusing on the box contents, St. James didn't notice Evans's expression shift to a worried look.

He came across a wooden case close to the bottom. It looked well made from quality wood, mahogany or cedar. With little light, he couldn't be sure.

A clasp at the front held the gold-coloured lid tightly in place. St. James worked the clip until the top lifted, hinges squeaking slightly as he slowly opened the cover. Inside was lined with thick green felt, recessed in a shape all too familiar to St. James, making the box's true purpose clear to anyone who viewed it. Lying snugly in the recessed area was a Ruger SR22.

Chapter 80

Evans covered her face in horror when she viewed the contents.

"Now I see why you were anxious to go back upstairs. You didn't want me to empty the box. You thought I'd just look at the tools and close the lid."

Evans didn't seem to hear.

"My God. Where did that come from?"

St. James studied her reaction closely. "I was hoping you would tell me."

Evans took a moment to gather herself. "You can't possibly think I put it there."

"Why not? Your house. Your inheritance. You live alone. And I'm sure the cats didn't put the gun there," he said sharply.

Evans began to cry. "I'm not used to nasty accusations like this."

St. James said nothing. He picked the gun case from the floor and stood. "I'm taking this to the Cambridge police," he said authoritatively.

Evans was still weeping when the two climbed the stairs to the main floor.

"You can't just take it without a warrant or something," she cried.

"Watch me," he said curtly and left.

Dozer was waiting in the Tucson when St. James exited Evans's home. St. James climbed in the passenger seat and flipped open the gun box without a word. Dozer's forehead creased when he saw its contents.

"What happened?"

St. James relayed the interview with Evans, including the rummaging that led to the discovery of the gun.

"What do you want to do?"

Go to the Cambridge police station. DI Harris offered to help if we had a need. Here's his chance."

Dozer nodded. "What's the address?"

St. James pulled out his cell and Googled the address.

"Seventy-four Parkside," he said as he entered it in Maps.

"Okay." Dozer cranked up the engine and pulled away.

St. James gave turn-by-turn directions as Dozer made his way to the police station.

They entered the main door, and St. James asked for DI Harris. A minute later, a short red-headed officer with boyish looks and freckles, wearing a slightly wrinkled light-grey suit, arrived at the front desk and introduced himself as Detective Inspector Harris. Harris studied the gun box under St. James's arm.

"Should I be worried?" he said with a faint smile.

Dozer laughed.

"No," St. James said. "Is there someplace we can talk privately?"

Harris nodded and led them to a meeting room where St. James filled Harris in on the interview with Barbara Evans and provided additional background on Taylor's case.

"My God!" Harris said. "Unbelievable! You fellows have your hands full. That's movie material."

Harris reminded Dozer of Baby Face Nelson, the American gangster from the 1920s.

"Do you think this is the gun that finished off this Chamberlain fellow?" Harris said to St. James.

"Don't know, but I'd like to find out."

"Lab boys are caught up on our work. Want me to have them check for prints?"

St. James smiled. "Thought you'd never ask."

Harris left the meeting room with the Ruger. Twenty minutes later, he returned, looking bewildered.

Dozer noticed it right away. "What's wrong, Detective?"

"Lab folks should be back to us soon," Harris said as if he hadn't heard Dozer.

St. James looked at Dozer first, then Harris. "I know we just met, Detective, but lab timing doesn't account for your concerned look."

Harris stared at St. James for several beats, then said, "I ran Barbara Evans through our databases…"

"And…?"

"She's been dead for two years!"

Chapter 81

Dozer and St. James were dumbfounded for several seconds, not saying a word.

"Well, who the hell did I just interview?" St. James said finally.

Dozer just shook his head.

"I'd like to keep the gun longer to conduct more tests," Harris said.

"Yes, of course," St. James said. "Whoever she is, she'll probably figure out that I'm onto whatever she's doing, even though I haven't a clue."

"I won't confront her before we know more, but I'll have her watched in case she decides to flee," Harris said.

St. James nodded. "Good idea." He thought of Chamberlain's picture, carefully pulled it from a coat pocket and handed it to Harris.

"I gave this to whoever I interviewed. Her prints will be on it."

Harris studied the picture for a second. "I'll have it tested," he said. "Where can I reach you in London?"

St. James gave Harris his coordinates.

"I've met DCI Kingston there, but he wouldn't be handling the case himself," Harris said.

"No. DI Joy is the lead detective; fraud, murder and whatever else we find. DS Billings is handling the murder investigation for her. I'll brief both when we get back to London," St. James explained.

"Okay."

St. James looked off for a couple of beats, considering what he'd just learned. "How did Evans die?" he said.

"Before my time. But the file said it was suspicious. Poison of some sort."

"Hmm. Treated as a murder?" St. James pressed.

"At the time, yes. But Evans lived alone. Recluse. No suspects. No prints anywhere in the house other than her own. Her husband died of natural causes a couple of years before her. More or less a dead-end street, if you'll pardon the choice of words."

St. James gave up a wan smile. "What about assets? Was there a will?"

Harris shrugged. "Not according to the investigating officer's report."

St. James peered off once again, running scenarios through his head at a rapid-fire pace. "What happened to her home?"

"Don't know," Harris said. "With cases that lead nowhere, officers eventually lose interest, sometimes quickly, especially with no relatives or loved ones to push them, and interesting new cases come along."

"How come nobody knew about this?"

"From what you told me about the case, I think you answered your question."

"You mean because her brother wiped her out of the system?" St. James said.

"Yes. No next of kin noted in the file."

"So you never solved the case?"

"Still open."

"Where is she buried?"

"Let me see." Harris pulled up a couple of files and an app, then tapped in a series of letters and numbers and waited for the results.

"Cambridge City Cemetery," he said finally.

"Probably a large one. What's the easiest way to find a grave?"

"The graveyard's on Newmarket Road close to the airport. Just key in her name on the website. That tells you the section and grave number of burial plots."

St. James and Dozer rose to leave.

"Thanks for your help," St. James said, shaking Harris's hand. "We appreciate what you're doing for us."

"Happy to help."

Sitting in the Tucson, Dozer Googled the address for the cemetery. "Little over two miles from here. Ten minutes," he said. He found Evans on the website and noted the coordinates of her grave.

Fifteen minutes later, St. James and Dozer walked among the rows of headstones, reading epitaphs.

The lawns were beautiful, perfectly manicured, hedges and trees immaculately trimmed.

Even with Evans's grave coordinates, it took ten minutes for them to locate her plot. They stood for several minutes staring at her headstone.

"Barbara Marie Evans. Born April 28, 1969," Dozer read quietly. "Died April 28, 2019. Her fiftieth birthday, for Christ's sake! What's the likelihood of that?"

"Don't know, Dozer." St. James stared thoughtfully at the headstone.

When they'd processed what they could, they walked back to the Tucson, climbed in and sat quietly for a time.

"I don't know what to make of this," Dozer said finally.

"Neither do I."

Chapter 82

Dozer drove back to London so St. James could make some calls. He phoned Anna first to say they were on their way and the three would have dinner when he and Dozer arrived. Then he phoned Joy and Billings and put them on speaker so Dozer could hear. St. James gave a complete account of the interview with whomever, their meeting with Harris, and their time in the cemetery.

"This case gets crazier with every turn," Joy said when St. James got to the death of Barbara Evans. "So who the hell did you interview? And why was she impersonating Evans?"

"Don't know, Phyllis," he said as if trying to answer the same questions in his head.

Billings had been unusually quiet. "*I'm* the DS investigating Chamberlain's murder, not this Harris guy," he growled when St. James finished recounting the trip.

Dozer passed a string of vehicles on the M11, looked over at St. James and smiled when he heard Billings.

"Don't worry, Bert. You're the man. At the moment, Cambridge's lab isn't as busy as the Yard's. Fingerprint work will be quicker, and results sent to us right away. Besides, we'd have to include Harris if anything criminal happened in his jurisdiction," St. James countered.

Billings made a scoffing sound.

Dozer's smile widened.

"In any case, we'll have lab results soon, and we'll see where that takes us," Joy said, cutting off Billing's second rant before it gathered steam. "Drive safely. You're important to us. At least until this mess is cleaned up!" she said with a snicker.

Chapter 83

Anna chose Granaio Piccadilly for dinner that evening.

The night was warm and comfortable with a gentle breeze playfully tormenting her hair. Streets were filled with people enjoying the spectacular London evening. Anna noticed an older couple strolling arm in arm and subtly pointed them out to St. James, who gave her a quizzical look.

"Nothing," Anna said. "They're just kind of adorable."

Although the restaurant featured beautiful gothic architecture inside, the fabulous evening seduced them to take an outside table.

Cathy, a thin twenty-something server with blue hair, a nose ring and tattoos covering most of her visible body, came by with menus and asked what they'd like. They rhymed off preferences, and Cathy moved to a group of young people four tables away.

"Speaking of Cathy, have you heard from her lately?" Anna said to Dozer.

Dozer had met a server, also named Cathy, in Ottawa when he was working with St. James. At the time, Cathy had been finishing a master's degree at an Ottawa university. Dozer lived in Toronto and commuted to Ottawa to see her on weekends.

Dozer shrugged. "Flame burned out."

Anna shrugged too. "Happens."

St. James didn't wish to get involved in Dozer's love life. "How is Denzel doing?" he said to Dozer.

St. James had employed Denzel White, Dozer's brother, to watch Anna's apartment during a Canadian case. Denzel's dependability impressed St. James. Convinced Denzel was capable of more than watching apartments, St. James had sent him to a school in Texas to hone his skills.

"He's great, thanks to you, Hamilton," Dozer said proudly. "Has a cell now, calls me most days wondering when we can get together. He has a part-time job in an Ottawa grocery store but keeps asking when he can work with you again."

"There will be room for him when the right job comes along," St. James said. "You give me too much credit for Denzel's success. He made it happen himself. I just facilitated."

Dozer looked at St. James and smiled. "Stick to arrogance. It suits you better than trying to be humble."

The three laughed.

St. James looked at Anna. "Where did you and Carolyn go?"

Anna suddenly became animated. "We had a wonderful day. This morning, I arranged a fabulous tour for us on a hop-on hop-off bus. It was thrilling to see the city from the London Eye, although I was scared to death when we reached the top. Couldn't look down. We spent time in the magnificent gardens at Buckingham Palace. I had no idea they were so huge. Thirty-nine acres. Can you imagine? The guide said it takes eight full-time gardeners and two or three part-timers to maintain it all. And what's a tour of London without the Tower of London and Big Ben? By then we were hungry and decided on lunch at Balthazar in Covent Garden. The lobster spaghetti was out of this world. After lunch we went to Warner Brothers studio. That's where they created *Harry Potter*."

St. James and Dozer were enjoying Anna's enthusiasm more than the description of her tour.

Dozer looked at St. James. "I'm exhausted just listening to her."

Anna smiled.

Cathy arrived with drinks.

Anna looked at St. James. "Hamilton, you haven't said much about your day in Cambridge."

St. James gave Anna the abbreviated version of the interview with whomever — the Ruger SR22, meeting with DI Harris and the lab work he was doing for them.

"Wow!" Anna said. "Now you have someone impersonating Barbara Evans, living in the dead woman's house, presumably with cats that were once hers. Bizarre!"

"*Bizarre* isn't a strong enough word for this case," Dozer mumbled and guzzled beer.

"Do you think you'll have the lab results tomorrow?" Anna said.

St. James sampled more scotch. "Possibly."

"Depending on who the woman is and whether the gun was the one used for Chamberlain's murder, we could be close to wrapping this thing up," Dozer said hopefully.

"Hope so," Anna said. "I'm tired of living out of a suitcase."

Dozer smiled. "Little homesick myself."

Cathy returned and recorded food choices.

Anna said, "What's on for tomorrow?"

"If we don't hear from Harris, I'll begin summarizing the case," St. James said casually.

Dozer's brow furrowed. "How the hell can you do that? You won't have all the evidence! There's still stuff you don't know."

"I have a lot of it, and what I do have won't change with whatever Harris finds."

"How can you be so sure?" Dozer pressed.

"Because I know where I am going with this."

Dozer looked at Anna. "There he goes again!"

Anna shook her head in frustration.

They finished drinks, and St. James ordered wine.

When the food arrived, they ate in silence — Dozer contemplating how St. James could solve the case without lab results; Anna pondering getting the hell out of London; St. James considering the few bits left he needed to solve the case.

Chapter 84

It was now a little over a month since St. James and Smythe first landed at Heathrow to investigate Taylor Supermarkets' profit discrepancy. The team was tired and a quarter of an inch this side of cranky. St. James knew he'd face a morale issue if they stayed in London much longer.

Even Smythe, who was now back home, was anxious about being on standby, knowing St. James could call him back to the United Kingdom or Germany or God knows where, at a moment's notice.

Then there was John Taylor. Distraught over the cost of everything, Taylor was appeased only by St. James's explanation that he could recover some, if not all, losses from funds sitting in IEI's bank account. The cost-sharing agreement with Scotland Yard and the German police gave him some additional peace of mind. Even not completely secure, Taylor had a reasonably good chance of a positive outcome.

St. James knew Taylor was struggling with more than just potential financial losses. Frayed emotionally, he could be close to a nervous breakdown. That alone was pressure enough to solve the case quickly.

***

Anna went to the hotel gym the following morning. Dozer, not convinced St. James was entirely out of danger, patrolled the grounds looking for threats. St. James was holed up in the room waiting for DI Harris to report lab results on the Ruger and Chamberlain's photograph.

Shortly after eleven, St. James's cell buzzed.

"St. James."

"DI Harris."

"What did you find?" St. James said anxiously, grabbing a notepad.

Harris went through the lab report in detail. St. James made notes as Harris went along, asking several questions to ensure he received what Harris was attempting to transmit.

"Wow!" St. James said, his brow wrinkled most of the call. "Really? Are you sure about this?"

"Very sure," Harris said confidently. "I went over it three times with the lab people in painful detail. You have a lot at stake. I wasn't going to accept the findings at first blush. So I verbally beat every fact and assumption to death to ensure the results were solid."

"I am grateful for your help, DI Harris, and even more grateful for your thoroughness," St. James said happily. "Thank you so much."

"You're most welcome. Should I forward this to the Yard today?"

"Give me a couple of days, if you don't mind. I'd like to have time to put the case together in a logical and organized way. Sometimes findings told in pieces leads to confusion because recipients aren't hearing the complete story at once."

"I understand," Harris said, promising to wait.

They ended the call.

St. James went to the window and stared down at Coventry. The street was crammed with vehicles creeping like turtles. On the sidewalk, a cyclist sideswiped an elderly lady selling flowers, sending her basket and her bundles of bouquets flying in every direction. The lady was fine, but her income for the day was ruined, as the flowers were trampled by thoughtless pedestrians.

Taking it all in, St. James thought, *That's about as chaotic as this case.*

He moved back to the small desk and reviewed what Harris's people found.

"It's time," he said aloud.

He called Kingston. "Can you arrange a large meeting room?" he said when Kingston picked up.

"Hello to you too," Kingston said sarcastically.

"Sorry, David. I'm distracted."

"I gathered that. Why do you want a large meeting room?"

"I think it's time to tell everyone what happened."

"Huh," Kingston said. "I know it's no use asking. I learned that long ago. But remember, Joy and Billings won't be expecting a show. They'll expect to know whatever you're harbouring before everyone else does."

"I thought of that and decided to take the risk. If Billings knows what happened, he'll mess everything up at the meeting."

"Can't argue with that. But he'll do it anyway."

"Yeah, but he won't have the facts to bully his way through."

Kingston laughed. "He'll bully his way with or without facts."

"Fair enough. I'll work around him."

"Then there's Joy. You crossed her once. How do you think this will go down?"

"No problem. Didn't you say she had a thing for me?"

"That and two pounds will get you a coffee," Kingston said lightheartedly. "I'll arrange a meeting room. Then you're on your own. When do you want this?"

"Let's try for Friday morning."

"Okay, my assistant will confirm when she locks something down."

St. James made a list of who he wanted to invite. There was no sense going further than that until Kingston's assistant confirmed a time and location. He glanced at his watch. Twelve thirty.

Anna walked into the room, tired and sweaty from her visit to the gym.

"Good workout, babe?"

"Yeah, pushed myself hard today. Badly in need of a shower, I'm afraid. So don't come any closer. I'm starving. Can we eat after?" she said, heading for the bathroom.

"Absolutely."

In ten minutes, Anna was showered and dressed in light-blue shorts and a white top, and they went to the dining room for lunch.

"What did you do this morning, dear?" she said when they were seated.

St. James gave Anna the rundown on what he'd accomplished — case summary, call with Harris, and conversation with Kingston.

"So you know what happened?"

"Yep."

"I won't even ask."

"Good."

Chapter 85

When they'd finished lunch St. James went back to the room to make some calls. Before doing so he opened an email from Kingston's assistant. She'd booked ample space to accommodate forty people at the Leonardo Royal London Tower Bridge Hotel on Prescot Street for nine o'clock Friday morning. She arranged coffee, muffins, bottled water and lunch for attendees.

St. James emailed Kingston, Joy and Billings inviting them to the meeting, providing particulars about the time and location of the reservation. Two minutes later St. James's cell vibrated.

"What the hell is this about, Hamilton?" Joy said curtly.

"It's a meeting to reveal what happened," St. James said calmly.

"You *do* remember that *I'm* the lead detective on the case, not *you*. That maybe *I* should know what happened. That maybe *I* should be unfolding the case," she said, tone shuffling between anger and sarcasm.

St. James was determined to remain composed until Joy's anger burned itself out and did not try to argue the merits of his methods. That would only fuel her rage, drive it up, not down.

"I remember, Phyllis."

Joy went from rage to borderline pleading. "Then why are you doing this to me?"

"There're several people important enough to hear what happened directly, one on one. But I can only tell the complete story once," he said mildly.

"Not everyone is the DI in charge of the goddamn case!"

"I know, Phyllis. I know."

"So what in the heck—"

"It's complicated and very entwined. Unfolding it will take some time. It's not practical to spend hours and hours telling the same long story over and over."

Joy hung up without another word.

"Well, that went well," St. James said, placing his cell on the small desk.

Before he could pick up a file, the cell buzzed a second time.

"I don't have time for this showman shit!" Billings snapped.

"Sorry to hear that, Bert," St. James said disingenuously.

Billings paused, not knowing how to react. Then he roared, "Who killed Chamberlain?"

"You're the detective for Chamberlain's murder, you tell me," St. James toyed.

Billings slammed down the office phone.

"Doing really well, now," St. James said, laughing.

He didn't hear from Kingston, nor did he expect to. Having solved cases together, Kingston knew St. James's methods well. Not always amused by his penchant for unfolding crimes in front of an audience, he greatly respected the man's abilities.

When St. James called Taylor to invite him and his three vice presidents, he was surprised by the lack of enthusiasm.

"Is this meeting going to make me happy, Hamilton?" Taylor said sullenly.

St. James's forehead crumpled. "I don't know, John," he said slowly, unsure how to answer.

"Don't know?"

"You'll have to come on Friday and judge for yourself."

"The four of us will be there," Taylor said and ended the call.

St. James shook his head.

St. James called Randall and Collins. They agreed to be at the meeting without question.

"Why are you inviting me to this thing?" Goldstein said when St. James called.

"I think you'll find it quite interesting, Harvey."

"You remember I have a court case on the go?"

"Yes, I do. But your assistant said court wasn't sitting this Friday," St. James said, smiling inwardly.

"You spoke to her?"

St. James smiled again. "No sense inviting you if you had to be in court."

"Right ... makes sense, I guess," Goldstein said slowly, embarrassed St. James caught him in a lie. "I'll be there."

Next, St. James called Frank Keller.

"What can I do for you, Hamilton?"

"I thought you might want to know what happened."

Keller paused a beat. "Could be interesting."

"We're having a meeting at the Leonardo Royal London Tower Bridge Hotel on Prescot Street at nine a.m. this Friday. Love to have you there if you can make it."

"Give me a second to check my schedule," Keller said. Back on the call seconds later, he said, "Yeah, I can make it."

St. James's final call was to Daniel Scrivens.

"Why me?" Scrivens said pleasantly.

"You were one of Chamberlain's lawyers. I thought you'd be interested in knowing what happened. Randall and Collins said they would come if you were coming," St. James lied.

Scrivens paused. St. James assumed to check his calendar.

"If I can move a couple of things around, I guess I could make it," he said reluctantly.

"Hope you can, Daniel."

Finally, he emailed Weber in Hamburg and Smythe in Ottawa. Both agreed to join the meeting on Friday by Zoom.

St. James stood, walked to the window and peered down on Coventry once again.

"Well, they've all been invited. We'll see how many of them show."

Chapter 86

Everyone showed. It was nine fifteen Friday morning by the time they all arrived, grabbed a coffee and muffin from a side table and seated themselves in one of the forty-two aqua-coloured leather chairs in the Leonardo meeting room. Six rows of chairs faced a TV suspended from a white ceiling.

A pleasant floral scent gently enhanced the room's atmosphere.

Anna arranged a table and chair at the front of the room to oblige St. James and his files.

The front row arrived first. For the most part, they were friendlies — Dozer and Kingston for sure; Joy, not so much at the moment. Arms folded tightly across her chest, Joy's expression could have frightened a black mamba.

Next to Joy, Taylor sat stone-faced, wearing what looked like a mortician's suit.

Anna chatted briefly with Joy and then sat next to St. James, ready to fulfill whatever need arose during the meeting.

Taylor's three vice presidents looked nervous as they seated themselves in the second row, along with Harvey Goldstein and Frank Keller, both sporting grave faces.

St. James was surprised to see Lucas Vanderbilt with a clean-shaven face and freshly washed hair, neatly brushed.

Taylor ordered a cleanup.

Harvey Goldstein's dark-grey suit looked too large for his slight frame; a Woody Allen look-alike except for the large white-rimmed glasses and an annoying grin.

Next to Goldstein, Frank Keller sat staring blankly at the table.

In the second-last row, Randall, Collins and Scrivens were vigorously debating the pros and cons of a recent court decision.

Only the grumpy Bert Billings squatted in the back row.

No one wanted to be there.

Anna brought Weber and Smythe up on Zoom and cast them to the overhead screen.

They were ready to begin.

St. James was statesmanlike in a charcoal suit and crisp white shirt, accented by a solid-red tie. He stood, shoved one hand into his pocket and raised the other to garner attention.

"Good morning, ladies and gentlemen," he said. "We have a lot to cover. I want to get started if you don't mind. This is a complicated and confusing case, so I will explain a couple of things up front. Hopefully, that will help with your understanding as we move along.

"Ordinarily, when we're called in to investigate a company, we examine documentation and interview everyone inside who we think might be relevant to the case. If we interview people outside or track external documentation, it's usually to corroborate what we've already discovered inside the organization. Rarely do we commence two parallel, seemingly unrelated investigations early in a case, hoping the facts in each will eventually meet up and merge to solve the case. This, I am afraid, is one of those cases," St. James explained.

Joy sat with her arms crossed, staring icily into the middle distance.

"We began investigating Taylor Supermarkets in the usual way, internally. Then certain external events took place that were seemingly unrelated. But it was plausible they could eventually merge with the internal investigation. These events were too compelling to ignore, and this forced us into parallel internal and external investigations. I will do my best to clarify which case I am referring to as we go, but I urge your full attention and absolute focus to follow and understand the whole case to the end. Any questions?"

Some shook their heads. Others just sat staring. Joy and Billings rolled their eyes from different parts of the room.

"Okay," St. James continued. "The first week of July, DCI Kingston called me to discuss what appeared to be a discrepancy in Taylor's profit. Taylor's management team had conducted a financial investigation and found nothing significant. In the absence of inferior performance or accounting errors, the logical next step for Taylor was to look for possible wrongdoing of some sort.

"DCI Kingston arranged a conference call with John Taylor the following day, resulting in Louis Smythe, my computer expert, who you see up there on the screen" — St. James pointed to Smythe — "and me flying to London to investigate Taylor's issue. When we arrived, Louis spent considerable time with Lucas Vanderbilt, analyzing Taylor's computer systems. In doing so, he discovered an add-on computer program that Vanderbilt designed himself. We considered the possibility that this program could have a nefarious purpose, possibly to divert money from the company. Further investigation eliminated it as a threat. It was, as Vanderbilt described it, a program to enhance system performance."

"Is this relevant to Chamberlain's murder?" Billings bellowed from the back row. Everyone turned to eye the disrupter.

St. James's eyes shifted to the back of the room. "Folks, this is DS Bert Billings. He's in charge of Nigel Chamberlain's murder investigation."

A few people craned their necks, then turned back to St. James.

"Bert, it's important for everyone to follow the lead-up to the case. Without that, nothing will make sense to fresh eyes."

Billings made an unpleasant sound.

St. James continued. "Then, unbeknown to us at the time, we experienced the first of a series of unrelated external events. Someone kidnapped Louis. At that point, we had no idea why Louis would be a target and to what end."

James pointed to Dozer in the front row. "Using apps to track Louis's cell phone, Dozer and I followed the kidnappers to a rundown house near Camden Station. When we overpowered them, we learned they worked for Wilhelm Schneider and Harry Fischer, senior management for International Enterprises Inc., or IEI, located in Gundelsheim, Germany. After a little persuasion, the two told us Fischer was IEI's CEO, and Schneider was, for want of a better term, Fischer's VP of Torture."

Snickers ran through the room.

"Schneider hired the kidnappers to steal a laptop belonging to Nigel Chamberlain, a wealthy businessman here in London, known as an importer/exporter of goods from East and Southeast Asia, according to the two thugs, anyway. They did manage to steal Chamberlain's laptop but weren't smart enough to open it. So, following Louis's kidnapping, we concluded Schneider, the man in charge of the caper, searched for someone capable of decrypting data vaults.

"To do so, he must have waded through countless websites, searched curriculum vitaes, and Googled who he thought was the most capable to enter and reveal the contents of computer hard drives without knowing the necessary security information. No doubt he found many people who could do the job. So I asked myself, why would he pick Louis out of a class of many? Even though I know Louis's capabilities well, I thought the answer may lie in Googling him myself, try to evaluate him through the eyes of someone looking for an advanced skill. Not surprisingly it showed Louis working with me, helping to detect fraud. So an expert known for detecting fraud would have considerable knowledge about how it was committed. Schneider would most likely see that as a valuable asset, perhaps even for the long run if Louis could be persuaded to join the dark side. Not knowing Louis, he wouldn't be expecting his resolve. When Louis refused to help, they beat him badly. But Louis was steadfast, held on without giving in until Dozer and I got there to rescue him. I am proud of his resilience," St. James said, glancing up at a smiling Smythe.

St. James opened a bottled water and drank some.

"How would Schneider discover Louis was in London?" Collins said.

"I don't know," St. James said. "I suppose once he settled on the best candidate, he would investigate everything about the person — where they lived, travels, habits, that sort of thing, trying to plan the best time and place to kidnap the person."

Collins nodded.

St. James continued. "As I mentioned, we came to London to be of service to Taylor only. Louis's kidnapping hit us from left field, not from the internal investigation into Taylor's business itself. Before Louis was kidnapped, there was no indication of anything out of the ordinary in Taylor's business, and we thought we might have come to London to find wrong where wrong didn't exist, that Taylor was paying us for nothing. This notion was helped along by another discovery I will explain in a few minutes.

"From here on, the case splits into two, an internal and external investigation, mushrooming into the bizarre."

Chapter 87

"Are we going to get to a point soon?" Billings blurted.

"Not if you keep interrupting, Bert," St. James said.

Joy smiled at St. James's quick retort.

"We brought the stolen laptop back to police headquarters. And the next day, Louis entered the data vault."

In the second-last row, Randall's hand went up.

"Lisa."

"If Louis's kidnapping hit you from left field, as you put it, how did you connect it with your work at Taylor in the first place?" she said.

"Excellent question. The answer is — I didn't!"

A look of wonder swept the room.

"We'd only been in the UK for a couple of days, and we spent those days entirely at Taylor's head office. Louis didn't know anyone here. He'd never been to Britain, so he couldn't have made enemies, at least not yet. And he's not wealthy or famous, so ransom as a reason for kidnapping didn't make sense. In the absence of any other information at that time, we thought Louis might be getting close to something at Taylor's that someone didn't want him to find. It was only later we learned Louis was picked for his computer skills, not for the knowledge of Taylor's business."

Randall nodded.

St. James continued. "When Louis entered the data vault, he found proof the laptop did belong to Nigel Chamberlain, just as the kidnappers said. Data showed £50 million hidden somewhere, with no clue as to where or why."

Several people helped themselves to water bottles while St. James added the next piece of the puzzle.

"You would only hide money to keep it from the authorities, a divorce lawyer or Revenue and Customs. Chamberlain wasn't married, so that ruled out divorce as a reason. Revenue and Customs had opened a file on him but not because of Chamberlain himself. This gentleman tipped them off," St. James said, pointing to Weber up on the screen. "Noah Weber is a senior investigator in the Federal Criminal Police Office in Hamburg."

Weber raised a hand to acknowledge the introduction.

"Noah opened a file on Harry Fischer and Wilhelm Schneider some years before, discovered a loose connection with Chamberlain here in Britain and asked the British government for help, so your government opened the file on Chamberlain to accommodate a request from Germany."

St. James said, "We are now in the external investigation. Noah believed Fischer was somehow defrauding companies through IEI but couldn't prove it because his technical people couldn't break into IEI's security system, which Fischer vainly referred to as Fischerlock. So at that point, we knew there was a potential link between Fischer and Chamberlain, but not with Taylor. And Chamberlain was becoming of interest to us because of Louis's kidnapping and what he found on Chamberlain's computer."

"But that had nothing to do with my company," Taylor said defensively.

"No, it didn't, John. But when DI Joy and I found Chamberlain lying on a bedroom floor with both hands missing and eight bullets in his chest, we felt a need to go further. To leave it there without ruling out a connection with you would have left a huge hole in the investigation."

Taylor nodded.

"The external investigation shifted our focus outside Taylor to the affairs of Fischer, IEI and Chamberlain."

"I don't see why you went down this path to begin with," Randall said, "other than to satisfy a curiosity that stemmed from a laptop that had nothing to do with Taylor Supermarkets."

"Your comment is an excellent one, Lisa," St. James said with a slight smile. "Given what we knew at the time, I was running on instinct, gambling that the hidden £50 million referred to on Chamberlain's laptop would somehow have something to do with Taylor's lost profit; a longshot at the time, I admit. The instinct led to a theory that something external could have harmed Taylor's business."

"Big gamble on your part," Randall mused.

"Yes, it was. But extremely complicated cases always begin with an instinct of some sort that eventually incubates into a theory if plausible information continues to breathe life into it. If I waited for hard facts and evidence to appear on its own before making a move, I would never solve anything."

Randall nodded slowly.

"Let's move on, Hamilton," Kingston said anxiously.

St. James agreed and returned to his notes. "The encrypted data noted Chamberlain instructed Randall and Collins to open two large safety deposit boxes in Zurich and make several trips to deposit packages. Randall and Collins never knew the contents of those packages but assumed they contained money because of their size and shape. More on this later."

Henry Collins concurred.

"The day after Chamberlain's murder, DI Joy and I" — St. James pointed to Joy in the front row — "went to Chamberlain's flat to conduct a more thorough search and were surprised we didn't find a cell phone. There wasn't one on Chamberlain's person or in his Rolls Royce. No cell was significant, especially for an international businessperson expected to communicate daily around the world."

"A closet full of women's clothes, size thirty-nine, was also a surprise find. A mixture of *E. coli* and low concentrations of hydrogen peroxide had damaged whatever DNA might have been there. Someone didn't want the clothes traced to them and knew how to prevent it chemically.

"No prints were found anywhere in the flat other than Chamberlain's and his housekeeper. And Chamberlain didn't have a girlfriend that Anna, my research assistant sitting next to me," he said, gesturing to Anna, "could determine. So the women's clothing was a mystery. More on this later too."

Billings let out a weird cough from the back — it sounded like he was saying "more later" while clearing his throat. St. James shot him a look and continued.

"The flat's small office contained the usual office paraphernalia. But we also found correspondence with Frank Keller." St. James pointed to Keller in the second row. "But Keller's correspondence was only a social exchange and added nothing to the case."

Keller smiled.

"After DI Joy and I finished with the flat, we drove to Chamberlain's primary residence in Wimbledon. As you would expect of a wealthy man, it was a huge mansion on an expensive street. Jones, Chamberlain's butler, delivered a grand tour of the place. Afterward, we landed in a study many times the size of the one in Chamberlain's Knightsbridge flat. And that's where we spent most of the time.

"When asked, Jones said Chamberlain had a cell, but that he'd given it up temporarily because it was dominating his life. Chamberlain wanted the odd day free of it altogether. On those days, Jones kept the cell in a wall safe. I spent time scrolling through text messages between Chamberlain and Schneider on the cell. Everything had been copied to Fischer. But stealing the laptop was confusing because Schneider's end of the exchange talked of doing business with Chamberlain. So why steal a partner's laptop if you want to do more business? It wasn't until much later that we learned Fischer and Schneider suspected Chamberlain of skimming funds that should have been transferred to IEI. The laptop was meant to prove whether Chamberlain actually was skimming.

"So now we had an additional connection between Fischer, Schneider and Chamberlain, and it was beginning to feel like Chamberlain might have been running UK fraud activity for Fischer's IEI."

"Skimming's a pretty good motive for murder," Joy offered, beginning to thaw as the meeting progressed.

"Certainly is," Collins agreed.

"If Fischer murdered Chamberlain, why are we spending all this time?" Keller said, checking his watch.

Goldstein, Collins and Randall nodded in agreement with Keller.

"We are spending all this time because this is a long, complicated and difficult case, and I've only just begun," St. James said authoritatively. "There are many surprises yet to come."

Chapter 88

Whispers washed over the room.

"Guess I'm not the only one thinking this is a waste of time, St. James," Billings said with a smirk of satisfaction.

St. James ignored Billings. "The cell wasn't the only thing we found in the wall safe," he said. "There was a second laptop. Louis examined it, as did Herb Johnson of Scotland Yard, and found two independent data sections within the hard drive, delivering two very different messages.

"One section contained what looked like legitimate business transactions for an import/export business. We suspected that was for show if authorities ever wanted proof Chamberlain actually was in the import/export business."

"The other section was a coded narrative Louis and Johnson eventually unravelled. They discovered Quantum, Chamberlain's operating company, had entered into a joint venture with IEI called ConQuest, one of many joint ventures managing similar fraud schemes in countries around the world. Quantum was responsible for managing UK fraud schemes. Keller reported to Quantum for some UK fraud schemes, and Quantum reported to IEI for all UK operations."

Keller stiffened. "I told you I had nothing to do with fraud anywhere," he said bluntly. "I was responsible for procurement from East and Southeast Asia, nothing more."

Taylor's three VPs remained stone-faced.

Eyes drifted to Keller.

Collins interjected with a puzzled look. "You keep referring to schemes. Some of us have no idea what you're talking about."

"Okay, Henry," St. James said and then looked around the room. "I wasn't planning to go through this until later, but now is as good a time as any.

"Think of the external investigation as having discovered a fraud pyramid. Harry Fischer sits at the top of IEI, Wilhelm Schneider immediately below. The world was divided into six sectors, according to the geographic proximity of each country. Sector chiefs managed fraud ventures in their sector and reported to Schneider on mandated swindle targets. They recruited country leaders who, in turn, organized companies within their country into smaller groups managed by local managers. It was a structure mirroring legitimate worldwide businesses with responsibility and power cascading from the very top, down to the lowest levels of an organization."

"Fischer defrauded 1,729 companies in fifty-seven countries."

"Sweet Jesus!" Randall blurted.

"I have photographs of the pyramid scheme in chart format." St. James handed pictures to Taylor and asked him to pass them on when he finished with them. "My verbal explanation doesn't do the complicated scheme justice, so the pictures circulating the room now will help with your understanding."

"I can't believe the magnitude," Collins said, shaking his head.

"I believe it to be the world's largest fraud scheme, billions in US dollars defrauded in relatively insignificant amounts, from 1,729 companies, monthly," St. James said.

"How was money extracted at the company level?" Scrivens asked.

"Companies Fischer wanted IEI to defraud were referred to as *targets*. Together with sector chiefs, country leaders developed detailed plans to successfully onboard a target. They took into account its revenue, earnings stability, and the amount of cash they could safely pilfer. IEI created a program to manage all this and assess the risk of extorting funds from each target without drawing suspicion from the target's management. Quite ingenious, actually," St. James said with a hint of admiration.

"Sweet Jesus," Randall said again.

The front row smiled at Randall's repetitive response.

"After they selected a target, how would they get away with actually executing the fraud?" Goldstein wondered aloud.

"Any one of several ways, Harvey," St. James said. "Fischer had scouts searching for disgruntled employees or those who may have overextended themselves with credit and needed extra cash, employees with the power to divert funds. In other instances, an IEI person would get a job with the target's cleaning or maintenance company or any other service having to be physically on-premises to deliver what the target purchased. Then all they had to do was insert a flash drive with a program that would somehow siphon or divert funds. A lot of diverse ways."

St. James stopped to drink water. "Let's take a ten-minute break. Please be back no later than ten forty-five," St. James requested.

Pandemonium ensued, chairs moving, people talking at once.

St. James thought he finally had their attention. Even Billings looked less crotchety.

Ain't heard nothin' yet.

Chapter 89

When the room cleared, three hotel staff in black uniforms with white lacy collars rushed in to remove dirty coffee cups, used napkins and other debris, and then brought in replacements and a second large container of coffee.

It was ten fifty by the time St. James herded the last straggler into the room.

Taking his place at the front of the room, St. James said, "Now I'd like to go back to what all this has to do with Taylor Supermarkets, the internal investigation."

He gestured to Taylor's VP finance, who now sat in a middle row. "At the beginning of each year, Cindy Woods prepares a profit forecast for Taylor to review and approve. Taylor focuses on the expectations for revenues and expenses and whether they're realistic for the coming year. An approved forecast becomes his benchmark to compare to actual financial performance. This is normal management procedure. When Taylor made the comparison halfway through this year, he discovered actual profit fell short of forecast by £185,000. It was this shortfall that triggered our involvement.

"When I analyzed the forecast, I discovered a major error. Several subtotals were double counted, artificially creating a greater difference between forecast and actual profit, giving the illusion of lost profit when there wasn't any. It looked like we ran up a huge bill trying to find something that wasn't there."

Woods hung her head.

Scrivens interjected. "Why didn't you end the investigation right there?"

"Without the external investigation, I would have ended the internal one then for sure. There was no indication of wrongdoing in Taylor at that point, only a faulty forecast creating the illusion. But I was too far along with the external investigation to let the internal one go."

Scrivens nodded.

"Then Louis's internal investigation resulted in a hard-earned breakthrough. After days grinding through Taylor's systems, he came across a well-disguised application — Pay Validation. It had no affiliation with a known manufacturer. To Louis, that's like waving a red flag in front of a bull. He runs every test, tracking software, and fraud detection program until an app is proven to be a threat or deemed harmless. After four fourteen-hour days, he found Pay Validation processed purchase orders and payments for only one particular supplier. Back to this in a few moments."

The room stirred.

"We met with Randall and Collins on two occasions. The first was immediately after Chamberlain's death when they confirmed Chamberlain asked them to open two safety deposit boxes in Zurich and make several trips to deposit multiple packages. We asked if they saw anyone suspicious. Henry said no, but Lisa had a faint recollection of a man wearing a long grey coat, matching hat, and aviator sunglasses, first at Heathrow, then walking between the UBS and Credit Suisse in Zurich. I thought nothing of it at the time. But I did later."

St. James glanced at Randall and Collins, who were seated together and following the presentation without expression.

"We met Randall and Collins the second time to arrange a visit to the Zurich safety deposit boxes to see what the packages contained. Lisa, DI Joy and I made the trek to the two Swiss banks. Dozer was in Germany working on the IEI external investigation but arranged to meet us in Zurich for the package unveiling. So the four of us entered UBS, and Lisa arranged access to the safety deposit box. For a brief time, we stood around, as nervous as a cat in a pack of dingoes," he said and got a small ripple of laughter. "When Lisa finally began pulling wrappers from packages, our jaws dropped."

St. James drank water.

Kingston smiled at his timing.

"Don't just leave us hanging, man," Goldstein said.

"Every package in both banks contained nothing but plain white paper cut to the size and shape of pound notes."

Gasps swept the room.

Scrivens was astounded. "Why in God's name would Chamberlain do that?"

"To make whoever may be following him think the money was out of their reach, locked in the Swiss banking system. Chamberlain even had the lawyers take some packages from one bank and place them in the other, all for show. A diversion."

"So at this point, we don't know where the money is?" Keller said cautiously.

"Correct," St. James said.

"At this point, we have a dead end on the money location. The Pay Validation program is being worked by Louis, as yet without a conclusion, and the IEI-Fischer-Schneider-Chamberlain relationship is confirmed by the external investigation but with no proven connection to Taylor," St. James recounted.

"What happened to Fischer and Schneider?" Collins said curiously.

"Short version. Schneider captured Dozer outside IEI's headquarters in Gundelsheim, Germany, yanked him inside to face justice at the hand of Fischer. Fischer couldn't decide what to do with him, so he had Schneider lock him in the basement until they could decide. But Dozer managed to escape and provide Noah with the evidence he needed for a court order to shut IEI down. To that point, no one other than an IEI employee had ever set foot inside IEI's head office. Being captured allowed Dozer to see the operation and what Fischer's computers were processing, and it wasn't East and Southeast Asian trading transactions. It was money flowing in from sector chiefs and joint ventures, money defrauded from the 1,729 companies in fifty-seven countries. They broke their own rule when they forced Dozer inside the fraud centre, bringing down an otherwise brilliant operation."

"Sounds stupid to me," said Randall.

Joy chimed in with a smile. "Certainly was."

Weber spoke on Zoom for the first time. "Fischer and Schneider have been charged. They're facing twenty to twenty-five years in prison," he said. "Thanks to Hamilton and his team."

"Good!" everyone said in unison.

Chapter 90

St. James wiped his brow with a handkerchief that matched his tie.

"Back to the external investigation. Some of you may not know Chamberlain had a sister, Barbara, married name Evans, living in Cambridge. Initial research showed Chamberlain didn't have a living relative. DS Billings discovered Evans when he interviewed Scrivens."

Everyone looked at Scrivens, who sat stone-faced, watching St. James.

"Chamberlain hired Scrivens to eradicate Barbara from every legal registry, tax roll and repository he could find because she was the sole beneficiary of their father's will. Chamberlain had received no inheritance from his father, infuriating him beyond logic and driving him to demand that his sister become nonexistent, at least on paper. I don't know how you did it, Daniel, nor do I want to. It's not relevant to the case."

Scrivens nodded.

"There was a second reason Chamberlain came to you, Daniel. And that was to obtain an opinion concerning a potential threat from Keller."

Keller stiffened again.

Scrivens nodded.

"Chamberlain owed you over a million pounds, Frank, and you threatened to go to the authorities if he didn't pay immediately. Chamberlain went to Scrivens to determine his exposure to criminal charges should Keller rat him out. Scrivens advised, and quite rightly so, that it was a commercial, not a criminal, matter."

Joy interjected, "But don't forget, Hamilton, we still consider the debt owing to Keller as a motive for him to kill Chamberlain."

Keller was visibly perturbed but sat still, arms crossed over his chest.

St. James drank water and eyed the room. "Okay, folks, that's Barbara and Nigel's sibling story. In and of itself, it sounds irrelevant, but it's important to the understanding of what comes later."

St. James looked at his watch. "What are hotel staff saying about luncheon arrangements, Anna?"

"Sandwiches, sweets, and hot and cold drinks will be here in twenty minutes."

"I'll try to arrive at a logical break for lunch." St. James paused to check his notes. "Okay, at this point in our external investigation, we have Fischer and Schneider out of the way, IEI shut down and all its cash secured in Hamburg by

Noah's people. We have Chamberlain and Evans's sibling relationship parked for the moment. And the internal investigation produced the Pay Validation program Louis found on Taylor's system."

St. James looked at the screen with Louis on it and then at Anna.

"Louis discovered the only company to transact through Pay Validation was Baker Sugars, a supplier of cookies, cakes and other sweets. Anna's research showed that a numbered company owned Baker. And the numbered company owning Baker was partially owned by three other numbered companies. Harvey incorporated all four. Of course, lawyers for anonymous companies won't divulge who the actual beneficial owners are. Otherwise, there wouldn't be anonymity. So when I asked Harvey for the beneficial owners, he couldn't say."

Goldstein smiled.

"In addition to Anna's research on Baker Sugars, Louis analyzed their website. He quickly discovered that the site lacked a valid trust certificate and was not secure. Louis found several spelling errors as well. The president of Baker was a woman named Francis O'Ceileachair. Louis could never reach her or any other live person at Baker. All this fostered considerable suspicion."

St. James paused to see if everyone was following him. When he saw a few blank faces, he moved to reassure them.

"These story bits and pieces seem confusing, I know, but each segment has to be brought to a certain level before they all knit together to make sense of the case."

Several heads nodded after the word *confusion*.

"This brings us back to the external investigation, to Chamberlain's murder. The lab people advised DI Joy and DS Billings the eight bullets found in Chamberlain's chest came from a Ruger SR22. For those of you unfamiliar with firearms, it's a model used mainly for target practice. Not the first choice of a professional killer. So DS Billings looked into Ruger SR22s purchased in the last six months, thinking the killer might be a first-time gun owner, buying for the sole purpose of killing Chamberlain."

Billings puffed himself up a bit and cleared his throat. St. James caught his little performance and kept going.

"There were three such purchases. DS Billings and I interviewed the three separately, and independently eliminated them as suspects. Each purchaser provided their contact list so DS Billings could determine if anyone had a connection to Chamberlain. DS Billings found no connections with Chamberlain. However, when I interviewed the new Ruger owners, I learned that one of them, Nancy Sweet, had overlooked two names on her contact list for DS Billings. More about this in a few minutes."

"This is impossible to follow, St. James," Billings barked. "There is no conclusion on anything. Everything is, *more later*."

St. James smiled. "That's what makes the case so complicated and why I asked you all here, so I would only have to explain it once. For those of you annoyed with me for not giving you a preview, perhaps you can now understand why I had to do it this way."

Joy avoided eye contact with St. James.

"Keep in mind, at this point, we don't know where the money is hidden or even if there is money to hide. All we have to go by is a few notes on Chamberlain's computer. We don't know why Chamberlain's hands were severed either." St. James continued. "It wasn't long before Chamberlain's hands showed up at Scotland Yard in a box addressed to DI Joy."

Joy cringed.

"The lab confirmed the fingerprints from the hands were, in fact, Chamberlain's but found no other prints on the box or on the note that came with the hands. The note read, *I heard the Yard was short-staffed. Thought you could use a couple of extra hands.*"

St. James studied faces around the room as he read the note. Some snickered, some looked appalled, others projected no emotion.

"Good thing the prints were Chamberlain's," Billings said with a grin. "Hate to think there's someone else walking around handless."

Dead silence followed Billings's tasteless remark, embarrassing to everyone but Billings himself.

St. James went on. "When DI Joy and I discussed the case, we concluded we'd overlooked a potentially large part of the external investigation. When Jones had given us the mansion tour, we had paid no attention to the cellar. So we returned to Wimbledon that afternoon to explore that space."

"The cellar had three separate rooms — a junk room, a cold room for food and another for wine. One by one, we went through each room, looking for openings, hidden doors, loose bricks or any other sign of a potential secret compartment where someone could hide money. It wasn't until we got to the wine room that we discovered a hidden area, purely by accident. When I pushed on two bottles stored in rack holders that were shaped differently than all of the others along the same wall, a portion of the wall slowly receded, revealing an inner door."

St. James didn't let hotel staff setting up lunch break his stride. "When I examined the door, wiping away soot and grime, I discovered a round patch resembling an eye on the right side of the door. At that moment, I knew precisely why Chamberlain's hands were severed."

The clinking of plates and cutlery being placed by staff grew louder.

"Good time to break for lunch," St James said.

Chapter 91

After lunch, everyone returned to their exact places. St. James flipped through notes for a few beats and then began. Still referring to the external investigation, he said, "The following day, we had millions of pounds removed from Chamberlain's cellar."

"Where is it now?" Keller interjected quickly.

"Safely stored in Her Majesty's vaults at the Bank of England. So the mystery of the hidden money's now solved. It did exist, and it was hidden.

"When the team waded through the Fischerlock security system, they uncovered every company Fischer had ever swindled. Now we are at the point where the internal and external investigations began to merge, validating the theory that Fischer and Taylor were somehow connected. Taylor Supermarkets was one of the companies Fischer defrauded.

"Chamberlain was the UK country leader for Fischer. But he had too many companies to manage by himself to ensure the fraud would go off without a hitch. So Chamberlain grouped smaller companies under local managers."

St. James's look toward Keller was sharp and piercing. "And you, sir, were one of those local managers, with fifteen company frauds under your tutelage, including Taylor Supermarkets," St. James said forcefully to emphasize the point.

Keller jumped to his feet. "This is outrageous!" he said aggressively in his thick Scottish accent. "You have no right to make such foul, unsubstantiated allegations. You have no proof. I didn't come here to be accused of something I didn't do. I'm out of here!"

DCI Kingston leapt to his feet. "Mr. Keller," he said calmly, "we'll be holding you for an interview under caution, pending further investigation. I suggest you sit down."

Keller thought the better of bolting and returned to his seat.

"Thank you," Kingston said.

St. James continued his focus on Keller. "I said earlier that the CEO of Baker Sugars was a woman named Francis O'Ceileachair. Not so. No woman with that name exists. But there is a man with that name, Frank, and that man is you! One of the many translations of the Gaelic surname O'Ceileachair is Keller."

The room gasped again.

"Thinking yourself clever by calling Baker Sugar's CEO Francis O'Ceileachair was a huge mistake. You thought a Gaelic surname no one could pronounce would go unnoticed. I can't tell you how many cases I've solved because of vain decisions like that."

The room broke into chatter.

Keller stared at the floor while Billings sat forward on the edge of his chair, now fully engaged.

St. James brought the room to order. "Taylor issued purchase orders to Baker Sugars to purchase goods," he said. "The fact that Pay Validation processed purchase orders and payments only for Baker Sugars and no other supplier was significant."

"Something else would have to be behind it," Randall said.

"And there certainly was, Lisa!" St. James said. He paused to drink water, and then looked up at them all. Taylor stared forward blankly, white as a ghost. St. James thought the man might faint.

"Early in the internal investigation, Anna researched Taylor's three vice presidents."

The second row re-entered the present from wherever their minds had been.

"Anna discovered several things. Daniel Sauvé had a car accident years ago, rendering a woman paralyzed. Settlement with her family wiped him out financially. Woods's husband has trouble holding a job. And the woman who raised Vanderbilt is cared for in a nursing home in Utrecht.

"The woman who was paralyzed is named Gerda Wagner. She's still alive in a long-term care home in Munich. The German government covers seventy-five percent of Wagner's health-care costs, and private insurance pays fifteen percent." St. James eyed Sauvé. "You cover the remaining ten percent, Daniel, either by an upfront settlement or an ongoing subsidy."

Sauvé remained stone-faced.

"During our interview, you referred to Wagner's health costs as an ongoing financial strain. So you either borrowed money for a settlement and were paying back the loan or regularly paid a subsidy to the home. Doesn't matter. Both are ongoing obligations and a strain on your cash flow. Money has to be tight, Daniel! Other sources of cash would be tempting, for sure. To clarify, you had motive to organize a fraud at Taylor's — but you didn't."

Sauvé's eyes never met St. James's, his ice-cold look focused at the front of the room.

St. James paused and turned to Woods.

"Your husband spends most of the time in pubs and can't keep a job. You have to raise the children on your own. Most young couples have to be two-income families to make ends meet. You're paid well but not enough to cover the cost of living, raising children in this society on your own. And not only does your husband not contribute to household expenses, but you have to be giving him money for pubs. Otherwise, he couldn't go. That's a double whammy on your cash flow. No money coming in from him, just money going out for his drink. To survive, you must be using one credit card to make minimum payments on another. Amounts on both cards have to be increasing monthly. You have motive to organize a theft at Taylor's too. But you didn't."

Woods broke down in tears.

St. James turned to Vanderbilt.

"Anna researched Utrecht nursing homes and found only one Visser, Hanna Visser, in the Bartholomeus Gasthuis, a beautiful facility. When I spoke with the administrator, she said you visited her several times. You contribute financially to her care. You had motive to steal from Taylor too. But you didn't."

John Taylor hadn't moved for forty-five minutes. He was pale as a corpse and almost catatonic.

"Where does all this lead us?" said a puzzled Goldstein.

"Well, Harvey, each VP had the motive to organize a fraud for Keller, but as I said, not one of them instigated a swindle."

Chapter 92

The room turned into chaos.

"This has gone on long enough," Billings bellowed.

"I've got clients to tend to, two I postponed to attend this circus," Scrivens said sharply.

"Us too," said Randall and Collins in unison.

"I have a lot of preparation for Monday court. I don't have time for all this. When I agreed to come, I couldn't imagine it taking more than an hour. So far, we've wasted most of the day," Goldstein grumbled.

The VPs' faces remained solemn, dour.

St. James quickly raised a hand. "Folks, please. Settle down. We're getting close to the end."

With everyone feeding off one another's grumbling, it took five minutes for the room to settle.

Suddenly John Taylor passed out, fell forward and smashed his head on the corner of the desk St. James was using.

The room succumbed to loud turmoil.

"Call an ambulance!" Joy yelled.

Within seconds, DCI Kingston was at Taylor's side. Taylor had crumpled to the floor and was bleeding from the forehead.

St. James tapped the UK emergency number, 999. The paramedics arrived ten minutes later.

"I'll make sure they look after you, John," Kingston told his friend. "Don't worry. They're taking you to emergency. I'll be there as quick as I can."

Taylor was beginning to come around but could only nod.

"Blood pressure's very high," one paramedic said, looking at a reading.

They whisked Taylor into the back of the ambulance and sped away in the direction of the Royal London Hospital, lights flashing, siren blasting.

"I pray he's all right," St. James said.

"Me too. This whole thing has been enormously difficult for him emotionally," Kingston said.

Everyone was talking at once and expressing their concern for Taylor when Kingston stood and faced the room.

"Please," he said, trying to keep the group calm. "The best thing we can do for John now is to finish this thing this afternoon, right now, without him, so he doesn't have to listen to any more."

Everyone agreed, but not without a few grumbles.

Kingston turned to St. James. "Hamilton, please continue," he said and sat down.

"We have Taylor paying Baker Sugars ostensibly for food purchases. But who benefits?" St. James turned to Harvey Goldstein. "When we spoke on the phone the first time, I told you I was doing work for Taylor Supermarkets, and you asked what I was doing for John Taylor, not Taylor Supermarkets. You gave John's full name. I asked if you knew him." St. James picked up a notepad to read verbatim: "You said, *Not really. I met Taylor once at a party. Know a couple of senior people working over there.*" He looked up from his notepad. "There are only three senior people at Taylor's, the three whose personal financial troubles we just discussed.

"It's a matter of public record that you incorporated four numbered companies with ownership directly or indirectly in Baker Sugars. We know Keller is the CEO of Baker Sugars. We also know Baker Sugars' website is poorly worded, without a trusted certificate and not secure. And there wasn't a live person to speak with there. Boiling everything down, it's a fake website for a fake company."

People shifted in their seats, trying to absorb it all.

St. James stared at Goldstein. "Harvey, although you're not obligated to tell us who the beneficial owner of the numbered company is, please think long and hard about what I'm about to say," St. James cautioned. "What do you think a well-informed judge would say if you withheld the names of beneficial owners in the largest international multi-country fraud scheme in history. Hundreds of companies bilked billions of dollars."

St. James let the question hang in the air before answering. "I think that judge would say, 'Do I want to be the judge who allows someone to profit from a fraud scheme because he hides behind a set of numbers called a company? Do I want to prevent the distribution of stolen funds to the rightful owners?' My bet, Harvey, is that the judge would do the right thing, and that you'd be on the losing side if you withheld the names of the beneficial owners."

St. James stared at Goldstein, who appeared to be disintegrating inside.

"Judges are human too," St. James said. "They don't want to have their decisions overturned or heralded as a precedent for every scumbag trying to weasel out of a criminal charge. They want to be known for making good law. If that's not enough, think about what the papers would write about you. Not worth it, Harvey," St. James concluded.

With every word emanating from St. James's mouth, Goldstein's face grew tighter and more troubled. He licked his dry lips. No matter his decision, Goldstein knew he couldn't avoid stark criticism.

Chapter 93

Goldstein was silent for what seemed an eternity. He weighed the potential force of anger from peers, every solicitor who had created anonymous companies for trusting clients. Those solicitors would face rage from clients who were beneficial owners of their companies; clients fearful of being exposed to the world. So revealing who was behind the numbered company that owned Baker Sugars was not a decision for Goldstein to take lightly.

Goldstein thought of the oath he took when he became a solicitor: *I will protect my independence as a lawyer, uphold the rule of law and act at all times with integrity. I will justify the confidence and trust that is placed in me by my clients, the courts, the public and by my profession.* Goldstein was facing a moral dilemma, a conflict between upholding the rule of law and maintaining the confidence and trust placed in him by his clients. As hard as it was, it all came down to the words — *protect my independence as a lawyer ... uphold the rule of law ... confidence and trust that is placed in me by the courts, the public and by my profession.* The more he thought, the more those words overcame the noise in his head.

So engrossed in his internal debate was he, Goldstein hadn't noticed everyone was up, milling about, getting coffee, waiting for him to say something.

Goldstein stood slowly, hesitated for a time and then spoke. "Frank Keller," he managed to squeak out in a weak voice.

The room went silent.

"I couldn't quite hear you, Harvey," St. James said hopefully.

"Frank Keller is the beneficial owner of the numbered company that owns Baker Sugars," Goldstein said finally in a loud and clear voice. He sat down and, for a time, stared blankly at the floor, wondering what he had just unleashed on himself.

Losing all hope, Keller leaned forward and buried his head in his hands.

Everyone took their seat.

"Thank you, Harvey — for doing the right thing," St. James said slowly. "To save time, Harvey, can we agree the three numbered companies with partial ownership in Keller's numbered company are beneficially owned by Sauvé, Woods and Vanderbilt?"

Goldstein nodded slowly.

Woods began to sob. Sauvé and Vanderbilt maintained their icy stares.

The room gasped.

"At this point," St. James said, "we have to return to the internal investigation because it makes sense to explain who has the authority to commit Taylor Supermarkets to liabilities, authorize payments, and at what level.

"Any one of the three VPs can approve purchases and payments up to £2,000; from £2,000 to £6,000 requires the signature of Cindy Woods as VP finance plus one other VP; from £6,000 to £9,000 requires all three VPs to approve; anything over that demands John Taylor's signature.

"Louis's review showed no purchases or payments transacted with Baker less than £6,000 or more than £9,000. That meant no one VP could have approved a purchase transaction. All were within the range requiring the three vice presidents to sign off. If the three tried to approve more than £9,000, Taylor would catch it."

"At first, Louis and I couldn't figure why Baker Sugars was the only supplier paid based on the balance owing to it. Other suppliers were paid when payables reached a certain age, some in thirty days, others in sixty or ninety, whatever Taylor could negotiate with a supplier. No connection with amounts owing. The only way cheques between £6,000 and £9,000 could leave the company was if all three VPs agreed the amount was owing and payment was due."

"You said the VPs didn't do it," Scrivens repeated with annoyance.

"And they didn't," St. James reiterated.

Chapter 94

"We'll finalize who orchestrated Taylor's fleecing in a minute. I will move to the external investigation now to deal with Nigel Chamberlain's murder," St. James said.

"Dozer and I went to Cambridge to meet with Barbara Evans, Chamberlain's shunned sister. She hadn't seen her brother in over ten years, so I showed her a recent picture. She held it for a time, then gave it back.

"I learned Evans's father left her the house, over a million pounds, and what she referred to as 'a box of junk' in the cellar. When I asked to see the box, she resisted. It would be a waste of my time, she said.

"I have a saying. When people *res*ist, I *pers*ist, and that's exactly what I did. The box wasn't full of junk. It contained several old but usable tools. When I was partway to the bottom, Barbara became anxious and wanted to go back upstairs. So I burrowed to the bottom of the box. There, I discovered the reason for Barbara's resistance; a superbly finished box containing a Ruger SR22."

Gasps rippled through the room again.

"Chamberlain's sister killed him?" Collins said bluntly.

St. James ignored Collins and continued. "The previous day, I spoke with DI Harris of the Cambridge police department to let him know we would be in his domain the following day. He offered his help if we needed it. So when I discovered the gun in Barbara's cellar, Dozer and I took it to Harris to check for prints. I also gave him the picture of Chamberlain that the woman handled. DI Joy and DS Billings were unhappy that I went to Harris for help. But for all I knew at the time, this could relate to something that happened in his jurisdiction. In any case, we were in for another shocker. Harris searched for Barbara Evans in his databases and discovered she'd been dead for two years, buried in Cambridge City Cemetery."

Once again, the room found itself catching its breath.

"This is gut-wrenching," Randall said with a pained look.

"At this stage, Dozer and I didn't believe anything or anyone. So we went to Cambridge City Cemetery and found Evans's grave. We stood there for a time, Dozer reading the headstone, me wondering who the hell I had just interviewed."

Chapter 95

"DI Harris called me this morning," St. James said. "He'd put a rush on the gun and Chamberlain's picture so I would have lab results for this meeting."

"Why didn't we get them?" Joy asked, obviously irritated.

"Probably sitting in your inbox," St. James said.

Joy nodded.

"What the hell did Harris say?" Billings said.

"There were two sets of prints on the gun," St. James said and drank water. Kingston smiled, sure St. James took time to drink just to aggravate Billings.

"One set belongs to Frank Keller," St. James said triumphantly.

"Who's the second?" Joy asked anxiously.

"The same prints on Chamberlain's picture," St. James said. "Mary Louise Kellar!"

Keller covered his face.

"Who the hell's Mary Louise Kellar?" Joy said abruptly.

"Frank's sister."

"I didn't know he had a sister!" Kingston said.

"Neither did we until Anna searched every way to spell Keller. Mary Louise spells it K-e-l-l-a-r, not K-e-l-l-e-r as Frank does. A Boolean search covers many variations of spelling the same name," St. James explained.

"Mary Louise was one of the two names Nancy Sweet forgot to list as a contact for DS Billings."

"Once Sweet told me that, and Harris confirmed it was her prints on the gun in Evans's cellar, the case fog began to lift."

"I believe DI Joy will prove Keller and Mary Louise conspired to take advantage of Chamberlain's madness when he eradicated Barbara on paper. Keller knew Barbara inherited more than a million from her father. So if Barbara was out of the way, Mary Louise could take her place, access the million pounds for her brother as payment for what Chamberlain refused to pay him. Then the two would split the balance of Barbara's assets. With no next of kin to inherit her estate, no one would be the wiser. All Mary Louise had to do was wait until the police lost interest in Barbara's death to move in. In the absence of anyone else in Evans's orbit, it would be easy for Kellar to slide into her house and take the million pounds she'd inherited, probably by forging her signature at the bank. Not that hard to do. Evans's husband left her money as well, so Keller and Mary Louise would also have that as a bonus."

Billings was stunned. "Holy Shit!"

Collins seemed oblivious to St. James's latest revelation. "How did Barbara die?" he asked.

"Suspiciously," St. James said. "Autopsy said poison, but they never solved the case. She was a recluse, and there were no relatives police could find because of what Chamberlain did to her identity."

Kingston was stupefied. "Are you saying Keller killed Barbara Evans?"

"I'm saying Keller and Mary Louise are the only known suspects."

St. James looked at Keller. "Given everything against you that we can prove, you'd be better off confessing to Evans's murder rather than denying it. But I leave that to DCI Kingston and DI Joy."

Joy looked at Kingston, astounded by the prospect of a second murder investigation connected to Chamberlain.

St. James looked at Joy. "Along with the lab results, I asked Harris to send what you need to compare bullets to those from Chamberlain's body. I'm sure they'll match the Cambridge Ruger," St. James said confidently. "You will have copies of all my notes and my help to wind everything up."

Joy was stunned by St. James's revelations.

"Was that one of the three Rugers recently purchased?" Scrivens asked.

"No. It was a gun already in circulation. I believe DI Harris will confirm with DI Joy the serial number is registered in Keller's name."

Taylor's three VPs remained frozen in the second row. Woods continued to weep. Goldstein was pondering the verbal persecution about to come his way. Randall, Collins and Scrivens looked as if they were beginning to understand the case. Billings remained confused.

"I interviewed Mary Louise, albeit thinking she was Barbara Evans," St. James said. "She would not have had the strength to sever Chamberlain's hands. That leaves Keller to do the dirty work, probably after asking Chamberlain several times where he hid the money and not getting a satisfactory answer. I don't know how Keller knew he needed Chamberlain's prints to access the money. Perhaps Chamberlain let it slip somewhere along the way. It's the only thing that makes sense. Otherwise, they'd have just shot him."

"After Keller severed the hands, Chamberlain would already be dead. Chamberlain not telling them where the money was hidden would have infuriated both Mary Louise and Keller beyond logic — enough to shoot the man eight times in a rage after he was dead."

St. James eyed Keller. "Torture was your only recourse to find the money. But you didn't allow for Chamberlain's resolve, his strength to hold back in the face of pain, never giving you the satisfaction of knowing where the money was. You were left to wander around with two hands, hoping to stumble on Chamberlain's hiding place. Knowing the hands would deteriorate with time, it was a race against the clock, and you knew, Frank, that you'd lose. So you sent the hands to DI Joy, thinking the Yard's resources might have a better chance of finding the money. You could always steal the money later. So, when I said we removed the cash from Chamberlain's cellar, I wasn't surprised how quickly you asked where it was."

St. James paused to drink water.

Keller's face remained engulfed in his hands.

"A couple of sidebars to reinforce the story," St. James said. "When I had lunch with you at the Westminster Arms, Frank, you arrived wearing a long grey coat and matching hat, aviator sunglass sticking from a handkerchief pocket, the very description of the man Lisa saw at Heathrow and in Zurich. You were following her to see if she would lead you to Chamberlain's money.

"The second tidbit is two men roughed me up one day walking back to the hotel from Taylor's office. When they tried a second time, Dozer was there to rescue me. Dozer, shall I say, charmed the two into telling us they worked for someone named Percy. The name didn't mean anything to me until Anna conducted a Boolean search that showed Frank was born Frank Percy Keller."

St. James turned to Keller. "You had more than enough money from the theft of Barbara's identity to repay what Chamberlain owed you. If you and Mary Louise had left it at that, you would have gotten away with it. Evans didn't have a will. And there was no one to fight over her estate. You would have been home free. But greed got the better of you, didn't it, Frank? You wanted whatever money Chamberlain had skimmed from IEI too."

Keller's head remained low, face tightly buried.

St. James continued. "It's one thing to steal from a dead person, Frank. Quite another to kill someone to steal. That unleashes a relentless pursuit. That's where you blew it. It was your bridge too far."

"You still haven't told us who orchestrated the fraud at Taylor's," said a frustrated Scrivens.

St. James nodded. "You remember I told you the ways Fischer onboarded targets around the world?"

Scrivens nodded.

"Well, Chamberlain and Keller decided they needed one of their own on the inside to bring Taylor into the fraud family. So that person got themselves hired and then scouted Taylor's employees, looking for cash-vulnerable people with power to divert money. When that person discovered the three VPs each needed cash for different reasons, they approached them with a solution. They all agreed and were introduced to Harvey Goldstein to incorporate numbered companies and prepare cash-sharing agreements among them, Chamberlain and Keller."

Goldstein remained quiet.

"Vanderbilt set Baker Sugars up as a supplier on Taylor's system so Sauvé could issue dummy purchase orders for goods that never arrived," St. James explained.

"Wouldn't that be caught when someone in receiving didn't receive goods listed on purchase orders?" Collins asked.

"Not if Sauvé was the one doing the checking."

Joy jumped in. "And Woods would be issuing the cheques to Baker, so no check there, either."

"Right," St. James said.

Randall interjected. "I can't believe Taylor wouldn't catch it."

"No reason he would, Lisa. No payments to Baker were less than £6,000 or more than £9,000. Taylor would never see anything related to Baker Sugars because the VPs controlled everything up to £9,000, and they made sure they never exceeded that threshold. Maybe he never even knew Baker was a supplier for that reason."

"You said earlier the VPs didn't orchestrate the fraud," Collins said.

"True, Henry. But they did benefit from it."

"Then who organized the fraud?" Goldstein pressed.

St. James continued. "I conducted some research on my own. Mary Louise Kellar was divorced for some time. She and her ex, Darin, had a daughter, a niece to Frank. When she divorced Darin, Mary Louise returned to her maiden name, Kellar. The daughter kept her father's name and eventually graduated at the top of her class with a degree from Cambridge University in drama. She became a damn good actor."

"For God's sake, Hamilton, who are you talking about?" Joy yelled.

"Deborah Singent-Smythe!"

"Who the hell is Deborah Singent-Smythe?" Billings barked.

"Taylor's assistant," St. James said.

"Taylor's assistant?" Randall said incredulously.

"Yes, Taylor's assistant," St. James repeated.

Scrivens was stymied. "How could an office assistant organize a fraud this complicated?"

St. James smiled. "As I said, she's a Cambridge graduate and a damn good actor. She is a lot more than an executive assistant but played the part to put herself between Taylor and the VPs. It was a perfect position to control the four of them, to set up and manage the fraud. And with mother and uncle well schooled in fraud, she had excellent training."

"Oh, what a tangled web we weave," Randall mumbled.

"Let me get this straight," said a stunned Collins. "What we use to call a secretary set up a complicated internal fraud scheme tied to numbered companies connected to a fraudster in Germany, controlled three VPs to make it work, and reported to her mother and uncle on Baker Sugars' cash flow?"

"That's right, Henry," St. James said.

"How did the VPs benefit?" Randall asked.

St. James cleared his throat. "Money sent to Baker for bogus goods was paid by Baker to Keller's numbered company by way of dividends. Once in Frank's account, it was divided among Quantum, IEI and the three VPs' numbered companies, paid to each as dividends. That's how the VPs benefited from the fraud scheme set up by Singent-Smythe."

Randall stared off. "So we have IEI owned by Fischer; Schneider was effectively his chief operating officer with six sector chiefs reporting to him. For his own United Kingdom section chief responsibilities, Schneider was accountable directly to Fischer. Am I right so far?"

"You are," St. James said.

Randall continued. "Then you have a leader for every country within each sector reporting to their sector chief. In this case, Chamberlain was the UK country leader reporting to Schneider, the de-facto sector chief. Is that correct?"

St. James smiled. "You're doing well, Lisa."

Tension ramped further as the room followed Lisa's interpretation of facts.

"Be patient with me, everyone. I have an overwhelming desire to get this straight in my head," Randall said.

"Keep going, Lisa," Scrivens said.

"Thank you. Then you have local fraud managers under each country leader, making sure each company toes the line and meets fraud targets set by Fischer and Schneider. In the case of the UK, Keller is one of those managers reporting to Chamberlain. Am I still on track?" Randall said.

"Bang on, Lisa," St. James said.

"Okay," she said. "And Keller managed fifteen company frauds for Chamberlain, one of which was Taylor Supermarkets."

"Correct," St. James said.

"And Keller sends his niece, Deborah Singent-Smythe, to apply for the job of assistant to Taylor himself. She lands the job, manages to learn the three VPs are strapped for cash, convinces them to go along with siphoning cash through the bogus Baker Sugars and helps them set up a numbered company structure to benefit from dividends along with Chamberlain and IEI."

St. James was impressed. "The lady deserves a star, everyone."

Except for the accused, everyone clapped.

Randall blushed.

"Thank you for that, Lisa. One final loose end," St. James said above the whispering. "Singent-Smythe always kept a change of clothes in the office in case she had to attend an after-hours function. When she left early one afternoon, I checked the size. Thirty-nine. I took notice of her provocative clothing preference my first day at Taylor's. The clothes in Chamberlain's flat were both her style and size.

"She kept clothes at Chamberlain's flat for convenience when Chamberlain and Keller were still on good terms. When the friendship ended over money owed to Keller, Chamberlain probably wouldn't let Singent-Smythe back in the flat to collect her clothes. DNA cleansing might have been done by Singent-

Smythe earlier as insurance to avoid a connection with Chamberlain should he become a liability for her later. Who knows? Graduating from Cambridge, she would probably have access to people in the chemistry department who could supply her with the chemical mixture and knowledge to eliminate DNA."

Billings stuck an unlit cigar in the corner of his mouth and chewed it out of frustration, realizing for the first time the case was out of his league.

Joy left the room to have Singent-Smythe picked up, arrange transportation of the four suspects to Scotland Yard and ask DI Harris to arrest Mary Louise Kellar in Cambridge.

"Jesus Christ!" Goldstein blurted.

"Goddamn convoluted mess," Scrivens called out.

"Are you finished, Hamilton?" Kingston said.

"Yes."

Kingston turned to the room. "Okay, everyone may leave except Keller, Sauvé, Woods and Vanderbilt. You four remain seated. DI Joy has gone to arrange police escorts."

Everyone but the four stood, all talking at once, babbling about how St. James unfolded the case, the length of time it took and how he possibly could have figured it out.

Chapter 96

St. James, Anna, Joy, Kingston and Dozer were sitting at a table in the Thistle Piccadilly Hotel bar. It was six o'clock Friday evening, the day St. James unfolded the case, and Prisha had just delivered a round of drinks.

Kingston raised a glass. "Here's to the four of you for doing one helluva of job," he said with admiration. "To think it took cracking the world's largest fraud scheme to get to the bottom of Taylor's relatively small profit issue is unfathomable," Kingston said, shaking his head.

Dozer nodded and launched into a slow tirade. "If Louis hadn't been kidnapped so the laptop could fall into our hands, all we would have found was Woods's forecast error. An error with no known fraud. We would have certainly gone home," he said. "Keller and Singent-Smythe would have continued milking Taylor undetected, and the large fraud operation would not have been taken down."

He looked at Joy before continuing.

"Putting the order of events together, it seems that if Hamilton and I hadn't taken the law into our own hands, we would never have solved Taylor's case, and *you* wouldn't be the envy of every police force in the fifty-seven countries Fischer swindled. You should have thanked us for bypassing the Yard to save Louis instead of punishing us."

Everyone but Kingston laughed.

"Don't push it, Dozer," Kingston said lightly.

"You missed a rather important step in the order of events, Dozer," St. James said.

"What's that?"

"If Woods hadn't made the forecasting error, Taylor would never have believed he was losing money. If he never thought profit was declining, Taylor would never have called, David." St. James turned to Kingston. "If you weren't called, we would not have been called. And none of what you said, Dozer, would have happened. Using your twisted logic, Woods initiated the investigation and deserves the credit for having herself caught." St. James laughed.

"Quit while you are ahead, boys," Joy suggested, shaking her head.

"Too bad Bert couldn't make it tonight," St. James said with a wink.

"What?" Joy yelped. "He wasn't invited, was he?"

"He's only winding you up, Phyllis," Kingston said with a smile.

Joy gave St. James a look. "I owe you an apology, Hamilton."

The others looked puzzled.

"What for?" St. James said.

"Chewing you out for not letting me in on the case solution before today."

St. James shrugged. "Water under the bridge."

"No, it's not," Joy insisted. "We both know I could not have done what you did today."

"It will come with time and experience," St. James consoled.

"Phyllis, Hamilton thinks you are a brilliant detective," Anna offered. "He told me he'd be happy to have you as a partner on any case."

Joy looked at St. James with raised eyebrows. "Really? Is that true?"

A smile crept across St. James's face. "Only if you promise not to get mad every time I say something just to annoy you on purpose."

"Agreed," Joy said with a smile.

Everyone laughed.

Chapter 97

Kingston and St. James grabbed a coffee from the hospital cafeteria at the nurse's suggestion. She needed another ten minutes to tend to Taylor properly, so they stood in the hallway outside Taylor's room sipping coffee, waiting for a signal he was ready for visitors.

The morning after the meeting was a warm August Saturday with occasional gusts, but not enough to discourage Kingston and St. James from wearing shorts and tee-shirts.

A faint smell of sanitizing cleaner made itself known as hospital staff darted in and out of patient rooms, going about daily routines. The PA system constantly summoned doctors and staff to different locations. A code blue triggered the mobilization of a cardiac team, doctors and nurses running past St. James and Kingston as they finished their coffees.

They wandered into Taylor's room and flanked the heavily sedated merchant when the nurse gave permission. Taylor slowly looked up, eying the two for a moment before speaking.

"Sorry I ruined your meeting, Hamilton," he said, words slightly slurred, his baritone voice weak.

"I don't care about that, John," St. James assured.

"Everyone at the meeting sends best wishes for a speedy recovery," Kingston said.

Taylor nodded. "Doctor said I had a mild stroke. 'Tiny,' he said. Doesn't think there is any permanent damage. Should recover completely."

"Good," Kingston said.

Taylor drifted off for a fleeting moment.

Taylor's room was small and scantily furnished with a tiny window overlooking a river of concrete. Not an enjoyable environment, but it wasn't meant to be. It was a place to recover.

"Don't know what I'm going to do, David," Taylor said when regaining consciousness. "Embezzled by my own team. I just want to cry. No one to run the place now. And I'm stuck in here. I'll lose everything."

"I thought about all that before David and I met for breakfast this morning," St. James said with an upbeat tone. "Subject to what you think, John, I believe I have a workable solution."

Taylor's eyes shot open as if suddenly shocked electrically. "How can that be when I have no one left?" he stammered.

"Vanderbilt has a senior person Louis thinks is rather good. He can keep the technical side running," St. James said. "I'll have Louis oversee him. He can do that virtually from Canada."

Taylor nodded. "Name's Dudley Whetstone," Taylor said. "Lucas said he's excellent."

St. James learned the key to keeping Taylor's morale fluffed was to offer a plausible way out of the very thing dragging it down. "I can ask the auditors to provide qualified help for Cindy's job until we find a replacement. They have a headhunter to help with that too," St. James said enthusiastically.

"What about operations?" Taylor mumbled.

"I looked at my notes and noticed you rated the Rupert Street store manager the highest for overall performance. He could run corporate operations from below head office with the occasional meeting upstairs if necessary."

Taylor thought about this for a bit. "Could work, I suppose," he said finally, sounding as convinced as a naturally pessimistic person could.

Taylor drifted off for another minute, came back and said, "Administration? I understand Deborah was part of the fraud too. Hard to believe the whole lot were disloyal."

Neither Kingston nor St. James thought it wise to say Deborah set up the whole scheme; could trigger a setback.

"I'll lend you Anna to manage the office for as long as it takes, John."

"Any good?"

"The best."

"Thank you."

Taylor's voice garnered more strength. "It will take a long time to get over this one; disloyalty, energy to rebuild a new team and company image. I'm completely gobsmacked!" he said.

"Important thing, John, is for you to start putting your health ahead of everything else," Kingston said.

"I know, David, I know," Taylor whispered.

"Then let Hamilton go ahead with his transition plan," Kingston said. "It'll afford you some peace in the interim."

"Hamilton," Taylor murmured. "I hate the way this turned out. But you did what you said you would do when we had the first conference call. It takes one hell of a man to stick with something like this when everyone around him doubts his every move. Thank you for your tenacity, strength and ability to see what no one else could. Prepare my third of your bill and bring me the company cheque book. Then put your transition plan into effect."

Kingston and St. James smiled at one another.

"Thank you, John. I'll set it up first thing Monday morning," St. James said.

But John Taylor didn't hear St. James. He had drifted into a deeper sleep.

THE END